A PLACE TO BELONG

Sister Circle

A Place to Belong

VONETTE BRIGHT
& NANCY MOSER

Tyndale House Publishers, Inc.
WHEATON, ILLINOIS

Visit Tyndale's exciting Web site at www.tyndale.com

TYNDALE is a registered trademark of Tyndale House Publishers, Inc.

Tyndale's quill logo is a trademark of Tyndale House Publishers, Inc.

Edited by Kathryn S. Olson

Designed by Catherine Bergstrom

Scripture quotations are taken from the *Holy Bible*, New Living Translation, copyright ©1996. Used by permission of Tyndale House Publishers, Inc., Wheaton, Illinois 60189. All rights reserved.

Lyrics to "The Joy of the Lord Will Be My Strength" by Twila Paris, © 1991 by Ariose Music, Nashville. Used by permission.

"Can you imagine stepping on shore and finding it heaven?" paraphrased from "Finally Home" by Don Wyrtzen. Used by permission of the author and Singspiration—Brentwood/Benson Music.

This novel is a work of fiction. Names, characters, places, and incidents are either the product of the authors' imaginations or are used fictitiously. Any resemblance to actual events, locales, organizations, or persons living or dead is entirely coincidental and beyond the intent of either the authors or publisher.

Sister Circle is a registered trademark of Tyndale House Publishers, Inc.

Library of Congress Cataloging-in-Publication Data

Bright, Vonette Z.
  A place to belong / Vonette Bright & Nancy Moser.
    p. cm. — (Sister circle)
  Includes index.
  ISBN 1-4143-0076-X (sc)
  1. Female friendship—Fiction. 2. Boardinghouses—Fiction. 3. Widows—Fiction. I. Moser, Nancy. II. Title.
PS3602.R5317P58 2005
813'.6—dc22   2004021287

Printed in the United States of America

11 10 09 08 07 06 05
 9   8   7   6   5   4   3   2   1

Vonette Bright dedicates this book to
my Orlando Sisters
who have been my greatest support group
during this year of 2003–2004.
Without you I would have been a lost lamb.
I love you all.
Thank you for giving me "a place to belong."

•   •   •

Nancy Moser dedicates this book to
Laurel, our youngest,
who will always find her place to belong
and fill it with freshness and enthusiasm.

The humble will see their God at work and be glad.
Let all who seek God's help live in joy.
PSALM 69:32

You can make many plans,
but the Lord's purpose will prevail.

PROVERBS 19:21

*A*ll she wanted was a little sun.

If all the world was indeed a stage, then Mae Ames was the director, star, and propmistress. The plan for today's scene was to portray an idyllic summer setting. A striking woman, who teased the edge of pretty when she tried, could be seen reading a book on the front lawn of a charming 1920s bungalow, bettering both her mind and her tan.

She'd started with just a book and a lawn chair. But once she got the chair positioned in the front yard, she quickly realized the June sun was hot and she needed her sunglasses, a straw hat, sunscreen, her pink Japanese fan, a glass of raspberry tea, and four Milano cookies on a plate. Never mind. Bring the bag.

Mae was just settling in—realizing to be *really* comfy she should go get one of the toss pillows from the couch—when she heard a familiar clearing of the throat. She didn't have to turn toward the porch. "You grunted, Mr. Husband?"

"What are you doing out here?"

She opened her paperback. "Reading a book."

"Looks like it would be easier sitting inside. Or on the porch swing."

"Easier, perhaps. But it's a proven fact that books read better when accompanied by the proper accoutrements."

"Want me to hire a neighbor kid to fan you with a palm leaf?"

She fluttered her own fan. "No need. I have it covered." She turned around to look at him. "Care to join me?"

"Nah. I'm not sure the recliner would fit through the door and I'd want—" His eyes moved to look at a car that was driving toward them.

Mae looked too. Then she popped out of her chair—or attempted to pop, as the lawn chair objected and tipped, forcing her to straddle it or put a foot *through* the webbing. Collier was halfway down the front walk when she finally got free of it, knocking over her tea. She tossed her hat toward the house like a Frisbee. It capped a mound of black-eyed Susans. She ran toward the car. "Ringo! Soon-ja!"

Ringo parked and Collier opened the door for their daughter-in-law, while Mae made a beeline for the backseat where the love of her life was seated backwards. She got him free of the car seat, pulling him to her shoulder. "Ricky, baby. How's my sweet-ums?"

Ringo came around the front of the car and kissed her cheek. "I'm fine, Mom. How are you?"

"Oh. Sorry, son. Never work with children or animals. Scene stealers, every one."

He flipped his head to get his longish hair out of his eyes. "I'll remember that."

Mae took a deep breath, filling her nostrils with the luscious smell of baby. If only they could bottle it. She turned her attention to Soon-ja. The girl's skin always looked pale against the black of her hair, but today, there was a pallor . . . "And how are you doing, Soonie?"

Soon-ja smiled, but looked to Ringo, as if needing advice on how to answer.

And she didn't answer.

Uh-oh. Something was up.

Collier led them to the porch where Soon-ja and Mae took seats on the swing. "What brings you to town?" he asked.

Ringo and Soon-ja exchanged that look again. "Life."

Double uh-oh. Mae held Ricky even closer. "Out with it. What's wrong?"

Ringo took a position against a column at the top of the steps as if positioning himself to flee. "I've lost my job."

Mae didn't quite understand. Ringo was a roadie with a rock band so the work always *was* seasonal. "The tour's over," Mae said. "You knew that was going to happen."

"But my next gig fell through." He glanced at Soon-ja, then at his son. "And I have responsibilities now."

"And no income," Soon-ja said.

Ringo gave her a look.

She gave him one back. "It has to be said, Go-Go. Now is not the time for subtlety—or pride." She angled in the swing toward Mae. "Can we move in here?"

"Just for a little while," Ringo added.

Mae sought her husband's eyes. Poor Collie. They'd only been married eighteen months and already they'd endured one adult child come home. Just last fall, Mae's daughter, Starr, had come to live with them while she and her fiancé worked things out. Now, to have her son's family move in . . . was she pushing the toleration limit of her darling Mr. Husband?

Probably. But that had never stopped her before. "Of course, you can," she said. She nuzzled Ricky's cheek. "It will give us a chance to spoil this precious baby."

"I *will* get a job," Ringo said. "I'll start looking tomorrow."

Collier stepped forward. "I had lunch with Joe Ambrose the other day and he needs workers. Construction."

"I could do that," Ringo said.

"Of course, you could, honey," Mae said.

There. Problem solved.

•   •   •

"There."

Evelyn smoothed the pastel quilt on Margaret's bed. The trouble was, it wasn't Margaret's bed anymore. Margaret Jensen had just moved out, moved away from Carson Creek altogether, and Evelyn was readying the room for a new boarder at Peerbaugh Place.

Another tenant, Piper Wellington, stood in the doorway with Peppers the cat rubbing against her legs. "It's hard, isn't it?"

Evelyn collected her cleaning supplies and put them in the handled tub. "I shouldn't get so attached to the ladies."

Piper picked up Peppers, snuggling her under her chin. "I suppose it would be less painful to just pass each other in the halls, and call each other, 'hey you.'"

Not funny. Especially since Piper would also be moving out in a few weeks to be married. "I just don't understand why Margaret felt the need to move hundreds of miles away. She had a teaching job here. Her parents are in Jackson."

"But Bobby is in Jackson."

Nuf said. Margaret had broken her engagement to Bobby when she'd caught him finagling some of the inheritance she was to receive from an old mentor. But their relationship had been doomed way before that. Bobby was not a nice man. Nice men didn't make their fiancées feel inferior. That wasn't love. Margaret's parents were no better. It was best she get away and start over. Sad, but best.

Piper let Peppers go and helped Evelyn by carrying the broom downstairs. "Are you ready for the meeting of the bridesmaids this morning?" The bridal party was meeting at Catherine's Wedding Creations to choose the style and fabric for the dresses.

"I must warn you, it's been nearly three decades since I've been a bridesmaid," Evelyn said. "I'm out of practice."

"But remember, you're not just a *maid;* you're the matron of honor," Piper said.

"'Matron.' Oh, yeah, that sounds loads better."

Piper laughed. They reached the kitchen where they put the cleaning supplies in the broom closet. Evelyn arched her back with a groan, feeling every one of her five-plus decades. She had an awful thought. "We're not going to wear anything strapless, or with a big bow in the back, are we?"

"Not unless you're outvoted," Piper said as she got a drink of water. "I must say it is a challenge to find a dress that will look good on two fifty-somethings, a twenty-five-year-old, and a woman over seventy."

"You will definitely get the grand prize for the most eclectic group of attendants."

"That's why I need you along, as a calming influence between Mae's madness and Tessa's prim and proper," Piper said. "Only you and Audra have taste I trust. Besides, with Mom gone, I don't know what I'd do without you helping with *all* the wedding plans." Piper's mother, Wanda, had died eleven months before.

"I'm happy to help or negotiate, as needed," Evelyn said.

Piper put her hands on Evelyn's shoulders, her face set in mock seriousness. "Knowing this group, you may need to add *arbitrate* and *mediate* to your job description."

"Okay, but that'll cost extra."

"Whatever it takes," Piper said.

✻   ●   ●

"Ladies! Ladies, please!"

The four women laughed at the sole male in their presence. Piper slipped her hand through Gregory's arm and kissed his shoulder. "You're not used to women oohing and ahhing over fabric swatches, are you?"

"Oohing and ahhing I can take. But swooning?"

"What's swooning, Mommy?" Seven-year-old Summer was serving lemonade like a professional waitress.

Audra touched her back. "It's what I do whenever I see your father. Let me rephrase that. It's what I *should* do whenever I see your father."

"Uh-oh," Tessa said. "Only seventeen months married and the swoon is gone? Shame on you!"

Gregory covered his ears. "Should I be listening to this?"

Evelyn batted one hand down. "Come on, Gregory, you're a doctor. Didn't you study the physiology of swooning?"

"I must have missed that day."

There was a knock on the door to Audra's garage that served as the office-showroom-workroom for Catherine's Wedding Creations, but before Summer could run to answer it, Mae burst in—with a baby in her arms. "Greetings!"

"Aunt Mae! Where'd you get the baby?" Summer asked.

She ruffled Summer's hair. "I found him on the doorstep."

Audra spoke up. "Mae, don't tell her that."

"Actually I'm not far off."

"Is that Ringo's son?" Evelyn asked.

Mae turned the six-week-old baby so he was sitting on her arm, viewing his crowd of admirers. "Ricky Fitzpatrick, meet your public."

If Gregory was overwhelmed by oohing and aahing about fabric he had to be blown away by the oohing and aahing over the baby. Somehow Ricky ended up in Audra's arms. A blessing—and a curse.

While Mae filled them in on the news of Ringo and Soon-ja, Audra walked around the room bouncing Ricky, cooing to him. Aching for one just like him. Would it ever happen?

She was beginning to doubt it. She and Russell had been trying to get pregnant for over a year—though they hadn't started to worry about it until the last few months. Audra had gone in for tests first. She was fine. Which meant . . . Russell had been dragging his feet about making an appointment to be tested but had finally gotten one set up for next Friday. She couldn't blame his reluctance. Hearing it from a doctor was so final. And yet, until the results *were* final, Audra knew they couldn't move on to the next step.

Which was?

Audra pulled Ricky close, kissing his forehead. She had no idea what they'd do if Russell was unable to father a baby. They hadn't let themselves talk about it. In fact, lately they didn't talk about much of anything. Shouldn't trying to have a baby bring a couple closer together?

If it works. Only if it works.

The worry verse in Matthew that had been her mantra popped to mind: *"Don't worry about tomorrow, for tomorrow will bring its own worries. Today's trouble is enough for today."*

Easier said than done. As far as she could tell, Russell was handling it far better than she—which added to the distance she felt. It wasn't that he didn't want a child of his own. He did. Although he'd adopted Summer, she knew he yearned for a baby that was theirs, together. As did she. She just wished it would happen so things could get back to normal.

Mae called to her. "Bring my grandbaby back here, Audra, and let's get down to the second reason I'm here—the first being to show off Mr. Ricky."

"The second being you can't drive past more than two cars in any driveway?" Gregory said.

She swatted his shoulder. "Watch it, mister. You're new to this Sister Circle, and we can have you expelled to some manly man gathering across town if you don't behave."

"Promise?" he said.

Piper slipped her hand through his arm. "He goes, I go!"

Mae rolled her eyes. "Ah, young love."

"I'm hardly young," Piper said. "I'm thirty-five."

"A chicklet." Mae bounced Ricky, then looked over the table of fabrics and drawings of dresses. "So, what are our choices here?"

"Hold up a minute," Gregory said. "I just had a scary thought: I don't need to have all my groomsmen together to choose the tuxes, do I?"

The women laughed. "Not necessary," Mae said. "We're very willing to pick those out too."

Evelyn turned to Audra. "Are you making a mother-of-the-groom dress for Gregory's mother?"

Audra felt a swell of panic. She really didn't have time . . . "I don't think so." She turned to the happy couple. "Am I?"

Piper looked at Gregory. "Uh . . . we don't know what she's wearing."

Audra picked up a fabric swatch. "Would she like a sample of the bridesmaid fabric after we decide?" She watched as Piper and Gregory had a discussion with their eyes.

"Uh-oh," Mae said. "What aren't you telling us?"

Gregory interlocked his fingers through Piper's. "Piper hasn't met Mother yet. We're going to dinner at her house in a couple weeks. She lives in Springfield."

"Ninety minutes. That's not far," Tessa said. "Or is it not far enough?"

Mae didn't let them answer. "What I want to know is *why* haven't you met? You've been engaged for months."

"It's complicated," Gregory said.

Mae pulled up a chair. "Out with it. All of it."

Gregory took a fresh breath. "As Piper probably told you, I grew up without any religious training. Dad was an Italian Catho-

lic and Mother was a Polish Jew. When they married their families
disowned them. So instead of having me benefit from both
cultures, they left them behind. I lived a pretty homogenized life."

"Skim or whole milk?" Mae asked.

Gregory laughed. "Skim, definitely skim."

Audra wasn't seeing the connection. "That's all very interesting but doesn't explain why Piper hasn't met your mother."

Gregory stood, put his hands in his pockets, and moved to
look out the window in the door. "My mother and I have been
estranged since Dad died five years ago. She blames me for his
death."

"Why?" Evelyn asked.

"Because I'm a heart surgeon and he died of heart problems.
If I couldn't save my own father what good am I?"

"Were you his surgeon?"

"No, no. I would never do that. But he had the best. It was no
one's fault."

Piper added, "Just like it wasn't anyone's fault that Mom
died."

That explained some of it to Audra, but still . . . "I'm sorry
about your dad," she said, "but surely your mom's happy that
you've found the love of your life."

When he turned to look at Piper Audra could see the love in
his eyes. But then his face clouded. "There's another complication.
In the past year, as I was discovering Jesus, Mother was rediscov-
ering her Jewish roots."

"Uh-oh," Mae said.

"Double uh-oh. When I called to tell her I had become
engaged, her first question was 'Is she a nice Jewish girl?' I had to
tell her no, and that I wasn't a Jewish boy either. Ethnically
maybe, but not in regard to my faith." He shook his head. "You
don't want to know what she said next."

Piper got up and hugged him from behind. They looked so perfect together. So unified. So . . .

"Are you nervous about the dinner?" Tessa asked.

Gregory pulled Piper's arms tighter. "We're trying not to be."

"Expect the worst and accept the best!" Mae said.

"That's not very helpful," Evelyn said.

"But it's the truth."

Piper let go and led Gregory back to the table. "I just want us to get along and find a level of mutual respect."

"Surely you can do that," Audra said.

Gregory snickered. "You don't know my mother."

There was a knock on the workroom door. Audra saw a flash of brown. It was Simon, the UPS man. "Excuse me a moment."

She got the door and Simon flashed her a smile. "Morning. I have three rolls and a box for you today." He peeked past her at all the people. "Oops. Having an important meeting?"

Mae waved him in. "Always room for one more, handsome."

Tessa flashed her a look. "Mae. Behave."

"Don't mind them, Simon. Come on in."

He brought the rolls in, then returned to his truck for the box. Audra was glad the ladies resumed their chatting. She liked Simon and actually looked forward to his near-daily deliveries. Like Mae said, he *was* handsome in a hometown-boy kind of way. And nice. And single. He'd just broken up with a girlfriend a month ago, and Audra had been teasing him about hooking him up with one of her single friends. Not that he would need anyone's help . . .

He put the box against the wall and held the clipboard toward her. "There you go. Lines nine through twelve."

Audra signed on the diagonal line he'd made. "Thanks, Simon. I'll see you tomorrow?"

"I wouldn't miss it." On his way out, he did a double take. "Dr. Baladino?"

Gregory turned to look at him. "Hey . . . Simon. I'm sorry, I'm up to my eyebrows in swatches. I didn't see it was you. How's your dad doing?"

"Fine, thanks to you." Simon took a step toward the table. "All this is for your wedding?"

Gregory let out an exaggerated sigh and picked up a sample board. "Yes, sir. And I'm having a terrible time choosing between periwinkle and cornflower. What do you suggest?"

Simon stroked his chin. "Periwinkle, definitely periwinkle."

"Good choice, handsome," Mae said with a clap.

Simon tipped an imaginary cap. "I aim to please." He seemed to remember he was on duty. "I'd better go. Nice talking with you." He nodded to Audra. "Bye, Aud."

"Bye." She let him out and returned to the table. All eyes were on her. "What?"

"*Aud*? My, my, you two seem to have hit it off," Mae said.

Audra felt herself blush and hated herself for it. She wasn't sure what to say.

Evelyn said it for her. "Enough of that, Mae. That's my daughter-in-law you're talking about."

Tessa shook her head. "You shouldn't imply such things about a happily married woman."

Piper joined in. "That *was* tacky, Mae."

"Fine, fine." Mae raised her hands in surrender. "Point taken. I was out of line." She swept a by-your-leave hand at Audra. "Sorry, sister. Simon's charm and dashing smile got the better of me." She paused. "But he is single, isn't he? I didn't see a ring."

"Yes, he's single."

"Perfect." Mae clasped her hands on the table and leaned forward confidentially. "We can't let a looker like Simon go to waste, ladies. I'm sure if we put our heads together we can think of a single sister in need of that smile, that red hair, and those blue eyes."

They laughed and got back to work.

None too soon.

●   ●   ●

Evelyn turned the flank steak in the marinade, put the cover back on the container, and put it back in the refrigerator. The smell of ginger, garlic, and soy sauce made her hungry. But it was hours until dinner.

But not hours before her newest tenant would arrive. Valerie Raines, budding author. She looked at the clock. Five minutes to two. Five minutes before the entire tone of Peerbaugh Place would change. Again. In truth, Evelyn was getting better at accepting the change that came with each new tenant. Yet after two and a half years it still surprised her that she was a landlord at all. The situation had been brought on by the death of her husband, Aaron, in a car accident and his lack of foresight in having any life insurance beyond funds to cover his funeral. She'd been a fifty-six-year-old widow in need of immediate income.

Whenever God closes a door, He opens a window. . . .

The door had been closed on her being a compliant, rather weak, doormat of a wife, and had opened for her to become a confident businesswoman with an ever-widening circle of friends. Of the original tenants, Mae, Audra, Summer, and Tessa were still around. Audra's wedding-business partner, the newly married Heddy Wainsworth Mannersmith, had been in the second group. And of the third? Margaret had just moved out and Piper was getting married in two months. Only Lucinda Van Horn was sticking around.

As if on cue, Lucinda came into the kitchen, carrying her "toolbox." It wasn't just any metal toolbox, but had been decoupaged with the faces of models and cutouts of makeup products. Inside were the tools of Lucinda's trade. Lucinda was a pro at all things cosmetic—she knew a zillion beauty tips. And a few pitfalls. As an ex-model and longtime divorcée who'd previously found her worth in her looks, Lucinda had gone under the knife a few too many times. Her current features were pulled and too tight, and when she'd come to Peerbaugh Place she'd brought to mind the aging star in *Sunset Boulevard*, her face a contorted mask of her youth. *"All right, Mr. DeMille, I'm ready for my close-up."* Only through the tough love of the other tenants had Lucinda found that less was more. At age fifty-nine, she looked nice now, though the aftereffects of all the surgeries were ever present.

"My, my, that smells wonderful," Lucinda said, setting her toolbox on the kitchen table.

Evelyn touched the top of the red-hots Jell-O salad, checking its progress. Her finger left an impression. She licked it off. "How many women are going to be at your workshop today?"

"Five have signed up. But there are always a few who stop by as they wander through the shelter. Pastor Enoch says my makeover sessions are creating the prettiest down-and-outers in a three-state area. I kidded him that we should have a Ms. Second Chance contest."

Evelyn was going to mention that Lucinda had received her own second chance through working at the shelter, but didn't. To go from a wealthy background, with her face gracing the pages of fashion magazines, to giving makeup tips to homeless women was a hard trip. "Are you going to be back for dinner?"

"Sure. I might even drag Enoch along—if that's all right," Lucinda said.

Evelyn grinned. "Of course." Lucinda and Pastor Enoch made a cute couple. He was a teddy bear of a man. Even his personality was cuddly.

Lucinda wagged a finger at her. "Don't give me that look. We're just dear friends. No romance involved."

"But he is cute, in a slightly balding, slightly overweight, slightly frumpy sort of way."

"What scares me is that your description is apt, and I agree with you completely." Lucinda opened the freezer and removed a half dozen makeup pencils and put them in her toolbox. Before Lucinda, Evelyn had never heard of such a thing, but apparently the pencils sharpened better when frozen. Lucinda continued, "Please keep in mind that I have finally found a purpose beyond being on the arm of a man, and I like it. Don't push, Evelyn."

Evelyn was taken aback. She'd just assumed . . . "Sorry. I'm glad you're so . . . fulfilled."

"Me too."

The doorbell rang and Evelyn was brought back to her landlord duties. "Can you wait just a few minutes? I'd like you to meet the new tenant."

"I suppose, but actually there's something else I wanted to talk with you about and—"

"Fine. But later please." Evelyn fluffed her hair, then opened the door. "Valerie! Welcome."

Valerie handed Evelyn one suitcase while she carried in another. She was wearing a pale yellow turban and a one-piece belted shorts outfit that reminded Evelyn of the forties. She couldn't think what to call it: a romper? a jumpsuit? It was flattering, and looked fabulous on Valerie's model-thin frame, but also a bit disconcerting. With only a hint of her black hair showing, she looked severe and of another time—a lot like Wallis Simpson, the chic divorcée who made a British king abdicate his throne back in the thirties.

Lucinda joined them in the foyer. "Goodness. Where *did* you find that outfit?"

Valerie pulled out the shorts, which were nearly as wide as a skirt. "At the Nearly New shop in Jackson. New fashions are so gauche. I much prefer vintage."

Before Lucinda could say something less than flattering, Evelyn intervened. "Valerie Raines, this is Lucinda Van Horn. Lucinda, Valerie."

They shook hands. "Charmed, I'm sure," Valerie said.

"Lucinda used to be a fashion model. In magazines."

Valerie's look of shock was not kind. "Really."

"That was a long time ago," Lucinda said. "What do you do?"

Valerie lifted her chin and made a pronouncement: "I am an author."

Evelyn checked Lucinda's reaction, but only received one raised eyebrow. "Valerie is writing a novel. Since we all like to read I thought she'd be a nice addition to Peerbaugh—"

"Those who read rule the world. What novels are you ladies reading now?" Valerie asked.

Oh dear. This is what Evelyn got for exaggerating. The only thing she'd ever seen Lucinda read was *Vogue*. And as for herself? She did love to read, but was suddenly afraid her book choices would not be up to Valerie's standards for worthy fiction.

Lucinda grabbed her keys from the table in the foyer. "Excuse me, I really have to get going. Welcome, Valerie."

And she was gone. Leaving Evelyn to sink or swim. But luckily Valerie left her question behind and looked up the stairs. "Is my room ready?"

Phew.

●　　●　　●

Evelyn sat on the window seat in Valerie's new room and ran a hand along the pink-and-green floral cushion. "When Summer and Audra had this room, Summer used to love to play with her dolls here."

Valerie leaned over the seat, parted the lace curtains, and

looked at the backyard. "Actually, this seat gets in the way. I'd rather it be an empty nook where I could place a desk."

What could Evelyn say? "I'm . . . sorry."

Valerie flipped a hand and let the curtain fall. She turned toward the room, placing her hands on her hips. "Could you help me move the bed, please?"

"Excuse me?"

Valerie pointed at the window-seat wall. "I need to move the bed against this wall so I have room for a desk over there." She pointed to the wall that contained a dresser and the door to the bathroom she shared with Lucinda.

Evelyn eyeballed the spaces. "But if you move the bed, it will overlap half the window seat."

"It can't be helped," Valerie said. "I must have a proper space to create."

Oh dear. "So you have a desk? Is someone bringing one over later?"

"No, no," Valerie said, pacing the room as if she was making mental calculations. "That desk you have in the parlor will work just fine."

"What?"

Valerie stopped pacing. "You did say this was a furnished room."

"Yes, but—"

"And you did say that you would do everything in your power to make me feel at home, make this room work for me."

She *had* said those things.

"When I first came to see the room and you showed me around, I noticed that walnut desk in the parlor. And since you have too much furniture in that room anyway, I thought it would work nicely in here."

I suppose I could move it. I could find another place to pay my bills and—

16

No! Evelyn was both shocked by the adamant thought and fueled by it. The old Evelyn would have given in, acquiesced to this ridiculous, rude suggestion. But the new Evelyn . . . "I'm sorry, Valerie. That's not possible. I use that desk nearly every day. It's the only desk I have in the entire house. It's not available."

Valerie's head snapped back as if she'd been slapped.

Evelyn felt a surge of power and liked it way too much. She took a step toward the hall. "However, I do believe there's an old library table up in the attic. You're welcome to use that, if you'd like. And I'm sure there's even an extra chair up there."

Valerie put a hand to her chest. "A dusty old table?"

"I'll get the Pledge."

Evelyn had herself a giggle as she went downstairs to get the cleaning supplies. But as she grabbed a dusting cloth, her satisfaction turned to trepidation. She'd won a battle. But was there going to be a war?

•   •   •

"Shh! Lower your voice," Evelyn told Piper in the kitchen before dinner.

Piper moved shoulder to shoulder as they cut French bread and buttered it. "She actually wanted you to give up your desk?"

"*Expected* me to. That's a key difference," Evelyn said.

"The gall."

"The gall."

"But you told her no."

"I did."

Piper put an arm around her shoulders and squeezed. "Your Aaron would be so proud."

Evelyn shook her head adamantly. "Actually, he wouldn't. He'd be appalled at the new me."

"Well, I'm proud of you."

"But there was a cost to all this assertiveness." Evelyn bent down and revealed a cut on her knee. "Wounds from the battle with the library table. It resisted coming down the attic ladder."

"You should have waited until I got home. Or called my dad. Or I could have gotten Gregory to help."

"It wasn't heavy, just unwieldy. We managed."

"So Valerie *did* help?"

"She had no choice."

"I love the part about you getting the Pledge for her."

"Actually . . . I *was* the one to dust it off."

"You pushover, you."

Evelyn shrugged. Her hard-nosed number went only so far.

Piper looked toward the kitchen door leading to the foyer. "Is she coming down for dinner?"

"She said yes. Lucinda called and should be here any minute. Pastor Enoch's not coming."

Piper checked on the steak broiling in the oven. "We could have used a man to help eat up this meat. You have tons."

Evelyn got an idea. "Why don't you call your father? I know it's short notice, but—"

Piper winked at her. "He does love your cooking." She went to the phone and within a short minute hung up. "He's on his way, says he can hardly wait to be in your presence."

"He did not say that."

Piper shrugged. "But he means it." She began to set the table for five. "How are things going on the love front?"

"Your father and I are not in love. We are in . . . in *like*."

"I'm his daughter and your best friend, and you have my approval, so I don't know what you're waiting for."

Evelyn checked on the meat. She wanted to say, "I don't either," but didn't dare. If Piper knew how much Evelyn loved Wayne Wellington, she'd say something to him, nudge him, even push him into making a commitment to her. And Evelyn didn't want a pushed man. She wanted Wayne to fall in love with her of his own free will.

But she did wish he'd get on with it. They weren't getting any younger.

She heard the front door open. Lucinda came in. "Hello, ladies. I'm starved."

"Five minutes," Evelyn said. "Wayne's on his way over. So sorry Pastor Enoch couldn't come."

"The life of running a shelter is ever changing. He had a whole family come in just as I was leaving."

"That's so sad."

"I know." Lucinda filled the glasses with iced tea. "Every time I go there I end up wanting to do more, help more." She stopped pouring. "Actually, that's what I wanted to talk to you about, Evelyn. This morning, when Valerie came I was going to tell you that—"

Valerie came into the kitchen just then and Evelyn moved to greet her. "Valerie! Good timing. Dinner's almost ready."

Evelyn heard the front door open again. Wayne appeared. "I have arrived! Bring on the food." He kissed Piper on the cheek and winked at Evelyn. Then, "Hello, Lucinda." He noticed Valerie for the first time. "And this must be the writer." He extended a hand. "Hi, I'm Wayne Wellington, Piper's dad."

Evelyn was disappointed he couldn't add, "and Evelyn's boyfriend."

Valerie shook his hand. "Author. And it's nice to meet you." A tuft of black hair had escaped the back of her yellow turban.

It was Piper's turn. "And I'm Piper Wellington."

"Soon to be Piper Baladino," Evelyn said.

Lucinda nodded. "She's marrying a doctor six weeks from today."

"Congratulations," Valerie said. But she didn't seem thrilled.

"Let's sit, people," Evelyn said. Once they were settled, they took each other's hands for grace. Valerie hesitated but let her hands be joined. Wayne gave a blessing and dinner was served.

"So, Valerie," Wayne said after all the food had been passed, "you're an author. What do you write?"

"I'm currently writing a novel."

"What's it about?" Piper asked.

"I'd rather not say," she said.

Movement stopped, then resumed. "A secret novel," Lucinda said. "Isn't that going to make publishing a bit difficult?"

"Many authors don't care to share the inner workings of their plot lines with neophytes."

What-a-phytes?

Valerie's eyes made the rounds. "No offense."

Tons taken.

Piper cleared her throat. "How far along are you?"

"Nearly done."

"What else have you published?" Lucinda asked.

There was a moment's hesitation. "This is my second novel. The first one is complete and is being looked at by a publisher."

"I bet it's hard getting published," Wayne said.

"It can be, but it won't be. Not for me."

Evelyn dropped her fork. She picked it up and asked, "So you have an inside connection or something?"

"No," Valerie said, cutting a piece of meat. "I just have a feeling."

So do I. Evelyn hated the negative feelings she was having about her newest tenant.

"Well then," Lucinda said.

Wayne changed the subject. "So how's the makeover queen doing?"

"I'm doing fine. In fact—" Lucinda set her fork down and looked in Evelyn's direction— "I've tried to say this twice but have been interrupted. Things are going so well at the shelter that I plan to work there more hours. Which makes the forty-minute drive from Carson Creek to Jackson seem a bit ridiculous."

Evelyn's stomach tightened. *No. No. No.*

"Which means I'm moving out. I'm moving to Jackson to be closer to my work."

Evelyn let Piper and Wayne do the exclaiming. She found herself incapable of making a sound. First Margaret moved out, soon Piper, and now Lucinda? Peerbaugh Place would be empty.

She glanced at Valerie, who was eating as if nothing was going on. Empty except for this egotistical . . . neophyte.

"Excuse me." Evelyn needed air. She went out onto the front porch, taking up residence on the swing. This couldn't be happening. Though she was doing a pretty good job at being a proper landlord, she was tired of the changeovers. She wanted people to come and stay. A long time. What was with people, anyway? She and Aaron had lived in this house for decades. Why did everyone else in the world seem content to move every few months?

She heard the screen door open but didn't look. She didn't want to talk to Lucinda. She needed time to adjust. She needed—

"Lucinda feels bad."

Evelyn looked up to see Wayne.

He motioned to the place beside her. "May I?"

She nodded. He sat and after a few moments the swing settled into a common rhythm. "Lucinda wanted to come out."

"I'm glad she didn't. I'm mad."

"She's not deserting you, Evelyn. She's moving on, living out the calling that you helped her discover."

"But Piper's moving out too."

"She has a good excuse."

They swung up and back a few times in silence. "Everyone leaves me. Everyone moves on without me. They use me, use my house, then discard it all as if it means nothing to them. I'm tired of it."

He angled to look at her. "My, my. Let your bitterness out, woman."

Evelyn felt silly. She hadn't meant to say so much—and worse, she didn't even know if she truly believed what she'd said. She leaned her head against the swing's chain. "Forget all that. I love having people here. And I don't begrudge them their new lives. But I do get tired of the finding-new-tenants part. Getting to know them. Adjusting."

He nodded once, paused, then said. "Are you happy with Valerie?"

She shook her head and shrugged at the same time. "I thought it would be inspiring to have a writer in the house."

"Author."

"Hmm. I always figured an author was someone who'd published something."

"According to Valerie, her break will come any day now."

"She certainly doesn't lack confidence." Evelyn sighed and looked out over the band of gladiolas that lined the porch. "She makes me feel inferior."

"Never, ever feel that, Evelyn. I'll help you find new tenants. And God will provide. You know that. He hasn't failed you yet, has He?"

"He certainly keeps me guessing."

"I think it's part of His job."

They watched Tommy Dillon roller-blade past them on the sidewalk. He waved and they waved back.

"Shall we go finish dinner?" Wayne asked.

Might as well.

'm old.

Evelyn pulled the dead geranium from its pot with extra vengeance. Out with the old, in with the new. She filled its place with a new, younger, prettier one and patted the soil around its roots. The new flower stood tall, strong on its stem, vibrant and very much alive. She gave it a *poing*, making it lose three red petals.

So there.

Evelyn set the newly planted pot on the porch railing, kicked a few sprinkles of dirt off the floor into the flower bed, took off her gardening gloves, and sat on the swing with an audible *"Oomph."*

This was pitiful. Couldn't she even bend down to pot a silly plant without having her muscles ache?

Obviously not. Especially not today when she was suddenly older than yesterday. She would never be fifty-eight again. *I'm being silly. I'm one day older than I was yesterday, not an entire year.*

Semantics.

She got the swing in motion and suddenly felt very alone. At breakfast no one had greeted her with shouts of "Happy birth-day!" Piper, Lucinda, and Valerie had sipped their tea or coffee, eaten their oatmeal, and gone on with their lives as if today was like any other day. As the hours passed since then, the reality of their actions hit. And hit hard.

They forgot. Everyone forgot. She was alone.

She glanced at the empty space beside her. This was a swing meant for two. The lyrics to a Leslie Gore song intruded and Evelyn found herself singing "It's My Party." Crying and parties. She let out a huff. "Nice pity party, Evelyn."

The mailman walked by and saw her. "Hey, Evelyn. Nice morning, isn't it?"

"Sure is." She stood to intercept him, but he motioned her down.

"Stay put. I'll bring it to you." He took the porch steps two at a time and brought her a nice pile of letters. "Looks like cards. You having a birthday?"

She felt the burden lift. A little. "Today," she said.

He gave her a salute as he headed back to the sidewalk. "Congrats. Have a good one."

Evelyn looked through the letters. There were two cards. She opened the pink one. It was from Gillie Danson. Gillie had been in their original Sister Circle. She'd moved to another state because of a job offer. How nice of her to remember.

The other card had Herb's return address on it. Herb Evans. The boyfriend she'd dumped to go after Wayne. She opened it.

But it wasn't a birthday card. It was a wedding invitation.

The other mail slid from her lap to the ground. She let it lie. Herb—her Herb—was getting married in a month. To Mary Gerber. Evelyn had never met her, but Mae had said she worked at Piggly Wiggly.

Evelyn found her head shaking no. Yet she'd known they

were dating. She'd seen them together, the first time way back at Tessa's costume fund-raiser.

But he proposed to me first.

He tried to propose, but you made it very clear you weren't interested. Face it, Evelyn. No one's interested.

And only one person had remembered her birthday.

Birthdays could be the pits.

•   •   •

Valerie sat at her computer and stared at the wall. It held no inspiration. She looked over her shoulder at the window on the opposite side of the room. A small window air conditioner did its work. Maybe she should rearrange the room so her desk faced the view—and the air?

Desk? Hardly. All Evelyn had been able to spare was a tottery and decrepit library table from the attic. If only that dratted window seat weren't in the way, Valerie would have a chance to create the proper setting that was most advantageous to the development of her craft. Last night, she'd taken off the cushion to see if complete removal was feasible. But the seat was built in and looked original to the house. If she was going to be a permanent tenant of Peerbaugh Place she might consider pushing the matter, but since her plan was to stay only until she got a contract for her first novel . . .

She looked back at the computer screen. This second novel wasn't going well. Every scene was hard fought. Every paragraph. Every word. The first manuscript, *Go Ask the Sunrise*, had poured out of her as if she had only to turn a spigot to get the ideas to flow. Sometimes her fingers could hardly keep up with her thoughts, and on more than one occasion she'd actually yelled aloud at her characters, "Talk slower! I can't keep up!"

She felt confident about the book's chances. She'd met her

agent, Carla Mandez, at a writers' conference. Carla signed her on the spot after reading only the first chapter and a synopsis. Within a month, they'd found a publisher who was interested in seeing the entire manuscript. Both Valerie and Carla were hopeful.

It had been Carla's suggestion that she start the next book and not waste time waiting. Getting a nay or yay from a publisher was often a very long process, taking months and months. Besides, waiting without *doing* was almost unbearable. Best to keep busy. And didn't good writers *have* to write?

Easier said than done. She closed her laptop. Maybe the mail was here. She went downstairs to check.

Once on the porch she heard, "I have it already, Valerie." Evelyn was seated on the swing, a pile of letters in her lap. "But there's nothing for you. Sorry."

Valerie tried to hold on to the adage "no news is good news," but only found the truism annoying. She started to head back inside when she noticed Evelyn dab one of her eyes. Had she been crying? She took a second look. Sure enough, Evelyn's eyes were red. Though she didn't relish getting involved, there was no polite way to leave. "Are you all right?"

Evelyn took a deep breath and let it out. "I'm suffering a bit of the blues this morning." She patted the space beside her.

Valerie had no choice but to sit. And what did she have to lose? It wasn't as if the ideas were champing at the bit, clamoring to get out.

"How old are you, Valerie?" Evelyn asked. "If you don't mind my asking."

"Twenty-nine."

"Hmm. It's a bit sobering to realize I'm old enough to be your mother. I don't think of myself as fifty-nine. Though my body sometimes reminds me of my real age, my mind has me sitting somewhere around forty—and holding."

"Interesting." She might be able to use this phenomenon in her book. . . .

Evelyn raised her feet and studied them. "Sometimes when I look at a certain outfit or pair of shoes I think, 'That's an old-lady sweater' or 'Those are old-lady shoes.' Then it will hit me fresh that I'm not young anymore."

"You're not old either." Valerie meant it. In order to write all the books she wanted to write she planned to live to be a hundred. *That* was old.

Evelyn tapped a piece of mail against her hand. "I got a wedding invitation today. From an ex-beau."

"Oh." She didn't know what else to say. "But you're a widow, correct?"

Evelyn nodded. "Aaron was killed in a car accident. It's coming up on two and a half years now."

"I'm sorry. I shouldn't have brought it up. Not now. Not with the invitation."

"It's okay."

Valerie shook her head. "No, it's not. I have a tendency to be too blunt. But it's not my fault—it's the fault of my characters."

"Oh?"

How could she explain? She tried to get comfortable on the hard swing. "If a writer is a good writer, she has to have an open relationship with her characters—anything goes. No secrets. Sometimes I forget that real people don't appreciate the candor."

"Sometimes I wish I could do that."

"Write?"

"No. Get people to open up and say what they think." The rhythm of the swing changed slightly. "It gets hard when you have to hold feelings inside, when other people don't notice." Evelyn suddenly stood and moved to capture the column at the top of the porch steps as if bracing herself for an earthquake. She closed her eyes, her face intense. "Sometimes I feel like standing here on this porch and yelling to the world. Yelling at the world."

Valerie was taken aback. In her one-week residence at Peerbaugh Place she'd observed that Evelyn was not a woman of high emotion but rather a woman of stability, who just *was*, who just went on day to day, not rocking any boats, and not wishing to be rocked.

Evelyn let the column loose, her smile self-conscious. "Sorry about that. Had a brain burst there."

"It happens."

"But I don't want you to think that I'm unappreciative of what I have."

"I—"

"Because I have a very good life. I love having you ladies living here at Peerbaugh Place. I have a fabulous son, a dear daughter-in-law, and a granddaughter who makes my heart ache just looking at her. Who could ask for more?"

Valerie studied her a few seconds. "You, perhaps?"

Evelyn looked toward the front yard, toward the place where she'd made her pronouncement. "I need to pick up my friend Accosta Rand. We volunteer together over at the hospital." She adjusted a pot of geraniums. "Maybe it will get me out of this mood."

"Being moody is not a bad thing, Evelyn. Writers are moody all the time. It's allowed."

Her landlady smiled wistfully and went inside.

$$\bullet \qquad \bullet \qquad \bullet$$

The bass beat of a stereo greeted Evelyn—as it always did when she went to Accosta's home. Yet it wasn't coming from her friend's house, but from one of the neighboring homes that had been bisected and dissected and turned into apartments. *Out* were most of the families that used to populate this street. *In* were the twenty-somethings with their cars, sacks of beer cans at the curb, and loud music. Though it bothered Evelyn, Accosta didn't seem to mind. Of course Accosta wasn't the kind to complain about anything.

When Evelyn had first met her—when Accosta had been in the hospital getting her gallbladder removed—Evelyn had thought *she* was the giver in the relationship. After all, at age eighty-three, with Accosta's son Eugene living five states away, the older woman needed the younger. But as the months passed Evelyn realized she was doing her share of taking from this frail woman with a heart as wide and booming as . . . as . . . as that incessant stereo!

Evelyn vowed not to let it bother her. Heading up the porch steps she noticed a blanket and pillow on an old wicker rocker nearby. What the—?

She knocked and Accosta answered immediately, her purse on her arm. "All ready," she said as she closed the door behind her.

Something wasn't right. Accosta always asked Evelyn inside for a moment before they left.

Accosta hung her cane on her arm when she got to the top of the steps, carefully taking the railing, readying for her descent. "I do hope there are some new babies today. I do love seeing the wee ones." She turned around, waiting for Evelyn's usual steadying arm. "Evelyn?"

Evelyn moved to the bedding. "What's this?"

"Oh, fiddle-dee. I forgot to bring it inside this morning."

"Did you sleep out here?"

Accosta glanced toward the door. "I think we can leave those there. I can't imagine anyone wanting to steal an old pillow and—"

"You slept in the rocking chair?"

Accosta held out her hand. "We really need to get going."

Evelyn picked up the bedding and held out her hand. "Keys please."

"No, it's fine. Just leave it be."

It was not fine. "What are you hiding in there?"

Accosta's face slipped from panic to teasing. She cupped her mouth into a whisper. "Actually, I have a boyfriend . . ."

Evelyn extended her hand a second time. "Keys please."

The old woman looked at the empty palm, sighed, then dug the keys out of her purse. "It's not as bad as it looks."

Oh dear! Evelyn opened the door and rushed inside, having no idea what she'd find. She couldn't imagine a reason for secrecy. For the pillow and blanket.

She was immediately assailed by the smell of dampness. The Persian rug in the parlor was pulled back. Small pieces of furniture were clumped together. Looking straight ahead toward the kitchen, she noticed a puddle on the floor and a moat of towels marking the doorway.

"Water? What happened?"

"A pipe broke under the kitchen sink."

Evelyn hurried to look, tiptoeing through the standing water. The cupboard doors were open. An old copper pipe hung askew. "When did this happen?"

"A couple days ago. The nice boy next door heard me scream and came over and turned off the water down in the basement. I don't know what I would have done if he hadn't known what to do. The water was shooting out everywhere and—"

Evelyn knew how old houses worked. There weren't separate water shutoffs at each sink and toilet. One valve served them all. Which meant . . . "You've been without water for two days?"

Accosta took the pillow and blanket from Evelyn and set them on the kitchen table. "I've been okay."

Evelyn noticed something else besides the wetness and the smell. "It seems awfully hot in here." The windows were open—which was good for the wetness, but not for the June heat.

"That's why I slept on the porch."

Evelyn made a beeline to the parlor. The air conditioner was off. She turned the switch. It didn't turn on. She flipped the switch on a nearby lamp. Nothing.

"You don't have electricity either?"

Accosta stood in the parlor, the slump of her shoulders even deeper than normal. "I . . . I'm a little behind on my bills."

Evelyn went to her side. "Oh, dear lady, why didn't you call me?"

Accosta glanced at the phone. Evelyn took the receiver off. It was dead. She felt sick to her stomach. She led Accosta to the couch and sat beside her. "Tell me what happened."

Accosta's voice was heavy. "Eugene lost his job. He can't send money anymore and I can't borrow more on the house."

"I would have thought your house was paid for by now."

"It was. But Eugene's kids wanted to go to certain schools; then he and his wife tried to start a business but it didn't—"

"You took out a new mortgage to help them?"

"Any mother would," she said. "But now, without him being able to pay me back . . . my Social Security doesn't cover . . ." She shrugged. "It will be all right."

Evelyn let out a bitter laugh, scanning the wet, hot, lightless room. "How? How will it be all right?"

"God will provide."

The phrase Evelyn had heard a hundred times suddenly sounded like the punch line of an awful joke. Yet she hesitated saying anything to shake her friend's faith. Accosta was fairly new to the believing business. "God will provide, but we're also put on this earth to help each other. But we can't help if we don't *know*."

"I'm sorry. I just didn't want to burden you—"

"Burden?" Evelyn ran a hand across Accosta's back. "You are a blessing in my life. Don't you ever think of yourself as a burden."

She nodded, but there was no strength behind it. "The neighbor boy says a lot of the pipes are rusted through. He said it will cost a lot of money to fix it."

Not good. Neither Evelyn nor any of her friends had a lot of extra money lying around. But she didn't let Accosta in on her worry. "We'll work something out. But for now, we're going to get you out of here."

"Out?"

Evelyn stood. "You're coming home to live with me."

"At Peerbaugh Place?"

"Lucinda's moving out this weekend. We'll make do until you can have her room."

"But I can't pay, Evelyn."

Evelyn touched a finger to the tip of Accosta's nose. "Enough of that. You're coming."

.   .   .

Lucinda packed the last of her things in a box and shut its lid. For the first time during the past two hours, she let herself stop. Look around. Breathe.

She'd miss Peerbaugh Place—which surprised her. When she'd first moved in last fall, she'd thought the boardinghouse below her station. She'd resented everything about it—and the women who lived here. She was Lucinda Van Horn, "of the Boston Van Horns." She laughed now, but it was an uneasy laugh. How many times had she introduced herself using that arrogant line? She suffered a shiver.

I was different then.

It was an understatement. Her whole identity had been dependent on her status as a Van Horn and as an ex-model, not on who she *was*, what she could contribute. But everything had changed at her fortieth high school reunion. She'd been humiliated by an ex-beau and old acquaintances, leading her to run into the night, into the dark streets of Boston, where she literally ran into Pastor Enoch Gunderson. He patched her scraped knee, fed her chocolate cake, and faded into the sunset. Only to be met again in nearby Jackson, where he ran the Haven's Rest Mission. Through a set of circumstances Lucinda had come to attribute to God, she now gave makeovers to down-and-out women hoping to get back in the workplace—or simply those who wanted to feel better about themselves.

She drew in a cleansing breath. What was that old ad? "You've come a long way, baby." And she had. She'd gone from an egotistical, desperate woman to one who had purpose and was finding peace with the idea of turning sixty next year *and* with the idea of not having a man in her life.

Not that Pastor Enoch wasn't a man. And single. And cute as a button. He was. But Lucinda was discovering that being friends with a man without the trappings—and traps—of a romance could be very satisfying. Maybe the facts that her marriage had failed and her numerous love affairs had fizzled were indicators that she shouldn't *be* married.

Fancy that.

She sat on the bed, running her hand over the quilt. One more night here and she was off to a new apartment in Jackson. She had landed a job at a local department store—in the cosmetics department—which would pay the rent. But her free time would be spent at the shelter, giving makeovers. Getting a hefty discount on supplies from the department store was an added bonus.

One more night.

But then . . . suddenly, she stood. All her thoughts were of tomorrow. Of the move. Of starting over. Of her new life. Was there any reason to stick around tonight? She shook her head and grabbed a box.

Surely Evelyn would understand.

•   •   •

Though Evelyn would have been fine with calling the hospital and telling them she and Accosta would not be in today, Accosta would have none of it. She would not shirk her volunteer duty. Evelyn was glad there was a new baby for Accosta to coo over. It was good for her too, making her forget—for a little while—that no one had remembered her birthday.

After their stint delivering flowers and spreading cheer at the hospital, they went to Peerbaugh Place. Evelyn was a little nervous about what would happen next. Not that she regretted her invitation to Accosta to stay with them. That decision was a no-brainer. But the logistics were weighty. Lucinda was moving out tomorrow. For tonight Evelyn planned to offer Accosta her own room and her own bed—even though she knew Accosta would object. But there was no way Evelyn could even think of Accosta sleeping on the couch in the sunroom or in the parlor. So exactly how did one convince a five-foot, eighty-pound, elderly woman to let herself be taken care of without coming across as a bully?

Evelyn lent a supportive arm as Accosta took the porch steps. "Oooh. The swing. I forgot you had a swing. Let's go sit."

It was a fine idea and would give Evelyn a chance to go inside and talk to Lucinda. With that thought she looked toward the street, checking. Lucinda's car was gone. Now what? She'd wanted to pin down exactly when Lucinda would have her things moved out.

When Accosta lowered herself into the swing, only her toes could touch the ground. "This is nice. What a wonderful place to sit. The flowers are beautiful. It's so quiet and peaceful."

Not a stereo in earshot. "Would you like some iced tea?"

"Don't go to any bother."

"No bother. You stay put. I'll be out in a minute."

Evelyn went inside and ran up the stairs to Lucinda's room. She prayed that most of her things were packed.

The door was open. The room was empty of all things Lucinda. Only the furniture remained. Evelyn opened the closet. It was empty. Turning back to the room she noticed a note on the dresser.

Dear Evelyn,

I got packed faster than I expected and was so excited . . . I decided to just do it now instead of hanging around another night. I hope you understand. I will always cherish my time at Peerbaugh Place and all the lovely sisters I've come to know. I'll be in touch.

Lucinda

A bevy of emotions rushed in. Sadness. Regret. Fear. Wistfulness.

And then glee.

The room was empty! *Thank You, Jesus!*

Evelyn ran downstairs.

.   .   .

"And this is your own private balcony."

Accosta stood in the doorway leading off her new bedroom, both hands at her chest.

Evelyn took one of them and gently pulled her outside. "Come on. Try it out. Have a seat."

Accosta came outside and sat in the wicker chair that overlooked the front yard. The branches of the trees seemed to bow at her presence.

"You can keep tabs on Mae and Collier from here. With Ringo, Soon-ja, and Ricky moved in, there's a lot going on over—"

She stopped when she noticed Accosta was crying. She knelt beside her. "What's wrong?"

Accosta shook her head. "It's so utterly perfect—and kind."

Evelyn put a hand on hers. "I'm thrilled to have you here."

And she was.

* * *

Evelyn left Accosta to take a nap in her new room. She went downstairs and saw the mail on the table in the entry. She took up the pink envelope and moved to the dining room, ready to place the birthday card from Gillie on the buffet—as she did every birthday.

But this time . . . she stopped herself. If she put the card on display the other ladies would see it. Then they could pretend they hadn't forgotten (when they really had) and slip in a belated greeting or present. But that was too easy. She didn't want to give them any help remembering.

You're playing the martyr.

Yeah? So be it.

* * *

Evelyn stared at the phone. She really should call Wayne to talk to him about getting Accosta's house fixed. Wayne was good at repairs, and being retired, he had the time. But if she called him . . . at this point she didn't want him to remember her birthday.

It was dumb and childish. But as the spurned birthday girl, she was allowed. *Evelyn! Why didn't you say something about it being your birthday? I feel horrible.*

Exactly.

Suddenly the phone rang and she jumped back. She calmed herself with a couple breaths before answering. "Hello?"

"Hey, Evelyn."

"Hi, Wayne." She hurried forward with her words, not wanting him to have time to make amends. "I was just going to call you . . ." She told him about Accosta's dilemma. "Can you take care of it?"

"Of course. I'll run over there now . . . which means . . . oh dear. I was going to see if you wanted to grab a bite at Ruby's. Piper is going to Gregory's mother's for dinner in a few days and she's nervous, so I thought maybe I could get some advice about how to help. But now . . . maybe we could go to lunch tomorrow?"

Evelyn set the stage for future punishment. "Sure. That's fine."

"Good. Then I'll get going. I'll let you know what I find out at Accosta's."

You do that.

* * *

If you would have asked Tessa Klein a year ago the odds of her ever meeting a Russian mail-order bride, she would have been aghast.

But that was before Ursola Shivikova Smith came into her life.

Tessa had known Ursola's American husband, Glenn, for years. He'd gone to school with Tessa's daughter, Naomi. They attended the same church. They worked on the same committees. When Glenn's first wife had died of breast cancer, Tessa had admired how Glenn had taken on the job of a single father, raising his son, Daryn, to adulthood. That job complete, it was appropriate and even advisable for Glenn to look for another wife.

But in Russia?

People had tried to talk him out of it, but after failing miserably with the regional dating scene, Glenn had been determined.

He'd taken two trips to Russia with the sole intent of meeting a wife. Tessa had heard stories of the planned gatherings where prospective wives met prospective husbands. No one would argue that it was far-fetched. Odd. Even bizarre.

But it had worked. Glenn, the middle-aged burly black man with the big laugh; and Ursola, the twenty-five-year-old petite, porcelain-skinned woman with the wistful look in her eye found . . . love? If not love, certainly a connection. Six months ago Ursola had arrived in Carson Creek. Tessa had attended the wedding.

And now the funeral.

For Glenn was dead. Dead of a heart attack at age fifty-two.

As Tessa climbed the steps of the church, she shivered in spite of the hot day. Every time someone young died—someone younger than her own seventy-seven years—Tessa felt a little guilty. Even a little humbled. Why was God allowing her these years? Had she used them well?

That would be up to Him to decide.

The sanctuary was nearly full, the organ music setting the mood with a legato piece where one note met another, leaving no space between them for silence or air. She accepted the arm of one of the ushers, took a program, and moved toward the center of the pew next to a couple she didn't recognize. She nodded a greeting and sat.

As she looked over the program of Glenn's too-short life, Tessa wondered if Glenn had had any existing heart problems. It wouldn't have surprised her. He'd been overweight and she'd often heard him puff after coming up the church steps. She looked up when Piper and Gregory slipped into the pew beside her, and she was tempted to ask him about Glenn's heart—he being Glenn's doctor and all—but decided it was none of her business. And what did it matter anyway? Dead was dead. Sorrow was sorrow.

Poor Ursola. To find happiness and then lose it.

She and Glenn *had* seemed happy. Ursola had made an effort to adjust to life in small-town America. Tessa and some of the other ladies of the church had given her a bridal shower and had taken turns picking her up for errands. Ursola nearly fainted when Tessa had first taken her into the Piggly Wiggly. Such immense choice and the sheer quantity of goods were a shock—and actually kind of embarrassing to Tessa. To have so much available at all times when much of the world struggled . . . it further reinforced Tessa's dedication to her international Sister Circle Network. She was working hard to reach women throughout the world, offering them the possibilities of sisterhood along with hope for improved living and social conditions, so the fact that a Russian had moved right into little Carson Creek was special. In a way, it brought her ministry home. Close.

Unfortunately, so far Ursola had not been too interested in Tessa's offers to introduce her to the ladies of Peerbaugh Place, or to join in a Bible study at church, or to even come over for dinner. So many people wanted to help, and yet after the initial excursions, Ursola had begged off, offering various excuses. And Tessa had backed off, realizing it took time to adapt to a new country, to a new language, *and* to a new husband.

But now Glenn was gone. Ursola was a widow in a strange land. Surely she'd ask for help now. Surely she'd *let* Tessa be a sister to her now.

She had a sudden thought and turned to Gregory. "Ursola doesn't have to go back to Russia, does she?"

Gregory leaned close. "I don't think so. She had temporary residency because of her marriage, which could have turned permanent. But when the spouse who's a citizen dies . . . I think it's a matter of paperwork—*if* she wants to stay, that is."

Tessa had never thought of that. "Surely she wouldn't want to go back."

He shrugged. "Home is home, Tessa. She has nothing to keep her here. Not now. I don't think she and Daryn are close."

"But life is better here. Mom. Apple pie."

"Maybe her mother's in Russia. And maybe she doesn't like apple pie."

Tessa tried to get her patriotism in check. If her world travels had taught her anything it was that people were proud of their roots. Gregory was right. Home was home.

And yet . . . the very fact that Ursola had signed up for one of those meet-and-greet events in Russia could well mean that she'd mentally cut the ties to her homeland long before she set foot on American soil.

There was movement at the back of the church and the congregation quieted as the family came in. Dozens and dozens of Glenn's extended family flowed down the center aisle, leaning on each other, comforting each other. Tessa recognized Glenn's son, Daryn, his arm around his wife, Shanna. But Ursola walked alone. Her face was drawn and seemed even paler than usual, especially in contrast to her long black hair and the rich chocolate skin of her in-laws.

Tessa whispered to Gregory. "She looks so tiny. So alone."

"She is."

There wasn't time to talk more. The service began.

•   •   •

I want to go home.

Ursola Shivikova Smith stood at the sink. She heard voices and even laughter in the next room. How could they laugh? Glenn was dead!

Her stepson, Daryn, came in the room and Ursola flipped away a tear and braced herself. "We need more meatballs," he said.

Ursola nodded toward the far counter. "There." She pointed

to the other counter. "You need more kolduny?" Needing to do *something* she'd made Glenn's favorite Russian dish of mushroom-and-meat-stuffed dumplings.

He snickered. "Hardly."

She turned back to the dishes, immersing her hands in the soapy suds rather than wrapping them around his arrogant neck. *Just go. Leave me alone. Totally alone is better than being around you.*

He paused at the kitchen door. "By the way, the lawyer wants to see us Monday. To go over the will."

"What is *will*?"

Daryn faced her, setting his feet. "The money. Dad's money, that will become *my* money now that he's gone." He popped a meatball into his mouth and she saw its shape in his cheek. "I wouldn't expect anything if I were you."

She forced a smile and offered Daryn a string of Russian cusswords in a tone that implied she was saying something nice.

He stared blankly, then shrugged. "Yeah. Whatever."

She shrugged back and was glad to see him leave. How could a wonderful man like Glenn have such an egotistical, mean, nasty, spiteful . . .

She forced herself to take a deep breath. This anger only drained her. Hopefully, she wouldn't have to deal with Daryn once they got past this will thing.

Money. She hated money. Lack of it had been a big part of her leaving Russia. Good jobs were scarce, the economy was bad, and the black market prospered. Most of the men she'd dated were alcoholics and had no more hope for the future than she did. But an American . . . the American dream . . .

She'd been attracted to Glenn the first time she'd met him. His smile. His laugh. It had been a long time since she'd heard laughter like his. Real laughter from deep down in his soul. And he hadn't hit on her like so many of the other men had. He'd talked to her in a voice that was as gentle as his laugh was boisterous.

He'd listened. Her broken English had made deep communication difficult and yet . . . after that first night spent talking, she'd wanted nothing more than to see him again, and longed to feel his strong arms around her, pulling her close. And safe.

She realized she hadn't washed a dish but was simply gliding her hands back and forth in the water.

The kitchen door opened and Daryn popped his head in. "People are leaving."

Good.

•   •   •

Russell Peerbaugh drove home from the doctor's office. This was not going to be an easy weekend. Waiting until Monday. Waiting for the results to see if it was his fault they couldn't have children.

What if it's a no-go?

He gripped the steering wheel and whispered, "'Don't worry about tomorrow, for tomorrow will bring its own worries. Today's trouble is enough for today. . . . Don't worry about tomorrow, for tomorrow will bring its own worries. Today's trouble is enough—'"

Trouble. Oh yes, there would be trouble in their marriage because of this. There already was. Not that he and Audra were on the verge of divorce or anything that drastic, but this baby thing had started to consume their lives. Audra didn't smile as much, and neither did he. There was always this should-do, want-to-do, can't-do aura surrounding them as if this one aspect of their lives could make or break what they had.

Ridiculous of course. Many couples dealt with infertility and developed a stronger bond because of it. It wasn't as if they weren't already enjoying the wonders of parenthood. His step-daughter, Summer, was a blessing he counted daily.

But . . . but there was something special about creating a child together. A definite, definitive product of two becoming one. Which meant if he didn't hold up his end of the deal, if the blame was within his faulty body . . .

He shook his head violently. He couldn't go there. Not yet. There would be plenty of time for blame. If and when.

•   •   •

That evening Valerie went out with friends. Piper went out with Gregory. Leaving Evelyn to spend the evening looking at old photo albums with Accosta. *Happy birthday to me.*

Not that Evelyn minded showing her friend pictures of Aaron and Russell and relatives long gone. It was fun seeing old pictures of Peerbaugh Place. Though she and Aaron had lived here for twenty-six of their thirty-one years together, it had been in the Peerbaugh family long before that—since 1900.

But with all the looking, all the reminiscing, Evelyn started having the strangest brush with weariness. All those years passing in the same place. Stuck. It was almost as if she'd been held captive by Peerbaugh Place. What would her life be like if it didn't revolve around this house? What if she sold it and took a world cruise like Tessa had done? Evelyn had seen so little of the world. The Eiffel Tower, St. Peter's, and Pompeii were pictures in a book, not in her memories. What sights had she seen?

There's a new sporting goods store on the edge of town . . .

She realized Accosta was telling her a story about when she and her husband and son had gone camping in Canada. She smiled and tried to be interested.

See? Even Accosta has been out of the country. She felt a sudden need to be alone—all successful pity parties were done solo. She waited for Accosta to finish her story, then closed the photo album and stood. "I'm a little tired. I think I'll turn in."

"Oh. I will too then."

Within five minutes they were in their respective rooms. As Evelyn got ready for bed she felt bad for cutting their evening short. Valerie had said writers were a moody lot? Move over.

She got in bed and was just about to turn out the bedside lamp when her eyes fell on a picture of Aaron, smiling from the porch swing. She picked it up and turned onto her back to look at it properly. "You wouldn't have forgotten my birthday, would you, Aaron?"

But as the memories of past birthdays came flooding back, she put the photo back in its place. Aaron *had* forgotten. More than once. Even when he remembered he'd never made a big thing about it. He wasn't very good at gift giving—usually giving something inappropriate or not giving anything. He always gave the impression that having to go out and buy a present was an imposition: "Oh great. It's your birthday *again*? Here's twenty bucks. Go buy yourself something."

Quite the sentimental guy.

So it's not like you're used to big to-dos on your birthday. Let it go. Get over it.

Maybe she was just a forgettable person.

As Mae would say: *Bummer*.

3

$\mathcal{R}$icky fidgeted in her arms. "Yes, yes, little man. Be patient."

With all the modern inventions of the new millennium, Mae couldn't believe no one had come up with a quicker way to heat baby bottles. She'd asked Soonie why they couldn't just use the microwave, only to be subjected to a mini sermon on the dangers of "hot spots." Gracious Gobstoppers. So here she was, waiting for a bottle to heat on the stove, just like when her own babies were little.

She looked at the kitchen clock. Collier looked at her looking. "He's not up, is he?"

Mae felt herself go on the defensive. "Soonie's getting him up."

"Ringo's a big boy; he should be able to get up for work on his own."

"He's used to working nights."

"It's Monday morning, the beginning of a new week. They've had nine mornings here. He's had the construction job with Ambrose Construction five of those days. Time enough to adjust to a normal work schedule."

Mae noted the "nine mornings." Not a rounded-off "ten," or a general, "week and a half." Nine. Specifically nine. As if he was counting. She sat at the kitchen table and lowered her voice. "How you doing with all this, Mr. Husband?"

Collier looked up from his crossword puzzle. "With having three extra people invade my house indefinitely? The key word being *indefinitely*?"

Mae heard two sets of footsteps moving around upstairs and glanced to the ceiling. At least Ringo was up. "You didn't mind when Starr was here last fall after she and Ted broke up."

He glared at her over his half-glasses.

"You *did* mind?"

He set down his pencil and took off his glasses.

Uh-oh.

"Not having any children of my own, I am thrilled to be given the experience through you. And a grandson . . ." He reached over the table and ran a finger along Ricky's arm.

"But?"

He withdrew his hand. "But I married you, Mae Fitzpatrick Ames. I married a grown woman with grown children, a woman who makes my blood flow at seventy miles per. When I wake up next to you each morning, freezing because you've stolen the covers, and experience the scent of your morning breath wafting toward me, and then see your messy hair consuming the pillow—"

"Hey!"

He touched her arm. "I love it. I love it all. And I love you."

That's better. "I love you too, Collie."

"But . . . I signed on to live with one Fitzpatrick. Not two and certainly not four. Call me selfish, call me rude, but I miss having you all to myself. That's a compliment, wifey. You are all I need and want in this life—at least on a daily basis. You are my every-thing."

Mae was once again amazed how Collier had the ability to melt her heart and make her want to fling herself into his arms—which she probably would have done if she hadn't been holding a baby. She kissed the air and blew it toward him. "You are my gift from God, Mr. Husband."

He made fists and took on a muscleman pose, making her laugh.

"I think you misunderstood. I said you were a gift *from* God. I didn't say you were a god."

"Oh." He dropped his arms and became her Collie again. Her Collie who let her hog the covers, who ran his fingers through her hair even on her numerous bad-hair days, and who kissed her, bad breath or otherwise. He was *her* everything. And she couldn't ruin that. She wouldn't.

•   •   •

Ringo was finally off to work, Soon-ja was cleaning up the kitchen, and Mae was dressed to go to work at her custom-jewelry store, Silver-Wear. She took her purse off the coat hook. "I'm off."

Collier was right behind her, keys in hand. "Me too."

"Where are you going this morning?" Mae asked. He was retired. He didn't *need* to go anywhere.

"I'm going to help Wayne work on Accosta's house some more. We have four fans going so the damage control is in place, but today we have to tackle the plumbing—or at least make a determination as to whether we need a professional on the job."

"That's nice of you," Soon-ja said.

Mae kissed his cheek. "Indeed it is. You're a good man, Charlie Brown. Call me later and let me know if you want to meet up for—"

Her eyes skimmed past him to the calendar that hung at the end of the cupboards. A red-star sticker grabbed her attention.

Every year she dotted the calendar with stickers on the birthdays she wanted to remember. But this star wasn't on this week. It was on last week. Last Friday.

She saw the name beside it: Evelyn. She pushed Collier aside and pegged the star with a finger. "I forgot Evelyn's birthday! It was Friday!"

Collier looked at the calendar with her. "I can't believe we forgot."

Mae racked her brain trying to remember what she had done on Friday that would explain her total brain freeze about her best friend's birthday. She could think of nothing. She had no excuse.

"I gotta go."

"To work?"

"To make amends."

• • •

"Yoo-hoo! It's me!"

Evelyn rushed toward the entry, a finger to her lips. "Shh, Mae. Valerie is working."

Mae looked upstairs and lowered her voice. "Which means you can't talk?"

I can't talk as loud as you talk. Evelyn crooked a finger and led them onto the front porch. "What's up?"

Mae pulled her into a bear hug. "Oh, Evie. I'm so sorry."

"For what?"

Mae let her go, but kept hold of her upper arms. "For forgetting your birthday. I can't believe it! Why didn't you say something?"

Evelyn strolled to the swing and Mae followed. A wave of satisfaction warmed her. Not telling everyone all weekend had been one of the hardest things she'd ever done, and variations on possible martyr scenes *had* kept her mind busy through too many free moments. She'd even kept it quiet when she'd had lunch with Wayne on Saturday. To hear Mae gush over her now . . . it felt good. "There was no reason to say anything. It was okay. I realize people have busy lives. Goodness, with Ringo home . . . you have plenty to think about besides my birthday. It was fine. Really."

Mae poked her thigh twice. "Don't give me that, Evelyn Peerbaugh. Don't go bland Evie on me. It had to have hurt and hurt bad. Admit it."

What could she say? This was Mae, and Evelyn knew her friend would practically stalk her until she told the truth, the whole truth, and nothing but the truth. "Fine. I admit it. It hurt. Bad."

"Good."

"What?"

"I mean *good* you admit it. But why didn't you tell anyone? Give us a hint?"

"I thought about it. But then . . ." She eyed Mae, then looked out across the yard. "There was a certain weird satisfaction in playing the martyr."

"Now there's a truth I can wrap my fingers around and shake in the palm of my hand."

"You've felt that way?"

"You betcha. I can't say as anyone's forgotten my birthday—fat chance, with all the hints I toss around, they wouldn't dare—but I've played Joan of Arc once or twice, and wanted everyone *else* to be burned at the stake for hurting me."

"It's kind of silly," Evelyn said. "A birthday shouldn't be that big a deal when you're fifty-nine."

"Gracious pony rides, Evie. Each of us gets only one special day a year. We deserve a little hoopla."

Hoopla would have been nice.

"So—" Mae stood—"better late than never. How about a belated birthday lunch today?"

That sounded nice but . . . "I told Wayne I'd bring sandwiches to Accosta's house. He's working so hard over there and—"

"And has commandeered Collie to help. So let's have a picnic. We'll surprise the guys. Two hopelessly beautiful women bearing food, frivolity, and fantastic company."

That sounded great. "Please don't tell Wayne about my birthday."

Mae shook her head, making a *tsk-tsk* sound. "Evie, Evie. The first thing you have to learn about gaining a man's attention so he'll stop being blind, stop taking you for granted, and finally look at you as the beaming, steaming woman you are—" she took an exaggerated breath and continued—"is learning when to utilize the power of guilt."

"But I don't want—"

She headed for the steps. "Leave it to me, Evie. I'll handle everything."

•   •   •

Mae carried the picnic basket and Evelyn carried the thermos of iced tea. The front door to Accosta's house was propped open. Even from the porch, Mae could smell a nasty dankness.

Mae stepped around a floor fan and peeked in the kitchen. The cabinet doors under the sink were open and the floor was littered with tools, but the men weren't around. She backtracked to the living room. "Oh, gentlemen?" she called. "Ollie ollie oxen free!"

Collier appeared at the top of the stairs. "Wifey, what are you doing here?"

"Where's Wayne?"

"I'm here." He stepped next to Collier.

Now that the audience was properly in place, Mae moved next to Evelyn, held up the picnic basket with one hand, and swept her other arm in a ta-da mode. "Lunch awaits. Come down and join your women."

The men looked at each other; then Collier said, "Give us three minutes." They disappeared.

The ladies moved into the kitchen and Evelyn whispered, "You shouldn't have called us 'your women.' Wayne doesn't think of me that way."

"But he should, and everyone knows it. Even he knows it. You two are the perfect couple and—"

"We're just friends."

Mae noticed the crease that had formed between Evelyn's eyes. "Friendship is nice, Evie. Friendship is good. But romance is better."

Evelyn busied herself unpacking the plates. "Like I told you, Wayne doesn't think of me in that way."

"You thought he did. A few months ago, you told me about the time he came out on the porch and held your hand and told you to look toward the future—with him."

Evelyn held a plastic fork in midair. She lowered her voice. "I must have overreacted. I thought it meant he cared, meant he thought of me romantically, but nothing's happened. I keep waiting and waiting."

"And feeling and feeling." Mae sighed. "Men can be as dense as a muddy river, Evie. The entire world can see what's deep in their hearts and they're clueless. And even if they do see it, they don't seem capable of doing anything about it."

"Was Collier that way?"

Oops. Mae took out the potato salad. "Collie is an exceptional man in that respect. Besides, I didn't give him a chance to get into the just-friends mode. Once we got past hating each other, he knew without a doubt that I'd cast my line right above his head, my hook was ready, and my bobber was waiting to be bobbed."

"But Wayne and I have slipped into this routine—"

"Rut. It's called a rut, Evie." Mae heard the men on the stairs.

Evelyn reached across the table and put a hand on her arm. "Don't say anything. Don't do anything."

"But it's the perfect time to do a little pushing."

"Don't. Please. I've got to do this my way."

"Your way is no way, Evie."

"Please . . ."

The men came in. But seeing the panicked look on Evelyn's face, Mae had no choice but to behave herself.

For now.

•   •   •

Ursola Shivikova Smith sat in the lawyer's office having no idea what to expect. Her stomach ached from worry. In Russia one did not go to an attorney for anything good. And the fact that Glenn's son wanted her there didn't help. He hated her. Not that she liked him much, but she would have—could have—if only he'd given her a chance.

Daryn sat in the far chair, with his wife Shanna between him and Ursola. He put his ankle on his knee, showing her the bottom of his shoe—an insult, though she wasn't sure he was smart enough to know that. The lawyer—a woman—sat behind a massive mahogany desk. She must be very rich. Ursola was suddenly worried about bribes. She wasn't sure how it was done here, but obviously this lawyer was used to getting many of them.

Ursola had no money except access to a few hundred dollars in her and Glenn's checking account. And she would need that and more to pay the house payment that was due in a few days. Then there were groceries, and the bills for the funeral.

Daryn had said this meeting was about money. She hoped so. She needed some. Now. At least enough so she could get by until she got a job and earned her own. She'd always wanted to work, but Glenn had told her to hold off for a while until she got used to the country and the language. *A while* was here. And as a foreigner, living on a visa, she wondered if there was paperwork to fill out. She had no idea.

The lawyer finished arranging her papers and looked up. She smiled. "Well then, first off I want to offer you my condolences. Though I only met Glenn the one time—years ago—he was an amiable, energetic man, a man far too young to be taken from his family."

Daryn put his feet on the floor and leaned forward. "Yes, yes, can we get on with this?"

The lawyer's smile disappeared, but she nodded and lifted a page. "Unfortunately, this will is an old will and Mr. Smith never made any changes that would include his new wife. I was unaware that he'd even married. If I'd known I would have advised—"

Daryn laughed. "Oh yeah . . . I see where this is going, and I like it."

Shanna put a hand on her husband's arm. "Daryn, behave yourself."

The lawyer's words . . . though Ursola wasn't exactly sure what they meant, she had a sinking feeling . . .

The lawyer looked directly at her. "I'm so sorry, Mrs. Smith. Though the funeral expenses are covered by a small life insurance policy, all the rest of your husband's assets will revert to his son."

"What assets are we talking about here?" Daryn asked.

The lawyer glanced at the page. "The house, the car, the furnishings. There's a little bit in savings, but not much."

Ursola's mind grabbed on to the word *house*. "The house? My house?"

Daryn grinned. "No, my house." He turned to his wife. "Our house."

"Daryn," Shanna said.

"Don't give me that tone, woman. You've been bugging me to get out of our apartment for months. Now we can."

Shanna glanced at Ursola. "But you shouldn't be so . . . so . . ."

Daryn stood. "I'll be how I want to be. She doesn't deserve anything. She doesn't even speak English. If I had my way she'd go back where she came from and—"

"Mr. Smith. That will be enough."

He shrugged. "Whatever."

"Mrs. Smith is your father's legal wife," the lawyer said. "Perhaps, for the sake of family unity and compassion you might agree to a compromise regarding the house and its possessions, as well as the timing of—"

"The timing is perfect." He looked at his watch and then at Ursola. "Today's the twenty-seventh. You have until the thirtieth, until the end of the month to get out."

Ursola popped to her feet. "Four days?"

The lawyer stood. "Mr. Smith, be reasonable."

"I'm within my legal rights, aren't I?"

"Yes, but your stepmother—"

"She's not my step anything. She's a gold digger who couldn't find a man in her own country so she conned her way over here. And I want her out. In four days. End of story."

He left the room. After an apologetic look, Shanna ran after him.

Ursola's legs gave out and she sank into the chair. The lawyer came around her desk, to her side. "I'm so sorry, Mrs. Smith. I wish there was something I could do. But unfortunately, your stepson is within his legal rights to be a miserable pain."

Ursola found herself staring at the navy fleck in the carpet. "I must leave?"

The lawyer put a hand on her shoulder. "Do you have a friend you could stay with until you get on your feet again?"

Get on my feet? What does that mean?

Yet even though the answer to the lawyer's question was no, Ursola found herself nodding yes.

The woman seemed relieved. "Good. Good." She reached back on her desk and retrieved a business card. "Here's my number. Please call if you need anything. I'm so sorry for your loss."

* * *

Ursola stood in the middle of her living room—strike that—Daryn and Shanna's living room. She did a slow turn, looking at the *things* for the first time since she'd moved in. In truth, there were very few things that were hers. Glenn had lived in this house for ten years. Except for a few wedding presents, plus the two brown suitcases full of clothes and mementos Ursola had brought with her from Russia, this was *his* house. These were *his* things.

Were. Past tense. In every sense of that awful word.

And now she had to leave.

But where would she go?

She sank to the floor, right there in the middle of the room, not wanting to sit on someone else's couch, not wanting to rest on anything that wasn't hers.

Go home.

It was a logical thought, but emotional. And impractical. She had no family back in Russia. *If* she got back there—and she didn't have money to even think of doing such a thing—she would have no place to stay. No roots to grab hold of.

I have to stay here.

But where, here? Though she'd met a number of people through Glenn's church, she'd made no effort to get to know them. She'd been too focused on getting to know her husband to worry about anyone else. She didn't even know their last names.

Suddenly overwhelmed with anger, she got to her feet. "I must do this!"

With new purpose she opened the coat closet and retrieved the two suitcases she'd brought with her from Russia. She tossed them on the bed in the master bedroom and filled them with her clothes and sundries, picking and choosing carefully. She folded and set them inside carefully as if each item had taken on more meaning because it was all she had. She added the tie that Glenn had worn the first time she'd seen him, and as an afterthought, took his favorite plaid shirt. She held it to her face a moment, drinking in his scent. She'd never wash it. Never.

The clothes also filled part of the second suitcase, but for the rest of the space . . . she walked through the house with an owner's eye. What did she want to take to commemorate this life spent with Glenn?

Her eyes lit on the matryoshka she'd brought with her from Russia. The nesting dolls had been in her family for three generations. The thought of Daryn even looking at them disgusted her. She put one inside the other and kept moving, spotting the photo album of their wedding, along with a little stuffed bear Glenn had bought her one Sunday at a craft fair.

In the dining room she stood before the china cabinet and looked longingly at the lovely china with the red and pink roses on it. It had belonged to Glenn's mother. When she'd first seen it Ursola had been hesitant to use it, but Glenn had told her what was his was hers and had brought her tea in one of the dainty cups and saucers that very evening. The idea of a man bringing a woman tea, serving *her*, had nearly moved her to tears. Ursola opened the cabinet and removed one cup and saucer. Now, she would never forget that moment. Not that she ever could.

She held the dishes to her chest and did a final scan. She spotted Glenn's Bible on the end table next to the couch and took it. How often had she seen him read it. How often had he read it to her, all excited with the stories and words as if he was sharing a favorite novel.

There. That was it. There was nothing else worth having.

She had one final thought. *Money*. She needed money. She had her checkbook—she could only assume Daryn would leave that alone. She backtracked to the kitchen, opened a cupboard, and took down a teapot from the top shelf. Inside she found a wad of bills: $183. It was more than she'd come with. It would have to do.

She closed her suitcases and took them to the front door. Though the June day was warm, she took a jacket, left the house and car keys on the front table, and closed the door.

•   •   •

If only it weren't summertime . . .

Ursola was weary. She'd left Glenn's house in the middle of the afternoon, carrying two suitcases. After only a few blocks she realized how odd she looked, how much she stood out. Luckily, most of her neighbors were at work, though there were plenty of children around. Bikes and trikes and skateboards. She got some odd looks, but tried to walk with confidence. They left her alone, but she quickly realized she had to lose the luggage until the cover of darkness. Unfortunately, during the summer months, that wouldn't happen until nearly nine.

Until then . . . she hid the cases in a backyard garden off a residential alley. The lilacs and dense flowers hid them well. She hoped the resident gardener would choose another day to tend her plants. Which took care of the luggage, but not Ursola. How could she spend the next six hours until dark? She walked toward Carson Creek's downtown. There weren't that many shops to keep her busy. An antique shop, a women's clothing store, a florist, a café, and a hardware store. All stores full of *things*. She didn't need things anymore. Not when she had to carry them. Not when her money needed to be used to survive.

One store grabbed her interest. Silver-Wear. The shopwindow was full of lovely silver creations. Ursola loved jewelry. She went inside. There was a woman at a workbench, her gray frizzy hair pulled into an impromptu clip in back. She looked up over half-glasses. "Hey there. Can I help you?"

Ursola repeated the phrase she'd heard Glenn say at such times. "Just looking."

"Have at it. Plenty to look at. Too much actually. I'm getting overstocked, but I just keep making more. I'll give you a good price if something catches your eye."

Ursola nodded and looked at the jewelry in the glass cases.

The woman got up from her workbench, taking off her glasses. "Speaking of catching the eye, that's a lovely brooch you're wearing."

Ursola's hand found the pin, remembering which one it was. "Thank you."

The woman leaned closer. "Is that embroidered?"

"*Da*. I made it."

"Well, well. A fellow artisan." She extended her hand over the counter. "I'm Mae Ames. And you are?"

A good question. Who was she *now*? "I'm Ursola Shivikova." She wasn't sure why she left off the Smith part, but it was too late to add it.

"I didn't think you sounded local. Russian? Polish?"

"Russian."

"A long way from home, are you?"

Ursola didn't want to get into it. "*Da*. Yes."

Mae pointed to the pin. "Can I see it up close?"

Ursola took it off. Mae put her glasses back on. "This is lovely. Do you have more?"

"More?"

"More pins. I'd put them on display. I'd sell them for you."

Money! "I . . . I have two more." She'd brought a total of three with her from Russia, intending to give two of them to Glenn's mother and any other female relative she met. But Glenn's mother was dead and she'd never been able to part with one to give to Shanna. Good thing.

"That's a start, but I'm talking *more*. A dozen would be best. We always get quite a crowd over the Fourth. Can you have some to me by then?"

"The Fourth?"

Mae spread her arms. "Very American holiday. The Fourth of July, which just so happens to be on the fourth of July. Independence Day. The day the guys who decided we should be a bunch of *united* states signed a paper announcing our intentions. Telling England *adios*." She put a hand to her mouth. "Oops. Wrong salutation. Make that *cheerio*."

Ursola nodded, remembering something Glenn had told her. An image came to mind but she couldn't think of the word to describe it. She made an exploding sound and flicked her hands in the air.

"Yeah. You got it. Fireworks. Everybody sets up lawn chairs and blankets around the square and we all go *ooh* and *ahh* together." Mae handed the brooch back. "But before we do that, everybody eats a lot, we listen to the mayor tell bad jokes, hear a few locals sing—some quite good—and then shop a lot. Loads of people come into town and set up booths of craft items. I put a table out front. Best sales of the year besides Christmas."

Ursola pinned the brooch back on her blouse. What a wonderful coincidence. But as soon as she thought that, she heard Glenn's voice in her head: *"There's no such thing as coincidence, babushka. It's God that does the arranging."*

Was he right?

At the moment it didn't matter. She needed money and she'd just been offered a way to make some. "I need thread, and uh . . ." She made a sewing motion.

"A needle? The Fabric Castle can fix you up." Mae came around the counter and pointed across the square. "They've got all sorts of craft supplies." .

For the first time since Glenn's death Ursola experienced hope. She hugged Mae and kissed each cheek. "Thank you, thank you."

Mae laughed. "A fellow hugger. Now I know we'll get along." She opened the door for her. "Now get. You have work to do."

Ursola nodded and hurried across the square. She heard Mae call after her, saying, "Hey, Ursola! I need a phone number!"

She pretended not to hear.

●   ●   ●

Evelyn dragged an empty garbage can to the far reaches of her garden. She'd neglected this area and it was getting overgrown. She wasn't sure if this was the right time of year to cut back her bushes, but she had no choice. It was a jungle.

She set the can between her zinnias and a hydrangea bush and began clipping branches. Then she saw something odd. Two brown suitcases were nestled under the branches. Definitely hidden.

She looked around the backyard and the yards of her neighbors for the suitcases' owner, then realized it was a ridiculous action. Whoever had hidden them wasn't going to be hanging around.

She looked across the yards again, for a different reason. Once she was assured she was alone, she pulled one of the suitcases out and opened it. It was full of women's clothes. Oddly, there was a man's shirt and tie. Just one.

In the other suitcase were a few more clothes, a cup and saucer, a Russian nesting doll, a Bible, and a photo album. She opened the pages. They were mostly wedding pictures of a large black man and a tiny pale woman with jet-black hair. He looked quite a bit older than she. Evelyn did not recognize them.

She looked for some identification but there was none. She closed the suitcases, sat back on the grass, and stared at them. What did it all mean? The only thing obvious was that they belonged to a woman. Was she running away? Was the husband abusive? And where was she? When was she coming back to get her things? Was she coming back?

Evelyn looked to the house, gauging whether she should take them inside.

No. What good would that do? If the woman was desperate enough to hide what seemed to constitute all her worldly goods, she'd be panicked if she came back to find them gone.

Evelyn set the suitcases back where she'd found them. Her work was done here. Best not to cut too much and ruin the hiding place, or make the woman wary by seeing evidence of recent work.

She carried the garbage can back toward the house. She went inside, but stood at the windows in the sunroom. She could see a glimpse of the brown luggage through the green. She stood there a good ten minutes before she realized she couldn't stand there all day and keep watch.

She pulled up a chair.

*   *   *

"Line two, Mr. Peerbaugh."

It had been a busy day at the bank, so Russell answered the call without a thought as to who it was, who it could be. "Russell Peerbaugh. How may I help you?"

"Russell, it's Dr. McCoy."

His nerves zinged as if he'd been shocked with an electrical charge. He sat straighter in the chair. Bracing himself? "You have the test results?"

"I do."

Russell couldn't help but notice there was no effusive, *"Good news! There's nothing wrong with you. It's just a matter of time before you and Audra are the proud parents of—"*

"I'm sorry."

"I can't—?"

"You can't father a child."

"Ever?"

"It's not a treatable condition." The doctor went on to tell him the details, but Russell barely heard. What did it matter *why*? The word *never* said it all.

The doctor wrapped up. "If you'd like to come in with Audra, I can explain it to her."

What's to explain? I've failed her. "That won't be necessary."

"Unfortunately, since there are no sperm, artificial insemination is not an option—unless you go to a sperm bank."

Russell stifled a bitter laugh. The vice president of a bank going to a sperm bank. *And what is your rate of exchange today, Mr. Peerbaugh?*

How about zero. Zilch. Nada.

Dr. McCoy was still talking. ". . . sorry. I know this is a disappointment."

Having a favorite team lose a ball game was a disappointment. Having to wait an hour to get a table at their favorite restaurant was a disappointment.

Russell felt the sudden need to be alone. "Thanks for the call, Dr. McCoy."

"You're welcome. Again, I'm—"

He hung up.

Russell turned off his calculator, stood, and walked out of his office, stopping only a moment to say to his secretary, "I'm going out for a while, Tina."

Her eyebrows dipped. "Is there anything wrong?"

He walked away.

* * *

Audra hated cutting out chiffon. Though it was lovely and draped like no other fabric, it squirmed and slithered on the table as if daring her to cut it accurately. But she was determined. Since starting Catherine's Wedding Creations she'd learned a ton about sewing, and the most important lesson was that accuracy was everything. A few extra minutes spent pinning or basting saved hours ripping up—or even throwing away. She had a bin full of her early mistakes, fabric she now let Summer play and sew with. And time wasn't the only factor. So was cost. Bridal fabrics were not cheap—even at wholesale. Mistakes cut directly into the profit margin.

She heard the door to the showroom open, but didn't dare look up from the scissors. "I'll be with you in a minute."

"I'll wait."

She stopped cutting. "Russell. What are you doing—?"

But when she saw his face, she knew. She knew he'd received an answer to the question that had taken over their lives. And it wasn't good.

She set the scissors down and removed the pincushion from her wrist. He just stood there like a dejected, rejected little boy, his head down, his arms limp.

As she crossed the room she fought a battle between her own sorrow and the needs of her husband. *Help me, Lord! Please don't let this be what I think it is. But if it is . . . help me not hurt him more than he already hurts.*

She stopped a few feet away. He didn't look up but just shook his head.

So it's true! Oh, Father, it's true!

Audra moved close and put a hand on his cheek. Then their arms slid around each other's torso, pulling two sorrows into one.

* * *

Evelyn flipped the recipe card over and read the last line into the phone for Manda, a friend from church. "Then bake at three hundred fifty for forty-five minutes."

Manda asked a few questions, gave her thanks, then said good-bye. As soon as Evelyn hung up she ran to the kitchen window to check on the suitcases.

They were gone.

"No!" Evelyn ran outside and down the path to the back garden, her eyes searching. She pushed her way between the lilacs and the hydrangeas, moving branches aside, knowing it was silly, knowing *if* the suitcases were still here, she would have seen them.

She stepped out of her plantings into the gravel alleyway that bisected the length of the block. Two kids were shooting baskets in a hoop on the Masons' shed, but that was it.

Let it go.

But she couldn't. She walked toward the boys. "Daniel?"

He held on to the ball. "Hi, Mrs. Peerbaugh."

"Did you see anyone walking down the alley with suitcases?"

The other boy spoke up. "Yeah. A lady."

Evelyn's heart skipped a beat. "Did you recognize her?"

"Nope," Daniel said, taking a shot that missed.

"What did she look like?"

Both boys shrugged. "Little. Skinny. Black hair."

"Kinda pretty, for an old lady."

"She was old?"

"Thirty maybe."

"Which way did she go?"

They both pointed.

"Thanks." Evelyn started to walk away.

"She do something wrong?"

"No. Nothing wrong." *Except make me crazy with curiosity.*

64

Evelyn walked home and went inside. She moved the chair away from the sunroom windows.

●   ●   ●

Ursola hadn't thought about hiding in the church until she'd bought her jewelry supplies and was heading back to her suit-cases in the bushes. It was a perfect solution to her problem. The church had pews to sleep on, a kitchen, a water closet, and even some classrooms in the basement that had no windows. She could work down there at night without her light being seen.

Plus, God was there. Maybe her notion that God could have been behind her going into Silver-Wear was real and true. So to live in this place—that Glenn loved so much—seemed appropri-ate and right.

Getting in hadn't been a problem. She remembered Glenn saying that the church office closed at five, so she made sure she slipped inside before then, taking a quick left toward the stairs, instead of right toward the office. She found the furnace room and hid inside until she heard footsteps and humming. When the slit of light that showed under the door went black she waited a few more minutes just to make sure, then came out. Into her new home. *In my Father's house I will find sanctuary.*

Ursola didn't know where she'd heard those words before, but she took comfort in them. She found a classroom without a window, put on Glenn's plaid shirt over her own, took a seat, and began to earn a living.

There is wonderful joy ahead,
even though it is necessary for you to endure
many trials for a while.
These trials are only to test your faith,
to show that it is strong and pure.

1 PETER 1:6-7

*E*velyn hesitated at the door. It was Wayne, but she was still in her robe. Yet for him to stop over unannounced at seven-thirty in the morning meant it was important. She fluffed her hair and opened the door. "Well, Wayne. To what do I owe the honor of this early morning visit?"

He stuck his head in the door, but whispered. "Is Accosta up yet?"

"No . . ."

"Good." He came all the way inside. "I have to talk to you."

They went into the kitchen and Evelyn poured him a cup of coffee, placing the sugar and a spoon close. Once they were both settled at the table, Evelyn said, "This sounds serious."

Wayne nodded. "The plumbing in Accosta's house needs to be completely redone."

"But I thought you and Collier were fixing it?"

"We were. But the more we got into it the more problems we uncovered. And the electrical? Marginal at best. We didn't dare go check on the furnace, afraid of what we'd find. It's beyond a fix-it job, Evelyn. It's major. And it's going to be expensive."

"Accosta doesn't have any money."

"I know."

She played with the salt and pepper shakers. "Can she sell the place?"

"With all the work that needs to be done she won't get anything for it. It would be better if we fixed it first and then she sold it."

"We?"

He sipped his coffee, then set it down. "I have some money put away and I was hoping maybe you did too. We could pool our funds and use it to get the work done."

Evelyn thought of her bank account. She'd managed to put some away. The good thing about living in a house that was paid for was that there were no house payments. The monthly rent from her tenants was above and beyond her financial needs. "I have *some* money. I've been saving for retirement."

Wayne nodded. "I understand. But we'd get our money back. Once Accosta sold the place she could repay us. I'd do my part of the labor for free." He pushed his coffee away and sighed. "I can't think of any other way to help her."

"And she does need our help. Her son . . . his job . . ."

"Exactly. The money she'd make after selling a house that's in good condition would give her a nest egg. A cushion for the coming years. She could even pay you rent."

"I don't care about that." And she didn't.

Wayne sat back. "So. What do you think?"

Evelyn did a quick scan of her thoughts and found no negatives. Apprehension? Sure. Questions? Many. But the overall feeling was one of assurance. But just to make sure . . . she extended her hand across the table. "Can we pray about this?"

He smiled. "That's my girl."

They bowed their heads and voiced their concerns aloud, each one taking up the prayer like a handoff in a relay. And just as if

Wayne had heard her thoughts, he quoted a verse: "'Let us run with endurance the race that God has set before us. We do this by keeping our eyes on Jesus, on whom our faith depends from start to finish.'"

She felt him stir.

"Yes?" he said.

"Yes," she said.

It would be done. With God's help it would be done.

* * *

Evelyn draped a sweater around Accosta's shoulders, fastening it at the neck with a chained sweater clip marked by two enameled posies. "There," she said. "All ready?"

"It's so nice of you and Wayne to take me out to lunch. And at a steak house too. That's special."

Evelyn exchanged a look with Wayne, cementing their conspiracy. Their ulterior motives weighed heavily. They didn't want to lie to Accosta about her situation, but they didn't want to alarm her either. They wanted to put a positive spin on things, yet to tell this dear woman that she was going to have to move out of the house she'd lived in for decades . . . Evelyn was glad for Wayne's presence.

Wayne drove and let Evelyn and Accosta off at the door to the Fireside Grill. Accosta took a deep breath. "Mmm. Do you smell that?"

It was a luscious smell of good food cooking inside. Evelyn thought of the meager fare at Accosta's house. A steak and a baked potato slathered with all the fixings were overdue.

Wayne joined them at the door. "Let's go in, ladies. I'm starved."

They got a table by a window and ordered. That done, Evelyn caught Wayne's eyes. He nodded slightly. It was time. *Please, God, help us say this right.*

Evelyn was relieved when Wayne made the first move. "Accosta, we have some news about your house."

She sipped iced tea from a straw, her tiny features making her look very vulnerable. "Good news or bad?"

"Both. I'm afraid a bit of both."

Accosta sat back, nodding. "The plumbing can't be fixed, can it?"

Evelyn was shocked by her knowledge but hurried to soften the truth. "It can't be quickly fixed, but it can be fixed."

"The plumbing's old. It needs a complete overhaul," Wayne said.

"I thought as much."

Wayne let a soft laugh escape. "You knew?"

She leaned forward and patted his hand. "I've lived in that house forty-two years. I know every squeak, creak, and crack. I just thank the Almighty that I've been able to get by this long. When it's time to sell, it's time to sell."

Evelyn's own laugh escaped. "So you realize you have to sell?"

"Of course."

Wayne's smile was full of relief and he ran a hand through his hair. "Well then. That certainly makes things easier."

Accosta looked from him to Evelyn and back again. "Oh, fiddle-dee. You two were all nervous about having to tell me about the house, weren't you?"

"Well, yes," Evelyn said. "Change is hard and we knew you'd lived there a long time."

"Change is hard, but change is inevitable," she said. "A person doesn't live to be eighty-three without learning to deal with change. Why, when I was young we didn't even have electricity or a bathroom in the house. Daddy used a horse and buggy until I was twelve. I've seen a passel of presidents, lived through too many wars, and seen skirts go up, down, out, and be tighter than skin on a sausage. Dealt with it all—I won't say without complaint, because I've done my share of that too—but the point is, I did it. I did it then and I'll do it now."

She waved a hand in the air and gave a hearty nod. "You tell me it's time to sell my house, then that's what I'll do. And if you'll let me stay at Peerbaugh Place, I'll be happy to spend the rest of my days right there, in that little room with the balcony in the trees. I'm content there—truth be told, probably more content than I was alone in that big old house. So, if you'll have me, I'm yours. And if you're willing, Wayne, I ask you to take care of the selling. Get it done so we can think of other things. All right?"

Evelyn's and Wayne's laughter caused other diners to look in their direction. Would wonders never cease?

* * *

Mae tossed her keys on the counter then kissed Collier on the cheek as he stirred something on the stove. "Chicken soup for lunch?" She'd been hoping for a nice cool salad. It was nearly ninety outside.

He glanced toward the front room. "Soonie doesn't feel well." He made a clenching motion at his midsection.

"The flu?"

He shook his head. "Your son."

"What's Ringo done?"

"He's your son."

She put her hands on her hips. "What's that supposed to mean?"

"He's independent, fancy-free, and a bit wild. Just like his mother."

And the problem is?

"Go talk to her."

Mae found Soon-ja in the front room, curled on the couch. Small in stature even when standing, in that position she looked childlike. And needy. Mae put a hand on her head. "Hey, Soonie. You're not feeling well?"

She sat up, shaking her head.

"Collie's making chicken soup—always good for what ails you."

She nodded.

"Ricky asleep?"

She nodded again. At this rate it was going to be a long conversation. Mae sat on the coffee table facing her. "So. Tell me what's got your stomach in knots?"

Soon-ja pulled her knees to her chest, that head shaking again. "You're his mother."

"Which means I am well aware of Ringo's faults. Spill it, girl. Maybe I can help."

She set her chin on her knees, then moved it back, giving herself room to talk. "He's been going out after work."

"I thought he was working late."

"No. Bars. He and this other guy from work go to bars."

Mae felt her eyebrows rise. "Really?"

"He's used to keeping late hours. Being up late. As a roadie the concerts were at night. By the time they broke it down, it was early morning. They slept until afternoon."

"But those kind of hours are unrealistic here."

"And thankfully gone. They don't work well with family life." She shrugged. "But Go-Go's been late to work twice already. I'm afraid he'll lose his job."

"He could."

"I'm not sure he cares. He calls it a grunt job."

"Everybody has to start at the bottom. Climb the ladder. Pay their dues."

Soon-ja spoke in Korean. *"Songkoto kutputo turokanda."* She translated. "Even a drill goes in from the tip."

Mae took a moment to let it sink in. "Maybe he's going out to fit in, get to know people. That's important on a new job."

Soon-ja nodded, but her forehead furrowed. "I miss seeing

him, talking to him. He comes home tired, then is off the next morning to work again. And Ricky misses him."

This was serious. Yet Mae wasn't sure what she could do.

"Can you talk to him?" Soon-ja asked.

A lot of good it will do. "I'll try."

Soon-ja stood. "That soup smells good."

.   .   .

Mae had everything out of the main jewelry showcase at Silver-Wear and was dusting and polishing. Menial, mindless work, but all she could handle as she pondered the Ringo problem. She hated being in the middle: between Ringo and Collier, and between Ringo and Soon-ja.

That boy.

The internal comment was of no use to anyone, and wasn't even definitive, and yet . . . it did express her lifelong exasperation with her son. If Mae was a free spirit, Ringo was a raging maverick. The job as a rock-band roadie had been perfect for him. Odd hours, loud music, and a frenzied pace. Rush, crash. Rush, crash.

His life had always been a bumper car, twirling madly until something hit him and spun him around another way. Soon-ja had done that to him. Ricky too. At least they'd spun him in one direction, but it seemed there was nothing on the other side to spin him back around toward them again. He had no brakes. He had no curbs to slow him to a halt. He lived in a free spin, in a wide-open expanse of nothing, *with* nothing to stop him or send him back where he belonged—to the side of his wife and son.

It wasn't that Ringo was a bad kid. Sure, he'd gotten in trouble with fast cars, underage drinking, smoking cigarettes. He'd even tried drugs in high school. But when his best friend had died of an overdose, he'd vowed never to touch them again.

He'd always been one to take the toughest road—for good or bad. And Mae guessed that one of the reasons he'd chosen to be a roadie was to purposely place himself in the path of drugs so he could fight the battle. And win. As far as she knew, he'd been victorious.

Mae found herself absently polishing a silver necklace and wondered how long she'd been working on it. She arranged it back in the case on a piece of olive velvet and tried to concentrate on what she was doing.

When Collier had first suggested that Ringo get a job with Joe Ambrose doing construction, Mae had been wary. Not that he couldn't do the work. Mae guessed he was a capable worker. When he got there. And it was nice that he was making friends. Good friends might be the cement that would keep Ringo and family in Carson Creek. But bar friends? Hmm. That was another—

When the door jingled, Mae looked up to see that Russian woman, Urma? Unna?

"Hello." She pointed at herself. "Ursola?"

Ursola! "The brooch lady. Did the Fabric Castle set you up with the necessary supplies?"

"*Da.*" She pulled four brooches from her purse and set them on the glass display case. "Four. I have four."

"Oooh." Mae studied them, one at a time. The backgrounds were different colors: black, white, navy, and green, and the flowers varied. "No two are alike, are they?"

"No."

"Do you have a pattern?"

Ursola touched her temple.

"Ah. The pattern of a creative mind."

Ursola's eyebrows dipped and Mae wished she knew some Russian words.

Ursola pointed at the pins. "How much?"

Though Mae had never had any intention of buying the pins outright—commission was the way to go—just the way Ursola asked spoke volumes. The woman needed money. Needed. Mae did a quick calculation in her head and was almost embarrassed at the low amount she came up with. Yet, art or no art, there was no way Mae could get more than ten or fifteen dollars for each of them. Meaning she should give Ursola five each, maybe seven-fifty. . . .

But she needs the money. A why? question surfaced. "Are you married?" Mae asked.

"Widow."

"Oh, I'm so sorry. You're so young. How long?"

"One week." She pointed at the pins again. "How much?"

Goodness. "I could give you ten each. Is that—"

"Da." Ursola held out her hand. Wanting cash? She *was* desperate.

But Mae remembered her previous oversight. She got paper and pen from the desk behind her. "Before I pay you, I really need you to write down your name—so I know the spelling—and your phone number so I can get in touch—"

"No." Ursola shook her head. "No phone."

Mae pulled the writing supplies to her chest. "Then how can I get ahold of you?"

Ursola glanced at the door, looking as if she wanted to flee. Mae was suddenly panicked. She didn't want her to go out the door, never to be seen again. Mae smiled and wrote something on the paper. "How about I give you my number, here and at home. You stay in touch. You call me. Any time. For whatever reason." Mae locked eyes with her. "Any reason. Okay?"

Ursola nodded, but looked down. Mae got forty dollars from the cash register. "Ten, twenty, thirty, forty. There you go."

Ursola clasped the money to her chest. "You want more?"

At ten bucks a pop Mae would be lucky to break even. "Sure.

Then she had an idea. "You want to sit with me in my booth on the Fourth? Sell the pins yourself?"

Ursola's eyes flit a moment, then settled. "Sure. I be there." She scurried toward the door, stopped, and said, "Thank you, Mae."

"Anytime." Mae set Ursola's brooches in the prime position in the display case and made quick work of a sign that said, "Hand-made Russian brooches: $10."

There were worse things than breaking even.

• • •

Ursola never expected to go back into her house. Glenn's house. Daryn's house. She never expected to need her sewing basket. But after the success of selling four brooches to Mae, and after weary-ing of making do with the craft scissors and supplies she found at the church, she decided she had to make a visit. And it had to be today. For tomorrow Daryn and Shanna were taking over. Moving in.

It was awkward even walking through the neighborhood. Though she'd not allowed herself to become close with her neigh-bors, they would surely recognize her and wonder why she was back.

But no. They didn't even know she was gone. At least not moved-out gone. And they wouldn't know until Daryn pulled up with a truck full of tacky furniture and his big-screen TV. Yet she still walked quickly and looked around for questioning eyes.

She met no resistance whatsoever—until she spotted Daryn's SUV in the driveway. She slipped behind a row of lilacs that marked the side boundary of the properties.

The front door was open and Daryn stormed out, closely followed by Shanna. Ursola didn't catch Shanna's words, but heard Daryn ask her, "But where did she go?"

Shanna moved to the front walk. "Who knows? You're the one who chased her out, Daryn. You were mean to her."

He pulled the door shut. "Don't start."

"Your father would be furious with—"

He pointed the car keys at her. "My father is dead and I only did what had to be done."

Shanna shook her head in disgust and walked to the car. Daryn ran after her. "What's that look supposed to mean?"

"You know what it means."

"And couldn't care less." He opened his car door. "We might as well go get a load."

"You want to move in a day early?"

"She's not here, is she? She left us the key."

One key. There's a spare . . .

"Barge in," Shanna said. "Take over. You're good at that."

They got in the car and took their argument on the road. Ursola loved it, but she also felt sorry for Shanna. The two women had gotten along pretty well on the few occasions they'd met before Glenn died.

She stepped out of her hiding place, got the spare key from under the mailbox by the door, and went inside. Odd how it truly didn't seem to be hers anymore. She retrieved her sewing basket and was about to leave when she had an idea.

She went into the kitchen and put a bag of popcorn in the microwave. Nothing smelled up a house more than popcorn. It would drive Daryn crazy.

When it was finished, she helped herself to a Diet Coke, made sure the aroma of popcorn was the only thing she left behind, and walked out.

As she was putting the spare key in its hiding place, she stopped. She smiled. Then she slipped the key into her pocket and walked away.

The possibilities were intriguing.

•   •   •

With her mind swimming with the issue of Accosta's house—and Wayne—Evelyn would have liked to put off making the cookies for the Fourth of July church bake sale, but decided not to. Soon-ja and little Ricky had come over, Audra and Summer would be here soon, and any moment, Piper would be home from having lunch with Gregory. There were too many hands prepared to work to not take advantage of them.

She set the counters with baking supplies while Accosta and Soon-ja covered the kitchen table with paper towels to hold the baked cookies. Ricky cooed contentedly in his infant seat on the counter. Evelyn heard the front door open and within seconds Summer burst into the kitchen, her little eyes taking it all in. "Wow, Grandma. Wow. We're going to make tons of cookies, aren't we?"

"Tons and tons."

Summer looked at the ingredients on the counter. "Chocolate chip *and* oatmeal raisin?"

"Both."

Accosta made a face. "But not in the same cookie. Ick."

Then Summer saw Ricky and the adults in the room became invisible. Evelyn heard voices in the hall; then Audra came in. "Hello, sisters."

"Hi, Audra," Evelyn said. "I heard voices—plural."

"Piper's here too. She's changing clothes."

Evelyn got out the mixing bowls. "How are things going? How's Russell?"

When there was no answer, Evelyn turned around to find her daughter-in-law fingering a cookie sheet.

Ricky had Summer's finger in his grip. "Mommy's sad," she said.

"Shh, baby. None of that."

The kitchen door swung open and Piper came in. "Give me a job to do. I'm ready to work."

No one said anything. Piper looked from face to face, coming back to Audra's. "What's wrong?"

"Mommy's sad," Summer said.

Suddenly, Audra grabbed Summer by the arm. "I told you to be quiet! If you can't be quiet then you can't help. You've got to learn when to keep your mouth shut. You're always—"

"Audra . . ." Evelyn put a hand on her arm.

Audra looked up, then let go of her daughter's arm.

Summer was crying. She wrapped her arms around Evelyn's waist. "Grandma . . ."

Oh dear. Something was very wrong. Evelyn hugged Summer and kissed the top of her head. Then she took her face in her hands, swiping the tears with her thumbs. "There, there. I think your mommy needs a good sister chat right now. Can you go up to my bedroom and play awhile? You can get out my jewelry box and play dress-up if you'd like."

"But the cookies . . ."

"We will not start without you. I promise."

"But Ricky gets to stay . . ."

Audra took a step toward her. "Baby, I'm so sorry."

Summer nodded, but left the room. They heard her feet on the stairs.

Piper pulled out one of the kitchen chairs and told Audra, "Sit."

Audra did as she was told, slumping into the chair like a sack of potatoes. They each found a seat.

"I'm sorry. I'm so sorry," Audra said.

"You can be as sorry as you want," Piper said, "as long as you come out with the truth. What's got you so upset?"

Tears started and Evelyn brought her a tissue. Her mind swarmed with thoughts of cancer or job loss or even divorce.

Horrible things worthy of Audra's tears. She did not expect to
hear . . .

"We can't have a baby."

Evelyn pressed a hand against her chest, keeping her heart
within its boundaries. "You're sure?"

Audra nodded. "We've both had tests. I was okay, but
Russell—" she looked at Evelyn nervously—"he can't father a child."

The Peerbaugh bloodline is dead.

Accosta said what Evelyn should have said. "I'm so sorry,
Audra."

"Me too," Soon-ja said.

"But you can adopt," Piper said. "I'm adopted. My parents
couldn't have children."

Evelyn realized this was a truth, but wondered if it was too
soon for Piper to bring it up, especially when Audra only
shrugged. Evelyn shoved aside her disappointment and touched
Audra's hand. "How is Russell taking this?"

"He's being brave. But I'm not. I'm mad." Her forehead crumpled into furrows. "I was looking forward to being pregnant
again, carrying the baby of the man I love. Now I won't ever have
that." Fresh tears came and she touched her stomach. "I'll never
feel a baby kick inside me again. I'll never have the experience of
a husband at my side when the baby is born. I'll never feel that
bond with him that says we created something together."

Evelyn didn't know what to say. Each of Audra's points was
valid.

Accosta stood. "I'll be right back."

Evelyn couldn't imagine where she was going, but concentrated on Audra. "Does Summer know?"

Audra blew her nose. "No. We thought we'd wait until *we*
had a full grasp of it before we brought her in on it. She'll be so
disappointed. She's been talking about having a brother or sister

for months. And with Ricky being around now—" she took a cleansing breath—"it's hard."

Accosta returned carrying a blue recipe box. Now was not the time to share a recipe. But Accosta moved in front of Audra, holding the box like it was full of treasures.

"What's this?" Audra asked.

"It's a worry box. Up until a moment ago it was *my* worry box. But now it's yours."

Audra opened it. It was empty. "I don't understand."

"You've been worrying a lot, haven't you?"

Audra snickered. "*A lot* is an understatement."

Accosta looked at the other ladies. "We all do. But we're not supposed to."

Piper nodded. "'Can all your worries add a single moment to your life? Of course not!'"

Even Evelyn knew another verse. "'Don't worry about anything; instead, pray about everything. Tell God what you need, and thank Him for all He has done.'"

Accosta beamed. "Well done, ladies!" She put a hand on the box. "When I'm worried about something, the first thing I do is get all prayed up about it. When I know I've poured out my heart and can't pour a single drop more, I write the worry on a piece of paper. Then I put it in the worry box and close the lid. It's giving it to God. It's letting Him have it and take care of it. Then I move on."

"I like that," Piper said.

"Me too," Evelyn said.

"Me three," Soon-ja said.

Accosta continued. "Every once in a while, I open the box and weed through the worries, taking out the ones God has handled then throwing them away." She cupped Audra's cheek in her hand. "Later on, when you're alone, get yourself prayed up about the baby. Let it all out, good and bad, tears and yelling. After that, write it down and tuck it away in this box for God to handle. Will you do that for me?"

Audra was crying and could only nod. Finally she stood and hugged Accosta close. They all hugged. And cried.

Then they made cookies.

·   ·   ·

Valerie slammed down the lid of her laptop. This boardinghouse was ridiculous. Grand Central Station. Women coming in and out, laughing right below her room, banging pans, running mixers. It was far worse than her last apartment where all she'd had to deal with were heavy footfalls, a few slammed doors, and the occasional bass beat of a stereo.

She moved to the bed and stretched out on her back, hands behind her head. She'd felt so sure moving to Peerbaugh Place had been a wise decision. Since deciding to concentrate on her writing full time, she'd found worrying about exorbitant rent a distraction to the creative process. Peerbaugh Place provided freedom from those worries, but in its place, constant annoyances. Although she knew she was allowed to use the public spaces of the house, she never felt comfortable setting up her computer in the sunroom or parlor, and the kitchen and dining room were not comfortable. Plus with Evelyn around most of each day, and now Accosta . . . Valerie had enough people populating her mind; she didn't need the real kind moving in and out, interfering with her other world.

Things were better in that world. If only she could stay there.

Valerie held her breath a moment as the sound of singing permeated the pitiful insulation between floors. She recognized some Elvis song: "'Precious Lord, take my hand, lead me on, let me stand. I'm tired, I'm weak, I'm worn.'"

With a sigh of disgust, she grabbed the pillow and wrapped it around her head.

*   *   *

Back home at her mother-in-law's, Soon-ja took Ricky out of his infant seat and held him close. Very close. Though he'd come into their lives sooner than they'd planned, he was such a blessing.

With the feel of his soft hair against her lips she felt totally blessed. She really should quit complaining about Ringo. Things could be worse. Much worse.

*   *   *

Ursola hunkered down in the furnace room and waited to make her move.

She'd seen the notices in the narthex for choir practice, and she remembered Glenn being gone Wednesday evenings, so she knew tonight was not a night she could hang around the church and work on her brooches. And it was too hot outside—even in the evenings—to sit long in the park.

Which meant only one thing. She had to join the choir.

Ursola *could* sing. She could read music enough to know whether she had to go up or down, but she was far from being a musician. The good thing was, from what she'd heard, she wasn't the only one with marginal abilities.

The smell of browning meat slid under the door. The added bonus to choir night was that it was also congregational dinner night. For two dollars she could get a good meal. She wondered what they did with the leftovers. She'd already found some left-over wedding cake in the church fridge. By slicing off skinny pieces she'd whittled it down without making it look like anything had been taken.

She vowed that food would never be an issue with her. Back in Russia she'd experienced shortages, long lines, and high prices. Coming to America with all its choices was a blessing. So what if she had to scrape a little now? One did what one had to do. And she *did* have money. But she didn't dare waste a penny. Her plan to spend two dollars on the dinner tonight was enough of a splurge.

Ursola heard people busy in the kitchen above her. Though the office workers had already left, the kitchen crew had come to make the dinner, creating a constant presence in the church. Within an hour enough people would be around . . .

Until then, she leaned her head back against the wall and dozed.

The sound of the door opening woke her and she stifled a gasp. Once the light was on, she'd be found out!

But the light didn't go on. And the door quickly closed. She let out the breath she'd been sav—

"Shh!"

"But Matthew . . ."

She was not alone. She heard the sound of kissing and the soft protests of the girl. Giggles. Then, "I have to go. The dinner's started. My parents will be waiting for me."

Another kiss. "Later then."

The door opened and closed again. Ursola's heart scuttled against her chest. Too close. And the dinner had already begun. She had to get out and blend into the flow of the church's Wednesday night busyness. She moved to the door, pressing her ear against it. She heard voices, but they seemed far away. Coming from the fellowship hall upstairs?

She cracked the door and listened again. Nothing close. In a bold move, she opened the door, stepped out, and closed it again. There. That wasn't so hard.

"Ursola?"

She turned toward the voice and saw a tiny old black woman at the end of the hall. They'd met but Ursola couldn't remember her name. "Hello," was all she said.

The woman came toward her. "What were you doing in the furnace room?"

"I . . ." She sighed. "Choir room? I want to sing."

The woman patted her on the back. "Good for you. We can always use another voice. Soprano or alto?"

She wasn't sure what those words meant. "High. I sing high."

"Soprano. I'm an alto myself. The choir room is down there, and rehearsal doesn't start for an hour." She put a hand to her chest. "Do you remember me? I'm Tessa Klein?"

Tessa. Yes, Tessa. Ursola nodded.

"So sorry about Glenn. How are you doing?"

"Fine." She pointed toward the stairs. She really wanted to get away from her hiding place. "You eat?"

"Whenever possible. It's chicken spaghetti tonight. Sounds odd, but it's really good. Shall we?"

• • •

Ann Mapes and Tessa walked to their cars in the church parking lot, "That new soprano is pretty good, but I do wish she was an alto. Your section really needs help, Tessa."

Yes, yes, and your section would be much improved if you weren't singing at all, Ann.

They reached Ann's car and she got in. "See you Sunday."

Tessa moved across the row to her own vehicle, then remembered she'd forgotten a book she'd borrowed from the choir director inside. Luckily, she had a key. As she was walking back to the church, she spotted a glimmer of light in one of the basement windows. *That's odd. Everyone's gone.*

She paused and looked at the light, trying to find an explanation. It wasn't as if the light was in the room that contained the window. It was subtler than that, as if the hallway light was on.

Tessa glanced around the parking lot, hoping to call someone over to look with her. But the lot was empty. She glanced at her car. What she really should do is get in and go home. Two clichés came to mind and offered conflicting views: *Curiosity killed the cat* and *Inquiring minds want to know.*

She wanted to know.

She walked off toward the side of the church, toward the window. It was a small window created by the addition of a window well to let in more natural light. In order to see inside, she had to bend over and—

Yes. There *was* a light on. In the hallway. No wonder the church's electrical bills were so high. If people were negligent . . .

She was just about to straighten up when a figure entered her field of vision. A figure wearing a red blouse.

By the time Tessa said, "Ursola?" the figure was gone. And a moment later, the hall light switched off.

What was Ursola doing in the church basement, after hours, in the dark?

She headed to the door.

.   .   .

Tessa flipped on only enough lights to get her from the front door to the stairwell. She hesitated. She didn't want to frighten Ursola by slipping in unannounced, yet she didn't want to make too big an announcement either. The young woman seemed the skittish sort who might run. Especially if she had something to hide. Which, apparently, she did.

Tessa held on to the stair railing and closed her eyes. *Father, I don't know what's going on but You have two women alone in Your house. I've got to believe You let me see that light for a reason. You wanted me to find Ursola. Help this come off as intended.*

She had an idea. She took a cleansing breath and flipped on

the light in the stairwell. Maybe if she made her presence known in segments it wouldn't be such a shock.

She had another idea, and started singing that Thomas Dorsey piece they'd practiced in choir. That way Ursola would know a woman was coming—an elderly woman with a slight crackle in her voice. A woman who was no threat.

"'Precious Lord, take my hand, lead me on, let me stand. I'm tired, I'm weak, I'm worn.'" She reached the bottom of the stairs and found the light switch for the hall. "'Through the storm, through the night, lead me on to the light. Take my hand precious Lord, lead me home.'"

Even though she knew she had no reason to be afraid, Tessa's heart pounded. Not knowing when and how Ursola would show herself . . .

She looked right, then left. Doorways led off the lit hall, most to classrooms. *Is she behind door number one? door number two?* She held her breath a moment, listening for any sound.

Nothing.

Suddenly, her patience left her. She knew who was down here, she'd prayed about it, she'd made her presence known. Enough. She cleared her throat. "Ursola? It's me, Tessa. Come out and talk to me, girl."

Nothing.

"Come on, dear. You know I couldn't hurt a bug on a berry. Come out and talk."

A door to the right opened. The furnace room again. Ursola stepped out. "Hi."

"Hi, yourself."

Ursola hugged herself. "How you know I here?"

Tessa pointed in the direction of the window. "I saw a light in the hallway, through a window."

Ursola looked in that direction as if trying to figure out where she'd gone wrong. She shifted her weight to the other foot.

"Well?" Tessa said. "Are you going to tell me why you've taken a liking to the furnace room?"

The young woman looked at the floor; then her face crumpled. "I sorry. I have no place to go."

Tessa chastised herself for playing the tough woman. She pulled the girl into a hug. "There, there. Let's go talk about it." She led them into a classroom, and pulled two chairs facing each other. She took a tissue from her purse.

Ursola got settled and dried her eyes. "Before? You ask how I am?"

"Yes, I did. And you said you were fine. But that's not the truth, is it, dear?"

She shook her head and began to shred the Kleenex. "Monday I go lawyer for will."

"To read the will. Okay. And what did he say?"

"Daryn get all. I get *nichto*. Nothing."

Tessa sat back. "I can't believe that. Glenn loved you. He wouldn't ignore you in the will. He wouldn't—"

She pointed to her wedding ring. "After . . . he not change."

"Oh." Tessa was going to say something about procrastination, but realized that was probably not a word Ursola would understand—though the girl certainly understood the concept. Her thoughts moved to the son. She'd only met Daryn once and hadn't been impressed—he'd seemed bossy and too gruff for her taste but . . . "Certainly Daryn will help out. Give you your due. It's only fair."

Ursola shook her head, dabbing at her nose with the tissue. "He want house. So I give him house."

Tessa was appalled. "He kicked you out?"

"I leave. Come here."

"You've been living here since Monday?"

She nodded. Then she smiled and stood. "Come."

Tessa followed her into another classroom. Ursola retrieved

a sewing bag from a storage cabinet. She pulled out a small embroidery hoop that was stretched with black fabric. Brilliant aqua and pink flowers took center stage. "See? I do."

Tessa ran a hand over the intricate crewel stitches. "This is beautiful."

Ursola reached deeper in the bag. "A pin. A brooch. I make money."

It was beautiful work and a nice concept but—

"Mae buy four. I make more."

"Mae? Mae Ames?"

"Silver-Wear. *Da.*"

"Does she know you're living in the church?"

Ursola's head was adamant. "*Nyet.*" She pointed to the embroidery again. "I start over. I work hard. I live."

Tessa made a decision. "Yes, you do. But you don't live here." She looked in the storage cabinet but saw only Sunday school supplies. "Where are the rest of your things?"

"Furnace."

"Get them."

"No, no. I be good. I not hurt church."

"I know you won't, dear, but you can't live here, and more than that, you don't have to. You're coming home with me."

●   ●   ●

The two-car garage had been turned into an apartment behind Tessa's daughter's home. Tessa kept apologizing for it, but Ursola thought it was quite lovely. Size-wise, it was similar to what she was used to in Russia. One small bedroom, barely big enough for a bed and a dresser, a minimal bath and kitchen, and a living area big enough for a couch, a small table to eat at, and a couple chairs. The odd thing about it was that every wall was a different, vibrant color that held pictures and shelves with knickknacks that didn't seem to match whatever was on the other walls. Each wall was distinct. Unique.

And odd.

Tessa came back in the living room carrying sheets and a blanket. "You've noticed my gallery, have you?"

Ursola shook her head and shrugged. She didn't understand *gallery*.

Tessa moved to the orange wall and adjusted a garish royal blue vase with gold curlicues that sat on a shelf. "I went on a world cruise. When I came home my souvenirs didn't match. They were distinct from each other. So I decided instead of trying to force them to blend, I would give each area its own space. This is my Italian wall. Italy just seems orange to me. Warm, vibrant, full of spunk."

She moved to the purple wall. "This is Japan. Exotic and regal. And this red wall is India. Spicy and striking. The green is Thailand, lush and expansive." She picked up a small wooden elephant, stroked its trunk, then set it down and turned to Ursola. "I met many women on my travels. Women who are desperate for sisterhood. But you're probably tired. We'll talk about my sister project another time. Let's get this couch made up for you."

Within a half hour Ursola was settled in. The moonlight came through the window above the couch, fell across her torso, and spilled onto the floor. Though she knew it didn't give off any heat, she felt warm within its beam.

Safe. Hopeful. Wanted.

She let sleep take her, willing to surrender today into tomorrow.

Rejoice. Change your ways.
Encourage each other.
Live in harmony and peace.
Then the God of love and peace
will be with you.

2 CORINTHIANS 13:11

*M*ae tried not to listen to the argument going on in the bedroom across the hall, but the trouble with old houses was their lack of insulation and the eerie way sound traveled through the grates in the floor.

"Stop listening," Collier said as he buttoned his shirt.

Mae realized she'd stopped brushing her hair midbrush. "It's hard not to."

"All couples argue."

"We don't. Not like that." She turned to face him. "Why don't we?"

"You want us to?"

"No. Not exactly. But don't you think it's kind of weird we get along so well?"

He left his shirt half open and put his hands on her shoulders. "Mae. Dear, dear wifey. We don't argue because we are both wise enough to know there are ways to disagree without straining the voice. Besides, I've mastered the art of letting you *think* you've gotten the upper hand, when actually—" he crooked his pinky in front of her face—"I've got you wrapped around this, darlin'."

91

She linked her pinky with his and they touched thumbs. Then she kissed him. "I don't deserve you."

"No one does, but you put up with me anyway." He finished buttoning his shirt. "Have you talked to Ringo like Soonie asked you to?"

"Not yet."

"Chicken?"

She looked toward the bedroom door. "I tend to embrace the hands-off method of parenting."

"Chicken." This time it wasn't a question and was accompanied by a nod.

He was right—as usual. Though Mae was hardly the non-confrontational type, and was very willing to share her opinions with friend and stranger alike, she had never been a controlling parent. Opinionated, yes; controlling, no. And if Ringo were staying here on his own as a single man, she wouldn't have hesitated—she hadn't hesitated to share when Starr had been staying with them. But once a child had been on his own awhile, once he got married, once he had a child . . .

The shouting from the other bedroom suddenly stopped. A door opened, then slammed. Mae heard Ricky crying from downstairs. Soon-ja must have taken the baby with her. She peeked out. The door across the hall was ajar and she saw Ringo walk past the opening.

She felt Collier's lips against her hair. "Now's your chance."

Goody. Mae opened the door and crossed the space between cowardice and courage. She knocked on the doorjamb. "Ringo?"

He whipped the door all the way open, startling her. "I suppose you heard?"

"We tried not to."

"I suppose you're on her side?"

"I'm on the side of your marriage. She misses you."

He sat on a bench at the foot of the bed and put on white

work socks. "I'm trying to earn a living so we can get our own place. I'm trying to provide for her and Ricky."

Mae stepped into the room. "And you're doing a fine job. It's not the work she objects to; it's the hours away after work."

"I have a right to relax, don't I?" Finished with the socks, he planted his feet and glared at her. "Don't I have a right to make friends?"

He seemed awfully into "rights" and it bothered her. "Living in a free country you have a *right* to do most anything, but that doesn't mean it *is* right. Not if it hurts someone you love and takes you away from your responsibilities."

He looked at the floor. "I hate that word."

She let out a huff of air. "Tough toenails! You're a married man. You're a father. Responsibilities go with the territory."

He raked his fingers through his hair. "Don't I know it."

Mae lowered her voice. "Surely you don't regret—?"

The shake of his head was adamant. "No. No. Not that. I love Soonie. I love Ricky. But up until now I've been leading another kind of life. The life of a roadie isn't exactly normal."

Ringo had never held normal in high regard. "Do you miss it?"

He shrugged. "I'll be okay."

Suddenly he was her little boy again. She nudged him over and sat beside him, wrapping an arm across his shoulders. "You're a good boy. A good man."

"Whose wife is miserable."

"She wants to spend time with you, Ringo. You can't blame her for that."

"I know. But it's nice having friends again. Me and the other roadies got real close. I guess I need that guy stuff."

"Nothing wrong with that. I don't know what I'd do without my circle of sisters close by." She smoothed a stray piece of hair above his ear and had an idea. "It's Friday. What if you take Soonie with you tonight?"

"Out with the guys?"

He'd missed her point. She compromised. "Do your friends have wives or girlfriends?"

"I think so."

"Make it a couples thing. Collie and I will babysit."

He sat still a moment, then nodded. "It's doable."

Mae slapped a hand on his knee. "See? That wasn't so hard. Now go tell your wife."

He rose, kissed the top of her head, and left.

Phew.

●　　●　　●

"Evelyn, I'd like a word with you."

What did Valerie want to complain about now? Yet being the dutiful landlady, Evelyn stopped emptying the dishes from the dishwasher and gave Valerie her full attention. "Is there a problem?"

Valerie pulled at the vintage peignoir set she was wearing, a pale blue tricot gown with a matching bed jacket and ruffled slippers. "It's unbearably hot in my room."

Wear cotton pj's instead of nylon and you'd be cooler. "Isn't the air conditioner working?"

"It's too loud."

Evelyn was confused. "It's not working?"

"It works, but when it's on it's so intrusive I can't think."

"But if you don't turn it on, it gets hot."

Valerie spread her hands. "You see my dilemma."

Evelyn went back to unloading dishes. It was a job steeped in logic—something her conversations with Valerie often lacked. "Perhaps you'll have to choose between temperature and noise?"

Valerie wrapped the tie of the bed jacket around a finger. "The point is, I don't think I should have to. Have you ever considered central air-conditioning?"

Evelyn knew her jaw had dropped into gawk mode, but she couldn't help it. "This house is a hundred years old. *If* such a thing were even possible, the cost would be . . . I couldn't afford it." *Especially not with my commitment to fix up Accosta's house.*

Valerie suffered an expansive sigh.

"I'm sorry, Valerie."

"While we're on the subject, there *is* something else."

Great. "Yes?"

"When I moved in I did not realize Peerbaugh Place was going to be the intersection for every life within a ten-block area. The other day, when you were cooking down here, the noise was quite unbearable."

"We were making cookies for our church, to sell at the Fourth of July bash."

"Commendable, but couldn't the cookies be made somewhere else?"

"I suppose, but considering three of the people who helped live *here*, and Soon-ja is just across the street . . ."

"I heard Audra's voice. And that little girl of hers. Couldn't you have baked at her house?"

Evelyn put the silverware away with as much clatter as possible. Who did this woman think she was? Evelyn would rather have an empty room than have the sisterly ambience of Peerbaugh Place sullied by this prima donna.

Valerie wasn't going to back down. "Couldn't you have gone elsewhere?"

Evelyn whipped around to face her. "No, we couldn't. Soon-ja is a guest at Mae's, and Audra's kitchen doesn't have enough counter space to make fifteen dozen cookies much less allow five women to move around without bumping, breaking, or burning each other."

Valerie clutched the opening of the bed jacket. "I only thought—"

Evelyn slammed the silverware drawer shut. "This is a board-inghouse, Valerie. When you moved in I told you that all the downstairs rooms were public. You can take that as a positive or a negative."

In true 1930s style, Valerie raised her chin. "Well!"

Evelyn mentally finished the line correctly. *Well, I never!* "Exactly."

After a perfect pirouette, Valerie strode out of the kitchen like Joan Crawford in a snit, her nightgown flowing behind her. A few moments later, Evelyn heard her bedroom door slam.

She stood in the middle of the kitchen and waited for a wave of regret to flow over her. When it didn't come she had the bizarre notion that perhaps, just maybe, she'd been justified. Being nice did not mean she should be a doormat.

She executed her own haughty pirouette and went on with her day.

●   ●   ●

"Hello, Mrs. Peerbaugh," said the bank's receptionist.

She looked toward her son's office. He was at his desk. "Hello to you, Sandy. Is Russell available?"

"Let me buzz him for you."

Within seconds, Russell was coming out to greet her with a hug. "Mom, to what do I owe this pleasure?"

She pointed to his office. "Do you have a few minutes?"

His right eyebrow rose. "Of course. Come on in."

They got settled in his office. Evelyn had two items on her agenda, but wasn't sure she should even mention the first: Did Russell know Audra had told the ladies about their fertility news? Did he mind?

Her choice was taken from her when Russell broke the ice on her other topic. "I ran into Wayne. He said you two are partnering on a project? Fixing up Accosta's house?"

"She's not going to get anything for it without major repairs. and she can't get the money to make the repairs without selling it. I have some money saved. I've been doing quite well at Peerbaugh Place and—"

Russell held up a hand. "You don't have to convince me. I think it's a fine idea."

Though surprised, she decided to get all the cards on the table. "Accosta wants to stay at Peerbaugh Place permanently."

"This is all right with you?"

"Absolutely."

"But from what Wayne said, the repairs are proving so costly that you might only break even when you sell her house. She might not be able to pay you. Ever."

Wayne hadn't told her this important bit of information, but Evelyn found it didn't matter. Money or no money, she wasn't about to kick Accosta out of her room. They'd work something out.

Russell sat back in his chair and rocked a few times. A conspiratorial grin appeared. "So. How are you and Wayne doing—beyond the construction partnership?"

"Fine." It was such an inept, incomplete answer, but she found she couldn't say more. Not with certainty.

"He speaks very highly of you."

"Really?"

Russell laughed. "You should see the way your face lit up just now. Are you in love with him?"

"Russell!"

"Well? Are you?"

When she felt her face redden she knew it was no use lying. "Yes."

He nodded. The grin remained.

"You approve?"

"Of course. Everybody does."

"They do?"

He leaned toward her, the smile gone. "We all want you and Wayne to be happy. You've both suffered. You're both wonderful people—people who would be happier together than apart."

It was hard not to grab on to his approval and run ahead to thoughts of a wedding and honeymoon and waking up in the morning snuggled on the shoulder of someone she loved. But reality returned with a slap. "I love *him* but he doesn't love me—not romantically."

"How do you know?"

She thought a moment. "He's never said . . . you know . . ."

"Have you ever told him 'I love you'?"

Evelyn was taken aback. "No. Of course not. It's up to the man to say it first."

Russell shook his head and went back to rocking. "Don't put it on us poor men, Mom. We're usually the last to know about such things. Sometimes it takes a nudge for us to realize our own feelings."

"So, I should say something to him?"

He shrugged. "When the time is right." He checked his watch and stood. "Is there anything else I can do for you today? Because I have a meeting in a few minutes."

They said their good-byes and Evelyn went to the car, her mind swimming with ways she could declare her love to Wayne. She was two blocks away before she realized she'd never asked Russell about the baby issue.

Maybe it was just as well.

•   •   •

Evelyn stopped home, changed into jeans and a "Grandmas are Purrfect!" T-shirt—with a Peppers look-alike on the front—

dropped Accosta off at her weekly bridge game, and headed over to Accosta's house. Wayne's Explorer was out front and her heart did a little flip.

Don't be silly now. Russell's talk of love has you acting like a teen-ager. She shut off her car, gripped the steering wheel, bowed her head, and prayed. *If You want me to say something, show me the right time. If not, help me be quiet.*

She started at a tap on the window. Wayne smiled at her. "What're you doing in there with your eyes closed? You can't be exhausted yet."

She opened the door and he extended a hand to help her exit. "Just doing a little preconstruction praying."

"Sent up my own earlier." He walked her toward the front porch, his arm strung over her shoulder.

Should I tell him now?

"The plumber should be here any moment," he said. "There's no water on so I hope you used the facilities before you came."

Nope. Now is not the time.

Instead of going inside, Wayne detoured to the driveway. "I borrowed some tables from church." Six long narrow tables lined the drive.

"What are those for?"

He nodded toward the house and they went in the side door. The smell of past dampness assailed her—would it ever go away? He led her into the living room, his hands spread wide, encom-passing the room. "All this stuff has to go."

Evelyn thought about the limited storage at Peerbaugh Place. "There's room in the attic for some of this, but—"

"No, not storage. It goes out on the tables, for the garage sale. Not this weekend, but the next, and—"

"Nuh-uh. I don't think so. This is Accosta's stuff. Her life."

He put a hand on her arm. "It's all right. I've already been over it with her." He pointed to a stack of boxes. "Yesterday, I helped her fill those three boxes with things she wanted to keep, and the two suitcases are full of the clothes she wants. The rest of it can go."

"Really?" Evelyn looked around. A lifetime of knickknacks and furniture surrounded her like a crowd awaiting further instruction.

"Really. Actually, she seemed ready to be rid of the things she's accumulated. I think it will be a relief to her."

"What about the son? Eugene? Surely he wants some of it."

"Accosta didn't think so. Apparently his tastes bend toward sleek and modern, and last time he was here she gave him a box full of sentimental things." He patted the top box. "I think she's been preparing herself for this a long time."

Evelyn ran a hand over an antique oak flip-down desk. "It seems so permanent. So drastic."

"It is, and it is. But it needs to be done, Evelyn. The construction can proceed a lot easier if things are cleared out, as will the cleaning afterward. And the house will sell a lot faster if it's a clean, neat slate. People need to see the architecture of the place, not Accosta's things."

She knew he was right, but it was sad. The end of a season. *"There is a time for everything, a season for every activity under heaven."*

He squeezed her shoulders, drawing her close. His lips were close to her ear. "It will be all right. I promise."

She got to work.

        •   •   •

Valerie poured herself more club soda, adding another slice of lime from her Tupperware cache. The phone rang and on the second ring she realized there was no one else at home to answer it. She hated taking messages and didn't understand why Evelyn didn't get herself an answering machine like the rest of the civilized world.

She took a sip and stared at the phone as it entered its third, then fourth ring. Five. A persistent caller.

In disgust she answered it. "Hello!"

"My, my, a bit edgy today, are we?"

Valerie chastised herself. It was her agent, Carla Mandez. "Sorry. I didn't know it was you."

"I think there's a compliment in there somewhere."

Valerie set the soda down and rubbed her forehead. This was not going well. "What can I do for you, Carla?"

"Actually, it's a question of what I can do for you."

Valerie pulled in a breath. "Good news?"

"The best. Red Stop Publishing wants your book."

Valerie fumbled to find a chair. Her throat tightened to such an extent she couldn't talk.

"Did you hear me? They want the book."

Valerie let her sobs do the talking for her.

*　　　*　　　*

After hanging up from talking to her agent, Valerie sat at the kitchen table at Peerbaugh Place, staring into nothingness. *I'm an author. I'm really an author!*

Suddenly, she jumped from the chair, pumped a fist in the air, and screamed. "Yes!"

But the sound died and did not return any congratulations. She was alone in the house. There was no one to share her joy. No one to give her a hug. No one to say, "Good job!"

I don't need them. I don't need that. The contract is my hug, my "Good job!"

Looking around the kitchen, she found herself feeling out of place. She didn't belong here, using the facilities in someone else's home. She was an author! The advance Carla was hoping to get for her wouldn't make the news, but it was more than she'd expected for a first timer.

It was more than enough to get her own place. An apartment? No. She didn't want to deal with close neighbors. But a house . . . what if she could rent an entire house? Nothing elaborate, but something with character and two bedrooms, one to use for her writing studio. Something with a nice view—and air-conditioning. She'd driven past a newer ranch house for rent on the edge of town. . . .

She checked the note Evelyn had left. She and Accosta wouldn't be home for hours. Plenty of time to arrange the next phase of her life. Her career. Her destiny.

•   •   •

All Evelyn wanted was a hot bath, bubbles mandatory. She'd spent most of the day sorting Accosta's possessions, getting them organized on tables in the garage. A lifetime of junk. Make that *junque*. No. Actually, no offense to Accosta, but most of it was just plain junk. If she wasn't so tired, she'd be inspired to do a thorough scavenging through the dubious treasures of Peerbaugh Place.

Worse yet, through it all, there had been no chance to declare her heart to Wayne.

She'd picked up Accosta from her bridge game and dropped her at another friend's house for dinner—which was good because Evelyn didn't feel up to cooking. With Piper and Gregory off for dinner at his mother's, and considering her earlier run-in with Valerie, she was sure she could get Valerie to find something to eat on her own.

She was halfway up the stairs, within a few feet of her soothing paradise, when Valerie cut her off at the landing. "I need to talk to you."

If Evelyn never again heard those words . . . "Can it wait?"

"Not really."

"Can I at least get off the stairs?" *To lessen the chance I'd fling myself down the entire flight.*

Valerie stepped back, allowing Evelyn access to the upstairs hall. She leaned against the railing, preparing herself for some inane ranting about Peerbaugh Place's shortcomings.

She was surprised to see Valerie bounce twice on her toes and smile. "I got a yes. My book is going to be published!"

Evelyn felt her eyebrows rise, and couldn't seem to lower them. She tried to disguise her shock with congratulations. "That's wonderful, Valerie. You should be very proud."

"Oh, I am! It's a great deal. Not loads of money, but plenty. Plenty to . . ." Her smile left her and she took a step back into the doorway of her room. It was then Evelyn noticed the suitcases. "I'm moving out. Today. I can afford a bigger place now—a place of my own—and this afternoon I remembered a house over on Wayfarer Road that was for rent, so I went and looked at it, and it's perfect, and I signed a lease and am moving in."

Evelyn closed her eyes slowly, then opened them. "But you have a lease here."

Valerie's smile was condescending. "I was hoping you'd let me out of it. Considering the circumstances. Considering my special news."

It was too much and Evelyn didn't feel like dealing with it. "Whatever." She shook Valerie's hand and added, "Congratulations. I wish you the best." Then she left her to take her own suitcases to her car.

A double dose of bubbles beckoned.

•   •   •

Evelyn stood at the bathroom mirror, combing her hair. But her mind wasn't on the mundane grooming but on her predicament. She was once again without a renter.

During her bubble bath, the water had practically boiled with the stewing going on in her mind. How dare Valerie leave her after less than two weeks?

Besides her anger at Valerie, Evelyn was mad at herself. Though she'd often bypassed the formalities of a signed lease, this time she had one. It was a legal document. Why had she let Valerie off the hook like that?

She stopped combing her hair and instead combed her eyes for the truth. *You wanted her gone. She was difficult and you're glad to see her go.*

True, all true. But that didn't change the reality of an empty room and no rent coming in. How bizarre to have a boarding-house with only one paid boarder—and that one leaving in a few short weeks to get married. She grabbed hold of the sink and bowed her head. "Father? What's going on?"

She heard the front door open and Mae's voice. "Yoo-hoo? It's me."

Evelyn looked at her reflection and nodded once. Maybe Mae would know what to do. If nothing else, misery loved company.

⋅ ⋅ ⋅

Mae stared at Valerie's empty closet. "I can't believe she moved out."

"She's going to be a famous author now. She doesn't dare live in a mere boardinghouse," Evelyn said.

"Did she say that?"

"Well, no . . . but she implied it. By moving out the same day she got news of her contract, she made it clear she thinks she's too good for us."

Mae was concerned about Evelyn's tone. It wasn't like her to be so bitter. She sat on the bed and patted the space beside her. "Have a seat, sister."

Evelyn surrendered even before she sat, sinking onto the mattress as if she had no bones to hold her. "Sorry. I'm being mean."

"You do have a right to be upset."

Evelyn looked at her, hope in her eyes. "I do?"

"Of course you do. Yell, scream, have a proper hissy fit if you want. She's left you in a lurch."

A nod. "I hate finding new tenants. It wears me out."

Mae couldn't disagree with her and felt bad that shortly there would be yet another room for rent when Piper moved out. She tried to think of something positive. "At least now you ladies can be as loud as you want, when you want." She sprang from the bed and did a few silly dance moves. "Party time at Peerbaugh Place!"

"We *are* such a wild bunch. That Accosta . . ." She shook her head as if in disgust.

"Remember the day we got Tessa dancing to Glenn Miller?"

"Was it 'In the Mood'?"

"'Little Brown Jug,'" Mae said. She grabbed Evelyn's hand and pulled her off the bed and under her arm in a jitterbug move, then back again in a fancy twirl.

Evelyn laughed and caught herself against the library table. "You're right. Valerie may be a talented author, but *fun* is not in her dictionary." She looked at the table, then gave it a pat. "Help me move this."

"Where to?"

"The attic. Let's get this room back the way it belongs."

●   ●   ●

Soon-ja wasn't thrilled about the Scoreboard as a restaurant because it was more bar than restaurant. The multiple televisions showing baseball were annoying. But she was so excited about spending time with her husband that she ignored anything that would cast a negative glow to the evening.

It wasn't easy. Only one of Ringo's coworkers had showed up—girlfriend in tow. She couldn't remember either of their names. The girl was all oozy over her guy, hanging on to his arm, kissing his shoulder. Not that the guy seemed to care. He ate his buffalo wings and fries, talking to Ringo about baseball most of the time. His hair was dirty and too long. Soon-ja didn't mind long hair—Ringo had long hair—but that didn't mean a guy couldn't keep it clean and neat.

Soon-ja was trying to pay attention because she really wanted this evening to work, but her thoughts kept straying to Ricky. Mae would be putting him to bed soon. It wasn't that her mother-in-law couldn't handle it—or hadn't done it before. The difference was that this was the first time Soon-ja hadn't been in the house when her baby had gone down for the night. The first time she hadn't been there to sing, "Oh Dear, What Can the Matter Be?" while rocking him.

Suddenly, her thoughts were brought back to the present when the friend asked, "You got a kid?"

He was looking right at Soon-ja. "Yes. A little boy." She was going to ask him if he had any children, but didn't think he was married.

"Kids are cool."

Ringo did the asking. "You got kids?"

"Yeah."

Soon-ja looked at the girlfriend—was her name Jane?—who let go of her beau's arm. "Hey, don't look at me."

"Not with her." He snickered. "But it does seem I can get a girl pregnant just by looking at her."

And this is a good thing? Soon-ja was going to ask if he ever saw his kids—it sounded like there was more than one—when the guy said, "Not that I ever wanted them. Surprises every one."

Okay. That was it. She thought of Audra and Russell and the

way they ached to have a baby, while this cretin had children he didn't even want.

He did a curlicue circle at Soon-ja's face. "You don't approve."

She glanced at Ringo who was clearly giving her a don't-push-it look. But since he'd asked . . . "It's just that some friends of mine want children desperately and can't have them. And when I see the pain in their eyes . . ."

"Yeah, that's the pits. But life ain't fair, is it?"

The girlfriend stood, pulling on his arm. "Come on, Mac. Let's go home. I want to get to bed early." Her grin said more than her words.

Mac put a few bills on the table, downed the rest of his beer, and got up. "See you Monday, eh, Ringo?"

Soon-ja was glad to see them leave. Now they could go home and see Ricky.

Ringo bit a fry in two with extra force. "Thanks a lot," he said.

Had she missed something? "What are you mad about?"

"You chased him off with the talk of babies."

"I didn't bring it up; he did. And you were the one who asked him if he had kids."

"But you turned it into a downer by bringing up Audra and Russell."

"Sorry." She wiped the condensation off her Diet Coke. "But truly, Go-Go, don't you think it's weird so many people who don't want kids have them, and so many who want them, don't?"

Ringo shoved his plate away and got out his wallet. "I'm tired. Let's go home."

So much for conversation and togetherness.

*   *   *

Piper put a hand to her stomach. "I feel sick."

"Do you want me to pull over?" Gregory asked.

She closed her eyes and shook her head. "I don't want to be late." She looked at her watch. Her mother-in-law-to-be lived ninety minutes from Carson Creek. They had fifteen minutes to go.

"You worry too much, sweetheart. We've prayed for a long time about this. God's not going to abandon us now. Besides, she's just my mother."

Piper managed a laugh. "Not to belittle God's power, but from what you've said she's quite a dynamo."

He smiled. "But still no match for the Father, Son, and Holy Spirit."

"Promise?"

"Absolutely."

They drove a few miles in silence but Piper couldn't stop thinking about it. "I want to be friends with her, Gregory. She's going to be a part of our lives for as long as we live."

"She doesn't have to be . . ."

She swatted his arm. "Don't even say that. You're an only child, I'm an only child, my mother is gone, your father is gone. Our family is small enough without us willingly excluding someone." *Or letting her exclude us.*

His voice was soft. "I *do* want her to be around, especially when we have children."

Just the thought of such a possibility made Piper feel warm inside. To go from a single woman who'd resigned herself to never having a husband and children to a woman on the verge of having both was heady stuff.

"Be yourself and you'll be fine," he said.

As nervous as she was, she wasn't sure "herself" had a chance.

•   •   •

Piper noticed a slim brass case set diagonally on the doorframe of the Baladino home. "What's this?" she asked Gregory.

He ran a finger over the Hebrew letters, but shook his head. "I have no idea."

Suddenly, before they'd even rung the bell, the door opened and Piper was confronted with Esther Baladino.

"Don't you dare come in without the proper respect," she said.

"Excuse me?" Gregory said.

She pushed past them, kissed her fingers, and touched the brass case. She glared at them, her eyes full of confrontation. "All who enter here must show their respect for God and His commandments by kissing the mezuzah."

Piper was stunned and waited for Gregory to say something. Do something. When he didn't, she kissed her fingers and touched the case.

Esther gave her one sharp nod. "Good. Gregory?"

He exchanged a glance with Piper and she tried to implore him with her eyes. What could it hurt? The premise was sound even if they didn't understand the details.

He kissed his fingers and touched it, then looked at his mother. "Hello, Mother."

He moved to hug her, but she held out a hand. "Inside, inside."

Okay then. Once inside, with the door shut, Esther allowed herself to be hugged. She looked much older than her sixty-one years. Though most people ended up having a vertical line between their brows, Esther's was a deep furrow as if she'd spent way too much time being serious, concerned—or angry?

Piper realized that Esther's hair was another factor that made her look old. No hair dye for Esther. Her hair was more salt than pepper and was cut in the nondescript short permed style that plagued women who didn't fight looking old. Her clothes were the only thing that prevented her from looking dowdy. She wore a coral-and-white floral skirt and a matching jacket that was worn closed. It was a happy outfit, which considering Esther's disposition, was disconcerting.

When it was Piper's turn to be greeted, Esther's furrow dug deeper. "So. This is her."

Her. Not "This is Piper." Not "This is the woman who's going to be my new daughter-in-law." And certainly not "This is the woman who's made my son so happy."

Piper didn't know whether to shake her hand, hug her, or—

Esther turned away. "Let's move to the dining room. Dinner's ready to be served. I don't like cold food."

Piper didn't think they were late . . .

"You said six-thirty, Mother. We're right on time."

She flashed him a look. "Did I say you weren't?"

Gregory took Piper's hand and they entered the dining room. Piper noticed that the flowers they'd sent—which were supposed to be delivered today—were nowhere in sight.

"You sit over here, Gregory," Esther said, "in your old place." Her tone flattened. "Piper, sit here. I'll be back in a moment to serve."

Gregory was holding her chair, but Piper stood. "Would you like some help, Mrs. Baladino?"

"No."

Piper sat out of necessity. Her legs were jelly. Gregory kissed her ear and whispered, "We'll be fine. I love you. You love me. Just remember that."

She nodded and he took his place across from her. She put her napkin in her lap, feeling foolish to be put in the position of being served. She was used to helping at any dinner party she attended.

But this was not *any* dinner. And the fact that Esther had refused her help could have been calculated to make her feel awkward. If so, mission accomplished.

But that's silly. She can't want me to feel bad. She doesn't even know me. She took a drink of water and had a fleeting thought that drowning herself was an option.

Esther came through the swinging kitchen door, carrying a large tureen—offering a moan at the effort. Gregory popped up to help.

"No, no. I can handle it. I'm used to being alone. Five years now, since your father died."

"I know, Mother. Five years ago September 23."

She set the tureen down and ladled out soup. "Matzoh-ball soup."

Piper nodded. "It smells delicious."

Esther handed a bowl to Piper, then wiped her hands on her apron. "Did you ever visit your father's grave, Gregory? Did you cover your mirrors in mourning and sit shiva for him, pray the prayer of the dead for him?"

As his mother handed him a bowl, he fumbled it, but caught it before soup spilled onto the white brocade tablecloth. "I don't even know what shiva is, Mother, but I have visited his grave."

"To sprinkle it with holy water, no doubt."

Gregory moved his napkin from lap to table. "May I speak with you a minute in the kitchen, please?"

"Not now. We're eating. There's more food to serve. You know I hate cold food."

"We'll be fine." He stood and moved toward the door, holding it open for her. She exited the room.

Piper bowed her head and prayed feverishly.

* * *

Piper didn't want to hear yet needed to hear. This was their future at stake.

She didn't have to make the choice. Gregory's and Esther's voices carried into the dining room, making her privy to every word.

"There's no need to be rude, Mother. Nor antagonistic. This is not a competition."

"You're right. It's not. It's a tragedy."

"What?"

"I just want one answer to one question."

"What is it?"

"How could you do this to me?"

"This?"

"Become a Christian. Abandon your heritage and faith." She repeated the question. "How could you do this to me?"

"I didn't do anything to you. I did it to me. For me. For Piper."

"So she's to blame?"

Piper caught her breath and doubt slid in. Was she to blame?

"No one's to blame. *Blame* is not a word that has anything to do with me becoming a Christian."

"How about the word *betrayal*?"

Piper heard footsteps. Was Gregory pacing?

"This is ridiculous—"

"I'm sorry you think your mother is ridiculous."

"Your idea of betrayal is ridiculous. Whom did I betray?"

"Forget about me. Think about your relatives who died in concentration camps. By believing in Jesus, you're betraying their memory."

The pacing stopped. Gregory's words became softer. "I'm not betraying them, Mother. And I'm certainly not forgetting them. Just as I'm not forgetting Dad's Italian roots."

"At least you're not Catholic."

"What's that supposed to mean?"

"Nothing."

"We're getting off the subject, Mother."

"Which is?"

"Which is my marriage to Piper and the fact that we want to have a good relationship with you."

"Some way you show it."

Father, give him the right words! Heal the rift between them. Please!

"I loved Piper a long time before I proposed marriage. In fact, I wanted to marry her long before I was even a Christian."

"Are you saying it's her fault?"

"Mother! Please stop that. If you must know, Piper had nothing to do with my conversion, or my immersion into a life dedicated to Christ. I came to that decision on my own."

"Humph."

"Piper's influence had to do with her character and integrity. I had never met anyone with such deeply founded beliefs—Jewish or Christian. She gave me up because of those beliefs."

"Gave you up?"

"God does not want any two people to be 'unequally yoked.' He doesn't want a believer to be married to an unbeliever because they won't pull together. They'll base their lives on a different set of rules, going in different directions."

"A Jew should marry a Jew. I understand that."

"Or a Christian a Christian. That's probably the reason I grew up with no religious training. Because you and Dad were unequally yoked."

"So you're blaming us?"

Piper could hear Gregory's sigh from the dining room. "It's not about blame, Mother; it's about love and having a solid bond so a new family can be created. A strong family."

"So you're saying our family wasn't strong?"

Be careful, darling . . .

"It . . . it could have been stronger. You and Dad were estranged from your families, leaving me without the benefit of either heritage. I have no roots in religion. I grew up with nothing."

"Don't talk back to me."

"I'm sorry. Not *nothing*, but no basis for faith."

"Well . . . maybe so, but it isn't that way anymore. I want you to come to your senses and join me in embracing the Jewish faith."

"Mother, I can't. I've made my choice. I can't go back."

There was a pause and Piper held her breath. Then Esther said, "You've hurt me and I'd like you and your shiksa to leave."

Piper didn't have time for the words to register, but stood when they came through the door. Gregory's face was red. He held his hand in her direction. "Come on. We're leaving."

"Gregory . . ." she said. She didn't know what to say. They reached the front door and he hurried her down the steps to the car.

"Go ahead," Esther said from the doorway. "Leave me. Abandon your roots, your heritage, your blood."

Gregory pulled up short and turned around. Piper had never seen such pain in his eyes. "So you're willing to shun me like your parents shunned you? Some family tradition. Go back inside, Mother. The food's getting cold."

      •   •   •

Piper wished Gregory would rant and rave. This mile after mile of silence was excruciating. She kept her face forward, only risking a glance to see how he was doing. If his pulled mouth, dipped eyebrows, and heavy breathing were any indication, he was in a state she'd never witnessed. Was it fury? sorrow? frustration?

Probably all of the—

Suddenly, he pulled off the highway onto the shoulder, shut off the car, gripped the steering wheel at twelve o'clock, and brought his forehead to his hands. His eyes squeezed shut and his breathing turned ragged.

Piper's left hand found the back of his head and she leaned over the center console until her head rested against his shoulder. Her right arm covered his. They didn't say anything. They didn't have to.

A car honked as it sped by.

Your Father already knows your needs.
He will give you all you need from day to day
if you make the Kingdom of God
your primary concern.

LUKE 12:30-31

*A*udra tied the robe around her waist and watched from the window as Summer put the small American flags in the grass along the curb. She'd told her to put them two feet apart and had even offered to go mark the spacing, but no, Summer had said she could do it. And she could. Though the distance between flag 3 and flag 4 was a little tight, generally—

Summer backtracked and corrected the spacing. Good girl.

Cynthia came across the street carrying a softball. The two girls got a game of catch going in the front yard. They could both use the practice because they had a ball game in a few hours. Audra went to the kitchen to pack a picnic lunch. And then there was the festival later on, and the fireworks. A normal Fourth of July.

Russell was at the kitchen table, reading the paper. He lifted a mug. "Coffee's ready."

"Thanks." She poured herself a cup and went to join him. But as she was sitting down, she stopped short. Sitting front and center at her place was a pile of brochures. The top one was entitled *The Joy of Adoption.*

He glanced up from his reading. "Have a seat."

"No thanks." She strolled to the sliding-glass door leading to the back patio.

"At least look at them, Audra."

But I don't want to look at them! She kept her words inside and shook her head.

"You can't say no before you've even looked."

Wanna bet? She swung around to face him, her mug held with both hands as a barrier, protecting her heart. "I can't believe you can let go of our dream just like that, and—"

"The dream is to have children." He carefully folded the paper and set it aside.

"Have children," Audra said. She put one hand on her abdomen. "Have children. Our children."

"If you're trying to make me feel bad because it's my fault we can't, you're doing a good job."

Good. Because it is your fault. She forced herself to take a few breaths . . . in . . . then out. She turned back to the impartiality of the glass. "You have to give me some time. We just found out that the problem . . . what the problem is, and—"

"You mean who the problem is."

She sipped her coffee.

Russell pushed his chair back, the legs protesting against the floor. "I'm sorry, okay? I feel horrible about this, and believe me, I've done my share of screaming at God, asking Him why."

With the ease of Katharine Hepburn in a Spencer Tracy movie, she turned and offered him a condescending smile. "And how did the Almighty respond?"

Russell's forehead gained deep lines and she knew she'd hurt him. *Go to him. Comfort him.* But she stood her ground, hating, yet loving, the surge of power.

He took his mug to the sink, emptied it, and put it in the top rack of the dishwasher. Then he placed his feet, gathered a breath, and looked at her. "I know I've failed you. Because of me, you will never experience the joy of pregnancy."

"Actually, I have experienced it. Thank God."

His face jerked back as if she'd slapped him. Then his jaw clenched and he raised his chin. "Maybe you should find someone else to do what I can't."

He left the room.

The sounds of children playing outside was salt in the open wound.

.   .   .

It was like a sick game-show question: How many emotions can a human being experience in the span of a single minute?

Answer: too many.

Standing alone in the kitchen, Audra grabbed anger, fingered bitterness, touched hate, stroked sorrow, juggled frustration, closed her eyes against self-loathing, and slapped away—then embraced—the duo of regret and remorse.

When the last two emotions took over, her legs became wobbly. She managed to set her coffee on the table before she leaned against it, her head hung low between her shoulders. The adoption brochures came into view. She closed her eyes. "I'm so sorry. So sorry."

Tell him that.

She forced herself upright, looking in the direction of her victim's escape, but her feet were in no hurry to move. Why was it easier to apologize to God than it was to tell her husband she was sorry?

Because you know God will forgive you.

She knew in theory Russell was also supposed to forgive her. But he had every right not to. He'd done nothing to bring this disappointment into their lives. And she *had* experienced a pregnancy and birth. That had been a blessing in disguise, even if Luke—Summer's birth father—was not.

Luke. She hadn't thought about him in months. How ironic that he'd given her what her husband could not. At least their stormy relationship had been good for something.

Your husband. Think about your husband.

She shook away thoughts of the man who'd been the heel in her life and walked toward the heart.

• • •

"Come on, Summer! Wham it!"

Russell leaned toward Audra and whispered, "One does not *wham* it at this age. She'll be lucky if she tips it."

Audra squeezed his arm, once again thankful that she had such a loving, forgiving husband. If he weren't such a man, the entire holiday might have been ruined by their early morning argument.

As Summer approached the batter's box and the coach helped position her just so, Audra concentrated on the game. She had to admit it was a little hard witnessing Summer's lack of athletic ability when she herself had always excelled at sports.

Piper clapped. "Come on, pipsqueak!"

"You can do it!" Gregory yelled.

Summer flashed them a smile, then a wave, then addressed the ball, and as her father predicted, tipped it so it rolled three feet.

"Run!" the crowd roared.

Startled, Summer ran toward first base, easily beating the chaotic infielders who politely let the other players on their team have first dibs on touching the ball.

Summer's cheering section sprang from their seats, yelling like she'd made a home run. Piper and Audra synchronized a series of foot stomps on the metal bleachers that rang nicely. Everybody laughed, then sat down so the next Babe Ruth could come forward.

Audra immediately popped up. "I'm hungry. Anybody want anything?"

No's all around.

"I'll be back." She climbed down the bleachers and headed for the concession stand—which consisted of a little hut with a counter and a flip-up front. She was just paying for her popcorn and Dr Pepper . . .

"Hey, Aud."

She looked toward the familiar voice. "Simon! What are you doing here?"

He didn't answer, but turned to the concessions worker. "Red licorice, please." Then he winked at Audra. "My mother used to say I only liked red licorice because I was a redhead."

He looked great. She'd never seen him wearing something other than his uniform. Then she remembered they were at a kids' ball field. "Do you have a child playing here?"

"No, no. No children here, or anywhere. I do however, have a nephew. He's five." Simon pointed toward another field. "I'd better get back before I miss a home run or something."

"Me too." Suddenly, she didn't want him to go. She heard herself saying, "Simon? Are you going to be at the Fourth of July celebration tonight?"

"Wouldn't miss it. Will I see you there?"

"Absolutely." *We'll be there. Husband. Daughter* . . .

He turned to leave, then looked at her again, his head tilted. "Did you change your hair?"

She fingered the hair hanging down behind her ears. "I . . . I pulled some of it back into a barrette."

He nodded. "I like it. Well . . . see you tonight."

Audra hurried back to the bleachers.

* * *

Soon-ja slipped out of the bedroom. She felt bad for waking Ringo and kicking him out, but it was nearly noon and Ricky had to go down for a nap. She hoped the baby would sleep a few hours because it was going to be a long day and a cranky baby would definitely put a damper on the celebration. She wondered how Ricky would react to the fireworks. His first Fourth of July . . . so many firsts.

In her baby's life. And in hers.

To think that a year ago she'd graduated from college with a degree in business with high hopes of wowing the corporate world with her smarts. She'd had offers of ground-floor jobs in two reputable companies and had been on the verge of taking one when the chance to work as the assistant to the tour manager on a rock tour had fallen from the sky. Into her lap.

All common sense had told her to ignore it. It was a magenta stone in a rock garden of grays and tans. Corporate America, that's where she belonged. That fit into her family's American dream for their girl. Since her parents had been killed in an accident when she was young, she'd been raised by her grandparents and extended family. It had been hard enough getting them to understand that she needed to leave Korea and venture out on her own to an American college. They would never understand her picking up the magenta pebble and putting it in her pocket. Such obnoxious distractions were to be plucked out and tossed away, not embraced. Not cherished because they were so different. So exciting. So rebellious.

Soon-ja had never considered herself rebellious. In Korean society one was brought up to go along. Keep the peace. *The silence is golden* was a phrase oft repeated by her grandmother and aunties.

But when the friend of a friend had brought her the advertise-

ment for the job with a rock tour, and when that friend of a friend
had said "You know what? You should apply. You'd have a
blast," she'd found herself thinking that a "blast" was exactly
what she wanted to do at that postgraduation moment in her life.
The idea of doing something strange and funky, even daring and
a bit dangerous, had taken over until she'd found herself apply-
ing. Only after she'd progressed that far in the process had she
consulted God to find out what He preferred. That delay in apply-
ing her faith had caused her more than a little guilt. Her family
had brought her up praying before, during, and after all important decisions and events. So when she'd slipped into this life-
changing opportunity, seemingly under God's radar, she had
never expected to get the job. Wasn't even sure she should take it
when it was offered.

But after praying mightily at that point in the process, she'd
felt the peace that came with a right decision. And so she'd gone
on tour with a rock band and met Ringo Fitzpatrick. It had been
love at first sight. Who could resist Ringo's sly smile, or the way
he tossed his head to get the hair out of his eyes?

Obviously not Soon-ja. She'd become pregnant. The shame
had been a heavy shroud. Her family would never understand.
And so they'd eloped. As time passed, being a married pregnant
woman became acceptable, even if the cart had been before the
horse.

She put a hand on the sleeping baby's back, the baby who'd
been unplanned but completely loved. She'd never expected to
love anyone this much, and sometimes it scared her. Did she love
Ricky more than Ringo? She knew that wasn't right, yet sometimes . . .

She slipped out of the room knowing the current problems
with her husband were making her feel like this. She had plenty
of love for both men in her life, and in truth, they would probably
take turns rising to the top of her love list, or falling to second

position because of some infraction. Did such ups and downs make her love shallow? Or was it normal?

She went downstairs, looking for Ringo. The house was quiet. Her in-laws were gone; Collier was helping Mae set up for the festival. Through the front window she caught sight of Ringo sitting on the porch swing. She went outside.

"Hey," she said.

"Hey." His greeting was mumbled because of the wad of bread in his mouth. Soon-ja had never seen anyone eat bread plain, but Ringo liked it that way. He'd told her the habit had started when he was little. If he was hungry in between meals, he'd found it easy to sneak a piece of plain bread out of the kitchen.

Ringo was barefoot and shirtless, wearing only jeans. He was not a muscular man, rather skinny really, but Soon-ja loved the look of him. Yet she wasn't sure it was proper for him to sit shirtless in plain view of the neighbors. She held her tongue and joined him on the swing.

He held the bread toward her. "Want a bite?"

"No thanks."

He let her do the rocking and sat sideways, tucking his feet beneath her nearest leg. "What's up for today?" he asked.

"There's a big festival down on the square. Your mom's selling her jewelry, and there's entertainment. Then fireworks."

"I'll pass."

"You can't pass."

"Why not?"

"Because it's a holiday. Because your mom is expecting us. Because I want to show Ricky the fireworks."

"He'll sleep through it."

"That's not the point."

He shrugged and wriggled his toes against her thigh.

"What would you rather do?"

His toes stopped. He looked out over the yard and Soon-ja sensed her innocent question had taken a deeper meaning.

"I miss the tour."

She laughed. "You miss the weird hours, the backbreaking work, the long miles in a bus, being around obnoxious people who abuse booze and drugs?"

A glance, then away. "Well . . . yeah."

Soon-ja felt as if the wind had been knocked out of her. She'd guessed he missed the general excitement of being a roadie, but to miss the things she'd always considered a negative?

He pointed at her face. "Don't give me that disgusted look. You chose that life too, you know."

True. "I chose it out of curiosity and because it sounded glamorous. It was anything but."

"That's your opinion."

They swung back and forth, both looking out on the yard. They waved at Accosta as she came out of Peerbaugh Place and cut some roses to take inside. Soon-ja loved it here in Carson Creek. Loved the calm serenity. Even loved the predictability of life here.

She hadn't realized he'd been watching her until he leaned forward and touched her cheek. "It's like there are two parts of me—the life I had and the life I have. Both are good."

"But they can't be mixed, Go-Go."

His eyes flashed. "Can't they? I was talking to Gordie the other day and there's another tour starting. He says I could get on. Three months."

The airless feeling returned. "And what are Ricky and I supposed to do while you're gone?"

"Go with me."

"Don't be ridiculous."

Ringo stood and faced her, sending the swing into wild gyrations. "This is what's ridiculous. Expecting me to live in my mother's house, all crammed into one room, never being alone."

"We're alone now."

"We're never alone. Not really."

"We can get our own place, put down roots."

"Roots that will strangle me. I don't want to be stuck here in Carson Creek. And I certainly don't want to be working construction."

"You worked construction as a roadie."

"It was different."

And it was. Building an elaborate set for a rock band was far different than working on a two-bedroom bungalow. She couldn't argue.

He began to pace between her and the railing. "It's stifling here. I feel like I'm going to burst. I'm going crazy living like this."

There were no words. Soon-ja stood. "I'd better go check on the baby."

He followed her to the door. "Is that all you can say?"

It was.

●   ●   ●

Soon-ja looked down at her sleeping baby. Ricky's mouth moved in his sleep. Was he dreaming of eating his next meal? His little fists were clenched, his arms bent upward, framing his head. Sweet, sweet baby. A baby whose father was miserable and whose mother didn't know what to do about it.

What had made her think Ringo felt the same way she did about the roadie life? What had made her think they could live a normal life? Had she been totally blind?

Ricky drew in a sudden breath and let it out, but regained his peaceful rhythm within seconds. There would be no peace on the road. Buses, auditoriums, hotel rooms, restaurants. People everywhere at all hours. If Ringo was the rock star they could have their own bus where some semblance of family life could be created, but for a peon there would be no special concessions. None. Get along or get out. Deal with it or we'll deal you out.

But Ringo wanted to get *into* that lifestyle and *out* of the lifestyle Soon-ja and Ricky needed to survive.

I want to go home.

She looked up at the absurdity of the thought. She'd been in the United States for five years—since she was eighteen. And yet, the home that was connected to the emotional plea was seven thousand miles away in Korea. Her relatives still lived there. . . .

She looked back at Ricky. They'd never seen this baby.

They deserved to see this baby.

She headed for the phone.

◦　◦　◦

Soon-ja hung up the kitchen phone. Her heart raced. Her family was thrilled with the idea of a visit from her and Ricky. They readily offered to pay for a ticket.

"How long can you stay?" they'd asked.

"Can we keep it open?"

The fact she'd even suggested such a thing shocked her. Was she really thinking of leaving Ringo for good?

No, no. It's just a visit. It's just a chance for us to think things through.

Her biggest hope was that Ringo would miss them. Ache for them. Long to have them back. Give up his notion of returning to the roadie life and accept that that portion of his life was past. It was time to be a husband and father. It was time to grow up.

She stared at the phone and realized her hand was still on it. Was *she* acting grown up by running home to her family?

They deserve to see the newest addition.

She nodded, putting a period on the excuse. It was better than the truth.

She heard the front door open, then close. Ringo was coming back inside. But she heard Collier's and Mae's voices too. Back for lunch?

Her stomach wrenched. How could she tell them? When should she tell them?

Mae reached the kitchen first. "Happy Fourth, Miss Soonie. You should see the doings down on the square. It's going to be great. We came home to grab some lunch before manning my booth. How's tuna sound?"

"Fine," Soon-ja said.

She'd tell them later. She couldn't ruin the day. She couldn't.

•   •   •

The customer walked away with her package. "Thanks. Come again." Mae turned to Ursola, sitting beside her. "Way to go, Ursola! Two pins in the first hour. You're putting me to shame."

Ursola wasn't sure what that shame line meant, but it didn't sound good. "I'm sorry I take sales."

"Gracious gemstone, sister. This is what free enterprise is all about. Healthy competition never hurt anyone."

Tessa sat on the other side of Ursola and inspected a blue brooch. "I think I like this one best." She handed it to Ursola. "Yes. Give me this one."

Mae clapped. "Three!"

Ursola was thrilled with the income, but it was also embarrassing. Were they just buying to be nice to her?

No . . . the first two sales were from people she'd never met before—though Mae's oohing and aahing over the brooches clinched the sale. With a nod, Ursola decided that she'd try to do a sales pitch for Mae's jewelry to the next person who came to the table. If only her English were better . . .

Suddenly Mae waved at someone. "Oh! There's Evelyn." As a woman with a wonderful smile approached, Mae opened the cash box, then handed Ursola a ten-dollar bill. "Go get us some tea, will you, Ursola?"

It seemed a bit awkward to stand to leave just as the friend Evelyn was approaching the table, but Ursola did as she was told.

*   *   *

"Quick!" Mae said. "Before she gets back."

Evelyn looked at Tessa, who shrugged. "Who—?"

"What are you talking about, Mae?" Tessa asked.

Mae leaned forward conspiratorially. "Evelyn, that beautiful young thing that just left is Ursola Shivi-something Smith. She's a Russian mail-order bride whose husband just died and whose stepson just rooked her out of house and home."

Tessa nodded. "I found her sleeping in the church. She's been staying with me the last three nights. She's a dear. She makes these gorgeous brooches and—"

Mae flipped a hand. "More on her artistic ability later. Just a few moments ago, when I saw you across the square, my mind put two and two together and—"

"Exploded?" Tessa asked.

Mae gave her a look. "And got a smashing idea. Is Valerie's room still empty?"

"Yes . . ." Evelyn added the two and two herself. "You want Ursola to take it?"

"Exactly," Mae said. "However, *take* is the operative word."

"She doesn't have any money," Tessa said. "Though she *is* doing her best to start from scratch and earn a living. She works constantly on those brooches."

Evelyn's mind swam. She'd never even met this woman. And a Russian mail-order bride? That was bizarre.

"Here she comes," Mae said. "What'll it be, Evie?"

Evelyn didn't appreciate being put on the spot and yet, hadn't she taken in both Mae and Tessa as boarders without much introspection or to-do? And they'd turned out all right.

Ursola set a cardboard tray of four paper cups on the table. "I got one for friend, too."

Mae beamed at Evelyn. "That was very nice of you, Ursola. And I'd like you to meet that friend. Ursola, this is Evelyn Peerbaugh. Evelyn, Ursola Shiv . . ."

"Shivikova Smith," Ursola said. "Smith. Smith easy." She held out her hand to shake.

She was so petite, barely over five feet, and slim too. Her skin was almost transparent in its paleness, and was made more so by her jet-black hair. She looked slightly familiar. "Happy to meet you, Ursola."

Evelyn looked at Mae, who was giving her every kind of nonverbal push possible. How could she *not* offer the girl the room? She cleared her throat. "Ursola, I understand you've been staying with Tessa?"

The girl smiled at the matriarch of the group. "She very nice to me."

"She's a very nice lady. But I have a better solution for you. I have a boardinghouse and . . ."

Ursola's eyebrows dipped. She didn't understand.

"I rent rooms to women."

Ursola nodded.

"I have one that's empty. It's yours if you'd like."

"I . . ." She shook her head. "No money."

"Don't worry about that right now. We'll work something out."

Ursola was breathing heavily. Her eyes flitted from Tessa to Mae and back to Evelyn. Evelyn nodded, trying to encourage her.

Then she began to cry. "You are so nice. All so nice."

There, there. Evelyn took her tears as a yes. Peerbaugh Place
was full once more.

•   •   •

"Glad you're back," Wayne said to Evelyn as she returned to the
church's baked-goods table. "We had a run on the oatmeal-raisin
cookies and I nearly panicked."

Evelyn took her place behind the table. "Where's Accosta?"

She went off to have a look at the library's used books. She'll
be back soon." He made a face. "I've been all alone."

"Poor baby."

"How are Mae's sales going?"

Evelyn realized she hadn't asked—or even had a chance to
ask. She let out a heavy sigh.

"What's that for?" Wayne asked.

"Remember the empty room I had at Peerbaugh Place?"

"Sure. Valerie's."

"It's not empty anymore."

He slapped her on the back. "Congratulations! You walk
across the square and end up renting your last room? That was a
profitable little stroll."

Profitable? Hardly. She told him the details regarding her new
tenant.

"Let me get this straight," he said. "You had two rooms for
rent and you've given one to Accosta—for free. And now you've
given the other one to an immigrant—for free."

Evelyn covered her face with her hands. "What have I done? I
only have one room bringing in income—and Piper's moving out
in a few weeks. With the financial commitment I've made on
Accosta's house . . ."

"Do you want to back out?"

129

Though her first inclination was to say yes, she forced herself to remember how she and Wayne had prayed about the Accosta project. How she'd felt good about it. Right. She had to leave that decision alone. But this new one . . . "I'm still in. But you have to admit, having two nonpaying boarders doesn't make any sense."

Wayne nodded and fingered a plate of brownies. "It doesn't make sense to us, Evelyn. But helping a sister in need . . . that's a good thing. Maybe it's even a God thing." He put a hand on hers and looked into her eyes. "I think you've got to trust that God knows what He's doing."

She loved how intense his eyes got when he talked about God. She nodded but let out a little laugh. "And He'll provide, right? When my bills come due, He'll give me enough to pay them?"

"One way or another."

They had a customer, preventing Evelyn from delving deeper into exactly what that might mean.

*   *   *

Piper was glad she and Gregory hadn't brought lawn chairs. Chairs would have separated them. As it was, sitting on a blanket on the grass in the middle of the square, they could cuddle. Leaning against his chest, with his arm as a solid post behind her, she was content. If she closed her eyes she could imagine away the world and easily let *him* become her world.

It was a bit frightening. She, who'd always been the independent woman, secure in her identity, successful at her career, loving daughter, loved friend. Though she'd always wanted to be married and have a family, she'd come to terms with the fact it might never be. She'd found contentment in the life she had.

Then Gregory had come along. Dr. Baladino—warm heart,

strong hands, keen mind, and now, solid faith. He was an immense blessing.

With a mother who hates you.

She squeezed her eyes tight against the memory of the dinner at Esther's. *Lord, show us what to do.* As the fireworks began, she reluctantly opened her eyes and let the flashes and booms in. The crowd clapped and gasped with appreciation.

Appreciation. She regained her focus on what she *did* have.

Gregory nuzzled her ear and whispered. "These fireworks are nothing to the ones I see when I kiss you."

Yup. He was definitely a keeper.

* * *

Audra started to help Russell fold the lawn chairs but Summer intervened. "Let me, Mommy. I like to fold them."

Audra let her help, and picked up the empty pop cans and trash. "I'll be right back. Don't leave without me."

She made her way through the departing crowd to a trash barrel on the edge of the grass. A step away, she looked up. "Simon!"

He picked up the can she'd dropped and threw it away. "Hi, Aud. Did you like the fireworks?"

"Very much," she said. Her stomach did involuntary back-flips. "And you?"

He nodded, then smiled. "The band did a pretty good job playing 'Stars and Stripes Forever' during the finale, don't you think?"

"Uh . . ." Actually, they'd been horrible.

He winked, leaned close, and whispered, "I have to say nice things about them. A good friend of mine plays clarinet."

Girlfriend?

"Joel Smothers. You know him? He works at the Scoreboard."

She shook her head. "I've never been there."

"Really? You should try it. I eat there a couple times a week." He shrugged. "My bachelor cooking is pretty lame."

Speaking of friends and girlfriends . . . she didn't see anyone hovering close waiting for him. "You here alone?"

He glanced behind. "I'm here with a few people. In fact, I'd better find them or I'll lose my ride. Nice seeing you here. Happy Fourth."

"You too." She returned to her family.

Russell looked up from the cooler. "What took you so long?"

She busied herself with the lawn blanket. "Oh nothing. I just ran into a friend."

Just a friend.

•   •   •

Audra couldn't sleep. She turned her back on the sleeping Russell and looked into the blackness of their bedroom. Her thoughts swam with images of Simon that placed her close to him—too close to him—touching, talking. Hugging. Even kissing . . .

She flung back the covers and got out of bed. "No!" She'd only whispered it, but looked back at Russell, hoping he hadn't heard. *No* what?

The list was long. Too long.

She went to the kitchen, flipping on every light as she went. Maybe the reality of seeing the everyday trappings of her life would dispel the fantasies that had invaded her mind.

She got a drink of water, but found herself frozen with the glass halfway to her mouth as thoughts of Simon spun their web.

"No!" She banged the glass on the counter and it shattered.

It served her right. She had no business thinking about another man. It was dangerous. Far too—

"What happened?" Russell stood in the doorway.

"I broke a glass."

He got out the broom and dustpan. "Be careful not to hurt yourself."

Good advice. Very good advice.

7

Finally, all of you should be of one mind,
full of sympathy toward each other,
loving one another with tender hearts and humble minds.

1 PETER 3:8

*A*udra spent extra time getting dressed, putting on a new pink-and-yellow plaid blouse with her pink capris. Russell came into the bedroom from the master bath, adjusting his tie. "What are you so dressed up for?"

"I'm not dressed up."

He grabbed his suit coat. "You're usually not dressed at all when I leave for work."

She smoothed her hair and touched the barrette in the back. "I just felt I should get going early. I have a lot of sewing to do for Piper's wedding."

It *was* true. Kinda. Sorta.

•   •   •

Soon-ja sat at the kitchen table with an empty cereal bowl in front of her. She couldn't eat. Not with the news she had to share with Ringo. Not knowing how he'd react. It helped that Collier had left with Mae to help her with the post-Fourth reorganization at Silver-Wear. At least they had the house to themselves.

In case Ringo yelled.

Which he would.

Her stomach clenched. She shoved the bowl away and grabbed handfuls of hair. *Help me! Help me say this. Or help me not say this. Or—*

She heard Ringo on the stairs. She only had a few seconds to figure this out, to find the words. But her mind went blank and she panicked. She stood, toppling her chair. Ricky started in his infant's seat.

Ringo came in as she was setting the chair right. "You okay?"

Not really. "It fell."

"I heard." He got out a bowl and poured Cheerios, milk, and too much sugar. He touched the tip of his son's nose, then sat at the table, digging in. He didn't wait to finish chewing before he talked. "You think more about me going back on the road?"

She had difficulty finding a breath. "Actually, I have."

His eyes lit up. She hated that his eyes lit up. "So I can go?"

"You can, but—"

He was out of his chair, pulling her into a hug. "It'll be great, Soonie. You'll see."

She pushed away and began to cry. "You didn't let me finish. You can go but I'm not going with you. I'm going to visit my family."

"In Korea?"

"They haven't seen Ricky." She hurried on with the details. "They're excited. And it won't cost us a thing. They've already bought the ticket and—"

"Whoa! When did this happen?"

"Yesterday. After we talked I . . . uh . . . I . . ."

"You called them? You brought them into the middle of our argument?"

"They've been wanting to see Ricky. And me."

"Right now? They have to see you right now?"

"Now's good."

"And convenient."

She couldn't argue that one. She didn't want to argue. At all.

He grabbed his work boots and put them on. "I have to go. We'll talk about this later."

"I'm leaving on Saturday."

He froze. Then he turned his head slowly, his look weakening her knees.

She didn't know what to do. Should she say it was all a big mistake? run into his arms? remain silent? defend herself? "I know it's short notice, only four days but—"

He stood. "So it's 'have a nice life' and move on, is it?"

She took a step toward him. "No, Go-Go. It's just a visit. Really—"

He opened the kitchen door. "That's what you say, but you know the truth. We both do."

He slammed it. Ricky began to cry.

Soon-ja joined him.

●   ●   ●

Valerie Raines sat at her very own desk in her very own office, looking out at her very own backyard, in her very own house, and stared at the computer screen. The blank computer screen.

There was no reason—no excuse—why the words shouldn't be rushing onto the page. She had silence, space, a nice view, central air, a glass of club soda with lime, a lavender candle burning, and no interruptions. Most of all, she had what every writer craves: solitude and time.

She heard a soft rumbling and looked behind her, for a moment forgetting that it couldn't be Peppers purring against the doorjamb, coming to visit. Sitting at her feet—sometimes *on* her feet.

To dispel the coziness of the memory, Valerie reminded herself she hated cats, pulled off her turban so she could hear better, then got up to see what *was* making the sound. She paused in the empty living room. But not empty for long. Using a portion of the advance she was going to get for her book, she'd bought an entire set of furniture that was supposed to be delivered Friday. No more living like a starving artist. She was an author now. She had an image to maintain.

What a joke. Sure, she'd taken to wearing vintage clothing during the past year, trying to make herself stand out and appear more glamorous and sophisticated. But who was she kidding? She could *try* to have style like the female writers of the twenties and thirties—Dorothy Parker or Virginia Woolf—but she couldn't quite grasp the aura they'd had about them, though she *had* done a pretty good job grasping their bent toward the pessimistic side of life. Peerbaugh Place had not reacted well. Her severe hair and flowing outfits had made the ladies more uncomfortable than envious.

In truth she didn't have an image to maintain; she had one to create. From scratch. She had to create the image of who she wanted to be. *Whom* she wanted to be? She never could keep that rule of grammar straight. Either way it was a tall order.

Moving into the kitchen Valerie realized the refrigerator was the source of noise that had drawn her away from her computer, though up close, its purr was a poor second to the amazing hum of Peppers' motor. Since Valerie was in the vicinity, she peered inside the refrigerator, trying to gauge if there was some corner of her appetite that needed appeasement in order to ignite her creativity. The pickings were bleak: skim milk, blueberry yogurt, a tub of margarine, and eleven eggs—one had broken in transit. The cupboards were worse. A can of tuna, a loaf of bread—that would certainly get moldy before she used it all—and a box of Cap'n Crunch cereal.

The Cap'n beckoned. She poured herself a bowl, took it into the middle of the empty living room, sat on the floor, and had a sugar binge, albeit fortified with nine essential vitamins and minerals.

The epitome of a successful author. If her friends could see her now.

•   •   •

Evelyn was making her bed when she heard the front door open.

"Hell-ohh? Evelyn?"

"I'll be down in a minute," she called to Tessa as she pulled the quilt over the pillows.

"Don't bother. We're coming up."

We?

Evelyn moved into the upstairs hall just as Tessa and Ursola came up the stairs. It wasn't that she wasn't expecting Ursola to move in; she just hadn't expected her to show up at nine the next morning. Ursola was struggling with one of the suitcases. "Here, let me help—"

Halfway down the stairs, her hand extended to take one of the pieces of luggage, Evelyn realized she'd seen it before. In her garden. As she carried it upstairs, she tried to fit this information into what she'd heard about Ursola's predicament.

Accosta came out of her room, carrying a book. "I thought I heard voices. Is this our new sister?"

Once they all reached the landing, Tessa took charge by placing an arm around Ursola's waist. "Here she is."

Accosta gave Ursola a hug, making Evelyn a bit uneasy about so many women in so little space at the top of some very steep stairs. "Let me show you your room, Ursola." Evelyn set the suitcase on the bed. "The dresser is empty, as is the closet." She moved to a door. "You'll share a bathroom with Accosta—if that's all right?"

Ursola nodded, but was fingering the doily on the dresser, studying it. "Thank . . . thank you."

She did not meet their eyes. Evelyn understood. She stepped toward the door. "We'll let you get settled."

There was a time for sisterhood and a time for solitude, and it was important to know the difference.

*   *   *

Evelyn didn't want to think about whether her choice to weed the back garden on this particular morning was spurred by an innocent desire to conquer a chore, or because she was hoping her newest tenant would come join her. But when she heard the back screen door slam, and looked up to see Ursola strolling down the path toward her, she felt a surge of pleasure beyond the chore.

But don't say anything. Let her bring up the suitcases.

She stood from her weeding, wiping her forehead with the back of her arm. "You all settled in?"

Ursola walked with her arms clasped behind her back. Her pants and blouse seemed too large, as if she'd lost weight. "It's lovely room. I very happy."

"That's what I like to hear." Evelyn motioned toward the window of Ursola's room. "I've always liked that room with its window-seat view of the backyard."

Ursola looked back toward the house, nodding. Then suddenly, she looked at the lilac bushes near the alley, then back at the house. Evelyn heard a soft gasp.

"What is it?" Evelyn's heart raced, hoping . . .

Ursola put a hand to her mouth. "Garden . . ." She shook her head. "No. Nothing."

Evelyn removed her gloves and stepped onto the path. "Obviously it's something. What are you thinking about?"

Ursola seemed to study Evelyn's face. Then she took a few steps toward the alley. She pointed to the lilacs. "I been here. I hide suitcases. There."

"I know."

Ursola's eyes grew wide. "You know?"

"I found them. I wondered who they belonged to. I even watched to see who would pick them up."

"You saw?"

"No. I got busy. When I got back to watching, they were gone." Now was her chance. "Why did you put them there?"

Ursola looked upward and watched the branches of the elm dance. Then she looked at Evelyn. "Husband leave all to son." She shrugged. "No home. I leave. But carry . . . too heavy. I hide. See Mae. Make pins. Live church. I come get." She pointed at the place where the suitcases had sat.

Evelyn couldn't imagine the feeling of loneliness and fear Ursola must have felt—in a foreign country, widowed, cast out. There were all kinds of Bible passages about helping widows, and upon remembering that fact, Evelyn felt better about offering her home. It was the right thing to do. Evelyn gave her a hug. "You poor girl. You have a home now. Here. You're very welcome here. I won't turn you away."

Ursola's forehead dipped as she nodded. Then she pointed back to the lilacs. "Odd. My suitcases here, then I here."

Evelyn laughed. "Not odd. God."

Ursola's eyebrows rose.

"Don't fight it, honey. Nor argue about it. There's God's hand all over this place. The stories I could tell you . . ." She thought of something. "Did you know I'm a widow too?"

"No."

"See? We have a lot in common." Evelyn put an arm around her shoulders and led her back toward the house. "Let's get some iced tea, have a piece of chocolate cake, and chat about that odd God we have—and our husbands too if the subject comes up."

Which it would.

* * *

Summer ran in the exterior door of Audra's workroom. Audra looked up from the sewing machine and was immediately disappointed. "How many times have I told you not to barge in here, banging the door and—?"

Summer stopped in her tracks. "Oh. Sorry, Mommy."

The little girl looked stricken and Audra immediately felt bad. "I'm sorry. I'm just a little stressed about work." *And not seeing Simon. Surely he has a delivery for me today. Surely I didn't get all dressed up with my hair the way he likes it for nothing.* "What do you want, baby?"

"Cynthia and I want to have a lemonade stand. Can you make us a pitcher? Cynthia's mom will give us cups."

Sure. Why not? She didn't have anything better to do.

* * *

Mae looked up when the bell on the front door of Silver-Wear jingled. "Soonie and son! What a nice surprise." She snatched the darling boy out of his mother's arms. "And how's my sweet-ums?" Ricky smiled, making the world right and good. She snuggled him into her neck. Only then did she really look at her daughter-in-law. "Oh my. Soonie, what's wrong?"

Soon-ja burst into tears. "I'm going home. Saturday."

The words didn't make sense.

"Home to Korea."

Mae felt her chin drop. She held Ricky tighter. "For a visit." She made sure the question sounded like a statement.

Soon-ja's shrug said a thousand words. . . .

Mae moved into her work space, putting the display cases between them. "But I talked to Ringo for you. You went out together the other night. I thought things were getting better."

"He wants to go back on the road. He's been talking to Gordie about another gig."

Fear turned to anger. "He can't do that! He has a wife and son to think about. He has a job."

"He doesn't like his job. He's miserable."

Mae left her safe space behind and moved close to Soon-ja. "Tough toenails! A lot of people don't like their jobs. But sometimes you gotta do what you gotta do to handle the moment you're in. It's called life. He's got you; he's got Ricky; gracious gadfly, he's even got Collie and me. That's more than a lot of people have. He doesn't like his job? So what? That boy has got to learn to grow up; life isn't all fun and games. Responsibilities are a part of it, like it or not."

Suddenly, Soon-ja covered her face with her hands. Mae went to her, pulling her under her spare wing. "Oh, honey. I didn't mean to make it sound like having the responsibility of you and Ricky is a bad thing. Ringo loves you very much."

Soon-ja pulled a tissue out of the pocket of her shorts and blew her nose. Ricky reached for her and Mae was forced to let him go. "I don't know what I'm going to do, Mae. Not long term anyway. But it's true that my grandparents and the rest of my family haven't seen Ricky yet."

Mae reminded herself that Soon-ja's parents had died when she was young. She'd been raised by her grandparents. "So it's just a visit?"

There was that shrug again. Mae quelled the impulse to grab Ricky back. Instead she traced a finger down his arm and let him take hold of it. "He's changing so fast right now. I don't want to miss it."

"I know."

Mae felt a wave of desperation wash over her, forcing her to grab a fresh breath. "I'll talk to Ringo again. Or maybe we can help him find a job he likes better and—"

Soon-ja shook her head no. "My aunt and uncle already bought the ticket. I'm leaving Saturday."

"What does Ringo think of all this?"

She took a step toward the door. "I have packing to do."

Mae stopped her at the door. "Soonie?"

"He's mad. He thinks it's for good."

"And he's still letting you go?"

Soon-ja's eyes were dark and deep. "He can't stop me, Mae. I have to do this." She left the store.

And the world came a-tumbling down.

Mae managed to get to the chair by her workbench just in time. She shook her head no, wishing she could make the situation disappear. She looked heavenward and yelled, "What's with my kids anyway?"

Collie appeared in the doorway leading to the back room carrying a tray of Earl Grey tea and blueberry muffins. "Uh-oh. What happened?"

She filled him in. "First Starr has trouble with her relationship with Ted, now Ringo and Soonie."

He broke one muffin in half, slathered both halves with margarine, and handed one to her. "The job of parenting doesn't end when they turn eighteen."

"But shouldn't I be able to go part time? Look forward to retirement when I don't have to do the job anymore?"

"Is that what you really want?"

She set her muffin on a napkin without taking a bite. "What I want is to have some time to enjoy my new husband. In peace. During our golden years."

"Golden? I'm not *that* old."

She smiled. "But you do make me glow."

He winked. "I'm not sure there's anything we can do about all this, wifey."

She smushed a crumb with a finger and licked it. "Which drives me crazy."

"Maybe distance will make the heart grow fonder?"

Her thoughts had moved on to other points. "Maybe we can help Ringo find a job he likes better than construction. Maybe—"

"What do you think he'd be good at?"

She sighed. "Besides being a whiz at acting immature?"

"Don't be cynical."

She'd try. But when she thought about her son's attributes, his interests, his marketable skills, she went blank. Not a good sign.

She ate her muffin.

●　　●　　●

The day stretched long before her. Every time the door to Audra's workroom opened, she looked up from her sewing only to be disappointed when it was Summer asking for more lemonade, wanting lunch, asking if she could go swimming.

The last was a great idea. With her daughter gone to the pool with Cynthia and her mother, Audra had time to concentrate on the problem at hand.

No Simon.

Up until today, she'd never really paid that much attention to how often he made deliveries, or what time he usually showed up during the day. But today that was the only thing on her mind. And when he didn't show up at all . . .

Why did she feel so disappointed? She was acting stupid. Childish. Was she so desperate for some chatty conversation with a handsome man that the lack of it could ruin her day?

Summer came home from swimming and ran off to get

dressed. Audra found herself standing at the workroom door, looking outside. Waiting.

Suddenly, Russell's car drove up. Why was he home?

Then it hit her. *Dinner. Husband. Reality.*

She hurried to the kitchen to throw something together.

●   ●   ●

Mae had to get out of the house. Dinner had been sans Ringo—who was who knows where—and Soon-ja was consumed with packing for her trip to Korea. And if she heard Collier tell her to calm down one more time . . .

She didn't want to calm down. So she stormed across the street to Peerbaugh Place. "Yoo-hoo. It's me!"

"Back here," Evelyn called from the kitchen. She was getting a big pot from under the counter. "Evening, Mae. What's up?"

Mae took a peppermint from the candy jar and unwrapped it. "Plenty. Where's Accosta and Ursola?"

"Up in their rooms. I was about to make watermelon pickles. Want to help? Or do you want to go sit on the porch to talk?"

"Might as well work while I whine. It keeps the momentum going."

"Care to cut up some rind while you whine?"

"Absolutely. I'm in a slicing-dicing mood."

Evelyn sliced off the hard green rind, separating it from the soft white part they would use to make the cinnamon pickles. Mae cut the rind into bite-sized pieces. Once they were settled into their work, Evelyn said, "Now, give me the scoop."

Mae stopped slicing. "Soonie is going home to Korea Saturday to visit her family and is taking Ricky with her."

"That sounds nice. I'm sure her family is excited to see him."

"Yes, yes, but that's not the point."

"Which is . . . ?"

"Soonie and my dearly beloved—but clearly stubborn—son are having trouble." She told Evelyn about the late hours, and Ringo's wanting to go back on the roadie rock circuit. "He's miserable working construction."

Evelyn moved all the rind to a big kettle, covered it with hot water, and put it on the stove to boil. "It is important for a person to like their work—at least a little. Otherwise their anger overflows into the other areas of their life. I know. Aaron was always flitting from one job to another. He was never satisfied." She sighed. "But I'm not sure he was capable of that feeling. Being dissatisfied almost became a goal for him. Sometimes I think he liked being in a state of 'miserable.'"

"And making you miserable."

She shrugged. "I'll try to be content in whatever state I'm in, but if I have my choice, I want it to be the state of Hawaii."

Mae laughed. "Did Evie make a joke?"

"I have a few."

"Good for you."

They worked in silence a few minutes. Then Evelyn asked, "So what are you going to do about all this?"

"Stew. And pray. Otherwise, there isn't much I can do. Soonie's going. I can have another talk with Ringo, but I doubt he's up to my grow-up-silly-boy content."

"Makes me glad Russell's grown and truly on his own. My work's done."

Mae pointed a dish towel at her. "Don't count on it." She looked toward the front of the house as they heard the door open.

"Piper," Evelyn said, answering Mae's unspoken question. "She and Gregory went out to dinner to discuss wedding plans."

"How's that—?"

Piper burst through the swinging door of the kitchen, making it bang against the wall. Her jaw was set, her face flushed. She was consumed in her own world as she went to the refrigerator, opened the freezer door, and pulled out a pint of mint-chocolate-chip ice cream.

Bang went the door.

"Hello, Piper," Evelyn said.

"Hi." Piper got out a spoon, then paused. "Care to join me?"

"I'm in," Mae said.

"Sure," Evelyn said. She and Mae exchanged a look.

Piper got out two more spoons and slammed the drawer shut, sending the silverware inside clattering. She handed off the spoons, yanked out a chair, plopped the carton on the table, and sat. The lid came off, her spoon dipped, and the first bite was taken with a force usually reserved for digging in a garden.

Mae and Evelyn sat. Piper passed the carton. Once they were all fortified with the proper combination of sugar and fat, Mae jumped in. "Did you and Gregory have a fight?"

"No."

"A disagreement about the wedding?" Evelyn asked.

"No. He's wonderful. He's letting me have the wedding of my dreams."

Evelyn's mind obviously traveled elsewhere. "Is something wrong with your father?"

Piper was into her third bite, but at Evelyn's words, seemed to snap out of it. "No, he's fine." Piper really looked at them for the first time. "I'm sorry. You're all worried."

"Because you're upset," Evelyn said.

Piper snickered, passed the carton, then set her spoon down. "But not for any reason you could ever imagine."

Mae crossed her arms. "This I gotta hear."

Evelyn gave her encouragement with a nod.

Piper looked from one to the other, then at the table. "I'm . . . oh dear, this is going to sound . . . goodness, I don't even know how this is going to sound."

Mae had had enough. "Piper! Just say it."

Piper took a fresh breath. "I'm upset because I'm sexually frustrated."

Mae glanced at Evelyn, who looked as surprised as Mae felt.

"I knew it would come out sounding strange. Now you think I'm weird, or wild, or—"

"Human," Mae said. She reached over and patted Piper's hand. "You two are waiting, aren't you?"

Piper nodded. "I know God wants couples to wait to have sex until after marriage because it's best for all involved, and good, and right, and all that, so I was determined and told Gregory up front where I stood." Her sigh came from deep inside. "But I must admit when I'm in his arms the whole best-good-right thing fogs a bit. A lot, actually."

"What did Gregory think about all this?" Mae asked.

"He was reluctant, but then he agreed that waiting *would* make the honeymoon even more special."

"So what's the problem?" Evelyn asked.

"The problem is that now he's being all strong and I'm going crazy every time we have to leave each other. I just want to go home with him and be with him all the time—I mean *all* the time."

Mae had tried to keep a serious face, but she'd reached her limit. She laughed and Evelyn joined her.

"It's not funny!" Piper said.

"No, no," Mae said. "We're not laughing because it's funny but because Perfect Piper has suddenly shown she's like the rest of us."

"You've felt this way?"

"One big advantage to marriage is having your lovey-dovey available for lovey-dovey." Mae feigned an exaggerated shiver. "I still get all tingly when Collie walks in the room."

"But you're still a newlywed, Mae. And you're lucky," Evelyn said. She looked at both of them, then added. "Things aren't always wonderful like that."

Silence.

"Don't ask."

Poor Evelyn. The more Mae heard about Aaron and their marriage the more Mae was glad she'd never met the man. She decided to change the subject. "How many weeks until the wedded bliss begins?"

"Twenty-five days. I wish it were tomorrow."

"You'll survive," Mae said. "With lots and lots of cold showers."

"And ice cream," Piper said. "Gimme that ice cream."

•　　•　　•

Evelyn turned out the light and pulled the sheet over her shoulder. She missed winter nights when she could snuggle under a double deck of blankets. There was no coziness in a single sheet.

There's no coziness in an empty bed.

She was happy to see Piper so excited about being married—and all that that entailed. The two of them would be happy. Evelyn knew it. Every time she saw them, she was stunned by the love that flowed out of every look, every touch, every word.

I wish I'd had that.

She rolled onto her side and looked at the space that Aaron used to occupy. Their love life had been . . . tolerable. Aaron had never been a demonstrative man. There were no good-morning kisses or hugs upon parting. There was sex. But it had been done out of duty or pure physical need—on both their parts. There was no love in the act. No bonding two into one.

She turned on her back and let her thoughts stray to the only other man she'd ever slept with: Frank Albert Halvorson. The father of the baby girl she'd given up for adoption. They'd had passion. Fast and furious, and full of intensity.

But love? The image of Piper's and Gregory's evident, public love for each other, and even Mae's and Collier's, suddenly collided with her memory of the boy Frank and the girl Evelyn, going through the physical motions of love without ever really feeling the connective tissue that wrapped around the daily love that could last a lifetime.

If Frank hadn't died in Vietnam, if they'd married and raised their daughter, would they still be married? Would it have been a love to last a lifetime?

She turned toward the window. There was no way to know, but on this night, for the first time, she felt a wave of doubt. Did that mean she had never truly loved before?

Evelyn sat upright, consumed with the horrible thought. How could she be fifty-nine years old and have yet to experience true love?

She reached for the lamp on the bed stand, needing light to dispel this awful thought. With the addition of light her eyes fell upon a photo of Wayne. She took the picture into her lap and stroked his face. She felt a flutter in her stomach and realized she was smiling. Suddenly her heart felt larger, fuller. And a shiver coursed up and down her arms.

Oh my. Evelyn allowed herself a giggle, set the photo in its place, and went to sleep, hoping to dream of possibilities. There was still time. . . .

* * *

Ursola sat on the window seat, her legs drawn to her chest. The backyard of Peerbaugh Place was mottled with shadow and moonlight. Lovely by night. Lovelier still by daylight.

She wiped a tear and looked over her room. It was a nice space—charming, clean, and hers. Her gratitude toward Evelyn was great. For nearly a week she'd lived in limbo, in a no-man's-land of hiding and getting by. Peerbaugh Place was better than all of that. But it still wasn't home.

You have no home now. You have no husband. You have nothing.

She bowed her head against her knees and let the tears come.

8

My child, don't lose sight
of good planning and insight.
Hang on to them,
for they fill you with life
and bring you honor and respect.

PROVERBS 3:21-22

*T*he woman inspected a bud vase. "Will you take a dollar for this?"

"You bet," Evelyn said. Evelyn was getting into the swing of Accosta's garage sale. Preparation was everything. She and Wayne had spent hours during the past week, sorting, cleaning, and pricing Accosta's worldly goods—or at least the household items. An auction for the furniture was planned in a month. For now they'd placed an ad in the paper and had signs at the end of the block pointing the way. Though the prices were good to begin with, Evelyn enjoyed haggling and making a deal. One person's trash was definitely another person's treasure.

There was a lull in customers so she watched Wayne help a woman load three boxes of goodies into her trunk. He wasn't really helping with the garage sale, but was available to pull from his remodeling work if she needed him.

She found herself smiling. Goodness. She *was* smitten, wasn't she? There was no reason that the sight of a dirty, sweaty man, dressed in his oldest yucky clothes, his hair mussed, his spare tire evident, should make her all warm and fuzzy inside. But it did.

She'd meant to tell him so, in a dozen ways, at a dozen times as they'd worked on this project of theirs. But something had always slid into the moment, making her chicken out, or distracted her enough to forget what she'd intended to say. The delay was frustrating, but had also given Evelyn time to look for signs that Wayne felt the same toward her. Russell had told her that men were often the last to know they were in love, and she *had* caught Wayne looking at her at odd moments, as if he was studying her, trying to figure out . . .

Whether he loved her? Pooh. Maybe he was just studying a speck of spackle on her nose, or was silently repulsed by the crows-feet that no amount of wrinkle cream could erase.

Evelyn realized she was still holding the dollar for the vase. She put it in the cash box and closed the lid—on it and on her romantic notions.

•　　•　　•

A blonde woman carrying a padded notebook and wearing a gorgeous, dusty blue business suit came up the driveway. She did not look like she'd be interested in purchasing Accosta's old Tupperware or Avon bottles—even if the latter were worth something. Yet she walked toward Evelyn with purpose.

"May I help you?" Evelyn asked.

"I'm Karin Gustafson with Creekside Realty. Is Wayne Wellington here?"

Evelyn rose from her lawn chair, feeling decidedly under-dressed in her jeans and pink polo shirt. "He's inside. Come with me." Evelyn turned to Accosta who was talking to a customer about an ancient toaster. "Accosta? Can you handle things for a little while?"

"Sure. I'll have the whole kit and caboodle sold before you get back."

Evelyn wouldn't put it past her. Accosta was a good saleswoman. Evelyn moved to the side door leading from the driveway into the kitchen. She opened it for the woman, allowing her to go first.

"Wayne?" Evelyn called.

"Up here."

"Watch your step," Evelyn said, leading the way to the front stairs. "You'll have to excuse the mess. Wayne's been working very hard getting the house in salable condition."

"I understand," Karin said. Evelyn couldn't help but notice how she barely allowed her fingertips to touch the dusty handrail, or the way she walked on tiptoe through the debris left by the plumber and electrician.

They found Wayne working under the sink in the bathroom and stood outside the door. "Wayne?"

"If you can hold on just a minute, I'll be—"

"No problem, Mr. Wellington."

At the strange voice, Wayne hit his head on the cabinet. "Oh, I'm sorry. I didn't know we had company." He got to his feet and wiped his hands on a rag. He shook Karin's hand. "Nice to see you again, Ms. Gustafson."

"You too. I see you're working hard. You must be quite a handyman."

"We have a plumber and electrician doing the main work. I'm just helping where I can." He motioned toward the door. "Let's step out in the hall where there's more room."

Karin opened her notebook and handed some stapled pages to Wayne. Evelyn saw photos of houses on them. "I have some comps from the surrounding neighborhood, some already sold and some still on the market. They should give you a good idea of the property's value."

Evelyn wanted to ask what a "comp" was, but didn't.

Wayne seemed to know. He flipped through the pages. "So you think the house is worth only this much?"

"I know you're disappointed, but the market is slow in Carson Creek and with it being a neighborhood where most of the houses have already been subdivided into apartments . . ." She shrugged, taking no responsibility.

Wayne showed Evelyn the prices of the other houses. "That's all?" Evelyn asked. "Even after we do the improvements?"

"Without the improvements you wouldn't even get this price. In fact, without the improvements, it's unsalable," Karin said.

Evelyn sought out Wayne's eyes, but he was busy with the papers.

"Of course, you could get another Realtor's opinion. . . ."

Wayne folded the papers in half. "No. I'm sure you're right. This looks very thorough. Thanks for telling us."

"Sorry it wasn't better news." She opened her notebook again. "Would you like to fill out a listing agreement today? Even if the work isn't complete, I could start getting it into the system and—"

"No," Wayne said. "Not today. Let us think about it."

Karin's carefully groomed eyebrows rose. "Oh, well. I'll get back to you then."

Yes, you do that. Evelyn let Wayne show her the door. As he shut it behind Karin, Evelyn stood at the bottom of the stairs. "What are we going to do? By the time we pay off what it's costing us to fix this place up, and Accosta pays off the mortgage she got to help her son with *his* expenses, she's not going to have much of a nest egg to live on for the rest of her life."

Wayne leaned against the front door, his head shaking. "But if we don't fix it . . ." He pressed his hands over his eyes. "I'm so weary. I'm feeling muscles I haven't felt in twenty years."

Evelyn took his hand and pulled him to the steps. "Sit. Relax. You've been working way too hard."

"Out of necessity. If we don't put in sweat equity . . . we're paying plenty for the pros already. I have to keep working."

"I'll do more," Evelyn said. She edged by to sit on another step above him.

"You've been doing plenty," he said. "You have Peerbaugh Place to run. Those ladies depend on you."

"They can fend for themselves. I baby them. They'll step to the plate if I ask them to."

His head hung low and he rested his arms on his thighs. She leaned forward and rubbed the back of his neck, wanting to help more. Aching to help.

"I truly believe we're doing the right thing. It doesn't seem to make much sense now, but I still have a feeling about it."

"So do I," Evelyn said. And she meant it. "It'll work out. Somehow."

Through a window Evelyn saw a mother and three kids run up the driveway toward the sale tables. "I'd better get back to work."

He stood. "Me too." He went up the stairs, his hand lingering just a moment on the top of her head as he walked by.

•   •   •

Even Mae couldn't think of a way to ease the tension as they drove to the airport. Her usual banter seemed inappropriate, and turning on the radio where they'd be subjected to some DJ's banter would have been unbearable. So, silence reigned—except for the cooing and gurgling of Ricky in his car seat. The four adults sat in their respective places, facing forward, watching the miles whiz by.

Even Collier stared straight ahead, as if driving the ninety minutes to the airport demanded his full attention.

Exasperated, Mae closed her eyes and talked to the only One who'd listen. The only One who could help them get through this.

The sight of Ringo holding his son so tightly, the sight of Soon-ja's tears as she handed her ticket to the flight attendant . . .

"Here." Collier handed Mae a much-needed tissue.

She dabbed at her eyes.

But then she heard Ringo's voice. "Soonie! Don't go!"

Soon-ja stopped at the opening to the tunnel that led to the plane. Ringo tried to get to her, but a male attendant stopped him. "You can't go past this point, sir."

Ringo stepped to the side of the line, just a few feet away from his wife, yet unable to touch her. Reach her. She was crying now, her shoulders slumped with real, as well as emotional, weight. Her right arm looked strained from holding Ricky in his seat, her left steadied two carry-ons that were slung over her shoulder.

A female flight attendant touched her arm. "You need to step aside, miss. Or go onto the plane."

Ringo's voice was pleading now. Mae had never heard him sound so pitiful. "Please, Soonie. Stay. We'll work it out."

Soon-ja glanced nervously at their audience. Eyes respectfully looked away. She kept her voice low. "I have to go. My family—"

Suddenly, Ringo's back stiffened and he shook a finger at her. "Fine! Go. But don't expect me to be here if you come back."

He stormed past Mae and Collier. Mae didn't know what to do. Poor Soonie, still standing there with her burden doubled by the thoughtless words of her husband.

"I'll go after him," Collie whispered. "Go talk to her."

Mae approached Soonie. The girl had put Ricky and her luggage on the floor and was digging a tissue out of a pocket. "I'm so sorry, honey. He didn't mean that." Travelers walked between them.

Ricky started to whimper and Soon-ja set her own tears aside to kneel beside him, rocking his seat. "I don't know what to do, Mae." Her eyes were so plaintive. "Tell me what to do."

What Mae wanted to say and what she should say collided. "You go visit your family and let them see Ricky. But then you come back to us. Back to Ringo. You come back and work it out."

"But he said he won't be here."

"He'll be here. I'll make sure of it." She managed a smile. "Now go. Have a safe flight and a wonderful visit with your family."

Soon-ja took a ragged breath. "Thanks, Mae. I love you. I love all of you." Then she picked up her son and disappeared into the tunnel.

Mae fought the awful feeling that it might be the last time she'd see either of them.

●　　●　　●

Mae stood in the hall outside Ringo's bedroom door. "But, Ringo, we need to talk about this."

"Leave me alone!"

"Maybe you should do what he says," Collier said, from the hall near the stairs.

"He's acting like a child."

"But he's an adult. In the end he's going to have to sink or swim on his own."

Empty and spent, Mae stumbled toward her husband. He met her with open arms. "But I don't want him to sink," she whispered against his shoulder.

"I know."

●　　●　　●

Ursola still had a hard time getting used to American grocery stores. If she had to describe this entire country with one word she would say *choice*. Sometimes it was daunting. From the moment people got up they were given choices ranging from what to eat and wear, to how to spend their day. Besides a few basic laws, people could pretty much do whatever they wanted to do. They were free. Another good word.

Today she was free to help Evelyn by doing the grocery shopping. Evelyn had given her a list and money. Ursola felt bad about not being able to contribute more than a few dollars, but she had a surprise in store for them. Tonight she would make a Russian feast. It was the least she could do.

She was going up the pasta aisle when she saw Daryn coming toward her. She faced the food shelves, angling her back toward him, hoping he'd—

"Well, well, my dear stepmother."

She faced him. "Hello, Daryn."

"I'm surprised you're still in town."

"Where you want me to be?"

"Wow, is *that* a loaded question." He glanced down the aisle, then back again. "You have no ties here anymore. Dad's dead. Shouldn't you be going home?"

She was tempted to shove the cart into his fat belly. "I have right be here."

He smiled, but it wasn't pretty. "Who says?"

Her stomach grabbed. "I have visa. I okay."

He nodded at a woman walking by. "I wouldn't be too sure about that. You don't belong in this country. You're an outsider."

Ursola felt angry tears threaten. "I okay here. I have visa. I stay."

"Whatever you want to believe. What I don't get is why you'd want to stay in a place that doesn't want you. Call me crazy, but that's stupid."

She had a lot of things she could call *him*, and *crazy* wasn't one of them.

He started to move on. "Hope I don't see you again, Ursola. Have a nice day."

She wanted to scream at him. A stream of Russian epithets sat ready on her tongue. But she dare not cause a scene. She was suddenly filled with doubt. Though Daryn hadn't come out and said it, now that Glenn was gone could she be deported?

She faced the shelves, fighting tears. She'd look into it. But how? How could she look into it without drawing attention to herself? How could she—?

"Ursola? Are you all right?"

She turned toward the voice of her friend Tessa but could only manage to shake her head.

Tessa left her cart and was by her side immediately. "There, there. Let's get you out of here and make things right."

"No. I can't." She pointed at the cart of food.

Tessa looked down the aisle and called to a boy stocking milk. "Tim? Can you come over here a minute?" The boy came over, looking wary. "My friend and I have to step outside for a few minutes. Can you be a good kid and look after these carts for us? Maybe put that milk back on the shelf for me? We'll be right back."

"Well . . . sure, Mrs. Klein. I suppose so."

"Many thanks. I'll tell Sam you went the extra mile for a customer today." She slipped her hand through Ursola's arm. "Now, let's go fix what needs fixing."

●　　●　　●

Tessa didn't really know Daryn Smith, but after talking to Ursola, she didn't want to know him. How could a man be so completely rude, so horribly unfeeling of a widow? So he didn't want her as a stepmother—that didn't excuse his actions. Would it have been too much for him to exhibit simple manners?

They sat on a bench across the street from the grocery store. Ursola's shoulders were bent, her eyes on the shredded Kleenex in her lap. The poor girl was spent and scared. Tessa wished she knew something about the rules of immigration.

She rubbed a hand across Ursola's back. "I want you to stop worrying. I will do some research and find out where you stand and what we have to do next. Don't let that bully make you afraid. Did you know the Bible says not to be afraid 365 times? One for every day of the year. God didn't keep telling us that because He thought we *wouldn't* be afraid. He expected it and took care of it. He'll take care of this too."

Ursola's eyes contained a glimmer of hope.

Tessa took her hand. "It's His promise. Want to pray about it?"

Ursola shrugged, but Tessa forged ahead anyway. She kept hold of her hand, bowed her head, and prayed aloud: "Father, you have a child here who's hurting and feeling alone in a foreign land. She wants to stay here and we want her to stay. Help us make that happen." She noticed Ursola nod and added a final line. "And Jesus? Please keep that bully Daryn away from her. We both have our own idea of how we'd *like* to have him handled, but You being merciful and all that . . . we leave it to You. In Jesus' name, amen."

She offered Ursola a smile. "Feel better?"

"A little."

"Good. Now let's get our groceries bought."

*　　*　　*

Audra heard Russell shuffle through papers on the kitchen desk. "Audra? Where are the papers about adoption?"

She didn't look up from cutting the fabric on the dining-room table. She wished she could pretend she hadn't heard him. He wouldn't like her answer.

He came into the doorway. "Did you hear me?"

Her throat was tight. "I heard."

"Then answer me."

"I put them in the bottom drawer." She didn't dare tell him she came close to throwing them out.

He took two steps toward her, lowering his voice. Summer sat at the coffee table in the next room coloring and watching TV. "You're being stubborn. We have a problem. This is a solution. A good one."

She set the scissors down with a clatter. "How can you give up having a baby so easily?"

He shook his head in disbelief. "I want to have a baby with all my being. But I'm giving up fathering a child, not being a father *to* a child." He glanced at Summer, then back. "Besides, we don't have much choice in the matter. I can't. I can't . . . make it happen. I've taken full blame, but if you want me to say it a hundred more times, I will. I'm sorry. I'm to blame for all this. It's my fault."

She shook her head. This isn't what she wanted. She didn't blame him. She wasn't mad at him; she was mad at the situation. And it *was* different for a woman. Not being able to carry a child . . . it was decidedly more personal because pregnancy encompassed a woman's entire being. To accept that it was never going to happen again . . . she took a breath and looked at him. "I feel like I'm in mourning for the child we'll never have, Russell. And mourning takes time."

He came close and ran a hand up her arm, ending at her cheek. "I mourn too. But the adoption process takes a long time too. You're a practical woman. It only makes sense to get the paperwork going and do our mourning afterward."

The logic was sound, and Audra, a purveyor of all things logical, longed to grab hold of Russell's words and find comfort in them. But the emotional part of her couldn't do it. "I can't, Russell. I can't let it go. Not yet." She hurried toward the bedroom.

After she closed the door, after she flung herself onto the bed, she realized there was another spoon stirring her up, whipping her into this mental froth of confusion.

And his name was Simon.

• • •

Evelyn and Wayne set the last folding table against the garage. "There," Wayne said. "That should do it."

Evelyn arched her back. "My body says a big ditto to that statement."

"You tired?"

"Very." She wiped a smudge of construction dust off his cheek. "But I shouldn't be the one complaining. All I've had to do is sit and take the money. You're the one who's been doing the physical labor all day."

He flexed his biceps. "Before you know it I'll be another Ah-nold."

Evelyn saw Accosta waving from the porch. "Hey, you two. Come have tea and let's count the money."

"Be right there." Wayne pulled the pivoting garage door closed and whispered to Evelyn, "How well did you do money-wise?"

"I never counted, but we had a steady flow all day."

They walked toward the porch. "I feel like slipping a fifty into the pot to make her feel better," he said. "After all, this was the sale of her life's possessions."

Evelyn purposely bumped into him and whispered back, "But not her life's treasures, right?"

He flicked the end of her nose and they joined Accosta on the porch. She had three glasses of iced tea waiting—along with the cash box.

"Sit," she said. "You count it, Evelyn."

With a bit of trepidation, Evelyn did the honors, but as she formed the first stack equaling one hundred dollars—with a large wad of bills still left in her hand—she gained confidence. When she topped off the third hundred-dollar pile, Accosta clapped, and Wayne was definitely smiling.

"Three hundred sixty-one, sixty-two, sixty-three and forty-five cents," Evelyn said. "Wow!"

Wayne patted a pile, shaking his head. "A dollar here, a quarter there . . . it all adds up."

"Just wait until the auction. All that furniture . . . some of it is antique."

"It wasn't antique when I got it," Accosta said, laughing.

Evelyn started putting the money back in the cash box. "I'll take you to the bank tomorrow so you can put this into your—"

Accosta placed a hand on her arm. "No."

"No?"

Accosta finished putting the money away, closed the lid, then set it between them. "This is for the two of you."

"Absolutely not," Wayne said. "It's your money."

"Which I want you to use toward fixing up my house. I know this is a money pit, and it's only right that house money goes back into the house."

Evelyn shoved the box toward Accosta. "But you need—"

Accosta shoved it back. "I need you to take it. I'm living under your good graces at Peerbaugh Place, not paying a penny. What expenses do I have? I get a little Social Security every month. That's enough for me."

Evelyn looked at Wayne. He shrugged, then put a hand on the box. "If that's what you want."

"It is."

Every little bit helped.

. . . .

Audra was shocked when Russell agreed to go to the Scoreboard Bar & Grill for dinner. Shocked that he'd said yes, but also shocked at herself for even asking. It's not like either of them had ever been there before—a point Russell had mentioned. "I've heard it's a fun place," Audra said. Which was a lie. There was only one reason she wanted to go to that particular place tonight. Simon might be there.

Russell, being the good husband he was, being the kind of husband who didn't hold a grudge over arguments, the kind who took every advantage to spend time with his wife, had said yes, never knowing the horrid motives of his wife's heart.

The guilt and doubts began as they got dressed and continued as they dropped Summer off to spend the evening helping Piper and Gregory make little packets of birdseed to give guests to throw after the wedding.

The feelings intensified as she and Russell entered the parking lot of the Scoreboard. Suddenly, Audra couldn't move.

Russell got out and noticed she hadn't budged. He leaned down to speak to her through his opened door. "You coming?"

Tell him no. Don't do this, Audra. Go home. Now.

She was just about to shake her head, just about to say something, when he closed his door and came around, opening hers. "Come on," he said. "You were the one who wanted to come here."

"I know, but—"

He rolled his eyes. "But what?"

But we shouldn't go in.

He held out his hand, palm up. "Come on. It'll be fun."

She got out of the car, hoping he was right and her instincts were wrong.

•   •   •

He was there. Just like she'd wanted him to be.

Yet at the sight of Simon nursing a beer at the bar, Audra's stomach churned—and not in anticipation. Even as the hostess was leading them to their table, inner warning bells clanged violently. *Get out! Get out now!*

Then when Russell took the seat with his back to Simon, and she was seated so she couldn't help but watch him. . . . *"Don't let us yield to temptation, but deliver us from the evil one."*

Russell opened his menu. "I wonder what's good here."

The menu. It was a safe place to look.

But even as she perused the Touchdown Bacon Cheeseburger and the Hail Mary Hot Wings she found her gaze shifting upward, to see him, watch him.

Stop it!

She glanced at Russell. He was looking at her. "You seem nervous."

She laughed too loud. "Don't be silly. It's just a new place, that's all." She looked around for show. "It's kind of loud with all these televisions going."

Russell shrugged. "It's a sports bar and grill. It goes with the territory. Not like our Chez Garsaud, is it?"

Chez Garsaud was their restaurant, the scene of their first date and many commemorative dates since. White linens and violins. It was Russell's type of place, where the Scoreboard was certainly a better fit for—

Simon turned around. Their eyes met. She looked down— too quickly.

Russell looked over his shoulder to see what she had seen. When he turned back to her his face was stern. "Who's that?"

Audra was going to say, "Who's who?" but stopped herself. "Oh, that's just the UPS guy who delivers my supplies. Sam or Sid. Something like that." Audra was suddenly intent on the salad selections. *Go home. Now. Enough of this*. Being a coward on the retreat was far better than being a weak woman skirting the edge of temptation.

The waiter came and they ordered. So much for escape.

9

Truth stands the test of time;
lies are soon exposed.

PROVERBS 12:19

*M*ae knocked on the bedroom door. "Ringo? You're going to be late for work."

She took a step away, then realized he hadn't answered. She knocked again. "Ringo?"

Collier came out of their bedroom, buttoning his shirt. "What's going on?"

"He's not answering."

"Open the door."

Duh. Yet as Mae put her hand on the knob, she didn't want to open the door.

Collier nudged her away and did it for her. The room was empty. The bed hadn't been slept in.

"He's gone!"

Collier opened the closet. "His clothes are gone too."

Mae stomped a foot on the floor. "He can't do this!"

"When we took Soonie to the airport Saturday he told her he wouldn't be here when she got back."

"But I promised her he would be here."

"It's not your fault, wifey. This is something they have to work out."

"Yeah, but—"

"He'll be fine."

"But my baby . . ."

". . . has been on his own for years and can be on his own now." He led her toward the door. "Let's go downstairs. I'll make waffles, and we'll cover that boy with prayer. How's that sound?"

"Soonie too. And Ricky."

"You got it."

●   ●   ●

Piper came downstairs to find the dining-room table covered with glasses, crockery, and china. At first she didn't see Evelyn sitting on the floor in front of the buffet, dishes all around.

"What are you doing?" Piper asked.

"Mostly making a mess." Evelyn extended a hand. "Help me up. I think I've hemmed myself in."

Piper pulled her to her feet, then picked up a rose-patterned bowl. "You have pretty things."

"Too many pretty things. Putting together the garage sale for Accosta has given me the bug to simplify my life and rid it of all things extraneous."

"Uh-oh. Sounds dangerous."

"*Overdue* is the word. What are your plans for the day?"

Piper put the bowl down. "I was going to ask you to go with me somewhere, but since you're busy . . ."

Evelyn moved a few stacks from the floor to the table. "Don't be silly. This stuff has been around this long; one day isn't going to matter. What did you have in mind?"

"I wondered if you'd like to go shopping with me for my trousseau."

Evelyn put a vase on the buffet. "Are you kidding? A chance

to look at lacy, satiny, lovely pretties?" She high-stepped over a footed cake plate and headed to the stairs. Three steps up she paused. "I'm flattered, but wouldn't you rather have Audra go? She's your best friend and is more your age and—"

"I want you, Evelyn. If Mom were here I'd ask her, but since she isn't . . . I want you."

"Goodness sakes, girl. You sure know how to make a sister feel needed. Give me five minutes and I'm yours."

* * *

Evelyn held a red satin nightgown at arm's length. It had an oriental flavor and a matching robe. She rubbed the fabric against her cheek. Such luscious things. She couldn't remember the last time she'd worn anything so lovely. And it had little to do with her widowhood. Even before then, she'd chosen to wear a cotton nightie in the summer and a flannel one on colder nights. Sure, they had a sprinkling of lace on them, but they weren't anything like this.

"Why don't you try it on?"

Evelyn hadn't realized Piper was watching. She set the gown down. "I don't think so."

"Why not?"

"I don't have any reason to—"

"To feel good about yourself? To pamper yourself?" Piper moved close. "When was the last time you did something for Evelyn?"

Evelyn thought a moment. "I colored my hair a few weeks ago."

Piper raised her hands. "Well, stop all the buses!"

It did sound pitiful.

Piper pressed the gown and robe into Evelyn's hands. "Go. Try them on."

• • • •

Evelyn twisted back and forth, making the gown and robe dance around her legs. The set fit perfectly, sliding nicely past any bumps and bulges in her midsection and flowing gently to her ankles. She hadn't felt this pretty since . . . since . . .

Have I ever felt this pretty? When she was young she hadn't had the money for such luxurious things, and when she might have had the money, she hadn't had the inclination.

She had the inclination now.

• • •

Evelyn put her package in the trunk of Piper's car. "I feel absolutely decadent buying this."

"But excited too, right?" Piper asked.

Evelyn helped Piper lay her going-away suit flat on the packages. "I'm certainly pleased. It was fun getting something so special."

"And it will be fun wearing it."

I just wish I had someone to wear it for. *Like your father* . . .

Piper got in the driver's side. "Indulge in a proper bubble bath tonight, have a cup of tea, put on a Josh Groban CD, and relax. You deserve it. You and Dad have been working hard getting Accosta's house ready to sell."

With difficulty Evelyn transferred her Wayne thoughts from romance to finance. She put on the seat belt and was immediately struck by the way it pulled her down, tight and restrictive. The feeling that started at her torso quickly spread throughout her body. And mind. As Piper pulled into traffic she gave in to it.

Oh well. It had been nice feeling free and limitless for a little while.

• • •

Audra had come to recognize the sound of the UPS truck. She heard it now and left the bookwork to answer the workroom door. She opened it before Simon even had time to ring the bell.

"Morning, Aud," he said. "Got a bunch of rolls for you today." He brought in two long rolls of fabric covered in brown paper and headed back to the truck. He returned with three more.

Audra wondered if he would mention seeing her last night at the Scoreboard.

Clipboard signed, he did just that. "So you tried the Scoreboard. The food's good, isn't it?"

"Good and plentiful. I ended up bringing half home."

He nodded. "The man with you . . . that was your husband?"

Her stomach pulled. "Yes. That's Russell. He's a banker."

Simon's right eyebrow rose. "The smart successful type, huh."

Audra sped right in. "A man doesn't have to be the head of a bank to be successful. Or smart."

He smiled. "Good to know."

She felt herself redden. "I didn't mean . . . I—"

He headed for the door. "Actually, I'm pretty good with numbers myself. Did you know two times three is six?"

Relief engulfed her. "You don't say?"

He winked. "See you tomorrow. Happy sewing."

• • •

Should I get red geraniums or coral ones? Accosta walked in front of the racks of flowers. She couldn't do much to fix her house so it could sell, but adding a few pots of flowers couldn't hurt. She had just zeroed in on a coral one that looked especially healthy when she spotted Valerie Raines looking at hanging baskets. "Valerie!"

"Accosta. How are you?"

"Fine, just fine." She liked Valerie's thirties-era jumpsuit, and remembered she used to have one just like it. "How's the writing going?"

"Fine, just fine."

"And the new place?" Accosta braced herself for *Fine, just fine*.

"Fine."

She thought of a question that couldn't be answered with *fine*. "Getting flowers for it?"

"Uh-huh."

This was a woman who used words for a living? Accosta took the hint. "I'm sure everyone would love to see you again. Stop by sometime."

Valerie took a step away. "Maybe. I'd better be going. Nice seeing you."

"You too."

Hmm.

* * *

Valerie left without getting any flowers. When she got home she slammed the door, making a newly hung picture of the Eiffel Tower fall to the floor. When she went to put it back she saw the glass had cracked.

It was too much.

She pulled the picture to her chest and sank onto the new couch. She began to cry, then rock, as if the print of Paris was something dear to her and not merely a pretty picture she'd found at Hobby Lobby for half price.

She tossed it aside and wiped her tears roughly. "This is ridiculous. Why should running into Accosta upset me like this?"

It isn't Accosta and you know it.

Suddenly, she was across the room, pushing the Play button on her answering machine. The voice of her agent, Carla Mandez, filled the room: "Valerie? You really need to call me back. ASAP. Sorry to say, I have bad news. They're not pleased with your demands, in fact . . . just call me."

There were four other messages from Carla, showcasing vary-ing degrees of agitation and desperation. Each one made Valerie's stomach roll and clench. She hadn't meant to come off as demand-ing to the publisher as they dealt with the contract negotiations, but the way they'd praised her manuscript . . . didn't that mean they really, really wanted it?

In Carla's defense, as Valerie's agent she *had* warned her, had tried to talk her down off her pedestal. *You're a first-time novelist, Val. They want you. They want your work. But they do have limits.*

Apparently so. In the messages, Carla had all but said—

The phone rang, making her jump. Before she could tell herself not to, she answered it.

"Val!" It was Carla. "Finally. Where have you been?"

Hiding. "Around."

"Didn't you get my messages?"

"I got them."

"I'm really sorry. I tried my best; I really did. But the competi-tion is so fierce and most publishers don't have the patience to deal with . . . with . . ."

"Prima donnas?"

"Red Stop Publishing is a small house. They like their authors to feel like family."

"And I was being the annoying cousin?"

"Something like that."

Valerie moved into the doorway to the kitchen and leaned her forehead against the casing. "Can't we withdraw our demands? I'd do it for what they originally offered."

"It's a little late for that, girl. And I already tried. In their eyes you are too high maintenance. The editor made the comment that 'if she's hard to work with now, what's she going to be like when we start critiquing and editing her writing?'"

"I'd behave. I would."

Silence.

"Carla. Don't you believe me?"

"What can I say, Val? This is your first book with me too, and face it, you do have a tendency to be defensive and demanding."

Valerie shoved herself out of the doorway. "Then why did you take me on?"

"You're a good writer. I thought that would be enough."

"It should be."

"But it's not. Relationships, Val. That's what makes the world go round. If there's no chemistry, no respect, no common goal . . ." Carla sighed. "I think we need to call it quits too, Val."

"What?"

"We're not on the same page."

"But we have a common goal and—"

"One out of three isn't enough."

Valerie desperately tried to remember the other two traits . . . respect and . . .

"I'm not feeling it, girl. Not deep down."

Chemistry. Valerie paced from the couch to the kitchen and back. "This isn't fair. What am I supposed to do now?"

"Send your stuff out again. You'll find another agent. But . . ."

"But what?"

"But curb the attitude, okay? Thinking you're hot stuff when you are hot stuff is one thing, but playing the part when you're a wannabe is bad form."

"Thanks a lot."

"Hey, I'd be remiss if I didn't tell it like it is. I wish you all the best, Val. You're a good writer. Just keep plugging—"

Valerie hung up. Then hung up again. And again. How dare Carla abandon her like this! How dare Red Stop treat her work like litter on the floor, something offensive for them to wad up and discard!

How dare you act like an arrogant fool!

Valerie fell onto the couch and buried her face in a pillow.

*   *   *

Audra pulled into the driveway after dropping Summer off at the library's Reading Rodeo. She had two hours to herself. The summer was only a third over and she was already eager for school to start again. Not that she didn't like spending more time with her daughter, but after getting used to having her days to herself, the house to herself, she was feeling a bit put upon. Which probably made her a bad mother on some saintly motherhood scale that touted impossible perfection, a sunny disposition at all times, and a house smelling of fresh-baked cookies.

While she was at it, she might as well add the Bad Wife title to the mix. She and Russell had had another argument this morning. Over nothing. Arguing over nothing seemed to be the norm lately. That and making up in time for the next foray to begin. Hence the stop at the grocery store to get supplies for a special I'm-sorry dinner. If they didn't get their marriage under control soon, they were both going to gain weight.

Audra opened the screen door, then balanced the sack of groceries on her hip to put the key in the main door.

"Here. Let me help with that."

At the sound of Simon's voice, she dropped the keys. They nearly bonked heads as they both bent down to pick them up.

"Let me," he repeated, getting to them first. She saw his UPS truck out front, but wondered how it had gotten there. Had she been so preoccupied with her failings as a wife and mother that she hadn't even heard him drive up? Impossible. She lived for the sound of his truck.

She let him open the door. He stood aside. "There you go."

At this point she realized she hadn't said anything. She saw he had a small box in his hand, along with his ever-present clipboard. "Only one box today?"

"Just the one." Simon nodded toward the open door. "Take your groceries on in. I'll wait."

Audra remembered they were at the front door, not the door to Catherine's Wedding Creations. Simon was obviously aware of the distinction, even if she was not. She took the groceries inside, but as she put them on the counter she was suddenly overwhelmed with emotion. The argument with her husband, the handsome man just outside being nice to her, the line between business and home, the futility of it all.

The grocery sack tipped over and the carton of eggs slipped to the floor. "No!"

"Audra? Are you okay?"

She knelt beside the mess. Eleven eggs were either broken or cracked. Once good, now forever ruined. Only one left. One survivor. She picked it up, but saw that it too had a crack underneath. Hidden, but still there.

It was too much. Tears appeared.

"Audra?"

Simon. She swiped her cheeks with her hands and returned to the door. He stood poised by the entrance, ready to help, ready to cross the threshold of her home if she needed him. At the sight of her, he asked, "Are you all—?" His head jerked back. "Are you crying?"

So much for her acting abilities. She moved closer. He took a step back on the stoop, holding the screen door open with his shoulder. She stopped on the threshold, on the tenuous borderline between right and wrong. "I'm fine. I just broke the eggs."

He lowered his chin and gave her an I-don't-believe-you look.

She shrugged. "Plus, I'm having a bad day."

He slipped the clipboard under his arm, then reached out and touched her upper arm. "I'm sorry. Is there anything I can do to help?"

The possibilities raced through her mind, yet somehow she found the strength to say, "I'll be okay."

His hand lingered against her skin the briefest moment before lowering. "I hate to see you sad."

Audra managed a smile and took a cleansing breath. "Life's like that sometimes. I'll be fine." This had to be over—before she threw herself into his arms to be comforted, right there on the stoop, in front of the world. "My package?"

There. That's the way to do it. Back to business.

Too soon he was gone. And her day was worse for his absence.

*   *   *

Accosta wasn't comfortable driving Evelyn's car, but she did like the feeling of freedom she got being out and about on her own. Doing something. Helping to make her home salable. As she headed home with the flowers, a wave of wistfulness came over her. It wouldn't be her house much longer. Forty-two years of living set aside.

She acted brave in front of Wayne and Evelyn, pretending she didn't care about letting other people take her possessions away. But she did. A little. Every dish, every blouse, every book brought with it a memory.

But I'll still have those. No one can take the memories away from me.

She drove down the street where Audra and Russell lived, and her spirits lifted at the idea that she could stop and visit if she wanted to. Audra's car *was* in the driveway . . .

In fact, there was Audra at the door, talking to a UPS

deliveryman. Accosta slowed and got ready to pull to the curb, when she saw the man put his hand on Audra's arm—where it lingered. The exchange was short, the words few. But the expression . . . the bevy of emotions . . .

Rattled, Accosta kept driving. What she'd witnessed was not the quick, polite-but-distant exchange of deliveryman and homeowner. *Audra, what are you doing?*

At the corner, Accosta turned right, feeling the sudden need to go around the block, to go back so she could talk to Audra, warn her, stop her.

Of what? And how? She couldn't very well storm up to the front door and accuse her of treading where no married woman should tread.

Could she?

Accosta made a second right turn, getting closer. Maybe she was overreacting. Maybe she'd read more into the moment on the step than what really existed. There had to be a logical explanation. Audra and Russell hadn't been married very long. They were virtually newlyweds.

But remember Audra being all upset while you made cookies at Peerbaugh Place? Remember how you gave her your worry box because there was *something for her to worry about—to pray about?*

Accosta returned to Audra's street and made the final right-hand turn. Something had to be said. Accosta hadn't lived through the depth and breadth of life for nothing. It was her responsibility as an old woman to share her knowledge, her compassion, her lessons learned, so younger women didn't make the same—

Oh no! The UPS truck was still outside Audra's house. That, in itself, spoke volumes. Accosta had seen how fast those men worked. Most of them nearly ran between truck and door. They never sat still a moment. Had he gone inside? Certainly not. *Please no, Lord. Please no.*

She slowed and looked at Audra's house. The front door was closed. Oh dear. This was bad. But then, as she passed the brown truck, she saw that the driver was in his seat. Good. That was good.

Yet Accosta's relief was short-lived, for the man wasn't checking a clipboard for his next run; he was gripping the steering wheel, his head bowed against his hands in obvious anguish. She could see his lips moving—in a prayer? In a moment of self-admonishment for crossing a professional line?

Though she'd meant to stop at Audra's, she didn't. This was too serious to enter into without thought. She needed to get back to Peerbaugh Place. She had some hefty praying to do, her new worry box to fill, and some divine guidance to receive.

*   *   *

Accosta carefully wrote her concern on a slip of paper: *Audra and Russell's marriage*. She folded it in half and deposited it in her worry box. "There," she said. "It's Yours now, Father."

She felt better. She'd spent the last hour praying about the situation, and asking God for guidance about whether or not she should talk to Audra about what she'd seen with the UPS man. When Accosta had come across a passage in James, she knew that talking *was* her course of action: "My dear brothers and sisters, if anyone among you wanders away from the truth and is brought back again, you can be sure that the one who brings that person back will save that sinner from death and bring about the forgiveness of many sins."

She didn't know how far Audra's sin had gone, but Accosta hadn't lived eighty-three years without knowing a bit about temptation.

The only variable was timing—*when* should she talk to Audra? She'd keep her eyes and ears open. She only knew it had to be soon.

. . .

Audra curled up in the cushy chair, her feet on the ottoman. The sack of groceries sat on the counter; the broken eggs remained on the floor. Her eyes were closed, but she wasn't sleeping. Though she *was* dreaming. Daydreaming.

He puts his hand on my arm and I evaporate in tears. He gently leads me inside and closes the door. Then he takes me in his arms. "There, there, Audra. A beautiful woman like you shouldn't cry." Then I look up at him and he looks at me and wipes away a tear with his thumb. He kisses me, ever so gently and—

The phone yanked her away from the kiss and her mind spiraled into reality. As she got up to answer it, she glanced at the clock: 3:23.

"Summer!" She reached the phone. "Yes?"

"Mommy?"

"I'm coming, baby. I'm so sorry. I'll be there in two minutes."

She grabbed her keys and raced out the door. It was all Simon's fault. Simon and those stupid daydreams.

No more. No more!

. . .

Honk!

Tessa's eyes shot open. She swerved back into her lane.

I fell asleep!

Her heart beat in her throat. She sat straighter and leaned forward against the huge steering wheel of her Oldsmobile. A slew of could-have-beens flashed through her mind. *Thank You, sweet Jesus, for saving me!*

This time. Saving her this time. She couldn't test His driving mercies again.

Yet she knew there might be a second time. With her speaking schedule for the Sister Circle Network increasing, it was inevitable she would often be on the road, tired. So what was the solution? The network was a nonprofit organization in need of funding. If she didn't venture out to spread the word, the whole concept would die. And *that* had far-reaching ramifications. This was not a local ministry, but an international one. Rini Fudecio handled the hard stuff from Rome, reaching out to the rest of the world, finding key ladies in key places to spread the word and start up Sister Circles. Rini was also finding funding to help women financially whenever possible. Yet the main goal was to get women hooked up with other women, embracing their special God-given ability to bond. Rini was a godsend. But Tessa was responsible for getting things going in the United States.

As the adrenaline rush faded, Tessa felt the weariness return like a heavy blanket. Oh, to curl up in a blanket, close her eyes, and—

"No!" She shook her head vigorously and opened the car window. The humid July heat swarmed in like a suffocating cloud, immediately making her sweat. Yet being uncomfortable was a good thing. It was hard to sleep when one was too hot or too cold. It was the "just right" that was the killer.

She forced herself to think of her to-do list. But as the items vied for position, she felt weary again. This time mentally. Sometimes it seemed too much. What had she been thinking to attempt such a task at age seventy-seven? Though she had the support of all her dear sisters, and even her daughter, son-in-law, and grandson, sometimes she found herself wistfully thinking of spending lazy days visiting with Evelyn on the porch of Peerbaugh Place, or reading some book about Henry VIII or Catherine of Aragon.

"I'm tired, Lord!"

Her voice sounded testy, but she knew God wouldn't mind. He got testy too once in a while. But she decided to add a more plaintive plea to the moment: "Help!"

The verse that she had tacked above her desk came to mind, the words waving like a flag. *"Be strong, and do the work."*

Often easier said than done. "I'm feeling a bit frail at the moment, Lord. Not strong at all."

"Don't be dejected and sad, for the joy of the Lord is your strength!"

Tessa laughed. Many times in her life, verses she didn't even realize she knew popped into her head, always perfect, always appropriate. It was another reason to stand in awe of the Almighty. "Way to go, God. You got me again, brought me back from sorrow to joy with just a few words."

Then, following His direction to find joy in Him, she turned on the radio to find an uplifting song. She found one. After a few notes she recognized it and laughed again at the perfect provision of the Father as Twila Paris's voice filled the car with just the words she needed to hear:

> *"The joy of the Lord will be my strength*
> *I will not falter, I will not faint*
> *He is my Shepherd; I am not afraid*
> *The joy of the Lord is my strength!"*

She sang all the way home.

•   •   •

Mae shut off the light, climbed into bed, and snuggled into Collier's shoulder. She let the night settle in. "It's too quiet," she whispered.

"It's night. It's supposed to be quiet."

He was right, of course. But tonight was different. Tonight they were alone in the house and there was no risk—or hope— of hearing a baby's cry, or voices other than their own.

Collier kissed the top of her head. "We wanted the house to ourselves again."

"Not like this. Not all full of iffy."

"Iffy?"

"Iffiness. We don't know when or even if the kids will come back."

"We prayed. God's got 'em. There's nothing else we can do."

Bummer.

10

Never let loyalty and kindness
get away from you!
Wear them like a necklace;
write them deep within your heart.

PROVERBS 3:3

*M*ae sat on a kitchen chair and put her shoes on for work. Collier had a laundry basket on the table and was folding clothes—a job she hated. Yes indeedy, she'd sure found herself a gem in her Mr. Husband.

"You don't have to do that," she told him. "I'll do it when I get home. I'm closing up early because of Piper's bridal shower."

"I don't mind. Besides, you don't know how to properly fold my T-shirts."

"Since when?"

"Since ever." He plucked a T-shirt from the basket. "Here. I'll show you." He proceeded to fold it in half, fold the sleeves in, then fold the whole thing in thirds. It *did* make it nice. "See?"

She stood and gave him a by-your-leave wave along with a bow. "I forever defer that particular job to the expert." She took the pile of kitchen towels to the drawer. "I plan to be home for lunch unless I get busy and—"

When she turned around to leave, she caught her husband with one of Ricky's sleepers held against his cheek. Her heart pulled. "I miss him too."

Collie looked at the sleeper, obviously unaware of what he'd been doing. He folded it as if it were a holy shroud. "I thought I'd like having the house to ourselves, but now that we do . . ."

She could easily fill in the blanks. She moved close, snuggled her way onto his lap, and pulled his head to her shoulder.

•　　•　　•

Ursola hadn't planned to go past the house she'd shared with Glenn, but when she was out taking a walk, she'd suddenly found herself close by. And when she saw the Garage Sale sign on the corner with her address listed . . .

She had no wish to run into Daryn or Shanna, but felt compelled to see what they were selling. She approached warily. From a dozen yards away she recognized Glenn's oak buffet edging the driveway. And was that the rocker they'd had in their bedroom? Her anger made her walk faster. They had no right!

As she got closer, her eyes scanned the scattered belongings—that used to belong to her. She grabbed a heart-shaped china box that Glenn had given her their first Valentine's Day. How dare they sell this!

The door leading from the garage to the house opened and Shanna stepped out. "Hi, how are—?" She stopped on the steps. "Ursola."

She held up the china heart. "What this?"

Shanna glanced back at the house and came closer, keeping her voice down. "It's a box we found in the buffet."

Ursola pointed at the price sticker. "Twenty-five cents?"

"You want it? You can have—"

Ursola spread her arms, encompassing the entire stash. "This mine! Glenn's!"

Shanna bit her lower lip. "The stuff came with the house, Ursola. It's all legal. The lawyer said—"

The door opened a second time and Daryn rushed out. "The lawyer said it's ours. Not yours." He pulled the box from her hand. "Get out of here, Ursola. This has nothing to do with you."

She let her mouth drop into a gawk. "This mine. You not give to me, but sell for quarters?"

"We can do whatever we want with it."

Shanna looked around nervously. "Why not let her take what she wants, Daryn?"

He set the china box down hard. "Because it's not hers! It was Dad's and he gave it to me." He took on an evil grin. "Besides, what is she going to do with stuff? I hear she's freeloading over at Peerbaugh Place."

With great difficulty Ursola held back tears. She showed him her back and walked away.

Shanna went after her. "Ursola! Wait!"

She stopped. Shanna pressed the china box into her hands. "I'm so sorry. Take this. Please." She ran back to her husband and Ursola heard them yelling.

Let them have it out. Without her. She was done.

*   *   *

Evelyn set the glass punch cups on the lace tablecloth next to the punch bowl, and adjusted the fanned stack of pink-and-yellow floral napkins. In the center of the table was a vase of pink roses, yellow daisies, and orange asters. Lovely. Absolutely lovely— if she did say so herself.

The smell of the lemon cookies told her they were nearly done. She got a silver cookie tray out of the newly organized buffet. She was just taking it back to the kitchen when the phone rang. It was Lucinda Van Horn, her old tenant who'd moved to Jackson.

"You're not calling to say you can't come to the shower, are you?" Evelyn asked.

"No, no. I'll be there. But I have a favor to ask."

"Name it."

"You may not be so quick to say that after I tell you . . ."

Though her stomach pulled a bit, she said, "Lucinda, just say it."

"You know I've been working at Haven's Rest with Enoch—Pastor Enoch."

"Of course. How's that going?"

"I love it. Who knew that an ex-model could end up being a role model? I'm giving three classes a week on grooming and makeup, and Enoch wants me to start a fashion class to help the women who are trying to get back in the workforce look their best."

"It sounds perfect for you. You have to be pleased."

"I am. At fifty-nine I've found my true calling. Who'd have thought it?"

Evelyn laughed. It was wonderful to have witnessed Lucinda's transformation from an overly nipped-and-tucked gold digger into a woman who'd found her true beauty below the surface. The timer rang on the oven. Evelyn tucked the phone between cheek and shoulder and removed the cookie sheet. "What's the favor, Lucinda?"

"There's a young woman who came into the shelter last night. She had her four-year-old daughter with her, but the child's sick. Actually, they're in the area so the girl can have some tests at the hospital. She's going there special, to be under Gregory's care."

"It's a heart problem?" That was Gregory's forte.

"It is."

"Four years old. How horrible."

"Exactly. And here's the kicker. The woman has very little money and no place to stay. Naturally, she wants to be close to her daughter, so being here in Jackson does her no good. I was wondering if she could stay at Peerbaugh Place a few days."

"Of course, but . . . but I don't have any empty rooms right
now."

"She'll take a couch. Anything. She's going to be at the hospital most of the time anyway. She just needs a safe—and free—
place to lay her head."

Evelyn didn't have to think about it. "She's welcome here.
When would she be coming?"

"Actually, I thought I'd bring her when I come for the shower.
We were going to leave pretty quick here because the little girl has
an appointment with Dr. Baladino at the hospital. She—Jody, the
woman's name is Jody—won't be at the shower, but she will show
up tonight."

"No problem. She can sleep in the sunroom. I'll have it made
up for her."

"You're a peach, Evelyn. I'll see you soon."

Evelyn hung up, her mind whirling—with compassion for the
woman and child, as well as with the knowledge that yet another
room would be filled at Peerbaugh Place. With another nonpaying
guest.

She focused on the cookies. She had another batch to get in.

* * *

"Mommy? Mommy!"

Audra realized Summer was talking to her, and by the way
her hands were firmly placed on her hips, *had* been talking to her.
She looked down at the dress she was cutting out on the dining-
room table. She had scissors in hand . . . yet how long had it been
since she'd made the last cut? "I'm sorry, baby. Did you say something?"

"I wanted to know if I could wear my Easter dress to Aunt
Piper's shower."

"That would be perfect."

Summer skipped away then stopped. "Shouldn't you get ready?"

"I have plenty of time. We don't have to leave until one-thirty and—"

"It's one, Mommy." She pointed to the anniversary clock on the buffet.

Audra stared at it. It couldn't be. The last time she'd checked it was noon.

"You coming?"

She set the scissors down. "I'm coming."

As she passed the family room, Russell looked up from the recliner from where he was watching baseball. "I was wondering about the time too."

"Why didn't you say something?"

He shrugged. "You were deep in thought. Just standing there, staring off into nothing. You worried about something?"

Actually, her worry was twofold. She was worried that an hour had passed without her knowledge, but the biggest worry involved the reason behind the lapse in time. "I'm fine. I have to get dressed."

Audra hurried to the bedroom and put on a favorite skirt and summer sweater. She moved into the master bath and started on her makeup. Luckily, it was an action she could do by rote, because her mind was consumed with the thoughts that had just devoured an hour of her life. Thoughts of Simon. Stupid scenarios that involved bringing the two of them together. Alone. Harmless really.

Nothing intimate happened. It's not like I'm thinking about sex or anything.

Her fantasies didn't go that far.

But far enough.

She caught herself staring at the mirror. She let her eyes focus and realized she was smiling. "Stop it!"

"Stop what, Mommy?" Summer stood in the doorway, looking pretty in her pink Easter dress.

Audra forced a smile. "I'm telling myself to stop taking so long, that's all. I'm way behind. Will you get out my white sandals, baby?"

Audra turned back to the mirror, not liking the crease that had formed between her eyes.

•   •   •

Tessa was just going out the door to Piper's shower when the phone rang. It was Rini Fudecio, calling from Rome. She had to take the call.

"Rini. It's so good to hear from you. How are things going?"

"I've been waiting to hear from you in response to all the mail," Rini said.

Tessa thought back to the handful of correspondence she'd received during the past month. "What mail?"

"What—? I sent you a lot of mail. Mail I've gotten from around the world. Women starting Sister Circles. Some needing help. Some saying thank you. I sent it all . . . last week? Yes. A week ago yesterday."

"I haven't received it. How much is 'a lot of mail'?"

"Plenty," Rini said. "Oh. The other line is ringing. That's all for now. Call me when you get the mail. Ciao."

"Will do. Ciao."

A lot of mail. How wonderful. Tessa could hardly wait.

•   •   •

Mae knocked, then entered Peerbaugh Place. "Yoo-hoo. It's me, ready to help."

Evelyn poked her head out of the kitchen. "And I need it! Come make the punch."

"You got it." Mae went into the kitchen and was greeted by Piper, Accosta, and Ursola, all doing their parts.

"The recipe's on the counter." Evelyn pointed with her chin because her hands were full, carrying a tray of pastel mints.

"Are those the mints you made?" Mae asked.

"The very ones."

"I help push in mold," Ursola said, acting out the process.

"Over and over and over," Piper said. "You ladies went above and beyond . . ."

Mae read the ingredients for the punch, and went to the freezer for the frozen lemonade.

"Where's Soon-ja?" Accosta asked.

Though she'd kept Soon-ja's trip to Korea a secret for a week now—hoping the girl would come right back—Mae knew the time had come to let her sisters in on her pain. "She went to Korea to visit her family."

"When was this?" Piper put sprigs of real daisies around the cake.

"Last Saturday."

Evelyn stopped in the middle of the kitchen. "Why didn't you tell us?"

Mae shrugged. "I thought she'd come right back."

"She is coming back, isn't she?" Accosta asked.

"We . . . we hope so." Mae decided she might as well get the whole thing out. "Ringo's left too, but we don't know where he is."

"Oh dear."

Piper went to her side. "Is their marriage in trouble?"

"It's not flourishing."

"And it's not going to have an easy time flourishing with both of them in different places," Accosta said.

"In different countries," Piper added.

"Why did Ringo leave?" Evelyn asked.

"He didn't like his job. I'm afraid he went back to being a roadie."

Piper opened the lemonade can. "That lifestyle is not conducive to married life."

"I know."

Mae felt Evelyn's hand on her back. "What would you like us to do?"

"Pray, sisters, pray hard."

And so they did. Right there in the kitchen.

*   *   *

Peerbaugh Place was full of laughter and ladies. All for Piper.

While the guests chatted and settled into the parlor, Piper stood at the dining-room window, looking out. There were a few women who hadn't showed up yet, but the one absence that caused Piper concern was Gregory's mother, Esther. After their less-than-stellar dinner at Esther's house, Gregory had suggested Piper not even invite her to the shower. "Why give yourself the grief?" he'd said.

And though she'd been tempted, she'd let her own mother's lessons of etiquette and manners win out. The mother of the groom was always invited to the bridal showers. Whether she'd come was something else.

Evelyn came up behind her. "Valerie's not here either."

Piper hated to admit she hadn't even thought of Valerie. "Maybe we shouldn't have invited her. She wasn't around Peerbaugh Place that long and didn't exactly bond with any of us—not that we didn't try."

"You were being polite, trying to include her. And she did RSVP, saying she was coming."

"Hmm." Piper's thoughts returned to her missing future mother-in-law. "Did Esther RSVP?"

"She did, and she said she'd come." Evelyn rubbed a hand across Piper's shoulders. "She'll be here."

Piper nodded, but her insides were uneasy at the thought.

When she heard a car pull up, her eyes were drawn back to the window. "It's her!" She put a hand to her stomach. The thought of eating anything . . .

Evelyn took her hands. "This is *your* shower, Piper. I will not let anyone ruin it for you."

"But what if she says something—?"

"Then she says something. This house is full of sisters who love you. Just be yourself and let them be themselves. Whatever happens happens."

That's exactly what Piper was afraid of.

The doorbell rang and Evelyn answered it, letting Esther in with kind greetings. Piper took a deep breath and did the same. She gave Esther an awkward hug. "Hello, Mrs. Baladino. I'm so glad you could come."

"It *was* a long drive."

"One we're all glad you made. Come meet everyone." Evelyn led her into the parlor and made introductions.

Mae patted the seat beside herself on the couch, "Come sit over here, Esther, next to me. Piper can sit catty-corner to us."

Piper's first reaction was one of panic. Of all people to chat with Esther . . . but as her future mother-in-law took her place next to Mae, and as Piper sat in the chair nearby, Piper wondered if Mae wasn't the perfect person to fill the position. No one fazed Mae and Mae fazed *everyone*, so maybe between those two truths, there would be peace at Peerbaugh Place this afternoon.

Mae touched Esther's knee and it began. "So, Esther. How does it feel to be gaining a wonderful daughter like Piper?"

"Daughter-in-law."

"Gracious gardenias, law-shmaw. You'll come to love Piper as a daughter, and that's a fact. She's one of the kindest, sweetest, most God-fearing women I've ever—"

"I'm Jewish."

The room quieted. "So we heard," Mae said.

Esther turned toward Piper, her eyes accusing. Piper jumped in with an explanation. "I told them you'd rediscovered your Jewish roots."

"Gregory's Jewish roots."

Mae spread her arms to take in the room. "We all have Jewish roots. That's what's so wonderful."

Esther slowly turned her gaze back on Mae. "But you're Gentiles. Christians, the lot of you."

Mae laughed. "Yes, there are a lot of us, and yes, we are Christians. But I for one have always been fascinated with the Jewish traditions. Do you keep a kosher kitchen?"

Esther straightened her spine, her hands still clutching the pocketbook in her lap. "My traditions are not to be studied like I'm some freak show."

"No, no, Mrs. Baladino," Piper said. "Mae didn't mean—"

"Of course I didn't mean *any* disrespect, Esther," Mae said. "I just think it's wonderful that you—and your son—have embraced faith as an important part of every—"

"Gregory betrayed his faith. The faith of his fathers."

"But wasn't his father Catholic?" Mae asked.

Piper wanted to shrink into the crack between the sofa cushions.

"I meant the faith of his Hebrew fathers, his heritage spanning back to David and Moses and—"

"Moses is one of my favorite people," Mae said. "At first he was scared and unsure of himself, but he obeyed God and did what he had to do. He had guts. Chutzpah?"

Esther seemed dumbstruck, but nodded.

Tessa piped in for the first time. "And David's psalms . . . I read a different one every day. They speak to me."

There were nods all around.

"Which psalm is your favorite, Esther?" Mae asked.

Suddenly Esther stood. "I have to go."

Piper stood too. "Mrs. Baladino . . . no."

"Oh dear," Evelyn said from across the room.

Mae put a hand on her arm. "Esther . . . I don't understand. Did I say something—?"

Esther sidestepped around the coffee table and headed for the door. "I shouldn't have come. I knew there would be trouble."

"Trouble?" Mae stood. "Esther, if I offended you in any way, I apologize."

Tessa tried to help. "Mae was only pointing out our shared heritage, Mrs. Baladino. It's something to be celebrated. We can learn a lot from each other."

Evelyn rushed to the door as if she wanted to block it, but Esther beat her to it, placing her hand on the knob. "I don't want to learn anything from any of you. I don't belong here. I belong with my own kind. I must bear the burden of having a son who's betrayed me by becoming engaged to a . . . a . . . shiksa."

There was that name again. Piper had first heard it at Esther's dinner. She didn't know what it meant, but felt as if she'd been called something nasty. Just the tone of Esther's voice . . . "Please, Mrs. Baladino. Come back and stay."

"There's good food," Mae said. "And games and—"

With a shake to her head Esther opened the door. "I bid you good day."

The door closed and the room was silent. Everyone looked at everyone else, not knowing what to do. It was like a dream. Piper burst into tears and received hugs and kindness. An apology from Mae. She was on the verge of telling everyone to go home when Accosta's words broke through the chaos of the moment.

"We need to pray for Esther," Accosta said, "pray that she stops feeling threatened by us."

"Pray that she's forgiven," Mae said.

"And us too," Tessa said.

Mae nodded and the women joined hands and prayed for Esther Baladino.

This was certainly the prayingest shower Piper had ever attended.

●   ●   ●

Piper was glad Evelyn had had the foresight to ask Mae to handle the party games. She was a natural, and that left Evelyn free to be hostess and concentrate on the food—which was a big hit. Everyone oohed and aahed at the pistachio dessert and the handmade mints.

Mae stood in the middle of the parlor holding a tray of miscellaneous items. "Attention, ladies. Listen up. On this tray I have placed fifteen items. I'm going to move around the circle slowly—once. Your job is to memorize what's on the tray. After everyone's seen the tray, I will leave the room and you will have to write down what you remember."

Lucinda raised her hand. "I can't remember what I had for breakfast and you expect me to remember fifteen things?"

"I certainly do," Mae said. "Quit complaining."

Summer tugged on Lucinda's skirt. "The winner gets a prize, Aunt Lucinda."

"Exactly," Mae said. "A prize worth hundreds of pennies is at stake. Put on your thinking caps." She started moving around the circle. Piper watched as the ladies leaned forward, scoping out the items as if their lives depended on the answer. Well, well. Games always did bring out people's competitive side.

As the tray came by, Piper found it hard to concentrate. She tried to make a mental list, then tried to take a mental picture, but she knew neither one was going to stick in her memory bank successfully. Oh well. She'd already received so many lovely presents. Actually, she hoped Summer would win. That little pipsqueak was so adorable, seated among the twenty other ladies like a little princess. Not many seven-year-olds would be comfortable as the only child present. But Summer was no ordinary child. Piper hoped to have many children of her own. Just as sweet. Just as special.

Tears threatened as once again, she felt the weight of Esther's departure coupled with the knowledge of her immense blessings. The dream of marriage and a family was happening. In just a few weeks . . . *But will Esther be there?*

Mae interrupted her thoughts. "Piper? You're not writing."

Everyone else was frantically scribbling down their list. Piper laid her hands across her piece of paper. "I defer to more able minds."

Heddy Wainsworth Mannersmith laughed. "I understand completely. When I was this close to our wedding, I couldn't add two plus two."

"That's four!" Summer said.

The ladies' laughter was added to Piper's list of blessings.

*   *   *

Valerie was dressed in a luscious gray voile tea dress she'd found at a vintage store online. She'd taken nearly an hour getting her hair pulled into an updo with soft tendrils framing her face. A beautifully wrapped present sat next to her on the seat of the car. She was all ready for Piper's shower.

In theory.

But in action, she couldn't get herself to go. She'd driven past Peerbaugh Place four times already. She'd seen the cars out front.

She'd seen the lights on in the dining room and parlor. If she rolled down her window, she bet she could even hear laughter.

Which is why she left the windows up.

Though dressed for a party, she was not in a party mood. Her entire life had just crumbled. There was no book contract forthcoming. No agent. No future. She'd blown it. And she didn't want to ruin Piper's shower by clouding it with any hint of gloom and negativity—

It was a lie. She wasn't driving around in circles because she was afraid of ruining anyone else's time but her own. If she went to the shower they'd ask about the book, giving her all the glorious attention she craved. She'd have to tell them the truth, and that would kill her.

Actually, she wouldn't *have* to tell them the truth. She could play the part of published author awhile longer. People would lose interest. And maybe she could find another agent and another publisher by then.

But maybe not. The publishing world was vast, yet very small. Inbred. Everybody had worked for everybody else. Word would get around about the difficult rookie writer who thought she deserved the world when she really should have realized that she had more to learn than to teach.

Valerie slowed in order to get a tissue from her purse. Suddenly, she saw Mae and Evelyn come out on the porch with Tessa. They were carrying cups of punch and talking.

If she drove too fast, the ladies would look up. If she stopped completely in front of the neighbor's house, it would look suspicious. Best to drive at a normal speed, hoping they wouldn't recognize her car.

No such luck. Mae looked up at just the wrong time, waved, and called out, "Valerie! Come on in!"

Valerie accelerated, her heart racing along with the engine. This wasn't good. Wasn't good at all.

• • •

Mae stood at the railing, looking down the street where Valerie's car had gone. This didn't make any sense. She turned back to Evelyn and Tessa. "Why didn't she stop?"

"Why did she speed up as if she wanted to get away?" Evelyn asked.

"It looked like she was dressed up," Tessa said.

"It's like she was avoiding us."

"The question is why?"

"I haven't been over to visit her since she moved," Evelyn admitted. "I really should. I do have a couple pieces of mail—junk mail—but it would give me an excuse."

"Let me take it over tomorrow afternoon," Mae said. "I'll get to the bottom of things."

With an approving nod, Tessa raised her glass. "I bet you will."

They clinked glasses. They could count on it.

• • •

All during the shower Accosta's insides felt like a sparrow fluttering its wings against a closed window. She'd hoped that the gathering would be a place where she could pull Audra aside and chat about what she'd seen on Audra's front stoop, but the time was never right. And they were never alone.

Until . . . she'd brought a couple dirty plates into the kitchen and found Audra at the sink rinsing them. *Now, Lord?*

Audra glanced over her shoulder. "Thanks, Accosta. Set them over here and I'll get to them. Wasn't Evelyn's dessert yummy? I really have to get the recipe. I'm sure Russell would love it."

"How is Russell?" *How's your marriage going?*

"He's fine. Busy at the bank."

Her answer revealed nothing. "So he's gone a lot?"

Audra hesitated then looked at her warily. "Not more than usual."

"So everything's okay? I mean, between you two?"

Audra shut the water off. "These are odd questions, Accosta. What are you getting—?"

The kitchen door swung open and two past tenants, Margaret Jensen and Gail Saunders, came in with more dishes. "Got more for you, Audra," Gail said.

Margaret set her dishes down. "I've been meaning to ask you, what color are the bridesmaids' dresses?"

"Very pale periwinkle."

"Ooh, that sounds pretty," Margaret said.

"I bet it was a challenge finding a style that looks good on Evelyn, Mae, Tessa, and yourself."

Audra shrugged. "A bit. But I think we came to a good solution. It's a simple sheath dress in crepe covered by a shimmery organza overshirt-jacket that is worn buttoned . . ."

Accosta left the room for more dishes. Today was not the day. The sparrows returned.

* * *

Everyone was gone from the shower and Ursola was glad. There was only so much girly-girl froufrou she could take. The women were all nice—it wasn't that—but the more she heard about weddings and true love, the more she wanted to run into her room and wrap a pillow around her ears.

Now that she had a chance to do just that, she realized her room was too confining. Best to escape into the backyard, sit among the dahlias and zinnias where air could reach her and prevent her from being suffocated by grief, longing, and regret.

And now a new woman was coming to Peerbaugh Place

tonight? A woman with a sick child? She didn't feel up to dealing with her either.

Either they're too happy or too sad. There's no pleasing you, is there?

Probably not. And the truth was, she didn't even want to try. While the other ladies of the house were rehashing the afternoon, Ursola slipped out back. The humidity was at its peak and she realized being revitalized by fresh air was not going to happen. But she didn't retreat. Alone and sticky was better than chatty and cool.

She sat on the small bench in the corner garden, the canopy of a shade tree providing a smidgen of relief. She wedged her hands beneath her thighs and leaned forward, eyeing the blooms. A butterfly flitted from one orange blossom to another. Such beautiful flowers. Glenn loved flowers. Roses had been his specialty. "I want to grow my own so I can keep my lovely wife supplied," he'd always said.

And he had. She'd even come to learn their special names: Dainty Bess, Belami, and Glenn's favorite, the beautifully red Forgotten Dreams.

Forgotten Dreams. She snickered. How ironic. Her dreams of house, family, and husband were far gone now. Would she ever—?

"Ursola?"

She looked up and found Evelyn standing on the path. She swiped a hand over her cheeks. *"Da?"*

"Are you all right?"

She nodded yes, even as the tears said no.

Evelyn was immediately by her side, on the bench. "There, there. What's wrong?"

Ursola tried to be strong. "Nothing. Pretty shower."

"Yes, it was. But you didn't have a good time?"

"No. Yes. I have good time."

"Then what's upset you so?"

Ursola didn't realize she was twisting her wedding ring

around her finger until Evelyn touched her hand. "The talk of weddings and marriage made you think of Glenn, didn't it?"

She nodded, then grabbed a hunk of her blouse in her fist. "It hurt. Deep."

"Oh, honey. I know, I know." As a widow Evelyn *did* know. "How long hurt?"

"I'm afraid there's no set time, and truth is, the grief will probably hit you at odd times for years. Sometimes it comes like a whack with a two-by-four, and other times it sneaks up on you like water seeping under the door. Aaron's been gone two and a half years and I still have bouts of missing him. Love doesn't die with them, Ursola. It just bends itself into a new shape."

She liked that.

Evelyn laughed. "That was quite eloquent, wasn't it?" She stood. "Loving is a good thing, and if we are to learn anything from our sorrow, it's that we need to grab every moment we can. You coming in?"

"Not yet."

"Take your time. We'll be there."

* * *

Piper tucked the sheet around the cushions of the couch in the sunroom.

Evelyn came in the back door from checking on Ursola. "You don't have to do that," she said. "I'll make up the bed."

"You've done enough today." Piper crossed the room to give her friend a hug. "Thank you. For everything."

"Glad to do it." Evelyn picked up a pillow and started to put it in a pillowcase, but held it instead. She looked out toward the backyard.

"Is Ursola all right?"

"She's grieving. It's tough being a widow."

"Or a widower. Dad still has painful times. He misses Mom." When Evelyn nodded and hugged the pillow tighter, Piper hastened to add, "He misses her, but he's doing all right. He's ready to move on." Was she saying this right? "He really likes spending time with you, Evelyn."

Evelyn sat on the couch, still clutching the pillow. "I just told Ursola that if our widowhood teaches us anything, it's that we need to grab every moment we can."

The look on Evelyn's face was so serious. Piper spoke carefully. "Good advice."

Evelyn nodded, but her forehead was tight in thought.

"What's going on in that brain of yours?"

Evelyn patted the couch beside her. "Sit."

Piper hesitated. She'd rarely seen Evelyn so intent. But she did as she was told.

"I love your father."

Piper let out a breath. "I know that."

"But *he* doesn't know that. And he should know. I've wanted to tell him for a long time now."

"Why haven't you?"

Evelyn sighed. "I'm chicken."

Piper laughed. "Don't be. We both know Dad likes you a lot; he might even love you. Either way he'd be flattered."

"But we're business partners. Is it appropriate to love your business partner?"

Piper stifled a laugh. "I don't think there's a rule about it. You love whom you love, Evelyn."

"I didn't plan on loving him."

Piper stood and pulled Evelyn to her feet. "But you do. So go over and tell him."

"Now?"

"Grab every moment. . . ."

Evelyn pointed to the couch. "But Jody's going to be calling any time and I need to pick her up at the hospital and—"

"And when she does, I'll go get her."

"But don't you want to see Gregory? Talk to him about the shower and his mother and—?"

There was plenty of time to talk to Gregory about his mother. "He's working. I can't see him until tomorrow. Which leaves you no more excuses."

"But it's my responsibility to be here."

"It's your responsibility to go see my father and declare your love. Now git."

*   *   *

Evelyn stood in the hall outside Wayne's apartment. She shifted her weight from foot to foot and back again. The last time she'd felt this nervous heading to see someone of the opposite sex was . . . she couldn't member, but most likely she had braces at the time. On the way over she'd tried to practice what to say, but everything sounded wrong. And yet, she was determined to do it. She was tired of thinking about it. Now was the—

Suddenly, the door opened. "Evelyn." Wayne was holding a bag of trash.

She stepped aside. "Go ahead."

He put the bag down and opened the door fully. "Nonsense. Come in, come in."

She was immediately struck by the smell of chocolate. The buzzer on the oven rang. "Oops. I was trying to race the timer down to the Dumpster." He grabbed a hot pad, opened the oven door, and removed a pan of brownies.

"Yum," she said.

"Yeah, well . . . every once in a while I have a craving."

"Glad to know I'm not the only one."

"But at least you have a houseful of people to help you eat it." He got out two plates. "Dig in and save me from myself."

They sat on the stools at the kitchen bar and dove in. The brownie was so hot it crumbled into wonderful gooey bites. Evelyn had no idea how she was going to segue from brownies to love. Yet maybe the correlation wasn't so far—

"To what do I owe the pleasure of your visit?"

Evelyn pointed to her full mouth, using the brownie as an excuse for not answering.

"Piper just called."

Uh-oh. She ignored the brownie to ask, "What did she say?"

"She said the shower was beautiful."

Okay then.

"And she also said you have something important to tell me?"

You'll pay for this, Piper!

He squished a crumb, licked his finger, and looked at Evelyn expectantly. "So?"

This was not happening. Evelyn pushed the plate aside, making it rattle. She stood and stepped away from the stools. "Piper had no right telling you that."

"Telling me what? She didn't *tell* me anything."

"She told you I had something to tell you."

"Which you have yet to tell me."

"Because she warned you that I was going to tell you."

"Warned me?"

"Told you."

"Evelyn . . ."

She grabbed a fresh breath. "I love you, okay?" She waited for the earth to open and swallow her whole but was relieved when it didn't. She grabbed her purse and headed for the door. "I can't believe I said that."

He barred her way. "So you didn't mean it?"

He was only a foot away. If she looked up she'd be looking into his eyes.

"Evelyn. Look at me."

What did she have to lose? She looked at him.

He was smiling. His eyes were kind and held a depth she'd never seen before. He took her hand. "I love you too."

Her free hand went to her mouth. "You do?"

He pulled her close. Life was good beyond measure.

*   *   *

Evelyn didn't drive home—she flew. An old twenties song came to mind and she tried her best to sing it:

> *"Life was a song, you came along*
> *I lay awake the whole night through*
> *If I should dare, to think you care*
> *This is what I'd say to you*
> *You were meant for me,*
> *And I was meant for you."*

It was true! It was all true! Wayne was meant for her and she was meant for him. She knew it and felt it deep inside. Her only regret was waiting so long to tell him. And if she had it to do over again she wouldn't have blurted it out like that. But what did it matter how it happened? Her declaration of love was a done deal. Now they could move onward. To the next step.

Which was . . . ?

She forced herself to stifle her planning mode. She truly didn't need to know the next step. Now was good. Now was right. The rest would come.

She pulled into the driveway and shut her car door quietly. It was after eleven-thirty—she couldn't remember the last time she'd been out this late. She quietly slipped in the side door, and flipped on the light in the kitchen. The closed French doors leading to the sunroom got her attention. They were never closed.

Then she remembered Jody! Sure, Piper had said not to worry, they'd take care of her, but for Evelyn to completely forget?

She flipped off the light so as not to wake her, and slipped into the foyer to head upstairs. She'd make amends tomorrow and give Jody her full attention.

Piper surprised her by meeting her on the stairs. "Well?" she whispered.

Evelyn put a finger to her lips and pointed to her bedroom. Once they were inside, with Evelyn seated on the bed and Piper in the chair, she told her story.

"I knew it!" Piper popped out of the chair and pulled her into a hug. "I knew he loved you. Who couldn't love you?"

"You're too kind."

Piper sat again. "Wouldn't it be amazing if you got married and you were my stepmother and—"

"Whoa there, Piper!"

"I know I'm running ahead."

"Sprinting."

"But wouldn't it be wonderful?"

Evelyn had to admit she *had* thought of it.

Down, girl.

11

Temptation comes from the lure
of our own evil desires.
These evil desires lead to evil actions,
and evil actions lead to death.
So don't be misled,
my dear brothers and sisters.

JAMES 1:14-16

*W*hen Evelyn went downstairs to make coffee in the morning she found the kitchen occupied by a stranger. The stranger who had been sleeping in the sunroom. "Good morning," Evelyn said.

The woman stood quickly, nearly toppling her chair. She had long straight hair the color of wheat. The style made her look fifteen, but her eyes and the pallor in her skin made her look forty. "Hi. I'm Jody Harper."

Evelyn extended her hand. "And I'm Evelyn Peerbaugh. I'm so sorry I wasn't here last night to greet you." She headed to the coffeepot but found the coffee already brewed.

"I made coffee. I hope you don't mind."

"Not at all. My home is your home. Would you like some eggs? Or pancakes maybe?"

Jody pushed her chair in. "No thank you. I want to get to the hospital to be with Kimberly. She's my daughter. She's four."

"How's she doing?"

Jody took her mug to the sink, emptied it, and put it in the dishwasher. "Dr. Baladino says she's a fighter but she might need a new valve in her heart."

"Oh dear."

"He'll fix it. Then she'll be good as new. I know it."

Evelyn trusted Gregory's doctoring skills but also knew his human limitations.

Jody gathered her purse. "I'll be going now. I may be late getting back. I don't like leaving Kimberly alone."

Evelyn felt for her. There was nothing worse than a hospital vigil. She wished there was something she could do.

There was. She got out a pad of paper and a pencil. "This is the phone number here. You call if you need anything. Even if you just want to be spelled a bit, call and one of us will come over and sit with Kimberly."

Jody's eyebrows dipped, she pursed her lips, and nodded. Then she was gone.

Evelyn strolled into the sunroom to tidy the bedding but found it neatly folded on a chair. The fact that Jody took time to clean up after herself when her mind had to be pulled a thousand ways said a lot for her character. Evelyn was glad to have her around.

◦   ◦   ◦

I hate him.

Ursola knew hate wasn't a proper emotion to have in church, but she couldn't help it. Seeing Daryn parade in with Shanna, shaking hands like a politician, grinning like he owned the world.

He owns your world. He stole your world!

And wasn't that one of Ursola's scarves around Shanna's neck? It was a slap, a personal affront. Shanna had no right to wear *her* clothes.

Ursola couldn't forget the sight of all her things strewn on the driveway and lawn like junk, selling for a quarter or a dollar. If the things meant so little to Daryn, why not give them back to her? With those *things* she could rebuild a life, remember a life. As it was . . . she appreciated the room she had at Peerbaugh Place, and she was working hard, making pins for Mae to sell. But there were only so many pins people would buy. And she didn't *want* to be a charity case at Evelyn's. Not forever. She had to get another job—a real job. But as an immigrant, could she?

Tessa sat on the pew beside her, also watching Daryn and Shanna pay court. "What's got into them?" she asked Ursola. "It's like they're glad Glenn's gone and are trying to take his place."

Tessa's words pegged Daryn's attitude. Ursola wanted to jump to her feet and yell at him for all to hear: *You think you can take your father's place in this church? in this town? You're wrong! You're nothing! You're a mean, evil-hearted man, Daryn Smith, and the world needs to see your true—*

She felt Tessa's hand on her leg. "Are you all right?"

Ursola realized she was breathing heavily. She stood. "I must go."

"Go? But church is going to start and—"

"Stay. I fine. I must go."

Ursola hurried out of the church.

* * *

Ursola walked to Daryn's house as fast as she could. If she could have run without drawing attention, she would have. She didn't have much time to do what needed to be done.

And what exactly is that?

She had no idea. But after getting worked up at church and walking out, she'd found herself walking toward her old house. Daryn's house. And along the way, she'd dug the spare house key from her purse. Which must mean she planned to go inside . . .

To do what?

She had no idea.

No. That wasn't entirely true. Because as she walked, one thought kept surfacing: *revenge.*

When she was a few houses away, she forced herself to slow her stride into a stroll. She spotted the neighbor on the far side cutting some roses. She held back. She didn't want to chat. She wanted to slip in and out unnoticed.

The neighbor went inside and Ursola used her key and entered the house. She closed the door, and allowed herself a breath. The house had changed completely. Gone was the tasteful but simple furniture, the homey touches that had merged Ursola's Russian taste with Glenn's American roots. A large, white-leather sectional took the living room captive and a giant TV covered the opposite wall. Above the couch hung a hideous painting that looked as if a child had gotten mad and brushed paint on a canvas in sweeping, ragged bands. Where was her picture of the mountains? Where was Glenn's mother's quilt that used to lay on the back of their couch?

She moved into the dining room. The oak table and chairs had been replaced with polished black lacquer ones. In the center was a vase with a bunch of bamboo poles in it. Where was her pretty floral arrangement?

Ursola stormed through the rest of the house. Everything had changed. Even the dishes in the kitchen cabinets were different. The only thing she recognized were two mugs on a counter mug tree. One said *His* and another said *Hers*. Every morning, for the short breadth of their married life, Glenn and Ursola had enjoyed their coffee in those mugs.

She snatched them off their pegs, feeling oddly triumphant. Realizing that more of her and Glenn's things might still be in the garage left over from the sale, she opened the door. Sure enough, there were boxes of *her* things lining the walls. *I should borrow a car and come get—*

Ursola was suddenly weary. It really wasn't the *things* she wanted. A few possessions couldn't make time rewind. She closed the door to the garage, ready to leave. She was through here. But then she noticed some papers on the kitchen table. The letters CIS stood out. Citizen and Immigration Services. Immigration papers? What would Daryn be doing with such a thing?

Getting you in trouble. Getting you deported.

She scanned the pages but much of the English was over her head. She could tell they were in regard to her visa, the one that Glenn had obtained so she could come over and become his wife. Was something wrong with it?

She remembered the run-in at the grocery store, when Daryn had made comments about her not belonging in this country. She looked at the government papers. Was he figuring out a way to get her sent home?

Then she remembered the rest of that day. Tessa had comforted her and told her she would look into it. But had she? Ursola had forgotten all about it.

She couldn't forget about it any longer. She grabbed her mugs, went out the front door, and headed to Tessa's. She'd be there when Tessa got home from church.

•   •   •

Tessa decided to skip brunch with her daughter's family today. Ever since Ursola had hurried out of the church, Tessa's stomach had lost its desire for an omelet or a Belgian waffle. She had her son-in-law drop her off at the house, and she walked up the drive-way toward her garage apartment. There, on the step sat Ursola.

"Ursola. I'm so glad you're here. I was worried."

The girl stood, hugging herself. "Daryn has CIS papers. I need help."

They went inside and Tessa chastised herself for not following through with her promise to look into Ursola's immigration status. She'd been so busy with her Sister Circle work that she'd completely forgotten. If this poor girl got in trouble because of *her* neglect . . .

They sat in the tiny living room. "Tell me what Daryn has."

Ursola told her about some visa . . . Tessa didn't understand much of it.

Ursola stood. "I must get papers. I must stay."

"You will stay. I'll call tomorrow morning and find out what's what. I promise."

●   ●   ●

Evelyn got in Wayne's car after church. "Thanks for doing this," she said.

He leaned down and kissed her cheek. "Glad to be of assistance."

As he walked around to the driver's side, Accosta whispered to Evelyn from the backseat. "I just love seeing two people in love!"

"Shh!"

Wayne drove them to the hospital. Evelyn's plan was to have Accosta stay with Kimberly awhile so Wayne and Evelyn could take Jody out for a proper lunch. She'd probably been eating hospital food—or nothing.

"I'm really proud of you, Evelyn," Wayne said. "Taking Jody in . . . how long is she going to be staying?"

"I don't know. Kimberly might need surgery. Then there will be a recuperation time. What bothers me is where they'll stay after the surgery. If only I had a proper room for her."

"That poor little girl. I'd give her some good grandma love if . I could," Accosta said.

Wayne hit his hand on the steering wheel. "I've got it!"

"The solution?"

"Absolutely. Piper's moving out in two weeks. I'm sure she wouldn't mind moving in with me for that short a time. After all, my apartment used to be *her* apartment. Then you'd have her room available for Jody and Kimberly."

Accosta clapped.

My last paying tenant moving out ahead of schedule?

Wayne glanced at her. "Evelyn? You don't seem thrilled with the idea."

Evelyn didn't want to say anything with Accosta in the car. She didn't want to make her friend feel guilty for being one of the nonpaying boarders. "I think it's a great idea. If Piper will agree."

"I'll use my fatherly influence."

•   •   •

Lucinda looked up from the tables where she was setting out makeup for her Sunday afternoon makeover session at the shelter. A scraggly man stood nearby. "May I help you?" she asked.

"I came in last night. Pastor Enoch said he'd have something for me to do this morning."

She looked around for Enoch. He wasn't in the dining room. "Try the kitchen."

A few minutes later, Enoch and the man came out of the kitchen. "Lucinda! I want you to meet someone from your past."

Her past had been all about high society and country clubs—far, far from the world of this man standing before her. She studied his face, trying to make the connection. "I'm sorry. I just don't remember."

The man laughed. "I didn't either, until Pastor told me. I was in a horizontal position at the time we met. In a doorway? In Boston. I scared you."

Lucinda took a step back as the memories of running away from the humiliation of her high school reunion returned. She'd ventured into the Boston night into a neighborhood not used to fifty-something women walking around alone, in heels and dressed to the hilt. Not nice fifty-something women anyway.

"How . . . why . . . ?"

". . . am I here?"

She nodded.

"Remember the good ol' pastor taking me to the shelter that night? You too, for your hurt knee?"

"I do."

"He ended up giving me his address here in Jackson, and time and my hitchhiking thumb did the rest."

Enoch slapped him on the back. "God did the rest. Danny's going to help with repairs around here."

"You bet. Whatever's needed."

Enoch poked Danny with an elbow. "Tell her the other connection."

Danny grinned. "I think you know my wife. Mae?"

Lucinda stumbled into a chair.

"Ex-wife, actually. As of 1974 to be exact. I ain't been around since."

Lucinda gathered her voice. "Does she know you're here in Jackson?"

"Not yet."

Lucinda realized the better answer might be "not ever." She couldn't imagine that Mae—with her new husband—would want an old one making contact. She looked at Enoch, trying to ask him with her eyes, *Do you approve of this?*

But Enoch's answer was a pat on Danny's back. "I have a call in to Mae."

"He doesn't want me to surprise her."

Imagine that.

"Come on, Danny," Enoch said. "Let's put you to work."

Small world. Tiny world. Miniscule world.

• • •

After church they sat in a booth by the window and ordered lunch. Summer started coloring the place mat. Russell excused himself to go to the restroom. Audra took a sip of her water. She rearranged the salt and pepper shakers, and the mustard and ketchup. She looked out the window—

And saw Simon sitting in a car in the parking lot.

"Mommy?"

She looked at Summer. "What?"

"Why did you just go *huhhh*?"

Audra hadn't realized she'd gasped aloud. "No reason." She pointed to the cat on Summer's place mat. "What color are you going to color the kitty?"

"Orange and brown. Like Peppers. Do you know what Peppers did the other day when I was at Grandma's?"

"No, what?"

Summer started telling her story as she colored, while Audra made comments in all the right places. But her true attention was focused outside. Why was Simon here? He had to have followed them from church. Had he been *in* church? There was something dangerous about the idea that he was following her, skimming the edge of her life. But also something exciting and flattering. To see him in a nonworking situation . . . it was just what she'd dreamed of.

Russell slid in next to Summer. He noticed the place mat. "That looks just like Peppers."

Summer beamed. Audra risked a look outside.

Simon was gone.

Why was she disappointed?

• • •

Piper kissed Gregory hello and they got in line for lunch in the hospital cafeteria. "You're looking lovely today," he said.

"You always say that."

He winked at her. "I always mean that. Sorry to miss church." They got their food and sat. Then came the question Piper had been dreading. "Tell me all about the shower."

"It was lovely. Evelyn and the other ladies outdid themselves."

"Did we get tons of good stuff?"

She laughed. "Yes, we did. We even have two toasters."

His eyebrows rose. "One for you and one for me?"

"No way. We share everything. One's going back."

He opened his carton of milk and poured it into a glass. "And how was my mother?"

Piper had tried to think of a way to couch the truth to make it more palatable, but there was no way. "She missed some of it. She left early."

He stopped his glass halfway to his mouth. "How much of it?"

"Most."

"Meaning?"

"She was only there ten minutes."

"What happened?"

Piper told him about Mae and Tessa and . . . "It wasn't really Mae's fault. Your mother didn't want to hear that Jews and Christians had anything in common. She was offended when Mae and Tessa mentioned they liked Moses and David."

"She probably considers them her territory now, seeing's how they're Old Testament men."

"But they're our territory too," Piper said. "Doesn't she realize that?"

Gregory twirled the spaghetti on his fork and took a bite. "You want to know the truth? I'm not sure Mother has even read the Bible. She's embraced the Jewish traditions, but not their source. Maybe your knowledge of what she *should* know shamed her." He shook his head. "Mother does not like being shamed."

Piper sat back in her chair. "We didn't mean to do that. We just got on the subject of our common ground. She took it wrong."

"A common reaction. If there's any offense to be taken she'll take it. Then she'll make you feel guilty."

Although all he said about his mother made her feel sad, Piper also felt a bit relieved. At least it wasn't her.

He put a hand on hers. "Knowing Mother, she was probably looking for a reason to leave early from the moment she left her house. Don't worry about it, sweetheart."

"But I want us to like each other. I want her to be at the wedding. I want her to be a part of our lives."

"Be careful what you wish for."

* * *

Ringo felt like a failure, like a ship without a port. He'd left his mom's house to take the roadie job with Monsoon Iggies, just sure he was coming back to the place his life belonged. As far as the work, he really liked setting up the stage and tearing it down. No problem. Even some of the company wasn't bad.

But the partying was. Bad. Very bad. Or real good depending on whether or not you wanted to get drunk or high. Maybe once, in another life, but now . . . the whole thing turned him off. All he could think about was Soonie and Ricky while he sat on a couch, nursing a beer, watching the members of the band and crew make out with groupies, the air heavy with all kinds of smoke. Soonie had said this life wasn't the life for them anymore. And she was right.

Ringo hated that she was right. And actually, it had taken him two days to push down his pride enough to want to call her to tell her so. But so far he hadn't been able to get ahold of her. He'd left a generic message on her grandparents' machine, saying he'd try later.

But this morning, he'd had an even better idea. He'd awakened early, woke his boss up, quit, and was on his way back to . . . .

His home? Carson Creek was his mother's town, not his. Not that he had anything against it. But at the moment, as he was running away from a life he'd had the courage to shove into his past, it was better than nothing. One step at a time.

He was only a half hour away. His stomach fluttered with the thought of walking into his mom's house and surprising her. Her hugs. Her making him feel welcome. Hey, maybe everyone should go away once in a while, just to have a cool homecoming.

.   .   .

Mae parked in front of Valerie's rental house and shut off the engine. The house was nice, in a blah, generic, cookie-cutter sort of way, but totally lacked the charm of Peerbaugh Place. And the trees—or one tree—out front? Mae could have wrapped one hand around its trunk. Add to that two sickly globs of impatiens by the front walk . . .

She chastised herself for being so judgmental. She wasn't here to rate the accommodations but to check on a friend who'd acted strangely. Mae could think of no reason why Valerie had driven by Piper's shower and not stopped.

She rang the doorbell and waited, and was nearly going to leave when Valerie came to the door, running a hand through her hair. "Oh. Hi, Mae."

Valerie looked awful. Gone were her eclectic vintage clothes and her perfect grooming. She was barefoot, and wore sweatpants and a T-shirt that had some Realtor's logo on it with the slogan We Sell Better Faster. Her hair was pulled into a halfhearted ponytail. She wore no makeup.

Mae tried not to stare. "How you doing, Val? We missed you at the shower."

Valerie swung the door so it covered half of her body. "Sorry. I wasn't feeling well."

Mae jumped on the explanation. "Are you sick? Can I get you anything?"

"No, no. I mean, I'm feeling better now."

You don't look better.

"When I said I was stopping by to see you, Evelyn asked me to bring over some mail that came to Peerbaugh Place."

"Thanks."

Mae realized Valerie was not going to ask her in. So she would have to do it herself. "Show me your place. Let me see that office of yours. I'm sure you have it set up just right."

Valerie was clearly flustered, but opened the door.

Mae went inside. The place was nice enough. It certainly was . . . white. White walls, white woodwork, white appliances. Light carpet. Sterile. The only splashes of dubious color were the couch, love seat, and coffee table—which were various shades of tan. "New furniture?"

"Yeah, well . . . I think I'm going to send it back."

"Why?"

Valerie pressed two fingers to her lips. Her head began to shake in short movements.

"Val?"

Her forehead tightened and her chin quivered. "I lost the contract."

Mae pulled in a breath. "How? Why?"

When she started to cry, Mae led her to the couch. Valerie pulled up short. "I can't sit there. Truly, I have to send it back. I don't have the money . . ."

Mae spotted a couple of folding chairs next to a card table in the kitchen and led her in that direction. "Let me make you some tea."

"I don't have any tea."

"Coffee then."

Valerie sank onto a chair. "No thanks." She sighed deeply. "I can't believe this happened."

"Exactly what *did* happen?"

Valerie avoided Mae's eyes. "I was a pain. I asked for too much. Acted like I was a big-time author when I was just a rookie." She looked at Mae. "I lost my agent too."

"Oh no . . ."

Valerie popped out of the chair and flailed her arms as she paced. "I left Evelyn's because it wasn't good enough for me, I spent money I didn't have, I acted like an arrogant fool, and I blew everything. I have nothing now."

Mae didn't know what to say.

Valerie stopped directly in front of her. "I want to come back to Peerbaugh Place. I *need* to come back. Will you talk to Evelyn for me? I know I didn't leave on the best of terms and left her in a lurch without another tenant, and I'll pay for the time I was gone but—"

Oh no. "Your room's filled. All the rooms are filled. In fact, they have another lady sleeping on the couch in the sunroom while her little girl's in the hospital."

Valerie expelled her air, deflated. "What am I going to do?"

"Don't give up on your writing. It must have been good for a publisher and an agent to be interested in it. You'll get hooked up again."

"But until then?"

"You get a regular job."

"Been there, done that. I wanted to make it as an author."

"And maybe you will, but for now, you gotta do what you gotta do." Mae thought of a Help Wanted sign she'd seen recently. "Ruby's is looking for a waitress."

Valerie snickered. "It's a diner."

"It'd pay the bills. You might even be able to keep the furniture."

"I've never been a waitress."

"You'll learn. I'll call Ruby first thing in the morning and put in a good word for you. How's that?"

Valerie nodded. "Thanks, Mae."

•   •   •

When Mae drove up to her house, she noticed Collier sitting on the porch with two other men. One was leaning against the railing and had his back to her, but the other one . . . no! It couldn't be!

She pulled into the driveway and burst from the car. "Ringo! Baby boy! You're back!"

Ringo met her on the steps and gave her a hug.

Collier stood up from the swing. "I'd just gotten back from errands when who shows up? The prodigal son returns, hey, Mae?" He motioned to the other man. "And then . . . you have another visitor. Says he's an old friend of yours?"

The other man stood and grinned at her.

Mae's heart stopped. She put one hand to her chest and with the other grabbed the railing to prevent herself from keeling over.

Ringo looked between them. "Mom? What's wrong?"

The man winked at her. "Hi-ya, Mae-Mae."

The words came out with difficulty. "Hi, Danny."

Ringo's jaw dropped. "Danny?"

Mae gathered her wits and finished coming up the steps, standing beside her son. "Ringo, meet your father, Danny Fitzpatrick."

•   •   •

Ringo escaped inside. Collier went after him. Mae couldn't blame them. The whole situation was the epitome of awkward. And bizarre. Danny was back?

But why? Sure Mae had prayed for Danny's return when he'd first walked out in 1974—when Ringo was a baby. But she'd soon realized she didn't really want God to say yes to that particular prayer and had let it fade away. Life was better with Danny gone. Not easier, but better. Calmer.

To have him turn up now, when she was so happy with Collier . . . there'd been nearly thirty years between husbands. Why did he show up now?

Mae realized she might not get an answer, and for now, she had to deal with it. With Danny, sitting here on the porch. Her porch. Gracious gadfly, what was she supposed to do with him?

Danny patted the space beside him on the swing. "Join me, Mae-Mae."

She sat on the rocker. "I think I'll keep my distance, if you don't mind."

Danny pulled his shirt to his nose and took a whiff. "I am kinda rank, ain't I?"

"It has nothing to do with your aroma."

He swung up and back. "I gotta tell ya that you being in the next town shocked me as much as it's shocking you. When I showed up at the shelter in Jackson and Pastor Enoch mentioned he knew another Fitzpatrick . . . then to have it be you? Hey, if that ain't good karma, I don't know what is."

"How about cruel fate?"

"Don't be mean. I'm not hurting anything."

She pointed toward the house and lowered her voice. "What about your son? You really think popping back into his life now is a good thing?"

"He was just a baby when I left."

Mae bolted from the rocker. "Exactly. You left me with two babies, Danny. Starr was three, Ringo still in diapers."

"Yeah, well . . ."

Mae tossed her hands in the air. "Oh, that explains it. Thanks for making it clear."

He opened his mouth to speak, closed it, then opened it again. "You're looking good, Mae-Mae. You've aged well."

She had to laugh. "Three decades hasn't improved your way with words." ·

"What'd I say?"

"Nothing. *You're* looking old, Danny."

"Yeah, well . . . whatever."

She sat down again, and forced her decades-old bitterness to back off. It wasn't doing anybody any good. "What have you been doing with yourself? Did you remarry? Do you have kids? other kids?"

"No and no. I wasn't the marrying kind, Mae. You know that."

"I know that."

He raised his feet off the floor and looked at them. "Sorry 'bout that. 'Bout being such a bad husband."

She opened her mouth to be sarcastic, but realized this "sorry" was more than she'd ever expected from him.

"When we were talking here on the porch . . . Ringo said he has a wife and kid?"

Mae raised an eyebrow. "They're in Korea visiting right now."

"I'm a grandpa?"

Oh dear. "Don't push it, Danny."

He nodded and looked over his shoulder at the house. "You think he'll talk to me, I mean . . . now that he knows?"

She was going to say, "Give it time" but realized she didn't want Danny around for any more time than necessary. She ended up saying, "I don't know."

He nodded, then asked, "How's Starr?"

"Doing well. She's engaged to a nice man. She's a book editor." She left out the part about where she lived.

"Wow. Books. Who'd a thought?"

It was a valid point. She'd never seen Danny even open a book.

She looked toward the door. She desperately wanted to get inside and be with Ringo. As rude as it would sound, she needed to wrap this up. "So what are you doing around here, Danny?"

"I'm going to help Pastor Enoch at the shelter. I met up with him in Boston. I came this direction 'cause a him. Just made my way. A little at a time. A job at a time. Weren't no plan to it."

Somehow the fact he hadn't sought her out made it better.

Danny shrugged. "But when I realized you were here, I . . ." He looked to the porch, then up at her again. Mae recognized a flirty look she'd seen many a time before. "I had to come see you, Mae-Mae."

She took a deep breath. "I guess I am glad to see you're well."

He nodded. "You gotta admit it's pretty funky, me finding you. Over and over in these shelters minister types keep telling me there ain't no such thing as coincidence. Guess this proves it, huh?"

It did that.

He stood. "I'll be going now."

Mae stood too. She looked to the curb. There was no car there. "How did you get here? How will you get back—?"

He smiled and held out his thumb. "Handy thing, this thumb. Don't know what I'd do without it."

Mae thought of offering to drive him, yet didn't want to be alone with him that long. But then, out of nowhere, Collier came outside. "I'll take you back," he said.

It *was* a solution.

"Cool," Danny said. "That would be awesome."

Collier caught Mae's eyes. "That okay with you, wifey?"

She nodded, her throat tight with love for him.

"Let me get my keys."

Mae turned back to Danny, unsure what to say.

He did the saying for her. "Nice to see you again, Mae-Mae. You were always my favorite wife."

Ha-ha.

Collier returned. "Ready." The two men headed down the front steps and over to the driveway. As Collier backed into the street, Danny gave Mae a little salute. "Tell Ringo g'bye for me."

She watched her first and last husbands drive away, then went inside to check on her only son.

*   *   *

Mae found Ringo in the kitchen, nursing a root beer. He looked up when she came in. "Is he gone?"

"Collie's taking him to the shelter in Jackson."

Ringo nodded.

"Did you want to talk to him?"

He shook his head vigorously. "I didn't know, Mom. I came home and was talking to Collier and this man shows up, gets dropped off here, said he was an old friend, and . . . I didn't know who he was."

"Of course you didn't."

"But shouldn't I have recognized him?"

"You were a baby when he left. And the pictures I had . . . he's changed, honey. He's been away a lifetime—your lifetime."

Ringo held the can with both hands. "For him to be my dad . . . it's too weird."

"That it is."

While he pondered this, she took a seat catty-corner from him. She'd let him ask the questions, hoping there wouldn't be many and they wouldn't be hard.

But they were. "Why did he leave?"

Because he was an immature, lazy, goofy man who had no concept of responsibility and what marriage and family were about and—

No. That would never do. It was old news and in a way had no relevance at this late date. She tried to think of an answer that would help Ringo now, as a man, as a husband and father. Suddenly, she thought of something he and his father had in common. "He left his family to find himself." *Like you just did.*

"Oh." Ringo took two breaths in and out. "Do you think he succeeded?"

"No. But there's still time. He's staying at Pastor Enoch's in Jackson. Maybe Enoch can help him find whatever 'self' there's left of him after all these years."

When Ringo met her eyes they were shiny with tears. "I hope so."

12

*E*velyn stood in the doorway to Piper's room at Peerbaugh Place and watched her pack. "I don't like this," she said. "I know you would have been moving out in a couple weeks anyway, but . . ."

"This is the right thing, Evelyn. It will give Jody a room, and Kimberly too when she gets out of the hospital. Think of it this way: it will be like having Audra and Summer back."

No it wouldn't. Why did people have to leave? Leave *her* behind.

Piper packed some books in a box. "Can I ask your advice?"

"Always."

"Gregory says not to worry about his mother and all that happened at the shower. He's more than willing to *not* have her at the wedding."

"And you?"

"I don't relish the hubbub that comes with every meeting, but I think she should be there. For Gregory's sake. And mine."

"And how do you plan to make this miracle happen?"

"I want to talk to her again. Alone. I thought I'd ask her out to dinner. Just the two of us. Try to find a middle ground."

"That sounds nice, but what if she doesn't want to find that middle?"

"Then I'll know I've done everything I could do."

"What's Gregory think about this?"

"I haven't told him yet. I wanted a second opinion first. Your opinion."

Evelyn was honored. "I think dinner is a nice idea."

"Good. I'll call her later." She closed the last box and took a fresh breath. "Okay. I'm ready. Let's load up the car. Dad's waiting on his end."

At least Evelyn would get to see Wayne.

•   •   •

Wayne went through some boxes from the bedroom closet. Though Piper had said not to make a fuss—she'd put her things down in the storage area of the apartment complex—he wanted her to feel welcome. He wanted her to have space so she didn't feel crowded.

Which is why he was giving her the bedroom. She'd object, but he'd win the argument. The pull-out sofa was fine for him. Besides, this was a way to repay *her* hospitality for moving out of the apartment way back when Wanda had first gotten sick while they were RVing. Before heading out on what was supposed to be the adventure of their retirement years, they'd sold their house, so when they'd come back to Carson Creek for medical reasons, they had no place to live. That's when Piper had first moved into Peerbaugh Place. One good turn deserved another.

It was going to be odd having Piper living with him again, but he welcomed the experience. Though she'd been on her own for fifteen years, he knew that soon she would be a married woman and his position as the man in her life would be usurped by Gregory. As it should be.

He also knew that all this was tough on Evelyn—on many levels. To see Piper leave Peerbaugh Place, and to give her room to yet another nonpaying tenant . . . Wayne was big on telling Evelyn that God would provide, but that didn't prevent him from getting a slight hitch in his gut as he wondered how and when.

He pulled down a box labeled Sentimental Clothes and another one labeled Piper—Baby. Two good contenders for the storage unit. He was curious as to what constituted Sentimental Clothes and took off the lid. Folded on top was a pink dress of Wanda's. He couldn't remember the occasion, but his mind retrieved an image that made him smile. Underneath the dress he found his navy blazer. How many business meetings and church services had it seen? If he remembered correctly, it was the first blazer he'd purchased after their marriage, bought at Miller & Paine for more money than they could afford, but next to nothing in today's dollars. He put his arm in the sleeve—which was as far as it got. He was no longer a size 40-Regular.

He skimmed the rest of the contents and moved on to the Piper—Baby box. She'd want these things someday for her own children. Grandpa Wayne. What an awesome title.

Inside this box were a few frilly dresses, a baby book neatly filled out in Wanda's lovely cursive, a well-worn stuffed bunny, a pink baby blanket. . . .

He spotted a red drawstring pouch. He emptied its contents into his hand. It was a gold locket that had initials engraved on it: ERW. *What?* Then he remembered that the locket had come with Piper's things from the adoption agency. It had been a gift from the birth mother to her daughter. Wayne felt a piece of paper still in the pouch. He pulled it out: *Give this to my darling daughter on her wedding day. Tell her I love her. ERW.* Talk about good timing . . . Piper would be so pleased.

The phone rang. "We're on our way over, Dad. You ready for us?"

"I'll meet you in the parking lot."

He slipped the locket into a dresser drawer, stacked the boxes one on the other, and took them down to the storage room.

●   ●   ●

Ursola didn't like answering the door of Peerbaugh Place, but with Evelyn and Piper moving Piper's things out, with Jody at the hospital, it was between Accosta or herself, and since Accosta was upstairs . . .

But as soon as she opened it, she wished she'd let Accosta handle it.

Daryn stood outside. "What do you know? I found you," he said.

I wasn't lost. "What you want?" Her voice sounded strong, but inside she was quaking. Did he know she'd been inside his house?

Accosta called down from the landing. "Ursola? Who is it?"

"No one."

Daryn pushed past her into the foyer. "I'm Daryn Smith, her stepson—though let me tell you, it's no honor. I'm here to collect the mugs she stole from my house."

Ursola took hold of the stairs' newel post.

Accosta carefully made her way down the stairs. Ursola moved to help her, but Accosta waved her away. "Young man, I think you should leave. You cannot come into this house and accuse anyone of stealing."

"Even if it's true?"

When she reached the bottom of the stairs, Accosta put a protective arm around Ursola's shoulders. "You need to apologize to this girl. From what I've heard, you are the one who could be accused of stealing. Taking her house away from her when she's reeling from the death of her husband? *Tsk, tsk.* Shame on you."

Daryn pointed a pudgy finger at Accosta. "I got the house fair and square. Dad left it to me, which only proves he loved me most."

Accosta shoved his finger aside and strode to the door. "Out. Now. And don't you dare bother this girl again."

Ursola was surprised when Daryn moved to leave. "If you think you can make me do anything, old woman, you're wrong."

Accosta took hold of the door and began closing it, with him in it. Daryn had no choice but to step out to the porch.

As he tripped over the threshold he said, "You haven't heard the last of me, Ursola!"

Accosta shut the door and Ursola threw the dead bolt. They froze until they heard Daryn's footsteps fade and a car pull away. Then they both let out the breath they'd been holding. They laughed nervously; then Ursola hugged Accosta. "Thank you. You very brave."

Accosta patted her back. "Fiddle-dee. I've dealt with my share of bullies. They push; I push back. Frankly, my guts and gumption surprise them and they back off."

"Always?"

"Enough."

"What if they don't?"

"Run?"

Ursola held out a hand. "Come. I show you something."

She led Accosta upstairs to her room. From a drawer she pulled out the two mugs: *His* and *Hers*.

"Oh my."

"I do it. I take."

"I see that."

Ursola held Glenn's mug to her chest. "Glenn drink . . ." Then she set it down again. "Daryn not care mugs! He sell. Garage sale. My things. Our things. Our life!"

"Not your life, Ursola. Things aren't life. Though sometimes it *is* hard to let them go."

Ursola suddenly remembered that Accosta had just sold many of her possessions at a garage sale. If anyone understood, Accosta did. She looked at the mugs. "I not want give back."

"You should. 'Thou shalt not steal.'"

"But *he* steal!"

Accosta nodded. "'Never pay back evil for evil to anyone.'"

"Anyone?"

"That's what the Bible says."

That was way too much to ask. Ursola decided it was not a good idea to tell Accosta that she still had a key to Daryn's house. Bible or no Bible, she wasn't done with him yet. Surely God would understand.

●　　●　　●

Accosta sat on the chair in her room, reading the Bible and praying for Ursola. Though it had been a long time ago, Accosta remembered how devastated she had been when her husband died. Broken, angry, sad, shocked. For Ursola to also have to deal with a devilish stepson . . . the man had no shame. Yet Accosta also saw hints that Ursola was susceptible to her own form of temptation. She was vulnerable right now. And choices were so important.

Accosta looked back to the passage she'd looked up about resisting temptation to do wrong: "If you think you are standing strong, be careful, for you, too, may fall into the same sin. But remember that the temptations that come into your life are no different from what others experience. And God is faithful. He will keep the temptation from becoming so strong that you can't stand up against it. When you are tempted, he will show you a way out so that you will not give in to it."

Good words. Important words.

Then suddenly, Accosta thought of Audra. How odd to be thinking of one sister, only to suddenly think of another. Yet it was as if Audra had just opened a door and entered the room where Accosta's thoughts were stored. *Audra's in trouble!*

She stood up so fast, the Bible slipped to the floor. She had to go to Audra's—now! She'd been waiting for an opening to talk with her alone, but that opportunity had never come. But now . . . was it too late?

Accosta moved to the door, then realized there was no one home who had a car. Evelyn and Piper were both gone. She back-tracked to the front window. Even Mae's car was gone.

I'll walk to Audra's!

But even as she headed to her closet to get her most comfy Hush Puppies, she realized that wasn't a sane thought. Carson Creek was small, but not *that* small. Audra and Russell lived many blocks away and Accosta's walking speed was like a snail on a stroll. By the time Accosta got there . . .

Call!

That she could do. Audra's number was posted next to the kitchen phone.

•   •   •

Audra stopped the sewing machine, lifted her wrist to her nose, and inhaled. She loved the spicy scent of the new cologne she'd

bought. She felt pretty in it. Sexy. When she'd gone to the drug-
store yesterday, she'd found herself sampling the fragrances, and
before she knew it, she'd had one in her basket. A total splurge for
a scent totally different from the one she usually wore. Russell
preferred florals.

She took advantage of the break in her work and reapplied
some pink-tinted lip gloss. She looked at her watch. Russell was
at work, Summer was across the street playing with Cynthia, so
Audra was alone. Simon would be by with a delivery within the
hour. If he had a delivery today. He *had* to have a delivery today.
She needed to see him.

And obviously he needed to see her too. Why else had he
been sitting in the parking lot of the restaurant yesterday? Her
stomach did a little flip at the thought. She closed her eyes and let
the memory segue into one of her fantasies.

Knock, knock, knock.

He was here! She leapt out of her chair and got the door.
"Simon!"

"Good morning to you, beautiful."

He'd never called her "beautiful" before. Suddenly, she
noticed he wasn't wearing his uniform. And he wasn't carrying
a package and a clipboard. "Aren't you working today?"

He shook his head. "Can I come in?"

"Of course."

Simon entered and closed the door behind him. That one
action flipped a switch in Audra's mind. *I've never been alone with
him in a room that had the door closed.*

He looked a bit uncomfortable and wiped his palms on his
jeans. "I took the day off."

"Why?"

"Because I needed to do something." Suddenly he took a step
toward her and pulled her into his arms. He kissed her. The shock
of it prevented her from enjoying it, though her mind was cogni-

zant enough to put together the thought: *This is your fantasy come to life! This is what you've been hoping for.*

But it wasn't. It was wrong. All wrong.

She struggled against him but he held her tight against his body.

The phone rang. She tried to push away.

He was unrelenting.

Audra squirmed in a different direction. But as she tried to turn her face to the left, she saw something that made her want to die.

Summer stood at the door, peering at them. Her jaw was dropped.

With a burst of superhuman strength, Audra managed to push Simon away. "No!"

He stumbled back. "Hey! That hurt!"

She didn't care about him.

Summer bolted. Audra ripped open the door and ran after her. "Baby!"

Summer ran toward the backyard. Audra caught her near the swing set and wrapped her arms around her. Summer resisted. "Leave me alone!"

"Summer, baby . . . it's not what you think."

Her daughter pushed her away just like she'd pushed Simon away only moments before. Audra had never seen such fire in Summer's eyes. "You were kissing him!"

"No. He was kissing me. I was trying to get away." Audra reached to wipe Summer's tears away, but the little girl parried.

"Are you and Daddy getting a divorce?"

"No, baby. No!"

"But that man . . . he's the delivery guy."

Audra was surprised Summer recognized him. To her knowledge she had only seen Simon a few fleeting times. "Yes, that's him, but—"

"I don't want to live with him!"

Audra shook her head vehemently. "That's not going to happen, baby! I promise."

"Then what was he doing here? Kissing you?"

Good question. She decided Summer could handle part of the truth. "He's interested in me. I was telling him to leave me alone." *After I led him on. After he took the bait and kissed me.* She took Summer's hand and was relieved when it wasn't pulled away. "I love your daddy very much. I will *not* do anything to jeopardize our family. I won't." *I've done enough.*

Summer stood still a few moments and Audra could see the turmoil on her face. "My friend Tammy's parents got a divorce."

"I know. It's not going to happen to us."

"You promise?"

"I promise."

Summer flew into her arms and they clung to each other.

* * *

When Audra and Summer came around the house, Simon was gone. His car was gone. And Audra prayed she would never, ever see it again. She'd even call UPS and see if she could request another driver. For his sake as well as hers.

With the amazing resilience of children, Summer went back to her play.

Leaving Audra alone.

But not alone.

She sank into her favorite chair, bowed her head, and began to pray. She had a lot of repenting to do.

Blessedly God was right there, ready to listen—and to forgive.

• • •

Accosta hung up the phone and called out to the empty kitchen, "Audra doesn't answer! I don't know what to do!"

She'd let the phone ring enough times to get Audra's answering machine. She'd done that three times, leaving a message once.

Obviously Audra wasn't home.

Or isn't picking up.

Accosta paced between phone and counter. *Father, what should I do now? I'll never forgive myself if something happens to her. I've been meaning to talk to her, I really have, but the time never seemed right. I was waiting for Your guidance. . . . Did I miss it?*

She stopped pacing and leaned against the table, dropping her head. "Father? What should I do?"

Accosta let three breaths come in and go out. With each batch of fresh air, she was filled with a feeling of calm. Peace.

Interesting. She raised her face to the ceiling. "Are You saying everything's all right now, Lord? Has the crisis passed?"

The calm settled in, deeper. Accosta looked at the phone, wondering if she should make one last attempt. She felt no compulsion to do so. But calm or no calm, she knew she'd feel better if she kept the prayers going awhile longer.

She took a seat and dug in. It never hurt to provide extra prayer cover.

• • •

After an hour figuratively—and often literally—on her knees, Audra felt cleansed. And extremely grateful. Though the consequences of her fantasies about Simon had not been fully played out, during her prayer time the consequences of what *could* have happened were presented to her with horrifying clarity. She could have lost everything. And gained nothing.

How could I have been so dumb? To risk it all for a few flirting, fleeting moments? To waste hours fantasizing about a man she barely knew? To anticipate seeing him? To get a thrill out of seeing him? To dress for him, do her hair for him, buy new cologne for him?

What bothered Audra the most was the way she'd rationalized it all: *Certainly God wanted her happy. If happiness was a right, and her life was lacking . . . if feeling special in Simon's presence made her happy . . .* Though she hadn't had an affair, she saw with sudden clarity that she was guilty of all but the final act. Her desire for something new and exciting was the lit fuse between teasing temptation and following through with it.

The way the daydreams had absorbed her time was frightening. She could almost understand what a person with a mental illness felt like—the cloudiness that stood between reality and cognizant thoughts. She'd been so enraptured, so shrouded, so deceived. The odd thing was, during it all, she'd known the truth yet hadn't been able to grasp it—and more so, didn't want to. She'd liked the way she felt in the fantasy. Special, as if anything were possible. Exciting and excited.

But why had God let her be tempted in the first place?

I do not tempt. But I allow temptation in order to teach you and help you learn to trust Me. I allow it to make you strong.

Audra nodded, knowing this was true. She clasped her hands and leaned her head against them. "Thank You for saving me, Lord! Now keep temptation far away. Help me keep my eyes on You. Let me focus on You and Russell and our wonderful life. Lead me not into temptation and deliver me from evil." She sat in silence a moment, then added, "Amen."

So close. So frighteningly close.

Though she felt better, she was left with one question: Should she tell Russell? Was that the last step in the process of repentance? Or would it do more harm than good? She needed to think on that one.

She headed to the kitchen to start dinner when she saw the light on the answering machine blinking. This must have been the caller who'd interrupted the kiss. She pushed the button for the message: "Audra, this is Accosta. I felt the most desperate nudge to call you. Are you okay? If I had a car, I'd be over there in a blink, but I don't, so . . . just know I'm thinking of you, and praying for you. Call me when you can."

Audra shivered. The knowledge that Accosta had gotten a nudge to call and had sensed Audra's trouble . . . God continued to amaze.

She dialed the phone. Accosta answered on the second ring. "Audra? Oh, I'm so glad it's you! What was going on? I felt such unrest, but then peace."

Unrest, then peace. A good description of her day. She told Accosta the entire story.

"I should have talked to you sooner," Accosta said.

"Talked to me?"

"I drove by your house last Wednesday. I saw the UPS man put his hand on your arm. I sensed then that there was something between you. I drove around the block and saw the man in his truck, all bent over the wheel, upset."

"He was upset?"

"Don't sound happy about it, missy."

Audra chastised herself. She apparently still had a ways to go to completely rid herself of all this. She leaned against the counter. "I'm so sorry about everything. I don't know what came over me."

"Sure you do. Satan was involved in this as surely as you and Simon."

Audra shivered. "I think you're overreacting."

"No, ma'am, I don't believe I am. Fantasies and daydreams aren't real. They're illusions. And the devil would like nothing better than for us to focus on them so we'll mess up our lives and fall into his trap."

She *had* felt trapped.

Accosta continued. "But that doesn't take you off the hook, missy. Your flesh was definitely guilty. Everybody has fleeting thoughts that aren't right, but when you let them continue, you risk giving Satan an in. And believe you me, he's all too willing to pounce. Once he does, the thoughts take over and take on a life of their own."

Which is exactly what had happened. "But it's hard to imagine Satan bothering with the likes of me."

"You think Satan is only involved in the actions of the Hitlers and Husseins of the world? Think again. His biggest lie is making us believe he doesn't exist in the lives of ordinary folk like you and me. Once we think we're in the clear, he's able to slip in the cracks and do his stuff."

Audra shuddered. "Oh, Accosta . . . all this talk of Satan . . . it creeps me out."

"Good. A dose of fear is healthy and keeps us on our toes. The devil prowls like a roaring lion, looking for someone to eat. We need to stand against him and be strong, and remember that others are going through the same kind of things we are. We're not alone."

"I felt alone."

"Another of his lies."

So many lies. She vowed to be more alert. She'd come too close to destruction.

"Are you going to tell Russell about it?"

Audra nearly laughed at God's provision. "I was just thinking about that before I called you. Do you think I should?"

"Absolutely. Secrets kill. 'And the truth will set you free.'"

"The book of John."

"See? You know the truth. You've come through the fog. The veil has been lifted! Alleluia!"

This time Audra did laugh. "You're wonderful, Accosta."

"I'll take the compliment, but God's the one who's wonderful. He's the one who got you through this. He's the one who saved you."

Audra hung up and gave credit where it was due.

* * *

As soon as she was off the phone, Accosta went upstairs and got out her worry box. She found the slip of paper she'd placed inside that said *Audra and Russell's marriage* and had the pleasure of tearing it in two.

Mission accomplished. Amen.

* * *

Audra heard Russell's car drive up. As her stomach did the flamenco, she sent up a flock of last-minute prayers. *Give me the right words, Father!*

He came in the front door. "Hey, hon. I'm home."

She dropped a pan.

When he came into the kitchen, she looked up at him sheepishly. "I dropped a pan."

"I see that." He moved to the stove and lifted the lid off a pot. "What's this? It smells wonderful."

"It's a peanut sauce. I have a salad and bread too."

He eyed her warily. "Sounds too special for Monday night. What's up?"

She took his hands but couldn't meet his eyes. "I have to talk to you about something."

"Sounds serious."

She nodded. "Summer's eating at the Baileys'."

"Sounds double serious."

It was, but she didn't dare say so and get him overly worried. She managed a smile and kissed his cheek. "Go change and it will be time to eat."

The right words, Father, the right words . . .

      •   •   •

Dinner was lovely—and delicious. And though Russell had asked her twice to tell him what was going on, she'd begged off until the end of the meal. After eating the French silk pie and serving coffee, it was time.

"Let's move to the living room, okay?"

He put a hand on the back of her neck and she loved him for it. They sat on the couch. Audra moved a few feet away, angling her body toward his. She pulled a pillow into her lap.

"So. Out with it."

She nodded and began. She told him everything, the words coming out in a rush and tumble like water in a mountain stream. She even told about having fantasies—though she didn't feel any compulsion to share the details. "When he showed up today and kissed me, I felt—"

"He kissed you?"

"I . . . I have to admit I wanted him to. At least in theory. But when he actually did it, then I *didn't* want him to. I tried to push him away but he was so strong, and then the phone rang and I saw Summer looking at us and—"

"You let Summer see you?"

"I didn't *let* Summer see us."

He looked away briefly. "What did she do?"

"She ran. And I ran after her to the backyard. I caught up with her and explained. She's okay. But it was horrible. When we came back around, Simon was gone."

Russell stood. "He'd better be gone! He'd better think twice about ever showing his face in our lives again."

"We're bound to run into him. He lives here, works here."

He began to pace. "I'll get a restraining order if I have to."

He was overreacting. "I'm sure that won't be necessary."

"You don't know. He had no qualms about going after a married woman. What he wants, he takes."

What he tried to take, I offered . . . Audra appreciated his anger—mostly because it deflected the fault from her own shoulders. And yet it didn't seem right. She held out her hand and pulled him down to the cushion beside her. "It's not all his fault, Russell. I'm to blame too. I led him on. I tempted him. And I was tempted."

He extracted his hand from hers, his head shaking. "This whole thing is like a bad dream. Aren't I enough for you?"

The comment surprised her. "Of course you are. I'm very happy with you, with our—"

He stood again and looked down at her. "You obviously aren't happy with me or you wouldn't have had those thoughts, and kissed that kiss." His hands waved wildly. "Who knows where it would have gone."

Suddenly any quick-fix response seemed inadequate. *Who knows, indeed?* Though the rational part of Audra's character could promise from today until Christmas that nothing more would have happened other than the kiss, the shadowed, secret side that had revealed itself during this entire ordeal poked at her easy answer with whispers of *Wanna bet?* A blanket statement like *It wouldn't have gone anywhere* expressed way too much confidence in her own strength. Right now, she didn't feel strong enough to walk across the room.

Audra put her head in her hands and sobbed. "I'm so sorry, so so sorry."

She'd hoped to immediately feel Russell's arms around her,

to hear his gentle, "Shhhh. It will be all right." And he *did* come through with both modes of comfort—eventually. But the few moments of delay between tears and redemption expressed the seriousness of her folly more than any lengthy discourse. The whole situation was out in the open now—which was good. But it was far from invisible, or even handily hidden in a corner. It *was*. Right there between them. And probably would *be* for quite a while.

With her husband's arms holding her close, with his head melded to hers, her tears did dry. But the consequence of her actions was a lingering unease and distance, no matter how close his body was to hers.

Then suddenly, everything changed. Russell sat up, took her hands, and found her eyes. "To be honest with you . . . I've been tempted too, Audra."

She was shocked at the immediacy of her anger. And fear. What was he going to confess? She found a fresh breath. "You have?"

He looked at his hands. "Remember that banking conference I went to last spring?"

"Chicago."

"Chicago. There was a woman there who was very attentive. She asked me to dinner. Just the two of us."

Audra felt a bit queasy. "Did you go?"

"No. But I wanted to."

Though Audra didn't want to feel it, a surge of jealousy coursed through her. "Was she pretty?"

"Very." He turned her hand over in his. "I . . . I came way too close to . . ." He shrugged.

Though his confession vindicated her own actions, the satisfaction was tainted with a horrible ache. *So this is how Russell felt when he found out about Simon.*

Russell traced a finger along the back of her hand, watching its progress as if he were Rembrandt perfecting a paint stroke. "I didn't tell you because nothing happened, but . . ."

"But?"

He stopped his tracing. "We need to face something, Audra. There are a lot of pretty and handsome people out there. Nice people too. Interesting people. Unless we're hermits, we're going to see them, talk to them, even work with them. And we *will* be tempted. But that doesn't mean we have to act on it." He looked toward the window. "After not going to dinner with the woman, I went back to my room and prayed—just like you did this afternoon."

Finally. Something positive they had in common. Audra grabbed on to it like a lifeline that would lead them back to their marriage. She pulled his hand to her lips and kissed it. "You're a strong man. An honorable man."

"Don't give me more credit than I'm due. Want to hear a verse I memorized for such times?"

"Of course."

He cleared his throat. "'Keep alert and pray. Otherwise temptation will overpower you. For though the spirit is willing enough, the body is weak!'"

"The Bible has an answer for every situation, doesn't it?"

"Thank God."

They snuggled on the couch. Audra felt closer to Russell than she had *before* her fall. She vowed to never hold anything between them again. One prayer kept flowing through her mind—a prayer that would solve everything: *Lord, please help me fall madly in love with my husband again.*

With God's help, love *would* conquer all.

*   *   *

Ursola couldn't sleep. With the darkness of night came a darkness of thoughts. Hate reigned. Ever since Daryn had sold most of her things in a garage sale, ever since he had come to Peerbaugh Place whining over two mugs that had no meaning to him, her hate had grown like a strangling vine, wrapping around the image of her stepson, encircling him, holding him captive, tightening, strangling. . . .

He deserved all of it. He was a mean man. Nothing like his father. If Glenn knew how Daryn was treating her, he would have . . . he would have . . .

Done nothing. Or next to nothing.

Her darling Glenn had been nice to a fault. Polite. Sweet. They'd never even had an argument. At his funeral the friend giving the eulogy had said that Glenn had "a servant's heart." It was completely true. Ursola had only to ask for something to have Glenn make it real. Once, while taking a walk around the square, she'd commented that a scarf in the dress shop was pretty. The next day it had been on her dresser. She supposed if she were another sort of woman, she could have taken advantage of him, but instead of making her greedy, her dear husband's generosity only made her humble.

Then be like Glenn now. Be kind. Be sweet. Be—

Thoughts of Daryn invaded such sentiments like a nasty soldier bursting through a door with evil on his mind. Her body tensed. Her heart pounded, and she found herself gripping the pillow as if it were Daryn's neck.

She sat upright, trying to shake it off. But the anger seized her, a constricting garment making it hard to breathe. *He's evil. He doesn't deserve anything he has. He doesn't deserve our house, our things, our life. He doesn't deserve to live; he—*

Ursola put a hand to her chest. How easy her life would be if Daryn weren't around. If he were gone, wiped off the face of the earth.

Burn the house. Let it be a funeral pyre to a man who doesn't respect anything beyond his own selfishness. Put an end to this evil man! Only

*then can your life be free. Only then can you honor your husband and
the life you built together.*

A warm satisfaction rushed over her. The idea was perfect:
a fire to purify, to purge the world of this evil.

Ursola smiled, returned to the confines of the covers, and
found the sleep of someone who'd determined her true purpose.

13

*Never seek revenge or bear a grudge
against anyone,
but love your neighbor as yourself.
I am the Lord.*

LEVITICUS 19:18

$\mathscr{T}$he day of Ursola's revenge passed slowly. Though there were the usual goings-on at Peerbaugh Place, Ursola wanted no part of them. She couldn't let herself dip into normal. She had to concentrate on her mission. To do so she pretended she wasn't feeling well and stayed in her room all day. Accosta even brought her chicken noodle soup. "If you need anything else, Ursola, you call me. I'll say a prayer you feel better."

You do that. And I will *feel a lot better when I have avenged Glenn's death.* For it had come to that. It wasn't about losing the house, the garage sale, or even Daryn butting into any immigration issue she might have. It was about Glenn and his death that had come far too soon. It was about Daryn causing the last few years of his father's life to be stressful. It was about being a widow and being due *something.* If Daryn wouldn't accept her, at least he would respect her courage. Like the poet Dylan Thomas said, "Do not go gentle into that good night." And she would not.

Finally night fell. It was time. When Evelyn, Accosta, and Jody were in their rooms, Ursola put on dark clothes and soft shoes. She slipped out of her room and out the back door, carrying with her only a lighter she'd found in a drawer by the fireplace in the parlor. She felt like a member of the Resistance or the black market. Her adrenaline flowed.

She wanted to run through backyards, but was afraid of security systems, electric-eye lighting, and barking dogs. Better to run on the sidewalks like a late-evening jogger. With each stride a mantra repeated itself in her head: *Get him, avenge Glenn. Get him, avenge Glenn. . . .*

Soon the world would seem right again and Glenn could rest in peace.

And she would be free.

•   •   •

Tomorrow was garbage day. Two cans stood at the curb in front of Ursola's old house, along with items left over from the garage sale. Ursola recognized a basket she used to keep napkins in, a flower arrangement that used to sit on the TV, and a pile of paperback books. Glenn had loved to read. A vivid image came to mind of Glenn beside her in bed, his half-glasses perched on his nose, reading before he went to sleep. She loved watching his eyes move. And every once in a while he'd catch her looking and wink at her, or rub her back as he read. A lovely moment, forever gone. But tonight . . .

Avenged.

How appropriate that the last vestiges of her life were being discarded on this fateful night. And how symbolic if she could use some of them to ignite her revenge. Ursola grabbed a stack of paperbacks. Perfect fuel for her fire.

She snuck into the bushes in front of the living-room window. Decorative bark was the ground cover in the plantings—that were wilting for lack of watering and care. Dry wood that would burn and catch the siding of the house . . .

Ursola tore the pages from the books, spread them on the ground, and piled the wood chips on top. She set one bunch under a juniper shrub. Surely it would catch fire too, helping her vengeance spread.

Suddenly, the lights in the living room went on. Ursola ducked lower and froze. She heard the sound of the television. She moved to the corner of the window and peered in. The sheers veiled the view but did not cover it. Daryn and Shanna sat next to each other on the couch, his arm strung behind her. They snuggled. They watched TV. They laughed.

Just like we used to do.

But would never do again.

Anger seized her. It was time to burn the image from her mind. She got out the lighter and held it near the pages. *Flick! Flick! Flick!*

Nothing!

Work! Light! You have to work!

She flicked it some more and ignited one spark. But by the time she saw it and moved it closer to the paper, it was gone. "No!"

Realizing she'd spoken aloud, she glanced up into the window. Daryn stared back at her.

"What the—? Ursola!" She saw, more than heard, the words.

She got up to run, but tripped over the shrubbery. The front light came on. Daryn rushed onto the front stoop and before she could stand, he dragged her to her feet. "What are you doing out here?"

"Let go!"

"I will not let go until you tell me what you're doing skulking around in the bushes, peeping in our windows."

Shanna appeared on the stoop. She pointed to the bushes. "There's torn up books down there."

Keeping hold of her, Daryn stepped over to look. "What's all that?"

Then he saw the lighter in her hand and before she could put it away, he grabbed it. "You were going to set fire to our house?"

Ursola struggled against his grip.

His fingers dug into her upper arm. He said to Shanna, "Call the police."

"Daryn, I don't think that's necess—"

"Call!"

She disappeared inside.

Ursola realized the trouble she was in. They'd arrest her. They'd put her in jail. She wasn't a citizen. They'd kick her out of the country!

A frenzy took over. She fought him, flailing, kicking, thrashing, biting . . .

He adjusted his hold, grabbing her from behind, locking his hefty arms around her torso. She was caged. She couldn't be caged. She had to get free!

Ursola screamed as she'd never screamed before.

"Stop that!" he said. He held her even tighter.

The porch light across the street came on and a neighbor man came out, then his wife. The man called, "What's going on over there?"

Ursola wished she'd paid more attention to names when Glenn had introduced her to their neighbors. But she didn't wait for Daryn to answer. "I Ursola! Glenn's wife."

The couple came across the street, and a few moments later, were joined by neighbors on either side. An audience! She had an audience for her grievances.

Heartened, with a burst of strength she freed herself from him. She stumbled toward the husband, nearly falling into his arms. "Help me!"

The man handed her over to his wife. Other neighbor ladies

comforted her. The husband stepped forward. "You're Glenn's son, right?"

"Absolutely. Which means I have all the rights here and you should leave—"

"But she's his wife. Or was his wife."

Shanna came onto the stoop again. "They're coming," she told Daryn.

Daryn nodded, then turned to the neighbors. "That woman," he pointed at Ursola, "tried to set our house on fire." He climbed into the plantings and yanked out a wad of paper and books. "See?" He held up the lighter.

Ursola felt their eyes. "Is it true?" the neighbor asked her.

She couldn't lie. The evidence was damning. Her scheme suddenly seemed so false, so odd, so beyond real. "I . . . he took everything! House, things." She stood away from the wives, gaining confidence from the sympathetic look in her neighbors' eyes. "He sell. My things. Glenn's things. I have nothing!"

"He said you moved away. He said you gave him the house," the husband said.

"He take!" She spit the word.

Daryn stepped forward. "Hold everything. I didn't take anything that wasn't given to me—by my father, all legal, fair and square—in his will."

The wife put a hand on her shoulders. "Glenn didn't leave you anything?"

"*Nyet.*"

"That doesn't make sense," said another neighbor. "Glenn adored you."

Someone else added, "He must've forgotten to change the will. That's all. It was just a mistake." He looked around the circle of friends. "We all do that. Put off stuff like wills."

There were many nods. The first neighbor took over again and spoke to Daryn. "You said you got everything fair and square, but if you were fair, you would have considered your father's intentions rather than the lack of a little paperwork. You know he never would have wanted her out on the streets without anything."

"So now I'm supposed to be a mind reader?" Daryn asked.

The neighbor rolled her eyes. "You're supposed to be a kind stepson. You're supposed to be compassionate to your stepmother. She's a widow now. She needs whatever help you can give her."

Daryn snickered. Then he smiled and pointed down the street at the police car coming their way. "Here's the help I can give her. She's wacko. Let the authorities handle her."

The police parked behind the group of neighbors and an officer got out. "What's going on here?"

Daryn pointed a finger at Ursola. "I want her arrested. She tried to burn down my house."

Everyone started talking at once. The policeman motioned for Ursola to come away from the others. His name tag said Dickerson. "Is this true?"

"*Da.* Yes."

His raised eyebrows indicated he didn't expect that answer. "What relation are you to this man?"

"I stepmother."

Officer Dickerson looked from the petite, white Ursola to the beefy black Daryn, then back again. Then his confusion faded. "You Glenn Smith's widow?"

Ursola had never felt such relief. "Yes!"

"You're from Russia, right?"

"Yes, I—"

Daryn took a few steps closer. "She's illegal. She doesn't even have a green card. She needs to go back where she came from."

Dickerson turned back to her. "Is this true?"

Fear took hold of her. "Yes. No. I . . . no green card but . . ."

How could she explain what she didn't understand? Then she

pounced on the one bit of information that might help. "Tessa Klein. She help me. Visa."

"I know Tessa. If she's working on it, I'm sure—"

Daryn tossed his hands in the air. "So that's it? Because some old lady's name is mentioned, you're letting it slide?"

The neighbor spoke up. "You could help her with all that immigration stuff, you know. Instead of hassling her."

"Hey, bud. It's not my job."

"So what is your job? Being a jerk?"

Daryn rushed at him and Officer Dickerson had to get between them. "Back!" he yelled. They both backed off. "Everybody needs to calm down so we can get this settled."

"There's no 'settled' to it," Daryn said, reclaiming his place near the front stoop. "She was committing arson. I want her arrested."

Ursola heard the neighbor say "jerk" under his breath.

Officer Dickerson shook his head, put his hands on his hips, and looked at the ground a minute. When he raised his chin and sighed, she knew she wasn't going to like what he had to say. "I'm sorry, Mrs. Smith, but I *do* need to take you in. Since he's pressing charges—"

"You bet I am!"

Dickerson flashed Daryn a look. His voice softened. "You need to come with me. Okay?"

Arrested. Held by police. Would they hurt her? Would they ever let her go?

Her life was over.

●   ●   ●

"I'll be right there!"

Tessa hung up the phone and grabbed her keys. The past minute seemed like a dream. Ursola arrested? For attempted arson? It didn't make sense.

She drove to the police station. She tried to pray but without more information, didn't even know what to pray for. A general, *Father, make it right!* seemed appropriate.

At the police station she spotted Ursola sitting in a glassed-in office with Len Dickerson. She'd been his Sunday school teacher when he was waist high. He'd married a nice girl. Tessa played bridge with his wife's mother. At least Ursola was in the hands of a good man.

Len rose to greet her. "In here, Mrs. Klein."

Ursola fell into her arms. "Tessa!"

"Sshh. I'm glad you called." She looked at Len. "Fill me in, please."

Len told her the incredible story and Ursola confirmed it. Len ended with, "Daryn's in the other office, waiting to give his statement so charges can be filed. He's pretty adamant."

This was totally ridiculous. "Oh, he is, is he?"

Len's eyes gained a twinkle. "Mrs. Klein, what are you—?"

Tessa stood. "I wish to speak with him. If that's all right with you."

Len smiled. "I don't see how it could hurt and if it will expedite matters . . . come right this way."

Tessa hooked her purse on her arm and strode after Officer Dickerson to another office where Daryn sat in front of an empty desk, his back to the door. Without turning around, Daryn said, "Can we get on with this? I don't want to spend my entire evening—"

Tessa moved into his sight line. "Hello, Daryn."

Daryn glanced at Len in the doorway. "What's she doing here?"

"She's a friend of the family, isn't she?"

"Not my family."

"You're not your father's son?"

"Sure, but—"

Tessa noticed the only other chair was the one behind the desk. She looked to Len for permission. "May I?"

"Have at it." He left, closing the door.

"Hey! Why's he leaving? I've been waiting a half hour to give my statement. I don't want to talk to you. You've got nothing to do with any of this."

"There's where you're wrong, Daryn Smith. Your father was an elder at our church. I am an elder."

He snickered. "You got that right."

Tessa slapped a hand on the desk. "You show some respect, young man!"

Daryn sat back in his chair. "What do you want?"

"I want you to ignore Ursola's little detour into the irrational and drop any thought of pressing charges."

He laughed. "And why exactly would I do that?"

"Because you've already done her wrong in more ways than I care to name. You have dishonored your father's memory by not taking care of his widow."

"She's nothing more than a mail-order bride."

"She may have started out that way, but Ursola and your father grew to truly love each other. Besides, that's none of your concern. How can we measure another person's love?" She leveled him with a look. "We can only measure our own. And yours, dear boy, is lacking."

"You're as wacko as she is."

Since he already felt that way . . . "I also want you to give Ursola the house back."

His jaw dropped.

"It would be a nice gesture."

Daryn nearly came out of his chair. "Gesture? You'd make us homeless to give her a place to live?"

Tessa shrugged. "Actually, I don't think she wants it." He seemed to relax. "So the next best thing is letting her tour through the house and take whatever means something to her—whatever you haven't sold, that is."

"I'm just supposed to let her take—"

"*And*, I want you to give her some of the money that's due her. Perhaps half the equity in the house? I think that would be fair."

He laughed. "Anything else?"

Tessa thought a moment. "I want you to lay off whatever scheme you had to complicate her position with immigration. Since you took her physical home, I will not have you taking her country too." She leaned toward him. "Leave her alone, Daryn. Respect her as a fellow human being, if not as your stepmother. Let the world see that you are indeed your father's son."

She stood and waited for his answer, feeling very much like Moses standing before Pharaoh and his hardened heart.

He kept shaking his head, glancing at her, looking around the room, opening his mouth, then closing it.

Come on, Father. Help him give in.

Finally he gripped the arms of the chair and stood. "Fine, fine. I'm done with it. I'm going home." He yanked the door open and went out in the hall.

"When can Ursola expect a check?"

Daryn looked down at her. "You are one gutsy lady, Tessa Klein."

"Thank you."

"Is next Monday satisfactory?"

"That will do quite nicely."

He left, shaking his head the whole way.

Victory is mine, saith the Lord!

· · ·

Tessa finished up the phone conversation. "Yes, she's fine, Evelyn, but she's going to be spending the night at my house. I'll bring her by in the morning."

Ursola sat on the couch and waited for Tessa to be through. It was wonderful to be in her care. She felt safe—but exhausted.

A few moments later, Tessa hung up and sat beside her, putting a hand on her knee. "I now declare the drama over. Care to tell me what it was all about?"

There *was* no explanation. No logical one anyway. "I mad at Daryn."

"So you chose to set his house on fire?"

Ursola folded the tissue in her lap. "Make no sense." And yet . . . "But it do make sense. Seem right." She had to try to explain it, for her own sake if not for Tessa's. She clutched a hand at her midsection. "I get work up inside."

"Worked up?"

"Yes." She flexed her fingers, trying to show the feeling of tension and unease that had held her captive. "I *so* mad. Want to hurt him."

"For taking the house?"

She hesitated, but nodded.

"Hmm." Tessa stood and walked to the other side of the coffee table, then faced her. "From a human point of view, your anger at Daryn is justified. But I don't think that's the total driving force at work here. You're also angry at the circumstances. The dearest person in all the world has been taken from you. It's natural to be angry. But you need to let God handle your anger."

"I can't."

"Why not?"

She couldn't say it. She could never admit such a thing.

"Ursola?"

"I . . . I mad . . . I mad at God."

Tessa flipped a hand. "You think He can't handle your anger? He's heard a lot worse. So let it out. Let Him handle it so you can move on and grieve."

Ursola shook her head vehemently. "I don't want grieve!"

"Why not?"

Enormous sobs took root in her chest. She had no choice but to let them out. "It hurt! Too much it hurt!"

Tessa sat and took Ursola in her arms. "Of course it hurts, honey. Losing someone you love is like having your heart scraped raw."

Ursola nodded against her shoulder. *Yes, yes! That was it.* "Why God take Glenn?"

"I don't know."

"Why He do that to me?"

"I don't know, honey. I don't know."

"I hate Him!"

"Go ahead. Hate and be mad. It won't change how God feels about you. He loves you and will continue loving you, right through this entire season."

"I don't feel love."

"You will. That's what grieving will do. Once you're there . . . it's only a matter of time. So go ahead and cry. I'm not going anywhere and neither is He."

Ursola wanted to stop crying, but suffered through a new bout of tears. Tessa would think she was a baby . . .

But Tessa didn't let go. "You know what, honey? Life's full of crises. They can make us bitter or better; it's our choice. But keep this in mind: God knows us from the beginning of our lives to the end. He knows the good and the bad. And He always takes what seems to be a tragedy and turns it into triumph—if we let Him. God's not punishing you by taking Glenn. He has left you here because He has more for you to do. Jesus came for Glenn when everything in heaven was ready for *him*. Glenn took his last breath here on earth, and his next breath in heaven." Tessa let go of Ursola, took a deep breath, and pounded her chest, as if she were warming up for calisthenics. "Think of it. Your lovely husband is breathing celestial air. He is very much alive. He is in the presence of God and has seen Jesus face-to-face. Can you imagine?"

Ursola tried to. She really tried to.

But Tessa wasn't through. "Remember when Jesus was talking to His disciples about the fact that He was going to leave them?" She got up and retrieved her Bible, returning to her seat. She flipped the pages. "Look at what He said about His death. Read it aloud."

Ursola began where Tessa pointed, "'If you really love Me, you will be very happy for Me, because now I can go to the Father, who is greater than I am.'" This was an entirely new way to look at things. "He . . . Glenn like it there?"

"I guarantee it. Dying and the idea of heaven seem scary to us because they are unknown. But God's promised us—not just told us, but promised us—that heaven's better." Tessa closed her eyes and recited from memory: "'He will remove all of their sorrows, and there will be no more death or sorrow or crying or pain. For the old world and its evils are gone forever.'" She opened her eyes.

Ursola suddenly felt bad for thinking only of herself.

Tessa stood and held out her hand. "Come with me; there's something I want you to see." Tessa led her back to her bedroom and stood before a picture that showcased lovely calligraphy. "This was such a comfort to me when I lost my husband. A friend made it for me. It's the refrain of a song, 'Finally Home' by Don Wyrtzen." She read the lyrics aloud, pointing at the words with a finger:

> "Can you imagine stepping on shore and finding it heaven?
> Can you imagine touching a hand and finding it God's?
> Can you imagine breathing new air and finding it celestial?
> Can you imagine waking in glory and finding it home?"

Home. Glenn was home.

Ursola's throat was tight. "I . . . I miss him."

Tessa pulled her close.

He reveals deep and mysterious things
and knows what lies hidden in darkness,
though He Himself is surrounded by light.

DANIEL 2:22

*M*ae put on her best mother smile. "Bye, Ringo. Have a good
day at work."

Ringo grunted and left.

Collier looked up from his paper. "Great conversationalist,
that boy of yours."

Mae held her mug of cinnamon-apple tea under her nose,
drinking in the spices.

Collier flipped pages. "Be happy he got his job back."

"A job he hates."

"Nobody works at their dream job all the time—some never.
A little sweat to earn a check isn't a bad thing. Besides, in the
mood he's in, physical labor seems like a great idea. Better pound-
ing nails with a little extra flourish than slamming doors around
here."

Ringo had always been a door slammer. "He's one confused
kid. The job thing, Soonie and Ricky still being gone . . ."

"His wayward father popping in out of nowhere."

Oh yeah. "I don't know what to do about that," Mae said:
"Lucinda called and said Danny's working at Haven's Rest now."

"At least he's in Jackson, not here."

It was still too close.

"Do you think Ringo wants to see him? get to know him?" Collier asked.

"I don't know."

"Do *you* want Ringo to see him and know him?"

A harder question with the same answer. "I don't know."

"Guess it's best to let God do the arranging on this one."

Mae was glad to oblige.

●   ●   ●

No more calling out for Russell to "Have a nice day" from the other room. Not anymore. Since Audra had asked God to help her fall madly in love with her husband she'd decided it was best to act as if it was a done deal. *If you have faith, have faith.* Hence, since her confession about Simon three days previous, she'd made sure Russell didn't leave for work without a proper hug and kiss.

Russell responded in kind. Not bad.

But this morning, she had something besides a kiss and kind words to make his day start off right. The idea had snuck into her consciousness the day before while watching Summer play house. Summer had placed a doll in her doll high chair, a stuffed monkey in the doll bed, and was cradling a white bunny with a pink ribbon around its neck, feeding it a bottle. "That's quite a diverse family you have there," Audra had said in passing.

Summer looked confused at the new word, but answered as if she'd made up her own definition. She pointed to the high chair. "I got Amanda from Grandma Evelyn, Sally kitty from Grandma Taylor, and Piper gave me Bunny when I was sick. They're all mine. I love them."

Three children from three different sources. *They're all mine. I love them.* Audra had thought about those six words ever since.

Prayed about those six words. Until this morning when she'd awakened with a decision front and center on her mind.

Russell got up from the kitchen table and put on his suit coat. "I might be a little late tonight. We have a meeting at four and it will probably run over."

Audra approached him for her good-bye hug and kiss. But when she was finished, she kept her arms around his neck. "I have something to tell you."

She regretted the flash of fear in his eyes. *I caused that.* She hastened to add, "A good thing."

His face relaxed. "What is it?"

She whispered in his ear. "I want to adopt a baby." She pulled back and watched his eyes scan hers for the truth.

When he was satisfied he pulled her close. "This is wonderful! What changed your mind?"

A doll, a kitty, and a bunny. She chose a more encompassing reply. "Love."

Good answer.

*　　*　　*

"Thanks for the help, Mr. Sandall. I'll be looking for those immigration forms. Ursola and I will be in next week."

Tessa got off the phone with the man who had been helping her work through Ursola's immigration problems. Nix "problems." Everything would be fine as long as Ursola let the agency know of her widowed status immediately. Tessa would make sure she did. Another crisis handled, praise the Lord.

Tessa looked at her watch. It was eleven and she needed Ursola to get up. In her small garage apartment there wasn't any place to go but the bedroom and the living room—where Ursola was sleeping on the couch. Tessa had already slipped out of her room at six-thirty to grab a banana for breakfast, then gone back, where she'd done a double dose of Bible study, read a chapter in her book on Catherine the Great, and taken care of the immigration problem. She'd been the polite hostess, but now her patience was as thin and tearable as a layer of phyllo dough.

She hated when her impatience interfered with her compassion. The poor girl. Being on the verge of burning down her stepson's house? Being arrested? No wonder she was sleeping hard. Ursola was distraught and vulnerable. Satan had had a field day. But no more. Now under Tessa's protective wing, and under the prayer cover of Tessa's prayers, Satan didn't have a chance. She'd memorized a new verse this morning that she would repeat as often as necessary until Ursola was free of his evil influences: *"Get away from me, Satan! You are a dangerous trap to me. You are seeing things merely from a human point of view, and not from God's."* Satan wasn't going to have another go at Ursola Shivikova Smith. Not while Tessa Klein was around.

That was yesterday. Today was a fresh day—that Tessa wanted to start. She went into the kitchenette and started making coffee. She made no attempt at being quiet, allowing the measuring spoon an extra *ching* by dropping it on the counter, and letting the cupboard door bump shut of its own volition.

Then she heard footsteps outside. Who was coming to visit? Looking out, she saw it was the postman. He never came back to her garage apartment. Tessa's mail just went into her family's box. She hurried to the door to intercept him. If he knocked on the door, he'd wake—

Exactly. She waited for him to do the dirty work for her. *Knock, knock, knock.*

Ursola stirred and Tessa answered the door. "Morning, Kyle."

"Morning, Mrs. Klein. I have some mail for you and wondered if you wanted it brought back here."

This was odd. "You can just put it in my daughter's mail box like you always—"

"You don't understand. It's a huge box."

"Oh? Well . . . bring it back then." She turned to Ursola who was sitting up on the couch. "Sorry to wake you, but we have a visitor."

Ursola nodded and escaped into the bathroom.

A minute later Kyle appeared with the box on a two-wheel cart. "It's that heavy?" she asked.

"It weighs a ton and came all the way from Italy."

She remembered all the Sister Circle letters Rini had told her to expect. She let Kyle bring the box inside and checked the return address. Yes, indeed, it was from Rini.

"Is someone sending you a gift?"

Tessa laughed. "Oh yes. It's a gift all right."

As she shut the door on Kyle, Ursola came out of the bathroom. "I sleep late. I sorry."

"No problem."

Ursola started folding the sheets on the couch. Tessa helped. When they were finished, Ursola pointed to the box. "What that?"

"Letters from women all over the world."

"Letters to you?"

Tessa got a knife from the kitchen and cut through the tape holding the box shut. "Not directly. To an organization I have called the Sister Circle Network." When she pulled back the flaps she was assailed with hundreds of letters. "Lord, have mercy."

"There are many."

Too many? "I had no idea . . ."

"You . . ." Ursola made a writing motion.

"Write back? Yes, I suppose that's what I have to do." She was suddenly overwhelmed.

"I help?"

Tessa let out the breath she'd been saving. Now *that* was a wonderful idea.

· · ·

Ursola was a good organizer. Within an hour they had all 523 letters divided according to country of origin. There were eighteen countries represented, from Nigeria to Belgium, Kuwait to Cyprus. It was overwhelming and humbling. Ursola seemed very interested in the whole Sister Circle idea.

Tessa stood back and looked at the piles spread across her living room. "I'm not sure what to do next. All these women, contacting us, needing us."

"What do they want?" Ursola asked.

"It's time we find out." Tessa sat at the letter-covered table and chose an envelope from North Wales. She opened it and read aloud:

> "Dear Sister Circle Network,
>
> I heard about your group from a cousin who lives in France, who saw your Web site. Women bonding with women as sisters in Christ. What a lovely idea! We were inspired to start our own Sister Circle groups with women around our neighborhoods. We are all so busy we don't get out and see other ladies as much as we'd like, so the Sister Circle is a good way to make an effort. Besides, one lady is going through a hard time with her husband, so she really needed to be around the rest of us. I think we helped her. Next week we're planning an outing to Liverpool, just us girls. It should be ever so nice. If there is anything we can do to help the Network, let us know."

"Nice," Ursola said.

"She enclosed a snapshot." Tessa showed it to Ursola and they studied it together. The women in the photo spanned a wide range of ages, from thirty-something to gray-haired. They were all smiling, with their arms around each other. Tessa's throat tightened. "They're so sisterly. This is just what I hoped would happen, but to really see it come about . . ."

"You write back now?"

"I should." She picked up another letter from Assisi, Italy. "But I don't speak these languages. How can I ever—?"

Ursola's eyes brightened. "I have friends in class. ESL class."

"What's ESL?"

"English as a Second Language. I learn English there. I meet people from world." She put a hand on a pile. "They help. They read."

Tessa spread her arms and raised her face to heaven. "Praise You, Lord Jesus for answering my prayers before I even asked!" She hugged Ursola. "It's no coincidence you being here, staying here. None at all."

"Coincidence?"

"It's not chance. Not luck. You are God sent, honey. You are just what I needed."

The girl seemed to stand a little straighter. She picked up the pile of letters from Russia.

It began.

• • •

Evelyn sat at the desk, paying bills. It was a bit harder this month. With Piper gone she had a house full of nonpaying tenants. If it were not so frightening, she'd laugh. *Father, I assume You know what You're doing but I wouldn't mind a little insight here.*

The phone rang, making her laugh. *Hello, Evelyn? This is God. Regarding that insight you asked for . . .*

She hurried into the kitchen to answer it. "Morning, Wayne. How went your second night of sleeping on the couch?"

"I will admit—only to you—that my back is having a problem adjusting, but I'll be fine. I like having Piper here. Changing the subject, did you know Piper's going to have dinner with Gregory's mother tomorrow night? Alone?"

"I did. Is she nervous about it?"

"Very. She and I have prayed about it together every night this week."

"Then it should go fine."

"She's a brave girl, that daughter of mine. I'm not sure I'd want to tackle a blunt and bitter mother-in-law."

"The bravest."

"How's the new boarder working out?" he asked.

"Jody's rarely here."

"How's her little girl?"

"Gregory's going to do the surgery." Though she didn't mind the small talk, she sensed it wasn't the real reason he'd called.

"That's a good thing, yes?"

"Yes. But frightening for such a little one."

Wayne hesitated a moment, then said. "I can't think of a good segue from surgery to the reason I called, so I'll just get on with it. I need you to come over to Accosta's today. At noon."

Evelyn glanced at the clock. It was already eleven-fifteen. "Is there a problem?"

"No. But I need you there."

She longed to return to the small talk. "Wayne, if there's something wrong, I wish—"

"Just be there."

●　　●　　●

Evelyn approached the steps of Accosta's home warily. What did Wayne want to see her about? Had he discovered some other costly problem? She wasn't sure she could handle any more financial strain.

When she reached the porch, she noticed the door was ajar. She pushed it open. "Wayne?"

She spotted a flowered tablecloth spread out on the living-room floor, the furniture that was to be auctioned off still pushed toward the center of the room. On the tablecloth were candles. And—

"Surprise!"

Wayne popped out of the kitchen, arms wide.

"What's all this?"

"It's a picnic to celebrate the completion of our project."

"It's done?"

"One hundred percent. Ready to sell." He hugged her, held her, and whispered in her ear. "We did it, Evelyn."

She closed her eyes and drank in his words, his smell, the feel of his shirt against her cheek, and the strength and safety of his arms. This was perfect. They didn't need a picnic. She was content to stay right here. *Don't move . . .*

But Wayne had other plans. "Come on. I want to give you the grand tour." He took her hand and pulled her through the house. Newly finished wood floors, fresh paint, new plumbing fixtures and appliances. Auction off the furniture and it was indeed ready for occupancy.

They ended up back in the living room where Wayne knelt at a picnic basket full of sandwiches, potato salad, carrot cake, and sparkling grape juice. He talked constantly as he arranged the food on the tablecloth, his words a steady thread that seemed to weave their lives together. She loved hearing his enthusiasm and basked in his—their—achievement.

"And the pièce de résistance? We have two parties interested in buying."

Evelyn stopped a bite of salad halfway to her mouth. "That's marvelous! Just like that?"

He laughed. "It's been weeks of hard work, Evelyn."

"I know; I just meant—"

"I know what you meant. And yet . . ." His eyes moved to the front window and she could tell she'd lost him.

"What?"

He let out an extravagant sigh. "I should be happy."

"Seems to me you *are* happy."

"Oh, I am. About being done. But these people who are interested . . . one wants to subdivide the place into apartments."

"After all your hard work making it nice the way it is?"

He nodded. "And the other interested party is a couple. A couple of professional types. They don't want kids—they told me that. And they want to make the second bedroom into a big closet, and the third bedroom into a master bath with a Jacuzzi and marble counters. They talked about bumping out the back wall and putting in a media room."

"A what?"

"A big room for a big TV."

Evelyn got caught up in his disappointment. "I don't like that everybody wants to change it."

"Change it into something it's not."

Evelyn had a wild thought and hesitated saying it aloud. "Maybe we should tell them no."

Wayne's face brightened. "You think so?"

"So you thought of it too?"

He shrugged. "I thought of it, then discounted it as dumb, then thought of it again. I know we took on this project with the sole intent of fixing it up so we could sell it and make Accosta—and ourselves—a little money, but shouldn't we have a say in how the house is used?"

"Absolutely."

He poured juice. "As I was working on it, I always pictured a family here. Or actually . . ." He shook his head.

"What?"

He looked her straight in the eye. "Actually . . . oh, I know this is odd, but . . ."

"But what?"

"I kept picturing *many* families here. Or partial families. Women with small children, women alone. Women in need of help."

"Like the women living at Peerbaugh Place."

Wayne blinked and his words came out slowly. "Just like them."

Evelyn felt a stitch in her stomach as if something amazing had just been set before her. She looked at Wayne. His eyes were wide and he was biting his lip. "Are you thinking what I'm thinking?" she asked.

He suddenly stood and scanned the entire room, as if seeing it for the first time. "Maybe there's a reason we haven't had the auction yet . . ." He strode into the dining room. "And this could be another bedroom. A big bedroom for a woman with a child. If we put bunk beds in here, it could sleep two children."

Evelyn *saw* it. She moved into the kitchen with Wayne. "But they'll need some place to eat. What if we closed in the back porch so there's room to bring the dining-room table here, into the kitchen?"

"Perfect," Wayne said. He opened the door to the tiny lavatory, then came out and looked at the odd-shaped closet under the stairs. "If we used some of this space we could put a tub in this bathroom."

"That would still only give us two baths for five bedrooms."

"It would have to do." Lunch forgotten, Wayne headed for the stairs. "Unless we could make that tiny bedroom into a bath."

They reached the landing and Evelyn looked up and saw the pull rope for the attic. She pointed at it. Wayne's face lit up. "Another bedroom!"

He pulled the rope and lowered the steps. He climbed them

with the vigor of a teenager and Evelyn followed. He yanked the pull chain for the two bare lightbulbs. Evelyn scanned the space. "It's like a dormitory. We could get in four or five single beds."

Wayne had moved to the attic window. "It's hot up here, but with a window air conditioner . . ."

Evelyn was suddenly overcome. With the tears she pulled in a ragged breath. "Wayne, what's happening?"

He faced her and took her hands. "I'm not sure, but I like it."

"Me too. But how . . . ? We need to sell this place. We can't open it up to women and kids for free. We can't—"

"You're right. *We* can't."

But God can.

Wayne pulled her into his arms. "I don't know the answers to your questions, Evelyn. And I've got as many as you do, if not more. But this feels right."

She nodded against his chest. Then with a sudden revelation, she pulled away. "Wayne, I think the only answer we have to give right now is yes."

"Before God even asks the question?"

With her nod the tears returned. They hugged in silence. Evelyn was scared to death and yet felt she was on the edge of the most important decision of her life.

No. That wasn't correct. She'd already made the most important decision of her life. She'd told God yes. The rest was just details.

. . .

Evelyn and Wayne talked about their idea all afternoon, energized, walking from room to room and back again as their vision for Accosta's house grew. But excited as they were, they made a pact not to tell anyone else. Not until they'd had a chance to let it sink in. Not until they had a chance to pray about it and ask God if it was His idea.

But that didn't mean their energy paled; it just changed locale. They ended up back at Peerbaugh Place where they could look through the attic to inventory the extra furniture that could be used to furnish the . . . the . . . house? retreat? haven? It was odd to have an idea yet have no clue what to call it.

Wayne held a pad of paper and a pen. Evelyn moved boxes to get to the far corners. "Here's another dresser and a desk chair," she said.

Wayne wrote it down. "Dresser. Desk chair. Check."

Evelyn caught sight of a box that was labeled *Linens*. They'd need linens for the many beds. She opened it and removed a needlepoint pillow that was on top. "Oh my . . . I made this when I was in college."

He glanced up, then looked at his list again. "Do you want me to write down the linen inventory too?"

"Might as well." She held the pillow for Wayne to see. "Do you think we can use this for decoration even if it does have my maiden-name monogram on it?"

They both looked at the orange initials ERW. Evelyn admired her handiwork. Though the orange *was* kind of obnoxious against the olive background, she remembered how much she had enjoyed making it. She should really take up needlepoint again. "It's still kind of pretty; don't you think?"

But when she looked at Wayne, his eyes were wide. He suddenly crossed the room and grabbed it from her.

It wasn't *that* bad. "Wayne . . ."

He stared at the letters. "This is yours? This is you?"

He was scaring her. "Of course it's mine. ERW: Evelyn Ruth Wilson. As I said, I made it before I married Aaron."

Wayne kept staring at the pillow.

"Wayne? What's wrong?"

He set the pillow down as if it were made of finest porcelain. "I have to go."

"But we were just getting started. The list?"

"Later. I have to go."

He left the attic and she heard his feet on the stairs, then on the porch. Evelyn looked out the attic window and watched him drive away.

What had just happened?

•   •   •

Wayne was glad Piper wasn't at the apartment. He needed time alone to think.

But first, he had to make sure.

He went to the bedroom dresser where he'd dropped the locket. He got it out and checked the monogram: ERW.

Evelyn Ruth Wilson?

He sank onto the bed. *Evelyn was . . . ? No, she couldn't be.*

Yet what were the chances of two women having the same three initials, in the same order? And what were the chances of . . .

After Wanda died, Evelyn had shared a time of her own deep sorrow with him, the fact that she'd given up a child she'd had out of wedlock. Wayne had been very honored that she'd felt comfortable enough to bare her past to him. But now that shared moment gained extra meaning.

He looked at the locket in the palm of his hand. ERW. Evelyn Ruth Wilson. ERW. Evelyn Ruth Wilson. One woman. One child.

He closed his hand around the necklace and held it to his face. "Father? Is this true? How could this be true?"

"How could what be true, Dad?"

Wayne hadn't heard Piper come in. "How was your fitting at Audra's?"

280

"Fine." She sat beside him. "But that doesn't answer my question. You look a little green." -

"I . . . I can't remember why I was saying . . . I don't remember what I was saying."

She pulled his hand upward. The chain was hanging out. No way did he want her to see the locket. The locket that had ERW on it.

She grinned, a child wanting a surprise. She fingered the free length of chain. "What's this?"

There was no way out. He opened his hand.

"Oooh, pretty," Piper said. She held it up, studying it. "ERW. Who does it belong to?"

He thought of a half answer that would have to do for now until he'd had some time . . . "It's a locket you're supposed to get on your wedding day."

She handed it back. "Oh. I'm sorry. I ruined a surprise?"

He pressed it into her hand. "No. It's yours. Take it now."

"Thank you. But I don't understand the initials. *W* for Wellington. But I don't remember a relative who's name starts with an *E*. Who's it from?"

Wilson. Wellington. "It's from your birth mother. I found it in a box of your baby things. There was a note. She wanted you to get it on your wedding day."

Wayne could tell she was looking at it with new eyes. She wrapped her arms around his neck and kissed him. "Thank you, Dad. Would you help me put it on?"

He'd never been very good with tiny clasps, but he did his best attaching Evelyn's locket around his daughter's neck.

15

The Lord says,
"I will guide you along the best pathway
for your life.
I will advise you and watch over you."

PSALM 32:8

*P*iper tried to be as quiet as possible as she got herself a bowl of cereal. Her dad was still asleep on the fold-out couch—which was a bit worrisome. He never slept past seven and it was 7:45. This, added to his oddish behavior last night about the locket. . . . He'd given it to her, but had seemed reluctant. Maybe she should give it back and let him give it to her on her wedding day, like her birth mother had instructed?

As she leaned against the counter to eat her cereal, she noticed the calendar on the wall. Today's square had a red circle around it. She caught her breath. Today was the first anniversary of her mother's death! No wonder he was reluctant to get up and face the day.

It wasn't that she'd forgotten. A week ago, she and her dad had discussed going to the cemetery today. But since then she'd let the busyness of the wedding preparations push the thought aside.

She looked into the darkened living room, the light of day seeping through the edges of the patio-door curtains. What did one say on such a day? *Morning Dad! Happy first anniversary!* It was absurd, of course, but Piper wasn't experienced in commemorating sorrowful events. What *was* the etiquette in such a thing?

Piper heard her father stir and realized—right or wrong—she would soon find out. He sat up, setting his feet on the floor. He looked in her direction. She stepped out of the shadows and tried on a smile. "Morning, Dad." Was it appropriate she left the *good* out of her greeting?

He squinted in her direction. "Morning."

"Did you sleep well?"

He ran his hands through his tousled hair. "Actually, no."

She wished she could have said, "Same here" but couldn't. She'd experienced the oblivious sleep of the ignorant and forgetful.

He stood, a bit bent over until he stretched. "Is there coffee?"

"You bet." She put her cereal bowl down and had a cup ready for him by the time he got to the kitchen.

"Thanks." He tried a sip, but it was too hot. "So. What are you doing today?"

Piper felt her eyebrows rise. Had he forgotten too? "I have some errands for the wedding, but I have plenty of time this afternoon to go . . . you know . . . with you . . ." She wanted him to remember.

"With me?"

She stepped toward the calendar, hoping he would look past her and see—

It worked. She watched his eyes skim over her shoulder and land on the red circle. "The cemetery!" His coffee sloshed over the cup onto the floor. Piper got a paper towel. "I can't believe I forgot!"

"I did too, Dad. Don't feel bad. We were both talking about it last week. We didn't forget. The day just crept up on us."

His shoulders slumped and one hand went to his face. She rescued his coffee cup, set it safely aside, and pulled him into her arms.

"A year ago . . . it's been a year without her . . ." He sobbed.

She didn't have any words that wouldn't sound trite or ridiculous. She just held him and added her tears to his.

•   •   •

The errands could wait. Wayne was glad Piper agreed to visit Wanda's grave first thing. They stopped at Flora and Funna and got a potted aster with vibrant purple blooms. Wanda had always loved purple.

Though Wayne had come to the graveside a few times, he wasn't into it like some people were. He didn't need to be next to a plot of ground to talk to Wanda, just like he didn't need to be in a church to pray. To each his own. But on this day, it did seem appropriate to go there with their daughter.

Evelyn's daughter.

He felt guilty because *that* piece of information had been the reason he hadn't slept well, not the fact that it was the eve of this somber anniversary. They parked and walked to the grave hand in hand. There was a bench close by and they sat, the stone warm in the sun. Suddenly, the light glinted off a piece of jewelry around Piper's neck. He leaned forward to see. It was the locket!

His first reaction was panic. "I don't think you should wear that."

She put a finger to it. "Why not?"

Yeah, why not? His mind scrambled for an explanation that didn't involve the truth behind his fear: that Evelyn would see it and recognize it and—

"Do you think it's an affront to Mom for me to wear it?" Piper reached for the clasp. "Because if you do, I'll take it off and—"

He stopped her hands and said, "No. It's all right." Even though it wasn't. She obviously liked it, liked receiving it. Who was he to take that away from her?

Yet he knew that the time was coming when she had to know. Evelyn had to know. But when? How? And how would they react? Would they be as confused as he was? as happy, yet sad? as in awe, yet afraid? The wedding was a week from Saturday. Should they know before then? Or would such a life-changing revelation be best kept for later when the hubbub of the wedding festivities died down?

What about his own relationship with Evelyn? He loved her and she loved him. What about the amazing vision they received yesterday regarding Accosta's house?

He couldn't think about that now. Not when the rest of his life, his daughter's life, and Evelyn's life was teetering.

Piper took his hand. "Are you okay?"

The guilt for *not* thinking of Wanda returned and was replaced by an even more distressing emotion. Anger. He got to his feet and let it out. "Exactly how am I supposed to be feeling today?"

"What?" She looked at him as if he were crazy.

Maybe he was. "Am I supposed to be falling down with grief? Am I supposed to cry out and curse God for taking my wife away from me? Am I supposed to ache inside for the lost year, the year I've had without her?"

"Dad . . . I don't think there's any set way to feel."

He moved to the headstone and shoved a leaf off the top. "I bet there is! I bet someone has created a list of ways to mourn and I'm not doing it right." He got down on his knees next to the grave. "Should I sprawl over the grass, a broken man?"

"Dad!" Piper got to her feet and tried to help him up, but he pushed her hands away and got up on his own.

"Or maybe I should be coming out here more often, having daily talks with Wanda like we used to at breakfast each morning?"

"Dad, stop it. No one's saying—"

"Am I supposed to have shriveled into nothing this last year? Should I have become a recluse? And how dare I fall in love!"

"You're scaring me . . ."

He knew he was out of control but couldn't help it. "Life is a scary place, Piper-girl. All sorts of things are going on behind our back, without our knowledge. Vast plans are whirling around us and we are just ignorant pawns." He laughed. "God's quite the plotter, He is. Withholding information for years until suddenly He sees fit to let us in on it."

"What are you talking about?"

He pulled in a breath. He'd nearly said too much. The information couldn't come out like this, in a wild rant at a graveside. Though Wayne didn't know when the proper time *was*, he was sure this wasn't it. He put his hands over his eyes, needing to press in sense and reason. He had no idea where all that had come from, but he regretted that his daughter had to witness it.

Evelyn's daughter.

"I have to go."

"But we just got here."

"Stay if you want. I have to go."

He strode to the car and she ran after him.

• • • •

Evelyn could hardly wait to see Wayne and talk to him more about their plans for Accosta's house. Plus, she wanted to find out why he'd run out of the attic yesterday. Probably just tired and overwhelmed. They did have a lot to think about.

Evelyn desperately wanted to tell Accosta about their plans, but knew it was too soon. Besides, Wayne needed to be in on that.

She called Wayne's house but no one was there, so she called his cell phone. He was probably out putting a few final touches on the house. If he was, she would drop everything and join him. She was thrilled when he answered.

"Morning, Wayne! It's a wonderful day, isn't it?"

"I'm busy, Evelyn. What do you need?"

Need? "I'm sorry. I was just hoping we could get together to talk about the house and—"

"Not today. I really have a lot going today."

She felt as if she'd been slugged in the stomach. It wasn't just his words; it was his tone, as if she were a pesky salesman and he wanted to be rid of her. "Well, okay . . . I'll talk to you later?"

"Sure. I'll get back to you in a few days."

Somehow the phone's receiver made its way back into its cradle. Somehow Evelyn found a chair. But after that there was only one "somehow" that mattered: Somehow, she'd done something that had caused Wayne to hate her.

Somehow the world had changed without her permission.

* * *

Wayne was glad Piper had dropped him off at the apartment and had gone on to do her errands. At least she hadn't been there to witness his dropping the atom bomb on Evelyn, causing total destruction in his wake. How could he have been so rude to her on the phone? And how could he have had a fit at the cemetery in front of his daughter? But even more: how could he ever handle the cacophony of thoughts and emotions that pummeled his soul?

I need to talk to Wanda. She'll know what to do.

As the thought materialized, he gasped. He really was losing it.

He stood at the patio door looking out on the green common area of the apartment complex, yet it brought him no comfort or pleasure. He pressed his hands on the glass and leaned his forehead against it. It was cool against the heat of his mood. Its solidity amid its transparency was a good representation of his current state. The truth was outside, in the common green, close but unattainable. He couldn't reach out and grasp it because this cold, hard wall kept him away.

What was *his* wall made of?

One word came to mind: *pride.*

As the word sank in, he moved his forehead away from the glass, dropped his hands, and turned back toward the room. "I'm not a proud man. I've taken everything You've thrown at me, Lord! I won't say I did it without complaining, but I did it. I admitted You were in control." His throat tightened. "I even surrendered my wife to You. My life. Those aren't the actions of a proud man."

You're proud of your strength in handling it.

Wayne didn't like that thought and shook his head against it. What had God wanted him to do this past year? Be a whimpering, simpering mess? Just because he'd been able to carry on, live life with some semblance of normalcy, he was being punished?

Punished?

Condemned by his own choice of words, Wayne sat on the chair by the sofa and put his head in his hands. Finding out Evelyn was Piper's birth mother was not a punishment. How could he even think that?

Because it was done without your consent.

That much was true. It was hard for him to fathom the extent of the events God had set in motion thirty-six years ago that were being culminated now. He counted off on his fingers. His marrying Wanda. Their not being able to have children. Evelyn having Piper out of wedlock. He and Wanda adopting Piper. Piper moving into Evelyn's home as a tenant. Wanda dying. And now, his falling in love with Evelyn.

He stared at his seven extended fingers, knowing there were hundreds of details that God had arranged in order for this outcome to take place. It was so beyond the scope of what man could coordinate that it had to be God. In a way it was frightening to know that he'd been a part of something so extensive, so utterly amazing.

He suddenly thought of a snippet of verse: *"My thoughts are completely different from yours. . . ."*

Isaiah something? Sensing it was important to read it all,

Wayne took up the Bible that sat on the coffee table before him. Sat waiting? He turned to Isaiah and after a few minutes, read the verses: "'My thoughts are completely different from yours,' says the Lord. 'And My ways are far beyond anything you could imagine. For just as the heavens are higher than the earth, so are My ways higher than your ways and My thoughts higher than your thoughts.'"

The words filled him up. It was true—all true. God's ways were beyond his imaginings. He needed to accept what had been revealed as a blessing and somehow learn how to fathom the miracle.

"But what about Piper and Evelyn?"

Another long list of questions surfaced. How would they react? He knew they would ultimately be pleased and as in awe of God's ways as he was. Timing was the issue. Piper was getting married in a week. Evelyn was the matron of honor. But now, in Wanda's absence, she was also mother of the bride? The logistics and implications were beyond complicated. If he didn't tell them before the wedding and they found out later, would they be angry? Would they be disappointed that he'd prevented them from experiencing the joy of the wedding to its fullest extent in their new mother-daughter roles? Yet wasn't there enough emotional turmoil as the wedding neared? He knew Piper was worried about her mother-in-law. Would adding issues about another mother be cruel?

He fell back into the cushions. "What should I do, Father? How should I tell them? When should I tell them?"

He sat in stillness hoping God would give him a clear answer such as "Tell them tomorrow at 2:30." Though Wayne felt God's presence, he did not receive a distinct answer.

Another worry surfaced. How could he ever be around Evelyn and Piper with this knowledge brewing and stewing inside him? Evelyn wanted to talk about their new plans for Accosta's house. Understandably. He wanted to talk about them too. But how could he be around her and act normal? Nothing was normal now. It was better than normal, but it would take some getting used to.

He closed his eyes, exhausted. *God, You started this. You work it out.*

This would be interesting.

•   •   •

Evelyn gathered a basket. She was going to cut a fresh bouquet to take to the hospital for little Kimberly when she and Accosta went on their volunteer rounds.

Accosta came into the kitchen and pointed at it. "Flowers for Kimberly?"

Evelyn nodded. "Want to help?"

"Of course." They went outside and Accosta held the basket while Evelyn did the stooping and cutting. The asters were especially lovely.

"You're quiet," Accosta said.

"I guess I don't have much to say."

"I'd guess you have too much to say."

Evelyn arched her back, the stretch both painful and exquisite. "I really wish you wouldn't be so good at figuring me out. It's very disconcerting."

"And annoying?"

"That too."

Accosta sat on the bench and patted the seat beside her. "Since there's no escaping the intuition of an old woman who loves you, I think it's time you fessed up."

Evelyn did as she was told, setting the basket of flowers on the path in front of them. "I did something to upset Wayne."

"What?"

"I don't know." She told Accosta about the phone call she'd made to Wayne, but didn't let it slip about their plans for her house. "He brushed me off. He said he'd get back to me in a few days. A few days!"

"Do I recognize the long-dormant essence of a teenage girl vying for attention?"

Her whining *did* sound adolescent. "It wasn't just his words; it was his tone."

"Maybe he was engrossed in something at the time. Maybe he was worried about something. Maybe he was upset about this being the anniversary of his wife's—"

"Wanda!" Evelyn angled her body toward her friend. "Piper mentioned they were going to the cemetery on the first anniversary. July 21. Today!"

Accosta spread her hands. "See? Worry over."

Evelyn stood and took up the basket. "This is such a relief. Thank you. I feel better. That explains everything."

Accosta held out her hand and let Evelyn help her up. But as they walked back to the house, a sliver of doubt stung Evelyn, causing her to stop. "But maybe there's something else I did to Wayne that I don't know about and—"

Accosta pointed a finger at her. "Hold it right there, sister. There will be no borrowing trouble on my watch."

Evelyn nodded, but the doubt remained.

●　　●　　●

Mae lowered the menu and leaned toward Collier, who was seated across from her at Ruby's. "Valerie looks as if she's doing all right, don't you think?"

They both watched Valerie refill coffee cups and chat with patrons at the counter. "It's got to be humbling for her," he said. "From budding author-to-be to serving burgers."

Since it had been her idea, Mae felt the need to defend Valerie's job. "She can earn decent money here."

"I'm sure she can. Money and sore feet."

Mae saw Valerie coming in their direction with two waters. "Shh!" She put on her best smile. "How's it going, Val?"

"Not bad." She patted her pocket, making coins jingle. "I may be paying my rent with quarters, but at least I'll be paying it."

"We promise to leave paper money for a tip."

"You'll make my day. What can I get for you?"

They ordered and Val took their menus. But as she was leaving, she turned back and leaned on their table. "Actually, I need to express my appreciation for your help in getting this job—for a reason other than the obvious monetary one."

"What's that?"

"All the people who come in here. Watching them, talking with them . . . it's like research for my books. There are some real characters in Carson Creek."

Mae laughed. "Who, in your able hands, will become real characters."

"Uh-oh, we'll have to behave ourselves," Collier said.

"Please don't. Normal is boring."

"I couldn't agree with you more," Mae said. "I just have one request."

"What's that?"

"When you write about me, make sure I'm fifteen pounds lighter and having a good-hair day."

"That's no fun." Valerie winked. "I'll be back with your tea in a minute."

They watched her go. "She looks happy enough," Mae said.

"At certain times in our lives 'happy enough' *is* all we can hope— Oh, there's Ringo."

Mae turned around to see the door. "Ringo!" Ringo was with another man—maybe someone from work? He waved at them but didn't come over. The two men sat at the counter.

Mae's thoughts strayed to her son's marriage. "Ringo needs to call Soonie and get her back here."

"Yes, he does."

"He does?" She was surprised Collier agreed. She'd expected him to say she was being a worrywart mother.

Collier set his silverware straight. "Absence may make the heart grow fonder, but it can also strain the ties that bind. Ringo had his fling back into the rock world and found it lacking. He got his construction job back. He's working. He's providing for his family."

"Who isn't here. But I'm tired of nagging him to call her. He told me to leave it alone."

Collier shook his head. "'Pride goes before destruction, and haughtiness before a fall.'"

"But I don't want him to fall. Not any more than he already has with the roadie stuff falling through, and Danny coming back . . ."

Collier reached across the table and took her hand. "Yet sometimes there's nothing else parents can do but let their children fall, then be there to pick them up."

"Messy business, parenting."

●   ●   ●

"How do I look?" Piper asked Gregory.

He glanced up from the baseball game he was starting to watch with her father. "You look fine."

That was not the answer she was looking for, and she stepped back into the apartment bedroom to check her appearance in the dresser mirror one more time.

"Wrong answer, Gregory," she heard her father say. "Let me give you some advice, 'Fine' is never an acceptable answer to the 'how do I look?' question."

"You got that right," called Piper from the bedroom. "*Lovely*, *breathtaking*, or *stunning* are the words I was searching for."

Gregory appeared at the bedroom door. "Point taken. You are all those things."

"Sorry. Too late. The five-second rule has passed. All compliments are now officially deemed afterthoughts and are no longer valid."

He snuggled close, wrapping his arms around her from behind. They looked at each other in the mirror. "Can't I get a special dispensation? Because you *are* lovely."

She leaned her head back against his and stroked his cheek. "Your wish is my command."

His eyes lit up. "Really?"

Uh-oh. Maybe she spoke too soon. "Am I going to regret those words?"

He turned her around to face him. "What I'd really like is for you to cancel this dinner with my mother. She's revealed herself to be a pain. You can't expect her to suddenly be nice. It's going to be an awful, stressful evening. You know I'm right."

"It's important we make amends. She's family."

"We don't need her. I've gotten along fine without her for years. Why start now?"

"Because it's the right thing to do."

"She'll argue and ruin the dinner."

Probably. And in truth, Piper didn't want to go. She hated confrontation and would much rather spend the evening with Gregory and her dad, grilling hamburgers and watching baseball. Yet sometimes the hard thing was the right thing. She put her head on Gregory's shoulder. "I really feel God wants me to do this. I need to make every attempt to find peace between us. I want her at the wedding."

"I don't."

She pushed away. "How can you say that? She's your mother."

"She'll ruin things. She'll be offended by any mention of Jesus and make a scene."

"She wouldn't do that." *Would she?*

Gregory took her chin and looked into her eyes intently. "You don't have to do this for me."

"I'm not. I'm doing it for us."

God, help me.

＊　　＊　　＊

Piper didn't merely drive to Jackson for her dinner with Esther Baladino; she prayed her way there. She couldn't remember going into another conversation with so much on the line. It would have been nerve-racking enough just to have dinner with a future mother-in-law, but add the fact that she was not the most amiable woman in the world, was opinionated, was newly passionate about her own Jewish faith, and unhappy with her son's Christianity. Piper just hoped the dinner would not turn into an incident in need of Middle East peace talks.

Piper had chosen Phillippe's. Hopefully, the quiet genteel atmosphere would make Esther feel special. And peaceful.

When Piper pulled past the front door into the parking lot, she spotted Esther waiting out front, her pocketbook hanging on her arm. Piper waved and offered a smile even though her nerves screamed. She wasn't late, but that wouldn't matter to Esther. When Piper and Gregory had gone to Esther's home for dinner, they'd been made to feel late. Obviously taking the upper hand in this way was Esther's habit.

Piper parked the car, glanced at her hair in the mirror, and told her reflection, "Let's do this thing." She sounded more confident than she felt and added a silent, *God! Help!* as she hurried toward the entrance.

"There you are," Esther said.

Piper's heart beat as though she'd run a marathon. She gave Esther a simple hug. "Have you been waiting long?"

"*Long* is in the eye of the beholder. My feet hurt."

Piper held the door and they went inside. The maitre d' greeted them, and they were seated at a nice table that was slightly secluded. A good conversation table. The maitre d' held their chairs, placed linen napkins in their laps, and handed them leather menus.

"It's in French," Esther said. "I don't know French." She closed her menu. "I don't like places that try to make you feel stupid."

Piper didn't know what to say. "The veal and the salmon are excellent."

Esther shrugged. "I like veal but who knows which one's which?" She eyed Piper. "I suppose you know French?" She made it sound like a character flaw.

"Not really. I just ask a lot of questions." Piper was glad when the waiter approached. "Can you tell us about the salmon and the veal?"

As he gave a vivid description of the dishes, Piper made a mental note to order whichever one Esther didn't. Luckily, the waiter asked Esther first.

"I suppose I'll take the veal. And a salad. With anchovies if you have them."

He smiled. "I'll see what we can do." He turned to Piper. "And you, mademoiselle?"

"I'll have the salmon and a salad—no anchovies, please."

When he left them, Piper wanted to call him back for his company, for mindless chitchat. Anything so she didn't have to face this gaping expanse of time that needed to be filled with talk. She had no idea what to say to start things—

"How are your friends from the shower?"

Piper was wary. "Fine . . ."

"That June woman certainly has an attitude."

June woman? Oh. "Mae? Yes, she does." Though Piper didn't want to rehash the shower, she thought it was an appropriate time to apologize. "I'm sorry if anyone hurt your feelings at the shower, Mrs. Baladino. Please know that wasn't their intent."

"I don't appreciate having Moses and David thrown in my face."

Piper felt her eyebrows rise, and forced them to lower. "I don't think that was the case, but—"

"It was the case. To have your friends flaunt their knowledge . . . I felt as if I was being quizzed."

"I assure you, you weren't. Mae and Tessa are very sincere about their appreciation for those two great men."

"Your friends are zealots."

"They *are* passionate about the Word."

"The Word?"

"The Bible." *We read it a lot. How about you?*

"The New Testament," Esther said. "Matthew, Mark, Paul . . . them."

"And the Old Testament. We study that too. After all, Jesus was a Jew."

Esther shook her head vehemently. "He threw all that away."

"No He didn't. He embraced all the Jewish holy days: Passover, Yom Kippur, Rosh Hashanah, the Sabbath. Jesus came to give salvation to the Jews."

"He's not ours. He's yours."

Piper's mind screamed for God to help. She didn't want to get into a theological discussion with a woman whose heart was so obviously hardened to the truth. But what could she say when Esther locked onto lies?

Piper fueled herself with a sip of water. "I'm not out to convert you, Mrs. Baladino. Neither is Gregory. That's not our job."

She snickered. "Sure it is. I know about Christians. All those missionaries wanting to save the damned for Jesus."

"I'm not a missionary. I'm going to be your daughter-in-law.

I respect your Jewish faith and am thrilled that you've found comfort in it. But you have to know that I'm also thrilled Gregory has found comfort in Jesus. It will be a bond that will unite us in our marriage. Gregory's told me how hard it was growing up in a household that was divided." As soon as she said it, Piper wished she could take it back. "I mean, to not have *any* religious upbringing must have been—"

"Yes, well, even an old woman like me is allowed a few regrets. But that doesn't mean Gregory should abandon half of his heritage. He had relatives murdered for their faith in the concentration camps. He can't throw that away."

"And I assure you, he isn't. He won't." Suddenly, Piper had an idea. "In fact, I would like to learn more about the Jewish traditions. Perhaps Gregory and I can incorporate some of them into our new home."

Esther sat back, appalled. "You can't do that. You can't combine Jesus and being Jewish."

"Actually, you can. Actually, it's quite logical to do so. Jews don't need to give up their culture to embrace Christ as *their* Messiah. He came for *you*, Esther. And me. We can share Him *and* share the traditions that are the basis of both faiths. No Jew has to walk away from their faith or their culture to embrace Jesus."

Esther's face seemed to vibrate with confusion, but blessedly there was no anger there. Had Piper gotten through? Had they truly found common ground?

"I suppose I could show you how to make gefilte fish or those matzoh balls I made when you came to dinner."

Piper nearly cried. "That would be wonderful."

"And maybe you could help me pick out a mother-of-the-groom dress—for the wedding?"

Their salads came at just the right time and Piper ate hers with glad thanksgiving. Praise the Lord!

● ● ●

Gregory stopped the swing with a foot. "My mother is going to do what?"

Piper laughed. His expression looked as if she'd told him his mother had taken up skydiving. "She's going to teach me to cook some Jewish dishes."

"Which *she* didn't know how to cook until recently. The only Jewish foods I had growing up were kosher pickles and bagels."

"It's not just the food, Gregory. She's celebrating the Jewish holy days."

"Does she even know what they mean? Or is she just hooked on the ceremony?"

Piper remembered Esther bristling at being made to feel stupid, yet there was a good possibility she *was* going through the motions without the knowledge of why. Piper still came to her defense. "When you first started embracing your faith did you understand the full background of baptism, Communion, Good Friday, Pentecost . . . ?"

He flicked the tip of her nose. "Point taken."

"Actually, the point we're talking about is that she's opened her mind and heart to God. It's up to Him to move her in the right direction, to a true faith, not fluff."

"But she's still making me feel guilty for becoming a Christian."

Piper laced her fingers through his. "Again, love, it's up to Him. Things are right between us now. She's coming to the wedding. The rest will fall into place, in His time."

Which she only hoped happened sooner rather than later.

16

$\mathcal{M}$ae had previously agreed with Collier that it was often in a child's best interest to let them fall and fail, then be there to pick them up. But she'd also agreed that parenting was messy business. And this morning when she awakened, she felt the nudge to get down and dirty, and mess things up a bit.

She looked at the clock by the bed. It was five-thirty. She really should wait for a decent hour to get her son out of bed. And yet . . . "the early bird catches the worm," "early to bed early to rise" . . . and her favorite by Sartre: "Three o'clock is always too late or too early for anything you want to do."

That may be true, but since it wasn't three . . .

She got up and put on her robe. Collier opened one eye, looked at her, then at the clock. "What's wrong?"

"It's seven-thirty—p.m.—in Korea."

"What?"

She leaned on the bed and kissed his cheek. "Go back to sleep. I'll handle it."

He grunted and turned over.

In the hall outside Ringo's room, Mae hesitated. She was

handling things all right, but *was* it right? She took a moment to check in. *Father, is this okay? I just want the kids to get back together. I want to hold Ricky. I want them to be a family again. Is that such a bad thing?*

She heard something fall onto the floor in Ringo's room. Then an epithet.

Perfect.

She knocked on Ringo's door and opened it. In the moonlight, she saw him on the floor using a wadded up T-shirt to sop up water from a toppled glass. "I musta hit it with my hand."

She flipped on the light. "I'll get a towel." On the way to and from the bathroom, Mae sent up a hearty thank-you. There was nothing better than getting the approval of the Almighty when it came to motherly choices.

Back in his room she finished what he'd started and gathered both damp cloths to take down to the laundry room. Ringo climbed back into bed. "What time is it?"

"Time to get up."

He glanced at the clock. "No it isn't. It's early."

"In Korea it's seven-thirty in the evening."

He tried to pull the covers up, but she held them back. "Mom, leave me alone."

"Nope. Not this time." She took his hand and pulled. "I am suffering from severe, debilitating baby withdrawal and you're the only one who can do anything about it."

He pulled his hand away and bent his pillow over his face. "I told you. Soonie is the one who left; she's the one—"

"Horse-hocky. You just remet your father who's been out of your life for thirty years. I think I can safely say it was not an altogether pleasant experience. So don't pull a Danny on us. Surely you don't want Ricky to live without a father like you did—not for one second longer. I will not allow it. So get up!" Mae pointed to the floor and held her stance until he peeked out from his pillow. "I'm not leaving."

He replaced the pillow over his eyes. "I can deal with that."

"Can you deal with this?" She began to sing the first song that came into her head. A Beatles tune. "'Well, she was just seventeen, . . .'"

By the time she got to the chorus of "I Saw Her Standing There"—complete with high *oohh*—she had him groaning.

And she'd gained an audience. Collier stood in the doorway. "What's going on in here?" he asked.

"I'm torturing my son. Care to join me?"

"Absolutely." He put an arm around her shoulders and they did the second verse together.

When they got to the chorus a second time, the pillow was gone and Ringo was up. "Stop already. Just give me a few minutes. I'll meet you downstairs."

Mae nodded, kept singing, took Collier's hand, and they danced their way to the kitchen. God, gumption, and rock and roll. Not a bad combination.

*   *   *

Mae wanted to yell, "Speak up! I can't hear you!" but didn't dare. She'd persuaded Ringo to call Soon-ja, so she didn't dare push it. When Ringo took the phone into the living room and began talking softly, she'd had to use all her questionable willpower to stay put at the kitchen table and not eavesdrop.

Collier looked up from his newspaper. "Thata girl, wifey. Timely restraint will earn you two sparkle stars."

"Pooh to sparkle stars. I want to know what they're saying."

"From the cooey tone of Ringo's voice, you know what they're saying. I'd guess your mission has been accomplished and Soonie and Ricky will be back in the family fold very soon."

"None too soon."

Ringo came back in the room. He was smiling.

"Well?" Mae asked.

"She was planning to come home tomorrow anyway. She was going to surprise me. She misses me."

"Of course she does."

He put the phone back in its charger. "I miss them."

"Of course you do."

Suddenly, he crossed the room, hugged Mae, and kissed her cheek. "Thanks, Mom."

Ah, yes. Parenting could be a messy business, but it could also be wonderfully rewarding.

• • •

Audra caught herself staring into space. She looked down at Evelyn's bridesmaid dress and saw the needle frozen in time, poised to take the next stitch. At first she felt a twinge of fear. Had she been daydreaming about Simon again?

She rewound her thoughts and discovered that Simon had not been the subject. Russell had. She laughed with relief. When she'd prayed for God to help her fall madly in love with her husband again, she hadn't truly expected Him to do it. Yet in the week since then, she'd found her heart dramatically changed. It was as if she saw Russell with new eyes. The things that used to annoy her weren't so earth-shattering after all. She found herself looking forward to the sound of his car in the driveway, and she actually made time to sit next to him just to cuddle.

Even more amazing than her change of heart was how Russell was changing because of it. This morning, before heading out the door to the bank, he'd backtracked to give her a kiss—on the lips. "Love you," he'd said.

Love you too.

So much for underestimating the power of God.

She felt as if the roots that had been yanked loose had regained their hold on the earth and were sinking deeper, spreading wider so nothing would ever loosen them again. She shook her head slightly, knowing it was too broad a statement, and their marriage had too many years to go for her to think there would never be other rough times. Yet she also sensed that each time the roots had to develop new shoots and new growth, they were a little more prepared for the next time. And the next. Didn't a pruned plant grow stronger and more lush? "I'm being pruned."

Summer looked up from the wedding card she was making for Piper and Gregory. "What did you say, Mommy?"

She set the sewing aside. "Let's go make Daddy a sandwich. He's coming home for a special lunch today."

Summer nodded. "He wants to tell me something." She gave her mother a sidelong grin. "What is it?"

"Be patient, baby." It was a good admonition to herself.

•   •   •

After eating half his tuna sandwich, Russell reached across the kitchen table and took the hands of both his girls. Audra's stomach hitched. She prayed that Summer wouldn't be upset by what they had to say.

"Is this it?" Summer asked. "Are you going to tell me the secret now?"

Russell squeezed her hand. "Yes, this is *it*. And the secret's a good one, but not in the way we expected."

"Are we pregnant?"

Audra heard herself gasp. "No, baby—"

"Not exactly," Russell said.

Summer pulled her hand away and crossed her arms, a pout starting. "I thought that was the secret. I want a baby."

Russell and Audra laughed. "We do too, chickie pie," Russell said. "But it turns out your mommy and I can't have one."

Audra put a hand to her stomach. "Not here. But we *can* get a baby by adopting one."

"Do you remember what adoption is?" Russell asked.

Summer looked at the ceiling a moment. "You 'dopted me when you married Mommy. And Piper's 'dopted too."

"Exactly," Audra said. "Wayne and Wanda adopted her when she was a baby."

"Didn't her mommy and daddy want her?"

Audra didn't know the specifics and didn't think Piper did either. She chose an answer that was always correct: "They felt they couldn't take care of her like she deserved so they let the Wellingtons do it for them. Her birth parents loved her enough to give her up."

Summer rearranged the bread crusts on her plate. "So who's giving us their baby?"

"We don't know yet. We'll go to an agency that helps parents and children find each other. First we have to fill out a bunch of papers telling the parents who have a baby all about us so they'll know if we're the right ones to love their child."

"Can I fill out something too? I'd tell them all about me being a good big sister."

Audra felt richly blessed. "That would be wonderful."

Summer pushed her chair back. "Can I do it now?"

"Sure."

When she left the room both Russell and Audra took a fresh breath. "Well then," Russell said, "that wasn't as hard as I thought it would be."

"She's a very giving child."

He took his plate to the sink. "Should we have warned her it might take a long time?"

Audra wasn't sure. "Let's not put time into the mix until we have to. Who knows? Maybe God will put us on the fast track for a baby."

He finished putting his dish in the dishwasher, put a hand behind her waist, and pulled her close until his face was nearly touching hers. "I adore you, you know." He kissed her once, then left to go back to work.

Well then indeed.

* * *

Piper shook Pastor Wilkins's hand. "Thank you for doing this, Pastor. I know it will mean a lot to my mother-in-law."

"Esther's a lucky one, getting you as a daughter."

"I don't know about that, but—"

He held one of her hands and put his other one on top, further sealing the transaction. "Not many brides would go to such lengths to make their husband's family comfortable. But are you sure you don't want to tell Gregory?"

She *wasn't* sure about keeping it secret and was completely relying on the fact that Gregory had let her have free rein over the ceremony. Free rein was free rein, wasn't it? "Gregory will be fine with it. I'm sure of it."

Almost sure.

* * *

Evelyn carefully applied a new shade of lipstick: Bahama Berry. She pursed her lips in front of the mirror, checking the result. It was a little more dramatic than she usually used, but desperate times demanded drama. She had to do *something* to get Wayne's attention back.

He was true to his word and had called her "in a few days." Those days had been torture for her. Sure, she'd seen him in church, where he'd been the essence of polite. They'd even talked about the Accosta project a few times on the phone and had come to the point that they felt they could share their vision with their friend. Yet something was wrong. Evelyn sensed it. While chatting with friends in the narthex after church, she'd even caught him looking at her oddly, as if studying her. Though she longed for his attention, this particular brand made her uneasy, like wondering if she had spinach in her teeth or a pen mark on her cheek.

This evening she vowed to *make* it different, make it get back to the way it used to be. Toward that end she'd asked Wayne, Piper, and Gregory over for a nice dinner. Certain they'd all been eating on the run during this last prewedding week, she'd enticed them with the promise of a home-cooked meal, a little calm before the wedding whirl.

She headed downstairs and checked on the setup in the dining room. She refolded a linen napkin and put it back under a fork, then adjusted a crystal goblet just so. Accosta came in the dining room and gasped. "It's beautiful!"

"You think so?"

"I know so. And the table's not the only thing that looks beautiful."

Evelyn felt herself blush. "Is the lipstick too much?"

Accosta came closer and held Evelyn's head in her hands. "Very Deborah Kerr."

"Not Marilyn Monroe?"

Accosta let go. "You were going for Marilyn?"

"No, no. Deborah Kerr is fine. I *don't* want to be vampish like Marilyn."

"Then you're a success. The dinner is a lovely idea. I'm sure they'll appreciate your effort."

Evelyn ran a hand over the lace tablecloth. "You don't mind being excluded?"

"Fiddle-dee, this is your home, Evelyn. You have a right to

give a private dinner party if you want. Ursola's eating with Tessa—they're working on answering a ton of Sister Circle letters. Jody, Kimberly, and I plan to eat in the kitchen and watch a movie."

"Which movie?"

"*Finding Nero.*"

Evelyn laughed. "*Finding Nemo.* I watched it with Summer. It's cute. It's about a fish."

"That's a relief. I couldn't imagine how Nero would fit into a kids' movie."

The front door opened. The guests had arrived. Wayne, Piper, and Gregory came into the dining room and gave Evelyn the reaction she'd hoped for. "You've outdone yourself, Evelyn." Piper gave her a hug.

"How special," Gregory said.

"Very pretty," Wayne said.

Evelyn accepted his nice words but noticed there was no hug. She tried not to feel disappointed as she stepped into the parlor. "Let's sit for a bit. Dinner won't be ready for a half hour."

As they took places in the room, Evelyn set her own need for accolades aside and put on her hostess cap. "I love your dress, Piper." And she did. "The peach color makes your cheeks glow. Or is that Gregory's doing?"

Piper snuggled against her fiancé on the couch. "I give him total credit." She played with her necklace. "Gregory did the nicest thing for me today . . ."

Evelyn stopped listening. Her eyes locked on Piper's jewelry. It was a locket with a monogram on it. Her first thought—*I had a locket like that once*—hurtled into the memory of what she'd done with that locket.

She was suddenly overcome with shivers. She clapped her hands to her mouth.

Piper stopped her story. "Evelyn?"

Evelyn stared at the monogram: ERW. She gasped, causing Piper to move away from Gregory's protective arm. "Evelyn . . . you're scaring me. What's wrong?"

Then Wayne came to her side and did an odd thing. He knelt beside her chair and took her hand, confusing her even more. "Yes, Evelyn. What you're thinking. It's true."

What's true?

But she knew *what*, even if she couldn't fathom it. Evelyn's hands shook and she began to cry. Her mind flew back to the moment when she'd taken the locket from her own neck and placed it in a red pouch for her daughter. She'd held that pouch to her heart a long time before she'd been able to let it go. . . .

"Would someone tell me what's going on?" Piper said.

Evelyn searched Wayne's face, needing to concentrate on someone who knew the truth, who could verify. "Wayne? How could this be?"

Piper threw her hands in the air. "Will someone tell me what's happening?"

Wayne squeezed Evelyn's hand. "How do you want to do this?"

Piper stood and stomped a foot. "Do what?"

Gregory stood beside her. "Come on, you two. You need to let us in on this—whatever *this* is. You're both acting strange."

Evelyn looked at Wayne, needing the answer to one more question. "How long have you known?"

"Since last Wednesday. I'd found it in a box in the apartment, but then, when I saw the pillow up in your attic with the same initials . . ."

It explained Wayne's sudden standoffishness.

"Initials?" Piper pulled the locket forward, trying to look at it. "ERW? These initials?"

Somehow Evelyn found the strength to stand. "Those initials

stand for Evelyn Ruth Wilson." She didn't add more, letting Piper assimilate one fact at a time.

"Is that you?" Gregory asked.

"Wilson was my maiden name."

Piper pushed past Gregory, finding space away from all of them. Her eyes found her father's. "You said this locket was left to me by my birth mother."

"It was."

The clock on the mantel counted the moments between ignorance and knowledge.

Gregory was the one to break the silence with three words that came out as individual sentences. "Oh. My. Goodness."

Evelyn sidled past Wayne and went to her daughter. "I had a baby nearly thirty-six years ago. I gave her up for adoption. I left her with a pink blanket and a locket with my initials on it." She breached the space between them by touching it now, for the first time since that emotion-filled day so long ago. "It appears that you are that baby. And I . . . I . . . somehow, I am your mother."

Piper's face crumpled and her knees buckled. Evelyn knelt beside her, giving her comfort as she had many times in the past two years.

But this time it was different.

* * *

The dinner had been forgotten and Piper felt bad about that. But there was no way she could eat. At the moment knowledge was her food and she ate it greedily. The four of them sat on the porch of Peerbaugh Place, she and Evelyn on the swing, her father in the wicker rocker, and Gregory leaning against the railing. Although she'd heard Evelyn's story of Frank during the years of their friendship, now it had new meaning.

"So my birth father died in Vietnam before knowing anything about me?"

"The news of my pregnancy and the news of his death—after only a few weeks in Vietnam—crossed in the mail. We would have been married. We loved each other very much."

Her father's name was Frank Albert Halvorson. No. That was only partly true. She looked at her father sitting across from her. Wayne Reginald Wellington was the only father she'd ever known. The only daddy.

Gregory raised a hand. "I just thought of something. You two ladies have been celebrating each other's birthdays for two years. Evelyn, surely you recognized that Piper's birthday was the same as your daughter's? And you knew she was adopted . . ." He shrugged. "I'm just surprised you didn't figure this out before."

Evelyn and Piper exchanged a look. "You were born on August 9," Evelyn said, "but that's not the birth date we've been celebrating."

Piper shook her head and looked to her father. "My birthday *is* August 9, but . . ."

Wayne took over. "Piper's mother and I decided to celebrate Piper's birthday on the date we got her. August 17 is the date she came into our lives, the date she was 'born' to us. We never thought much about it. It was within a week of her real birthday. It wasn't a big deal."

Piper nodded. "I never even think about it. Except on those rare occasions I've had to give my real birth date for some legal document, I consider the seventeenth my birthday."

Evelyn shook her head, incredulous. "And yet that one decision helped keep the secret once you moved into Peerbaugh Place and befriended me, your birth mother. That's amazing."

No one could argue.

Then Piper thought of another question. "But what would it matter if I'd found out two years ago when I moved in here?"

Her father's response was sobering. "Your mother was alive then. . . ."

Oh my. How would Wanda Wellington have reacted to having her daughter's birth mother suddenly show up in their lives?

"If Wanda had found out . . . it would have complicated things," Evelyn said. "I wouldn't have wanted to hurt or distress her for the world. She was a good friend."

"Your friendship with her is another miracle," Gregory said.

Piper wanted to bring up the fact that her father and her birth mother had fallen in love, but she knew it wasn't her place. Their burgeoning relationship had a lot to deal with now. It was best she leave it alone and let God handle the timing.

"God's timing is perfect, isn't it?" her father said.

"On that we all agree," Gregory said. "But speaking of timing—" he stood—"we have a long day tomorrow with the rehearsal and the rehearsal dinner."

Piper rose, fueled by the time *and* a sudden thought. "The wedding! Evelyn is the matron of honor yet she's also my mother . . ." She looked at them, frantic. "What's the etiquette for this situation? Should you sit with Dad as mother of the bride, or still be one of my attendants, or—"

Wayne laughed. "Instead of the matron of honor, she's the mother of honor."

Piper looked to Evelyn for her reaction.

"That's perfect," Evelyn said.

Wayne looked confused. "I was joking."

Piper took his hand. "No, Evelyn's right. It's perfect." She kissed his cheek. "Thanks, Dad."

Life was good. And God was an awesome God.

•   •   •

Though Piper was tired, though she knew she should really go home and get to sleep, she also realized there was one thing she and Evelyn needed to do. That night. Before either of them could rest.

They called Mae, Audra, Russell, and Tessa and issued a 9-1-1 call to come to Peerbaugh Place. By the time Evelyn had returned to the porch, Mae was rushing across the street barefoot, wearing a yellow chenille bathrobe over a nightgown. "What's the emergency?"

"Have a seat," Piper said. "We're waiting for the others."

Mae tightened the tie belt of her robe. "You cannot call me over here and make me wait."

Evelyn led Mae to the swing, where they both sat. "Five minutes, Mae. You can wait five minutes."

After we waited nearly thirty-six years . . .

It was difficult keeping Mae occupied until the others got there. The woman was brutal in her persistent queries. Audra and Russell arrived next, and had to join the waiting game. Then with one minute to spare, Tessa drove up. Piper had never seen Tessa hurry, but hurry she did, capturing the front walk with a run-walk, her head down in concentration. It moved Piper to witness her friends' immediate response to her call. And her brother . . . it was hard to fathom that Piper now had a brother. How would he feel about all this?

Speaking of . . . from her place on the swing, Evelyn held out her hand and Russell stood besider her, his face full of questions. She shook her head. Soon, soon there would be answers.

When Tessa reached the porch, Mae said, "Finally! They wouldn't tell me a thing and it's driving me crazy."

"Well, we're here now, so—" Tessa looked at Piper— "did you and Gregory break up?"

Piper never imagined they'd think such a thing. "No! No. We're fine. The wedding's on, as planned."

"It's a *good* emergency," Mae said. "They did tell me that much."

Piper saw Russell relax. It was time. She stood near the railing, setting her feet to supply the support she'd need. "We've recently discovered something very miraculous. Very 'of God.'" She looked to Evelyn, unsure who should say what.

Evelyn took over, first looking at each face. "There's no right way to say this, so I'll just let it out." She put a hand to her chest. "I am Piper's birth mother."

Silence.

Piper wasn't sure they heard. "I'm her daughter."

Mae gasped. "No way."

"Way."

Suddenly Tessa was out of her chair hugging Piper. And the swing gyrated wildly as Mae hugged Evelyn.

Then Piper noticed that Russell and Audra were not a part of the celebration. They stood apart; both clearly stunned.

Evelyn noticed the same thing, and she and Piper went to them. Evelyn took Russell's hand. "Son?"

Russell's head shook back and forth. "She's my sister?"

Piper's stomach tied a knot. The two women nodded.

"She's the baby I gave up before I married your father."

His head continued its back-and-forth path. "This is so . . ."

Piper braced herself for "horrible" or at the very least "bizarre."

Evelyn squeezed his hand and pushed the moment. "This is so . . . what, honey?"

With a glace to his wife, he sighed deeply and said, "So miraculous. He pulled his mother, wife, and sister into a group hug.

The details and the subsequent celebration of God's amazing ways lasted well past their normal bedtimes.

Truly, O God of Israel, our Savior,
You work in strange and mysterious ways.

ISAIAH 45:15

*P*iper's eyes opened and her first thought was *Today is my wedding day!* She rolled onto her back and adjusted the sheet and blanket neatly under her arms. This was her last day as Piper Wellington. Thirty-five years under that name, with that identity. She hoped to have more than as many years as Piper Baladino. Mrs. Gregory Baladino.

She stretched her arms to the ceiling, spread them to either side, then realized there would be no more sleeping in the middle of the bed, no more making a moat of three pillows around herself. Gregory would claim his rightful place, and she hoped the only pillow she'd need was his shoulder. She'd waited her entire life for this—and she was glad she'd waited. There was an exquisite sweetness having the knowledge that, though she'd certainly faced extreme temptation, with God's help she'd managed to resist and wait and agonize and wait and . . . and now she was getting the blessed reward.

She and Gregory had talked about their pasts—hopefully they had no secrets—and he had told her about a couple women who'd been in his life. He was not a virgin. He'd cried telling her, so sad that he couldn't bring himself to the marriage in the same state of purity she had maintained. In truth, he'd never regretted his past relationships until he met Piper. Only then had he recognized the triviality and awful self-seeking that had been the hallmark of his sexual past. He'd asked her forgiveness and received it, though Piper was quick to point out that Jesus was the true forgiver. And though she'd come into the marriage sexually pure, she was no saint. They both had their weaknesses and flaws to contend with. Some past, some present, and certainly, some future.

But wasn't that the essence of marriage? Dealing with *everything*? With all life had to throw at them? *Give us your best shot! We've got God by our side and on our side!*

There was a tap on the bedroom door. "Yes?"

Her father opened it a crack. "You awake?"

She nodded, sat up, and patted the side of the bed. He took a seat along with her hand. "Today's the day."

She nodded again, this time because her throat was tight.

"Are you ready?"

She swallowed and managed, "Very."

"I wish your mother could be here."

She found her voice. "Mom started all this. Remember the way she pushed Gregory and me together?"

"As subtle as a sixteen-wheeler."

Piper adjusted a pillow behind her. "Do you think she sees me today? Do you think somehow, God allows her to see?"

His face turned serious. "I do. I have no proof except to know how much God loves us and loves families. I think at special moments in our family's life, God lets us see."

Piper leaned forward. "She'll love the dress."

"That she will." He stood and offered her his hand. "Shall we have one last breakfast, Piper-girl?"

We shall.

"Soon-ja! You're back." Audra took the phone to the kitchen table. Everyone had been thrilled that Soon-ja was coming home in time for Piper's wedding. "When did you get in?"

"Last night. But—"

There was something odd about Soon-ja's voice. "Are you okay? Are Ricky and Ringo okay?"

"They're fine. I'm fine. But I have something important to talk to you about."

Audra's spine tingled. "What kind of something?"

"Is Russell home?"

"Yes . . ."

"Can I come over?"

"Of course, but Soon-ja? What's up?"

"I'll be right over. Three minutes."

Audra hung up but stared at the phone a full minute. Russell came into the kitchen, carrying his groomsman tux in a zipper bag. "I'm going to be so handsome today, you're going to drool."

"Don't be too beautiful. I wouldn't want to get my bridesmaid dress messy." She realized the tone of her voice hadn't matched the levity of her words.

It caused him to do a double take in her direction. "You seem upset."

"Soon-ja's on her way over. She has something to talk to us about."

"Us?" He hung the tux bag on the doorframe. "I barely know her."

"She specifically asked if you were home."

"Hasn't she been in Korea visiting her family?"

Audra nodded. "That's why I can't imagine why she wants—" She heard a car drive up and rushed to the living-room window. "She's here."

They met Soon-ja at the door. Her smile and greeting were tentative. "I'm sorry to bother you on such a busy day," she said. "Actually, I don't even know if I should be here."

Russell offered her a chair in the living room and he and Audra sat on the couch. "Soon-ja . . . just tell us."

Her hands kept each other company on her lap. "What I have to say is wonderful, but I hesitate because I don't know you that well, though Mom and Collier *have* talked a lot about you. But Ringo and I are outsiders here."

"You've been here six weeks."

She shrugged.

"How was your trip?" Russell asked. "How did you find your family?"

Audra wished he hadn't asked that now. She wasn't in the mood for polite chitchat.

"They're fine. Actually, they play a part in what I have to tell you . . ." She sighed. "Oh dear. There's no subtle way to do this."

Audra found Russell's hand. "Then just do it."

Soon-ja took another breath. "It all started while we were making cookies right before the Fourth."

It took Audra a moment to change her thoughts from Korea to Carson Creek. "At Evelyn's?"

Soon-ja nodded. "After hearing you that day, so upset . . ."

Her eyes searched theirs and Audra tried to pinpoint the day, the conversation. Then she remembered Accosta giving her a worry box—because . . . "I was upset about us not being able to have a baby."

Soon-ja's next words came out in a rush. "Exactly! And the thing is . . . I have a baby for you. Or rather, my grandmother has a neighbor girl in Korea who had a child that she wants to give up for adoption. The father was American so she wants an American couple to adopt him and when I heard—"

"Him?"

"A little boy, Chin. His name means 'precious.'"

Too many words. Too fast. Silence sat between them.

"Did you understand what I said?" Soon-ja asked.

Russell squeezed Audra's hand. Hard. She attempted to put the miracle into words. "You . . . you have a baby. For us."

"If you want him. Are you interested?"

Audra found Russell's arms and they held each other tight. *Yes, oh yes.*

* * *

Piper knew it was traditional for the bride and groom not to see each other before the wedding, but she couldn't wait. Though the rehearsal had gone smoothly last night, she had a surprise for Gregory regarding the ceremony. She'd decided just this morning that it was best to give him a little warning. So as soon as she reached the church, she called him on her cell phone.

"This is your bride to be—"

"Hello, dear bride to—"

"Meet me in the rose garden of the church. Ten minutes."

"Ooh, is this legal?"

"Shh," she said. "It's a secret rendezvous. Be there."

"I wouldn't miss it."

She headed for the garden, but was sidetracked when a deliveryman came in the front of the church. "Excuse me? We have a delivery of a—" he looked at his clipboard— "a chuppah?"

Piper caught sight of Evelyn at the end of the hall. "Evelyn? Could you come here a minute?" She gave Evelyn instructions, then went off to meet Gregory. There was no turning back now.

• • •

Piper found Gregory pacing in front of a bench in the rose garden. Like a caged animal?

Like a groom to be.

He turned when he heard her coming, and his smile . . . *soon. Soon.*

He took her hands and kissed her, then spread their arms wide. "Jeans and a T-shirt. You look lovely."

She blushed. "That's where I drew the line. I'll see you before the wedding but not in my dress. That comes later."

"Not so much later anymore." He sighed. "Just a few more hours." He moved to the bench. "So. Why the meeting?"

She pulled a jewelry box from her pocket. "I have a present for you."

He looked taken aback. "I don't have anything for you."

She kissed him. "You are my gift, dear one. All I want is you."

"But you have a present—"

She hated that he felt bad. "It's not much. It's just something I'd like you to wear today. It's symbolic."

He opened the box and pulled out a gold necklace. "It's a Star of David."

"With a cross in the middle. It represents both religions. It represents your Jewish heritage and your commitment to Christ."

His finger traced its edge. "It's beautiful. Thank you."

"You're welcome." Her relief was short-lived because now came the harder surprise. "There's something else . . . I've made a small change in the ceremony that you need to know about."

"Uh-oh. Do I need another rehearsal for this?"

"No, no, nothing like that. But to appease—to honor—your mother, I have had a chuppah delivered."

"A what?"

"A Jewish bridal canopy. You and I will stand beneath it during

322

the ceremony." His eyes were wary, so she hastened to explain. "The chuppah represents the home we're creating together. It has four posts but no walls, indicating that our new home will be open, a part of our extended family and community."

He considered this a moment. "I like that."

She let out a breath. "Good."

"Is Pastor Wilkins okay with it?"

"He thinks it's nice."

"You've covered all the bases, haven't you?"

"I tried to."

"Is there anything else?"

"Just one. When we have Communion, we'll drink from the same goblet and then Pastor Wilkins will hand it to you and you'll step on it, breaking it."

"And why do I do that?"

"In memory of the destruction of the temple in Jerusalem in the year 70 and the centuries of exile that followed."

Gregory nibbled her ear. "You've done your homework, wife."

She pulled away only because she had to read his face. "Do you think your mother will be pleased?"

He took both her hands. "She'd better be. But beyond that . . . I want you to know that I love *you*. I'm marrying you and you're marrying me. What Evelyn, Wayne, and my mother have to say has meaning, but in the end, it's our family—you and me—that counts. Understood?"

"Yes, husband."

He kissed her, then looked at his watch. "We'd better go. We have a wedding to attend."

●   ●   ●

Piper pointed at Evelyn. "Don't you dare cry!"

"But you're so beautiful!" Evelyn *did* hold the tears back. For now.

Mae put her hands on her hips. "We are not going to have to call an intermission at the wedding to accommodate a crying jag, are we?"

Evelyn dabbed a tissue to the corner of her eye. "It won't just be me crying."

Probably not.

Tessa adjusted Piper's veil. "You *are* magnificent, Piper. A vision."

They all looked at Piper's reflection in the huge wall mirror of the bridal room. The dress was strapless in white satin with a wide skirt. The bodice was covered with a waist-length, long-sleeved, lace jacket. Demure, feminine, stunning.

"It's Audra's doing," Piper said.

Audra stood behind her and leaned on her shoulder. "I just took care of the package. The true glow of beauty is coming from inside."

Mae gave her a look. Audra wasn't usually so flowery. Hmm . . . "Speaking of *glow of beauty*, you look a bit glowy yourself, young lady. Is there something you want to tell us?"

Audra blushed.

Evelyn gasped. "Are you pregnant?"

Piper ran toward Audra. "I can't believe it. This is—"

"No, no!" Audra waved the question away. Then she smiled. "But . . . there still might be a baby on the horizon."

After a pause, Tessa said, "An adoption?"

Audra slapped a hand to her mouth. "I shouldn't have said anything. Nothing's definite. And Russell should be here to tell the news, if and when."

Mae raised her right hand. "No problem. We do solemnly pledge to act surprised at all appropriate moments. And with that hope planted for a future celebration, I say it's time to gather for an important proclamation." The women arranged themselves around Piper, facing the mirror. Mae took a deep breath, then said, "Just as I thought. Face it, sisters; we are definitely a Sister Circle of very hot babes."

Summer rushed in front of the group. "Me too!"

"Babes and a babe-ette."

Tessa rolled her eyes. "You do *not* understand the meaning of decorum, Mae."

"I understand enough. I understand it will be inappropriate to hum 'Viva Las Vegas' during the wedding vows, and I understand I shouldn't wink at Collie when we're both up front, or blow him a kiss even though he's just asking for it by being so cute."

"I have to stand really still," Summer said. She practiced in front of the mirror, her basket of flower petals held just the way Evelyn had showed her.

Mae took a place beside her and they were serious statues— until Mae made a face, causing Summer to giggle.

"There will be none of that," Tessa said.

"Oh, Tessie, heaven forbid we have fun at a wedding," Mae said.

"Have fun at the reception. The ceremony is a very solemn occasion."

Piper put a hand to her midsection. "Oh dear. I'm suddenly nervous."

Tessa held out her hands. "Circle up, ladies." They formed a circle and one by one the women prayed aloud for God's blessings on the day, as well as their gratitude for their happy sisterhood. Nothing fancy, just heartfelt. Before meeting these women, Mae had never considered praying aloud, but now . . . it was a common event that always left her feeling filled up and whole.

It was Evelyn's turn. "Father, miracles abound. To be here at Piper's wedding, not just as her friend but as her birth mother . . ." She glanced up and caught Mae's wink.

There was a knock on the door. Mae was closest and opened it. "Starr baby!" Soon-ja came in next and everyone gathered round.

"Starr, we haven't seen you for months," Tessa said. "Not since you went back to New York. How's the publishing world? How's Ted?"

"Fine and very fine. He's here. Out front."

"Forget Ted," Mae said. "Though I love the man, where's Ricky? Where's my baby boy all dressed for a wedding?"

"He's sitting with Ringo," Soon-ja said. "Speaking of dressed for a wedding . . . Collier looks handsome in his tux."

"He cleans up good," Mae said. Collier and Russell were sharing the groomsmen duties with two of Gregory's hospital friends.

Soon-ja nodded back to the space where they'd been standing in a circle. "But we interrupted. What were you doing?"

Mae took the hands of her daughter and her daughter-in-law. "We had a little circle of sisters going. Praying, praising—"

"Count us in," Starr said.

Mae's jaw dropped. Had Starr opened herself to prayer and faith? Last fall Starr had left Ted and come to live with Mae and Collier specifically because Ted had become a Christian, a condition she found appalling. Apparently, she'd changed her mind. Mae would get the scoop later.

The women went back to their circle, now two sisters larger. There was always room for one more. . . .

*   *   *

With only ten minutes to show time there was a knock on the bridal-room door. "If that's Gregory, don't let him in!" Piper said.

Mae headed to the door. "If it's Gregory, I'll go have a talk with him about patience." She opened the door a crack and Piper heard an exchange of soft voices. The door closed.

"Who was it?"

"It was Esther."

Piper rushed toward the door. "Why didn't you invite her in?"

Mae barred her way, holding an envelope between them. "I did invite her in. She shook her head and asked me to give you this."

Piper looked at the envelope. It was small, the size of a note card. At first she thought it might be a wedding card, but then she noticed that only her name was on the front.

"What is it?" Audra asked.

Piper shook her head and opened it. She removed a card that had pink and orange flowers on the front. As she began to read the inside, she moved away from her friends, instinctively seeking privacy:

Dear Piper,

Though I'm never one to mince words, sometimes I do have trouble expressing what I really want to say. So I'll try writing it.

I've had a lot going on recently. Learning to be a widow, reclaiming my Jewishness, dealing with Gregory's Christianity, having my only son find a mate. I admit I've been more than a little confused about things. In my search for truth, I'm finding there's a lot I don't know. Too much. Frankly, it rattles me because I'm a woman who likes the status quo. All this has made me a bit gruff and brusque, and I've often spoken without thinking.

Bottom line? I've hurt you and made it hard for you. For that I'm sorry. You've been nothing but gracious. I should have been so gracious.

If there's one thing I've learned, it's the importance of family. So here's a truth for all of us: Gregory has chosen to love you. Because of that, I choose to love you too. The rest will come.

May you and Gregory find much happiness and many blessings.

Love,
Esther

Piper felt tears threaten. Evelyn put a hand on her arm. "What's wrong?"

She carefully put the note back in its envelope and took a cleansing breath. "Not a thing."

•   •   •

The ceremony was like a lovely dream from which Evelyn didn't want to awaken. Watching Piper and Gregory stand under the chuppah was very moving. The white satin of the cloth and its gold embroidery were elegant and Evelyn liked the symbolism. She risked a sidelong glance to Esther, sitting in the front pew. She was smiling. She had to be honored by Piper's gesture.

Evelyn was honored. *That's my girl!* was a gleeful exclamation that Evelyn wanted to shout to the world. But she had the rest of their lives to spread that news to all who would hear. Right now she wanted to concentrate on the ceremony.

Pastor Wilkins quoted from First Corinthians:

"'If I could speak in any language in heaven or on earth but didn't love others, I would only be making meaningless noise like a loud gong or a clanging cymbal. . . .'"

The fact that Evelyn even knew the verse came from First Corinthians was such a miracle. Before Aaron had been killed she'd had little use for God, and had experienced little love—either as a giver or a taker. Her life had often been meaningless, like a loud gong or a clanging cymbal.

She concentrated on the words again. "'Love is patient and kind. Love is not jealous or boastful or proud or rude. Love does not demand its own way. Love is not irritable, and it keeps no record of when it has been wronged. It is never glad about injustice but rejoices whenever the truth wins out. Love never gives up, never loses faith, is always hopeful, and endures through every circumstance.'"

So many circumstances. Getting pregnant with Piper, losing Frank in Vietnam. Choosing to love Piper the best she could by giving her up—to Wayne and Wanda. Marrying Aaron, having Russell. Living a life that had seen many happy times, but had also been steeped in times of great frustration. Had Frank been the love of her life? They hadn't been together long enough to find out. But Evelyn could safely and sadly say that Aaron had not earned that distinction.

The ceremony had moved on to the vows. "' . . . will you love her, comfort her, honor and keep her, in sickness and in health, for richer, for poorer, for better, for worse, in sadness and in joy, to cherish and continually bestow upon her your heart's deepest devotion, forsaking all others, keeping yourself only unto her as long as you both shall live?'"

Gregory's face was intent with devotion as he looked at his bride. "I will."

As the pastor turned to Piper's vows, Evelyn took to heart the words she'd heard at many wedding ceremonies through the years. Though her marriage to Aaron had left much to be desired, they had stood by each other. They had been faithful. They had persevered. And yet . . .

She caught sight of movement to her right. It was Wayne in his front pew. Alone. She longed to sit beside him and found it odd that she was torn between standing up with her daughter and wanting to sit beside her father. There was time enough for both roles, each in their proper moment.

"I will," Piper said softly.

Will. A person's will was such a strong and powerful thing. Evelyn had willed herself through the hard years with Aaron. She'd willed herself through his death and her early widowhood until finally she'd abandoned her will to the loving God who'd been there patiently waiting to get her attention. How much easier might her life have been if she'd turned to Him sooner?

As Piper and Gregory exchanged rings, Evelyn forced herself not to dwell on past mistakes of admission and omission. She'd learned from it all. That was the important thing. And the future was so amazingly full of promise. . . .

At her side, Summer wiggled, her time of being still reaching its limit. She held out her hand and Summer smiled up at her. There. That was better.

Another miracle. Russell marrying Audra and bringing into their lives this little girl who made air fresh and light bright. It saddened Evelyn that there would be no little one with the Peerbaugh nose—though perhaps that *could* be considered a blessing. Yet it was ironic that any future grandchildren would be adopted when she herself had given up a child for adoption.

She sought her son's eyes and they exchanged a smile. Then, both their eyes drifted toward Piper and suddenly, Evelyn realized there *would* be more babies! Her grandmotherhood was not just dependent on Russell anymore. Piper and Gregory would have children. Maybe many children. Oh happy day! Why hadn't she thought of this before now?

Because now is the perfect time to realize all your blessings.

It was nearly complete. She saw Pastor Wilkins raise his hand for a benediction. "From the Song of Songs I say, *Ani l'dodi v'dodi li*: 'I am my lover's, and my lover is mine.' I now pronounce you man and wife. You may kiss the bride."

Tears were inevitable. She'd almost made it. . . .

Then Pastor Wilkins put the glass from which Piper and Gregory had shared Communion on the floor in front of the groom.

With a flourish Gregory broke the glass under his foot and Evelyn heard Collier yell, "Mazel tov!"

Piper and Gregory turned toward the congregation, absolutely beaming. Pastor said, "I present to you Mr. and Mrs. Gregory Baladino!"

There were cheers and applause as the bride and groom walked past their loved ones as man and wife. Even Esther was clapping.

Praise God from whom all blessings flow.

.   .   .

The wedding reception and dance were a huge success. It was wonderful seeing past Peerbaugh Place tenants: Gillie, Gail, Margaret, Lucinda, and Valerie were all there. Even Jody and Kimberly had come. People ate hors d'oeuvres and cake. They danced and sat around tables talking.

In bringing the past tenants up to date, Accosta had told the others about her house and commended Wayne for all his hard work. Evelyn and Wayne still hadn't told her about their idea. Maybe now was the time? Evelyn leaned toward him to ask.

Mae wagged a finger at them. "Nope, nope. There are no secrets tonight. What are you two conspiring about over there?"

Wayne did the honors. "Actually, we have an idea for Accosta's house. . . ." He told them about his and Evelyn's disappointment and wariness with what prospective buyers had wanted to do with it, as well as their dream of opening it to women and children in need.

Tessa slapped a hand on the table. "The Sister Circle House!"

The table was totally silent; then everyone started talking at once.

"It's perfect!" Evelyn said.

"It fits in with our Sister Circle—and Tessa's Sister Circle Network."

"To think that my house could do such good," Accosta said.

The wonderful comments went on and on. Russell was the one to bring the whole thing back to reality. "How are you going to fund this thing?"

A different kind of silence swept over the table.

Audra swatted his arm. "Nothing like putting the kibosh on things, hon."

"Dreams are great, but money makes them happen."

Jody raised a tentative hand. "I think I might be able to help."

Evelyn couldn't imagine how.

Jody continued. "I work at the Mikelmass Foundation. We get grants for charitable projects that benefit the family. I could help get you the money the Sister Circle House will need."

Evelyn was at a momentary loss for words. Then she said, "I didn't know that's where you worked!"

Jody shrugged. "You wouldn't. I've taken a leave of absence to help Kimberly." She looked across the room where Kimberly was playing quietly with Summer and some other children. "But this *is* what I do. I can help. I'd love to help."

Gillie, one of the first tenants at Peerbaugh Place, also raised a hand. "I work for a foundation too. We'd help. I know we would."

Tessa took Ursola's arm and lifted it. "And here's your live-in administrator! She's been helping me with all the Sister Circle mail and she's shown a heart eager to meet women's needs."

Evelyn looked around the table, dumbstruck with the way God had brought all these women into her life.

"My, my," Wayne said, taking her hand. "Will you look at how God's provided exactly who we need, right in our own little circle of friends?"

"Almost like He had it planned all along," Mae said.

Tessa shook her head. "No *almost* to it. This is God's doing. Every bit of it, and I won't have anyone saying different."

Mae put up her hands in surrender. "We wouldn't dare!"

As everyone started brainstorming the idea, Wayne leaned close, whispering in Evelyn's ear. "It appears our partnership just got some divine approval, my dear."

She couldn't—and wouldn't—argue with him, for it was divine. In every way.

●　　●　　●

Evelyn shut the door of Peerbaugh Place and sat on the porch swing beside Wayne. His arm found her shoulders and she was content to swing without words. Words were unnecessary. It had been a perfect day.

"Yes, it was," Wayne said.

Evelyn was taken aback. It was as if he'd read her mind. "Yes, it was what?"

"A perfect day."

"But how . . . ?" She stopped. There was no need to dissect it. She leaned her head against his. "I love you, Wayne."

He kissed her forehead. "And I love you."

Evelyn cuddled even closer—content to have finally found the place she belonged.

The earth is the Lord's, and everything in it.
The world and all its people belong to Him.

PSALM 24:1

A Note from the Authors

$\mathcal{D}$ear Readers:

What do you do with twelve women who need resolution—all at the same time, all talking at once, giving their opinion of how *they* would like things to work out?

You ask them to be patient, wait their turn, and not be bossy. Sure—that works.

That was the situation we had in writing this fourth—and last—book in the Sister Circle series: *A Place to Belong*. We'd gathered quite a gaggle of ladies, and sometimes it was a little overwhelming. All the characters wanted time in the spotlight. Imagine telling Mae to back off. Or asking Tessa to hold her opinion. Good luck.

Yet despite juggling the logistics, it was a pleasure letting the sisters finally work things through. And it was just as satisfying to us (as we hope it was to you) to see where their stories had been heading through four books. You may find this hard to believe, but even *we* didn't know. That's the joy—and wonder—of writing fiction. The characters seem real, their lives intertwine with ours, and it's an adventure seeing those lives take off on their own. Sometimes it's hard to keep up with them!

There's a parallel between fictional characters and real-life sisters. For aren't *we* prone to demand resolution, talk all at once, give our opinion to God regarding how we'd like things to work out? Don't we often take off on our own, oblivious to how it affects others? And doesn't God tell us to be patient, wait our turn, and not be bossy? The question is, do we listen?

Hopefully we do. We want to. We try to. And blessedly, God in His mercy and love keeps working on us, keeps talking to us. He doesn't give up.

And neither should we. So toward that end, thank you for letting us share the Sister Circle books with you. We revel in the news of actual Sister Circles being created around the country—and the world.

You're still not sure what a Sister Circle is?

One more time before we go. . . . You probably have a circle of friends who get together for a specific reason: a Bible study, a bridal shower, a meeting to plan a school event, an evening of bunko. But wouldn't it be nice to have girlfriends who get together just to enjoy each other's company? That's what a Sister Circle is.

The only qualification for sisterhood is friendship. We hope you and your friends will read the novels and use the suggested discussion questions in the back of the books.

Once you get your Sister Circle started, it will become unique, just to fit you and your friends. Our dream is for you to bond with a group of ladies—for life. Let's recapture the joy of our grand-mother's era, when women gathered and talked. It's not that hard. You can do it. (If you bring a plate of sweets it will be that much easier.) So make your list of special sisters, pick up the phone, and ask them over. The rest will come.

Now, in parting, we'd both like to express our gratitude to a few sisters of our own. Special thanks to Brenda Josee, who's listened, advised, prayed, and provided chocolate at all the appropriate moments; and to Pearl Galpin who provided us a place on the beach to meet and be creative in style. Thanks to Ethel Herr and Ellen Cohen, two dear women of faith who helped with some of the Christian-Jewish issues. Thanks to Anne Goldsmith, Kathy Olson, and Becky Nesbitt at Tyndale House for all the wonderful suggestions, insight, and encouragement. And finally, ultimate thanks to God for bringing us together in the first place. The blessings of that miracle go far beyond a few books. . . .

You will find the discussion questions for each book and additional information on our Web site at www.sistercircles.com. (While you're at it, also check out www.nancymoser.com.)

Phew. That's it, ladies. Now go forth and bond. Sisters forever!

Vonette and Nancy

About the Authors

VONETTE BRIGHT is cofounder of Campus Crusade for Christ along with her late husband, Dr. William R. Bright. She earned a degree in home economics from Texas Women's University and did graduate work in the field of education at the University of Southern California. Vonette taught in Los Angeles City Schools before joining Bill full-time in Campus Crusade. Bill and Vonette have two married sons and four grandchildren. Vonette's commitment to help reach the world for Christ has fueled a passion for prayer and a desire to help others develop a heart for God. She founded the Great Commission Prayer Crusade and the National Prayer Committee, which helped to establish a National Day of Prayer in the U.S. with a permanent date of the first Thursday in May. She presently serves as chairperson for the Bright Media Foundation and maintains an amazing schedule from her home in Orlando. Vonette's desire is to see women of faith connecting, serving, and supporting each other with such genuine love that women who do not know Christ will be drawn to them and will want to meet Him.

NANCY MOSER is the author of three books of inspirational humor and eleven novels, including *The Seat Beside Me*, *Time Lottery*, and The Mustard Seed series. She teaches writing at a regional college and is a motivational speaker. Information about her Said So Sisters Seminars can be found at www.nancymoser.com. She and her husband have three nearly grown children and three corresponding nearly grown cats.

Scripture Verses in *A Place to Belong*

Chapter	Topic	Verse
Chapter 1	Plans	Proverbs 19:21
	Worry	Matthew 6:34
Chapter 2	Plans	Proverbs 16:9
	Worry	Matthew 6:34
Chapter 3	Sanctuary	Psalm 27:5
Chapter 4	Trials	1 Peter 1:6-7
	Victory	Hebrews 12:1-2
	Worry	Luke 12:25
	Worry	Philippians 4:6
Chapter 5	Change	2 Corinthians 13:11
	Time	Ecclesiastes 3:1
Chapter 6	Provision	Luke 12:30-31
Chapter 7	Love	1 Peter 3:8
Chapter 8	Planning	Proverbs 3:21-22
	Temptation	Matthew 6:13
Chapter 9	Truth	Proverbs 12:19
	Aid	James 5:19-20
	Work	1 Chronicles 28:10
	Joy	Nehemiah 8:10
Chapter 10	Loyalty	Proverbs 3:3
Chapter 11	Temptation	James 1:14-16

Chapter 12	Testing	James 1:12
	Honesty	Exodus 20:15
	Evil	Romans 12:17
	Temptation	1 Corinthians 10:12-13
	Devil	1 Peter 5:8-9 (paraphrased)
	Truth	John 8:32
	Temptation	Matthew 26:41
Chapter 13	Revenge	Leviticus 19:18
	Comfort	John 14:28
	Heaven	Revelation 21:4
Chapter 14	God's Ways	Daniel 2:22
	Satan	Matthew 16:23
Chapter 15	Guidance	Psalm 32:8
	God's Ways	Isaiah 55:8-9
	Pride	Proverbs 16:18
Chapter 16	God's Ways	Habakkuk 1:5
Chapter 17	God's Ways	Isaiah 45:15
	Love	1 Corinthians 13:1
	Love	1 Corinthians 13:4-7
	Union	Song of Songs 6:3
	World	Psalm 24:1

Discussion Questions

CHAPTER 1

1. As a landlord, Evelyn has to constantly deal with change and finds herself both accepting yet weary of it. How do you react to change?
2. Lucinda has had quite the career change from magazine model to teaching homeless women makeup tips—yet she's happy. What do you think about such a status change? Have you ever experienced something similar? How did you handle it?

Faith Issue

Evelyn thinks about the adage "When God closes a door He opens a window." When has this happened to you? Was the window a better experience than what was left behind?

CHAPTER 2

1. Has anyone ever forgotten your birthday? How did you react?
2. Valerie says her blunt nature is the fault of her characters. Sounds like an excuse, not holding herself accountable for her own flaws. Think of your own worst flaw. Do you pass over it by making excuses? What's the real cause/effect/solution for your flaw?

Faith Issue

The timing of Lucinda's moving out a day early, making room for Accosta to move in . . . God's timing is often amazing. Describe an incident when God's perfect timing was evident.

CHAPTER 3

1. It is often hard for a mother to balance her dedication and loyalty to her children with the dedication and loyalty her husband deserves. How have you handled such situations?
2. Evelyn is discouraged by Wayne's nonromantic interest in her but is hesitant to push the issue. What do you think she should do?

Faith Issue

Ursola is devastated by her husband's death, the meanness of her stepson, and life in general. How might someone with a strong faith react to such a situation? How about someone with no faith?

CHAPTER 4

1. Wayne and Evelyn take a risk by using their savings to help a friend. What financial risks have you taken? What were the results? How do we know which risks to take?
2. Though Soon-ja is having trouble with Ringo, by hearing Audra's no-baby news, she counts her blessings. When have someone else's troubles helped you put yours in perspective?

Faith Issue

What do you think about Accosta's worry box? How about making one of your own?

CHAPTER 5

1. There is a time to give in and a time to stand strong. Evelyn surprises herself by standing strong against Valerie's demands. What kind of woman are you? The give-in type? Or the type who stands strong? *Or . . .* one who makes demands like Valerie?
2. Evelyn is waiting for just the right time to declare her feelings for Wayne. Name a time you have been in such a waiting position to talk about something important. How did you know

when to speak up—or remain silent? Did you make the right timing choice?

Faith Issue

Soon-ja and Ringo are struggling. Ringo is hanging out with people who influence him badly. Though as believers, we are *not* to isolate ourselves, how do we handle the pressure and presence of acquaintances who live in conflict with our beliefs? How can we be a "light" in the darkness without turning them off?

CHAPTER 6

1. Simon has walked into Audra's life at the point when she is the most vulnerable. She feels herself succumbing to dangerous thoughts. What should she do?
2. Ringo is discontent, trapped into thinking that life will be happy all the time. He's putting his marriage at risk. If you were Soon-ja, how would you handle the situation?

Faith Issue

Peerbaugh Place is filling up—with nonpaying boarders! Evelyn is a little panicked, yet Wayne says it might be a God thing. What do you think God is up to?

CHAPTER 7

1. The entire time Valerie was at Peerbaugh Place she complained. Now that she's on her own with her dream in sight, she's discontent. Why? What went wrong?
2. Collier tells Mae that parenting doesn't end when the kids are eighteen. What's the best thing Mae can do about the Ringo–Soon-ja situation? What's the worst thing?

Faith Issue

The ladies discuss true love. Not everyone is supposed to be married, but for those who are . . . do you think there is one God-chosen love?

CHAPTER 8

1. Wayne and Evelyn are discouraged that their project to fix up and sell Accosta's house is not working out as well as they hoped. Yet they still feel God is behind it. When have you been discouraged during a "God project"? How did you get past it?
2. Tessa seemed to be at the right place at the right time to help Ursola deal with her anxiety and fear regarding Daryn. When has God put the right person into your path? Or when have you been that person?

Faith Issue

Audra is struggling with temptation. What is the source of temptation? Is there any way to avoid it?

CHAPTER 9

1. Ringo runs away. When have you run away from a situation/problem? Did it help?
2. Society tells us to be skinny. Most of us aren't. Yet we can still feel pretty. When was the last time you allowed yourself to feel pretty? How can we sisters help each other see our own beauty?

Faith Issue

We often can get so busy—even doing God's work—that we lose the joy. What ways can we get it back, and hold joy close?

CHAPTER 10

1. Piper is disturbed by Esther's constant disapproval of her. Have you ever had someone disapprove of you to this extent? How did you handle it? What worked? What didn't?
2. Finally, Evelyn tells Wayne she loves him. Why is it so hard to risk rejection? How can we find the courage to let others know how we feel?

Faith Issue

The sisters pray often, in many situations. It comes naturally to them and is part of their relationship with each other. Do you have this kind of relationship with other sisters in Christ? If not, how can you get it?

CHAPTER 11

1. Audra tries to stop the consequences of her temptation but it catches up with her. What's your opinion about how Audra handled this entire matter?
2. God hates a proud heart (Proverbs 21: 4). Valerie has just lost her dream because of her proud attitude. Describe a time when pride got you in trouble. How was the situation resolved?

Faith Issue

Evelyn is very willing to help the stranger Jody and her daughter in their time of need. And Jody is very gracious and appreciative. God wants us to help others whether they deserve it—or even appreciate it. Name a time you've dealt with both kinds of recipients of your help.

CHAPTER 12

1. When Piper moves out, Evelyn asks, "Why does everyone have to leave?" It's a life question we've all asked. How have you dealt with people coming and going in your life?
2. Audra is shamed and has to face the consequences of her temptation. Yet God is there. Have you ever gone through such a time of upheaval, confession, and forgiveness?

Faith Issue

Accosta receives a feeling that Audra is in trouble. She could ignore it, but she doesn't. She does all she can—and it turns out that her feeling was actually a nudge from God. When have you felt such a nudge? Did you ignore it? or obey it? Did it pan out to be a nudge from God or not? If not, what were you out but a little time?

CHAPTER 13

1. Accosta told Ursola to never "pay back evil for evil." Yet revenge is a strong emotion. Describe a time you've let the need for revenge get the best of you. What were the consequences? What could you have done differently?
2. Daryn is a mean man. Yet at the police station Tessa gives him his due. Do you believe that what goes around comes around?

Faith Issue

With Tessa's help Ursola comes to terms with her husband's death by thinking about the idea of him happy in heaven—in a better place. If you've had to grieve for a loved one, what has helped you get through the pain?

CHAPTER 14

1. Satan is at work in the world. Tessa believes he was partly responsible for Ursola's act of revenge. Do you agree? What is the danger of blaming our bad behavior on Satan?
2. Audra makes a decision for adoption by seeing Summer playing with her dolls—a seemingly inconsequential moment that changes everything. What ordinary moment in your life turned out to be of huge consequence, perhaps helping you make an important decision?

Faith Issue

Ursola's staying with Tessa, Tessa's needing help with letters from around the world, Ursola's having connections with foreign students . . . coincidence? or the implementation of a divine plan? Name a time things fell into place in your life.

CHAPTER 15

1. Wayne gets upset about what society expects of a widower. What are the rules of mourning now? What should be the rules?
2. Wayne learns the truth about Piper and Evelyn. It's a burden and he doesn't know what to do. Have you ever discovered a truth that was a burden? How did you handle it?

Faith Issue

Piper lives the commandment "Honor your mother and father" even though Esther Baladino doesn't make it easy. When have you had difficulty following this commandment? How could you do better?

CHAPTER 16

1. Mae tries to live out the directive that a parent needs to let children try and fail in order to learn their own lessons. She *tries* . . . When have you let your children fail? How did it turn out?
2. The man-woman mating game . . . Evelyn takes extra time to look pretty, makes a nice dinner, plays the game in order to make things right with Wayne. In your own relationship, what works in the making-up process?

Faith Issue

God is a God of details. Thirty-six years of planning, setting up, making sure Piper, Wayne, Wanda, and Evelyn were given every opportunity to play out His perfect plan for their relationship. Name a time when you can look back and see one of God's extensive plans in your life.

CHAPTER 17

1. In preparation for marriage, Piper and Gregory told each other about their pasts. Did you do this with your spouse? Is there a time when the whole truth may not be a good thing?

2. Evelyn finds her "place to belong," her purpose. It's an amazing process—one that each of us *will* experience if we ask God to show us. How has God revealed His purpose for your life? What do you think about your future living in this purpose?

Faith Issue

Piper goes to great lengths to combine Gregory's Jewish heritage with their Christian faith. What do you think about combining these two faiths? Is it possible?

Turn the page for

an exciting preview of

WEAVE
of the World

by Nancy Moser

AVAILABLE FALL 2005
AT A BOOKSTORE NEAR YOU

ISBN 1-4143-0161-8

Weave of the World

*C*rash.

Lavon Newsom ran toward his son's bedroom. Four-year-old Malachi looked up from his toppled tricycle. He'd run into his Lego tower.

"Sorry, Daddy." He didn't look sorry, but grabbed two chunks of the tower, rolled onto his back, and banged them against each other until no two pieces hung together.

Lavon took the surviving piece away. "*Shh*. Mama's sleeping, remember?"

"Oops."

Lavon took the trike into the hall, where there was a clear shot next time Malachi felt like riding. Yet how far could he really ride in their sixth-story apartment on the Upper East Side? Sure, they took the trike down the elevator and to the park when it was nice out, but that was always a chore, an expedition.

Enough mental complaining. Lavon returned to the bedroom, his finger to his lips, and whispered. "Come help me with breakfast, Chi-chi. I want to make something special for your mama." They made a big deal out of tiptoeing into the kitchen, where Lavon flipped on the TV and turned to a morning talk show.

Malachi found a shoe and, holding it like an airplane, flew into the living room. That kid had an imagination that could turn everything into anything. Malachi returned to base and landed the shoe on the counter.

"The runway's on the floor, please." Lavon stirred some orange juice. "So what'll it be? Pancakes or dirt?"

"Dirt!"

"Dirt it is." It was a daily exchange, but neither of them seemed in any hurry to change it. In fact, Lavon relished such silly moments and thrived on them. The thought of going back to work full time and not being home with Malachi made his stomach turn in a way that was not conducive to either pancakes or dirt. Getting laid off from his consulting job was the best thing that had ever happened to him. To them. Lavon knew God had done it. God had gotten him out of the office and into the home where he belonged. Sure, it made money tight, but they were getting by.

Until Patrice quit her job.

He couldn't blame her. She'd been working at the bank for seven years, working toward a vice presidency. Two days ago, when she'd gotten passed over, she'd quit. So now they were an ex-banker and an ex-consultant. At least one of them needed a job—and soon. Privately, he hoped Patrice got one first. He didn't want to relinquish his Mr. Mom role.

Sure, he got flack for his stay-at-home status from his buddies, but he could handle them. He purposely kept a few details to himself. They didn't need to know how much he enjoyed it, how he jumped out of bed each morning looking forward to the day in a way that would have been unthinkable when he worked outside the home. Who knew he'd be so good at kid rearing, kid talking, kid thinking, kid wrestling?

Speaking of which . . .

"Syrup run for the pancakes!"

Right on cue Malachi lifted his arms and Lavon scooped him

up, setting him against his hip like a bedroll. They moved to the refrigerator. Malachi opened the door and grabbed the syrup. With a quick angle of their bodies, his feet shut it. A few steps more and the syrup was on the counter. "Syrup run complete!"

As soon as Malachi's feet hit the floor, Lavon saw Patrice in the hallway, her pj's disheveled from sleep. Malachi ran into her arms. "Morning, Mommy!"

"Hey, bud."

"I was being real quiet so you could sleep."

"Mmm. I heard you being quiet."

"We're having dirt for breakfast."

"Again?"

Lavon met her halfway, giving her a kiss. "You look wiped out."

She fell into a kitchen chair and ran a hand over her head. She'd cut her hair short and looked a lot like Halle Berry. But prettier. "It's hard to sleep when my entire future has been ruined."

"It's not ruined; it's just taken a detour." But Lavon had to admit, he hadn't slept well the past few nights either.

While Malachi ran off to play, Lavon poured his wife some coffee and started making the pancakes. He glanced at the TV. A very stately, elderly white woman sat on a couch next to Chad Ames, the ever-smiling talk-show personality.

"Today our guest is an extraordinary woman who has an extraordinary offer to share. You might be seeing her ads in newspapers across the country this week, and today she's here in person. Madeline McHendry Weaver, of Weaver, Kansas." He turned toward her. "Welcome."

"Glad to be here. But it's McHenry. No *d*."

Chad glanced down at his notes, his façade broken. "McHenry. Sorry." The smile returned. "Tell us about the ads, about what you're offering our listeners."

Patrice leaned forward. "I've never seen ol' Chad falter like that. I like this woman already."

"*Shh*," Lavon said. "I want to hear."

The woman tried to lean forward, but it was evident the couch was too cushy for her frame. She put her hands on her knees. "I have lived in the town of Weaver, Kansas, my entire life."

"Your name is Weaver. Are you from one of the founding families?"

"By marriage. But even before marrying, Weaver was my home. It's still my home. It's a home I want to share with the world. By giving it away."

Lavon fumbled the pancake turner.

Chad displayed an ad for the camera. *FREE LAND!* screamed the heading. "You're giving away a town? By placing these ads, correct?"

Lavon hadn't seen any ads.

"That's how it will begin. Weaver was once a thriving town of 1,283. But due to economic and societal changes, it's emptying out."

"How many live there now?"

"Forty-two."

"Forty-two?" Patrice said. "I can't imagine."

Lavon was glad she didn't say more. He didn't want to shush her again, but he had to hear. He took the griddle off the burner and shut off the heat.

The woman's head shook back and forth. "Not enough people. Not enough. In October Weaver will be one hundred years old, and I don't want it to die. It will not die. In fact, I've dedicated myself to making it thrive again by buying up all the properties that were for sale. I've had them parceled into homesteads—similar to what was done for our ancestors a hundred and fifty years ago. I am offering these homesteads free to settlers who apply and qualify."

"She's giving away free land!" It had burst out of him.

"So?" Patrice said.

"Listen!"

Chad continued. "You said the word *qualify*. How do they qualify?"

"We have a Web site where people can find more information, including a list of the positions available and—"

"Positions?"

"Indeed. But remember, I am repopulating a town. There are certain needs that must be met."

"Such as?"

She counted off on her fingers. "Teacher, peace officer, librarian, postmaster, pastor, café owner, banker, maintenance manager—"

Lavon pointed at his wife. "A banker!"

"So what?"

Chad smiled. "Rich man, poor man, baker man, thief?"

Mrs. Weaver made a face, not amused. "The thief need not apply."

"But the rest?"

"They can fill out an application, write the required essay, and send it in. We will interview the finalists."

"So work experience is a determining factor."

"In regard to skills, yes." The woman tried to get comfortable, but seemed unsuccessful. "Yet an applicant's past is only consequential in as much as it helped create who this person is now, and who they'll strive to be in Weaver. You have to understand, I am giving the town to new 'settlers' who want to be there—need to be there. They fill a need in the town and we fill a need in their lives—the need to start over and put down roots."

As she talked, Lavon held the edge of the counter. His legs were weak, his heart racing. He absorbed every word.

"I'm searching for people with the pioneer spirit, people who are willing to leave their old lives behind to work hard and rebuild Weaver to its previous glory. In return for homes—plus storefronts or businesses—the winners will have to sign a contract to stay put for five years. If they give up before that time—I despise quitters—they will lose their property, including any improvements they've made. Such a no-turning-back obligation will weed out the weak or indifferent."

Chad's eyebrows rose. "You seem to have it all worked out."

"No *seemed* about it. I am determined."

"I'm sure you are." Chad's smile was condescending, and Lavon had the feeling the interviewer was *not* the kind of person this woman wanted to bring to Weaver.

Chad turned back to the camera and gave the Web site address. Then he thanked her. A commercial for lemon-fresh Lysol came on.

Lavon tried to calm himself, tried to collect the thoughts that were ricocheting through his mind.

"Can I talk now?" Patrice said.

He realized he'd been rude. "Sorry, but—" he pointed at the TV—"did you hear what that woman offered?"

"Land. In Kansas."

"They need a banker."

She put down her coffee mug. "Lots of places need bankers."

"But they *need* bankers. And they're offering free land and homes and—"

"Uh-uh. Surely you don't—?"

"Why not? You just quit your job. You want to be vice president of a bank, don't you?"

"Not in a town that has only forty-two people."

"It's going to have more. That's what she's doing with the giveaway. Bringing more people in."

Patrice shook her head. "But it's Kansas. We're lifelong New Yorkers. We've never been west of Ohio."

"A huge oversight on our part."

"We're city people. *Big-city* people."

Lavon spotted Malachi's trike in the hall. "We could have a house with a yard and place for Chi-chi to ride and play . . ."

"You've been watching *Leave It to Beaver* again."

Guilty as charged. He loved that show.

She nodded toward the window. It was snowing outside. "It snows in Kansas. A lot, from what I've seen. There would be no riding trikes outside in the winter there either."

"No, that's when they go sledding, and make snow angels and snowmen and—"

"Sledding and snow . . . you can romanticize anything. We should never have watched *It's a Wonderful Life* last Christmas."

He smiled. "It *would* be a wonderful life . . ."

"You're impossible."

Maybe. And he *was* mesmerized by shows depicting small-town life. Hometown settings. Hometown values. Hometown problems. He thought of something else. "You wouldn't be dealing with big corporations and bank politics, but with loans to help people start over. You'd make friends with your customers and—"

"Oh yeah. A black female banker in a tiny town populated by ninety-nine percent whites. Don't be naïve."

"There are blacks in small towns in Kansas."

"How do you know?"

He didn't. But surely with a project like this, there would be an air of community that would transcend the normal ethnic and racial issues.

Patrice pointed to the stove. "I'm hungry."

He stood and flipped the heat back on.

"What would you do in a tiny place like Weaver?" she asked.

Good question. "I'd do what I'm doing now. Or maybe I could start my own consulting firm. Have a home-based business with our computer."

Lavon was glad she didn't comment. A commercial came on with a car zooming down an open highway edged by fields of waving wheat. He pointed at the TV with the pancake turner. "Open spaces. Big sky country."

"That's Montana."

"I'm sure they have big sky in Kansas too."

She fingered the handle of her mug. "We don't even own a car."

"We could get one. A minivan."

"Get *you* a minivan, you mean," she said. "I want a Porsche."

"I'll get you any car you want—any car we can afford."

Patrice cocked her head. "You're serious, aren't you?"

He faced her. "I know it doesn't make sense, but I feel it's right. Deep down right." He put a hand to his gut. "At least let me look into it. Where's your pioneer spirit?"

"I don't have any. And neither do you. Our ancestors immigrated here from who knows where and stayed put. They never felt the need to move west. Why should we?" She got up to get more coffee. "We probably wouldn't get accepted anyway."

Lavon turned back to the stove. *But maybe we would. Maybe we would.*

Read the
Nonfiction Companion
to *The Sister Circle*

*D*esigned to complement *The Sister Circle, The Woman Within* will help you unleash the power and joy of a Spirit-filled life. As Vonette Bright shares her lifelong journey from being a self-doubting young wife and mother to becoming a woman influenced, nurtured, and guided by the Holy Spirit, she shows you how to live a life characterized by joy, energy, and purpose, despite the at-times burdensome stressors of life.

ISBN 1-4143-0052-2

Visit us at tyndalefiction.com

Check out the latest information on your

favorite fiction authors and upcoming new

books! While you're there, don't forget to

register to receive *Fiction First,* our e-newsletter

that will keep you up to date on all of

Tyndale's Fiction.